UP FROM THE DEEP

VAUGHN A. JACKSON

SEVERED PRESS
HOBART TASMANIA

UP FROM THE DEEP

Dedication

*To my parents, who to this day can't agree on who introduced
me to Godzilla
Thanks for showing me the power of the SKREEONK*

CHAPTER 1

"There she is," Raymond gestured at the monstrous iron structure on the horizon. He blew a stream of smoke from beneath his wide brimmed hat. "Gaia Station."

"Is that it?" Ishii asked, acting unimpressed. His once impeccable black suit clung too tightly to his skinny form. The moisture from the sea air glistened on the material, having already soaked it through.

Ishii clenched and unclenched his fists as he shifted in his seat. On his right, a bald man in sunglasses snored loudly. To his left, a young woman with blue hair and a tattoo that snaked up her calf, and presumably continued beneath her skirt, fiddled on her phone. She looked up and gazed absent-mindedly into the water.

"Is that it?" Raymond forced a chuckle. "My friend, that is the single most advanced oil drilling platform your money could buy. And it *was* a lot of money, am I right?"

"Yes. It was." Ishii grimaced, and loosened his tie. He clutched, white-knuckled, at the briefcase in his lap. "How long until we arrive?"

Raymond cocked his head back and glanced at the rig. "It'll be a bit. Just relax."

"The water makes me nervous." Ishii checked his watch.

"You should not fear the water," Raymond whispered in a menacing voice. "Fear what lurks below the surface."

"I don't appreciate your tone, Captain. Don't forget who we are."

Raymond didn't look up. He rested his chin on his hand and pretended to be deep in thought. "The Mob? No. Triads? Eh, oh, the Yakuza, right. You all threaten the same way and pay the same way. It doesn't matter to me. You'll get what you want, and I will return to the sea a richer man." He looked up and grinned wildly at Ishii.

Ishii looked to his companions for backup but deflated when he saw their disinterest. The bald man continued snoring, and the woman gave a disinterested shrug and continued to fiddle with her phone.

"He's right," she said without looking away from the screen. "With this we'll dominate the oil market. *He* will only walk away with that." She jerked a thumb at the briefcase in Ishii's lap.

"Let's just say, I'm not one for long games." Raymond scratched at his greying beard. He smirked at the woman. "What's your name, ma'am?"

"Not interested," she said with a scowl.

"I am not familiar with that name. Japanese I suppose?"

She rolled her eyes and looked away.

Raymond turned to Ishii and said, "You might want to watch her, I think she's falling for me." He adjusted the wheel to ensure the boat stayed on course.

Ishii gave a nervous laugh and wiped a shine of sweat and sea spray from his forehead. A wave crashed against the side of the boat, and he jumped, fumbling with the briefcase before settling back into his seat, paler than before.

Raymond's face darkened and took on a serious expression. "Mr. Ishii, I understand that you don't like the ocean, but let me tell you...most of the worst accidents at sea have been caused by a nervous man acting in his own self-interest. Do you understand?"

Ishii swallowed hard and nodded.

"Good."

The motorized boat carried them closer to the towering oil rig. Raymond's experience as a sailor made it easy enough to keep up the appearance of a sea captain, but the sun beat down without mercy. It was hot despite the coolness of the ocean spray.

"Wake up, my friend," Raymond said, shaking Ishii awake. "We're here."

Ishii's eyes widened. "But you said—"

"That it would be a bit, and it was. A little bit." Raymond flashed a wolf-like smile.

Ishii scowled. "Captain, I—"

"Here we are," Raymond said, reaching up to grab hold of a hanging ladder. "Ladies and landlubbers first," he extended a hand to the blue-haired woman. "Ms. Not Interested?" He motioned up the ladder.

"Bae Ling Zhang." She frowned. "If only so you'll never make that ridiculous joke again."

"Works every time." He made a sweeping motion with his arm. "After you, Ms. Zhang."

She looked at the ladder and cursed in Chinese. "Remind me again why we didn't take a helicopter?"

"Too conspicuous," a deep voice answered. The bald man had stirred from his sleep and levelled a pair of dark sunglasses on Raymond. "No government would suspect a rusty old fishing boat."

"She may be rusty, Mister...?" Raymond raised an eyebrow.

"You talk too much," the bald man said, moving Bae Ling to the side and beginning up the ladder himself. He pulled himself up by reaching for every third rung, and quickly made the ascent.

"And it seems you lack common manners," Raymond grumbled. "Ladies next then."

Bae Ling began to climb the ladder and Ishii followed after. Raymond put a hand on the man's chest.

"What are you—"

"Pretty lady wearing a skirt and you want to climb up right behind her?" He raised an eyebrow. "I don't think so. We'll wait until she is up and *then* you climb."

Ishii fidgeted with his tie some more. He kept casting nervous glances at the water and gasping every time the boat rocked on the crest of a wave.

Bae Ling Zhang made it to the top a few minutes later. Raymond watched Ishii go up next and followed when the trembling man was halfway up the ladder.

Raymond pulled himself up the last rung of the ladder and stepped onto the platform. He brushed off his ragged wool coat and straightened his hat. Ishii rested his hands on his knees, trying to catch his breath. The bald man scanned the area with sunglass-shaded eyes, while Bae Ling leaned against a wall with her arms folded across her chest.

"Is the crew all here?" the bald man asked.

Raymond turned to Ishii. "Yes, Mr. Ishii. But since this is meant to be covert, it's just a small staff. Skeleton crew. In the control room."

The bald man frowned, but he said nothing. Ishii looked back and forth between Raymond and the bald man and sighed.

"Captain, will you please take Mr. Han and I to the control room to meet the staff," he said at last with a resigned sigh.

"And Ms. Zhang?"

"Is here for security analysis. She will assess the station and make sure there is nothing unexpected waiting for us." He forced a smile and nodded at the Chinese woman.

"As you like." Raymond opened the nearest door. "This way."

When the two men crossed the threshold, he added, "Ms. Zhang, please don't lean too far off the edge of the platform. Water from this height...like being slammed into concrete." He pounded his fist into his hand in demonstration.

Bae Ling rolled her eyes again and disappeared up a nearby flight of stairs.

"Gentlemen," Raymond said, disappearing into the dark portal and sealing the door behind him. A crimson light flooded the narrow corridor. "I hope no one is claustrophobic."

They continued down the hallway. Ishii tripped over the raised lip of an open portal as they passed, almost tumbling to the cold iron floor. "Watch your step, Mr. Ishii," Raymond said, "everything in here is metal. Please don't crack your skull."

Han helped Ishii to his feet, and they continued until they came to a door labelled "CONTROL" in large red letters. The door opened onto a dim room lit by several flashing monitors. A few people sat at computer terminals glanced up as Raymond motioned the two men in. As soon as they crossed the threshold, Raymond sealed the door behind them. He looked in through the small porthole and gave a terse wave, all of his false demeanor dropped in an instant.

"Thank you for your cooperation," he said.

Han slammed his fists on the heavy metal door. "Open this door or—"

"Or what? You'll be trapped in a control room?"

Ishii's face appeared in the window. "Captain please, you're making a mistake."

"Says the man who has his back to a room full of assault rifles," Raymond said, motioning for the two men to turn around. He leaned against a nearby wall and pulled his smartphone from his coat pocket, connected his headphones, and selected his favorite song. His eyes stayed focused on the door for when Bae Ling arrived.

#

Ishii and Han wheeled around and came face to face with six soldiers in dark military fatigues. The two men's suits lit up with three laser points each.

"I am Commander Ira Shah. Under the jurisdiction of Interpol, you are under arrest! Put your hands above your heads." The foremost soldier motioned with his gun. "Now."

Ishii began to comply, but before he could, Han shoved him to the side with a loud grunt and dove to the floor.

4

"Goddamn it," Shah said. "Open fire."

The roar of bullets filled the room as all the soldiers opened fire.

"Please! Don't shoot," Ishii screamed, his voice cracking. "Mr. Han, stand down!"

"No." Han popped up to the left of the soldiers and fired twice. The first bullet struck one soldier dead center. There was no blood as they crumpled to the ground with a gasp.

The second shattered a monitor across the room, sending sparks flying and smoke billowing. He ducked back behind the computer desk before the next volley of bullets filled the space he left behind. "Bulletproof, of course," he growled.

Ishii covered his head and screamed as the soldier on the floor crawled to grab him and cuff him to a nearby pipe.

"Don't move." The voice was female and each breath coming from the masked face sounded laborious. "Stay low." She pressed her back against a nearby console. One hand clutched her chest where the bullet had struck the Kevlar, the second pointed a small handgun at him with unwavering focus.

Ishii nodded and sank down into as comfortable a position as he could. Tears and sweat coated his face, and his rumpled suit was more askew than before. "I hate this job," he said.

#

Raymond slowly took out his headphones as Bae Ling stormed into the metallic hallway, her gun aimed directly at him. In her other hand she clutched a radio, and Raymond cursed at the idea that her reinforcements might be en route.

"Open the door," she commanded.

Raymond sighed and tucked away his phone. The sounds of the gunfight made it hard to hear in the confined space. He wondered how long it took to subdue a coward and a brute. "I'd rather not be filled with lead."

"Open the door, or I will replace your fucking brains with lead," she said, holding the gun inches away from his face.

"Do you mind?" Raymond said, motioning to his hat. "The brim is low, and I find it impolite not to look you in the eyes while you threaten me. I'm just—"

He grabbed her wrist and jerked it to the side just as she fired. The report of the gun deafened his right ear. Raymond rotated so that his body was alongside hers, still gripping her wrist and pointed the gun away from both of them. He looped his hand around the trigger of her gun and fired six of her shots into the ground.

"I was hoping you'd just surrender," he said, as he kicked her in the back of her knee. Her grip on the gun loosened and he plucked it from her hand. Pointing it at the back of her head, he said, "Please do not move."

"Go fuck yourself," she said.

"I have the last one," Raymond shouted. "Hurry up in there."

As if in reply, another burst of noise from multiple rifles. Blood splattered the broken glass of the control room porthole. There was a moment of silence followed by "Shit!" in Shah's rasping voice.

"Ishii! Han!" Bae Ling shouted. "Damn it!"

She held up the radio and Raymond realized too late what it really was. He lunged forward but it was too late. She clamped down on the red button on the side. Immediately the whole platform shook with the force of the first explosion. A second and third sounded off shortly after.

Raymond tumbled to the ground but managed to hold on to the gun. Bae Ling took her chance and sprinted down the hallway to the platform deck door. She cranked the wheel and swung it wide open, letting in the mixing smells of sea and smoke.

The whole station groaned, and Raymond felt the platform lurch under his feet. He aimed for the back of her leg and fired. The bullet went wide ricocheting harmlessly off the metal doorframe.

Shah burst from the control room. "What the hell's going on?"

"I missed a detonator. Zhang must have suspected something and set up bombs. She's sinking the platform," Raymond said, rubbing a sore spot on his head. "My stupid mistake."

"Is she crazy? Doesn't she know she'll sink as well?"

"The boat," Raymond said. "She's going for the boat!" He righted himself and sprinted out the door after the fleeing woman.

"Lieutenant Greenwood has one of the men in custody," Shah shouted as he jogged to keep up with him.

Raymond gave a quick nod as he ran.

Smoke filled the air on the open deck. It whipped around his head, carried by the brisk ocean wind. Bae Ling had made it to the top of the ladder.

"Ms. Zhang!" Raymond drew a bead on her with the gun. "Surrender, now."

The oil platform lurched to the side, sending Zhang toppling. The whole structure was falling apart around them. She grabbed the side of the platform, hanging on by her fingertips. One of her shoes plummeted down into the churning ocean. She tried to pull herself up but couldn't. Instead she slipped farther down.

Raymond rushed over and grabbed at her wrist. "I've got you!"

"Get your hands off me," she screeched.

"Believe me when I say, you don't want that." He tried to pull her up as dizziness and nausea from his head injury mixed with the smoke-filled air crashed over him like the thrashing waves below.

Bae Ling let go of the platform with one hand, dragging Raymond forward.

"What the hell are you doing?" he growled.

"Death before dishonor." She slashed at his hand with razor sharp fingernails.

Raymond gasped in pain and jerked his arm away. Realizing what he had done, he lurched down to grab Bae Ling's wrist again, but was too late. Amongst the plunging debris from the platform and burning smoke in his eyes, he couldn't make out where she landed. He didn't see her resurface.

"Like hitting concrete," he said, rubbing his eyes with the sleeve of his jacket. "Damn, that stings."

The station shuddered again. Raymond knew it wasn't safe to stay any longer. He was thankful at least that the fire wasn't spreading fast.

Shah exited the station interior, followed by Lieutenant Greenwood pushing Ishii along in front of her. The four other soldiers carried a body bag between them.

"Zhang?" Shah asked.

Raymond shook his head. "Leave the body," he said, looking at the late Mr. Han.

Ishii rushed towards him. The soldiers raised their weapons, but Raymond waved them down. "He's unarmed and cuffed. What do you want, Mr. Ishii?"

"Captain, please, I'm sure this can be all sorted out with the right amount of payment."

An explosion from inside blasted a plume of smoke and debris from behind the four soldiers on body duty. The dead man thumped to the ground inside the latex sack.

"We don't have time for this," Raymond said as Shah reclaimed the prisoner. "Leave Han, get to the boat."

The soldiers made double time, filing down the ladder until only Greenwood and Raymond were left on the platform. Shah had escorted Ishii down first, strapping the struggling man to his back.

"You first, sir," Greenwood said.

"Look out!" Raymond yanked Greenwood out of the way of a collapsing pillar. The force of the impact tore a chunk out of the station and sent them flying. Their piece of the station teetered precariously above an exposed tangle of sparking electrical wires and jagged steel bars.

Raymond looked back at the main portion of the station deck. The split had shunted them a good eight feet from it. "Can you make that jump?"

"No sir, I don't think I can." Greenwood's voice came out strained. Sheet metal the size of a small dinner plate stuck out from an angry gash on her side. A red stain spread through the camouflage canvas material of her uniform. Their tiny platform groaned and tilted at an angle that made it difficult to stand. Greenwood began sliding towards the mechanical forest of certain death that sparked beneath them.

"You go on ahead, sir," she said. "I'll try and make the jump after you." Her hands trembled, but she gave him a thumbs up and the most confident smile her willpower could muster, though he couldn't see it behind her mask.

Raymond shook his head, pulled her in close and said, "This next part is going to suck. Mostly for me, but also for you. Take a deep breath and keep your back pressed to my chest."

He clamped his eyes shut, and leapt backwards off the collapsing platform, plummeting into the churning water below. The water rushed up to meet him, slamming into his back like a wall of bricks. His body surged with pain, and then went numb as he sunk down into the dark ocean.

The oil rig gave out with a thunderous roar. The four pylons holding it up crumpled, sliding the whole platform down into the sea around them.

#

Raymond came to on a cot in the old fishing boat. He blinked and went to sit up but found that he couldn't. A groan escaped his mouth as he realized he had no feeling from the waist down. Greenwood was looking at him from the opposite cot. She'd wrapped the top of her uniform around her waist and lay on her back in a white tank top. A thick pad of gauze was taped in place, but even that was tinged a deep scarlet.

"My back?" he asked.

She nodded. "Peters, the medic, says he thinks several of your vertebrae are shattered, but that your spinal cord is intact."

Raymond heaved out a sigh and rubbed his face. "And you?"

"Sprained some stuff, hell of a lot of bruises," she paused, "and this." It was obvious that her efforts to indicate the wound put her in a lot of pain. Raymond held up a hand.

"I can see it from here." He let out a pained laugh.

"Right," she said. "Point is, I'm alive. Thanks to you."

He closed his eyes and let out a deep breath. "That's good. Very good."

"Why'd you do it? You could have left me and got down the ladder before the platform sank."

He opened a single eye and stared into her intense gaze. "It seemed like the right thing to do at the time. Now, I won't lie, I'm kind of regretting it."

Greenwood stared at him, blinking, and then broke into a laugh so hard it made her clutch at her side before it broke into a painful sounding cough. She wiped tears from her eyes. "You're gonna tell me you risked your life on a spur of the moment decision."

"Ninety percent of being a detective is acting on gut instinct. Sometimes it gets you hurt, but sometimes you save someone's life."

"And sometimes both happen." Shah entered the small cabin and gave them both a concerned look. "Glad to have you back with us, Captain Dehane."

"Ha! Back." Raymond coughed, pushing himself up on his elbows. It felt like someone was shoving a hot iron bar down his back, forcing it down inch by inch as he rose. Finally, he set his back against the wall of the cabin. "A little support?" he gasped, motioning to a nearby pillow.

Shah gently leaned him forward and slid the pillow between his back and the wall. Raymond groaned with the extra movement. But once the pillow was nice and secure, he breathed a sigh of relief.

"Where are we?" he asked. "Near a bar, I hope."

Greenwood covered her mouth to stifle her laugh.

Shah's brow furrowed. "With the amount of morphine we had to pump into you, I don't think—"

"A joke, Commander, to cope. But please, where are we?"

"Exactly where we were, minus an oil rig," Commander Shah said, clearing his throat and looking decidedly embarrassed at not understanding the humor. "I figured it would be best to wait for evac here."

"I would have made the same decision. And how long have we been here?"

"Only about an hour since the rig went under."

"Anything interesting? Any sign of Bae Ling's body?"

Shah shook his head. "Nothing to report, it's just the ocean. And there's too much large debris to safely navigate. Hitting the water from that height," he paused, casting a wary glance out at the grey ocean, "it's unlikely she survived."

Both Raymond and Greenwood gave a solemn nod of agreement.

The boat shuddered and gently rolled to one side, then tipped back to the other. Raymond braced himself to keep from rolling onto the floor. "Is a storm coming?"

"Clear skies all around," Shah said, looking out the window. "Why?"

"Something feels off about the motion of the waves," Raymond said, craning his neck to look outside. For a clear and sunny day, one with little wind, the ocean swelled and churned as if their boat rested in a great pot being stirred by an angry god. "I used to sail quite often. I know the ocean."

A rogue wave hit the boat sending Raymond sprawling to the floor. He gasped as electric pain shot from the middle of his back down to his toes. A good sign, but an unwelcome one at the present moment. Shah's feet flew from under him, but he caught himself before hitting the ground.

The commander scrambled to his feet, and with an excruciating assist from Greenwood, managed to return Raymond to his previous position, strapping him in place with some rope and duct tape, but leaving his hands free.

"And now I feel just as much a prisoner as you, Mr. Ishii."

Masahiro Ishii had been curled up in the corner of the cabin, trying to stay as silent as possible. He must have hoped that no one would acknowledge him. His wrists were tied together down by his ankles and his eyes were puffy and red from crying. He gave Raymond an emotionless look before returning his gaze silently to his shoes.

Overtop of the roar of the ocean, a sound like concrete grinding on metal rose to a deafening crescendo. Raymond clamped his hands over his ears. As suddenly as it started, the noise stopped.

"Is that still the platform?" Greenwood asked.

"It should all be underwater by now," Shah said.

One of the other officers burst into the cabin. He began speaking German at a rapid-fire pace while flailing frantically and pointing outside the cabin.

"Peters, no one can understand you when you talk that fast. Calm down!" Shah grabbed the man by his shoulders and shook him. "What's wrong?"

"The water," he said in broken English with a thick accent. "It is rising. Like a mountain."

Shah let go of him and bolted out of the ship's cabin. No sooner had he walked out, he mumbled, "My god."

Raymond struggled to see what the commotion was about. Peters had not been joking. The water, no more than a mile away, peaked like a great wide mountain. Thunder split the air and the water mountain exploded sending a shockwave that knocked the boat forward. The wooden structure creaked and groaned under the force. What truly struck fear into Raymond's heart was the sound that came next. Deep and guttural, like the cry of a whale played from inside a massive meat grinder. A deep shadow appeared beneath the surface of the water where the "mountain" had been.

"We need to go. Now." Raymond's head swiveled from person to person as he shouted out the window. "Can any of you sail a ship?"

Spencer Chaplin, the youngest officer, hurried to the open window. "Is it, uh, much different than flying a plane, sir?"

"I trust you'll figure it out. Now learn quick, and get us out of here, Chaplin."

Raymond watched the shadow grow until it was at least ten times the size of the sloop. The water around the shadow began to rise, and as the shadow grew, a faint purple glow began to emanate from the water. He heard the boat's engine start up and it began to pull away from the rising shadow. The noise from earlier cut through the air again, and the purple glow from the water intensified. Rough waves pounded at the boat, even as it made its escape. That's when Raymond saw it. The head came out first, reptilian and grey-scaled as if its skin was part of the ocean itself. An elongated neck thick like a tree trunk followed, with a thin, fan-like membrane crowning its head and travelling down to a ring-like sac at its base. A hiss escaped its throat as it ran a malevolent gaze over the ship. Its neck extended, hovering over the ship, and gazing down at them through orange, snake-like eyes.

"What the hell is that?" Chaplin said, looking over his shoulder.

"It's huge," Greenwood whispered, her eyes wide.

"Do we shoot it?" Peters asked.

"Maybe it isn't a threat," Raymond said. "Let's not make it one. Focus on getting away."

The creature blinked, a pale film flicking over its golden eyes. Two arms encrusted in petrified rock, coral, and all manner of crustacean shells rose from the depths. It screeched, shaking the boat and sending a chill down Raymond's spine. The force of the noise alone made his eardrums throb. A pungent smell of fish and iodine filled the air. Raymond gagged, and covered his nose.

The creature's head swayed atop its serpentine neck, before retracting back to a stockier, coiled position. Its eyes remained locked onto the retreating boat.

"I think it sees us," Peters said, aiming his weapon.

The creature reared back, a mouth full of jagged fangs that sprung from its gums like switchblades, stretched open, pouring saliva and seawater into the ocean below. Its head shot forward, and Shah opened fire. Peters and the other two officers outside followed suit.

The creature shrieked and diverted its attack, plunging its head into the water just to the side of the boat. The rest of its body followed, revealing something that looked like a rocky-shelled alligator with a thrashing, webbed tail.

Raymond felt the vessel leave the water and crash back down far to the left of where it had been. He hissed as more pain shot down through his legs. The creature disappeared below the surface, pushing the boat around on the force of the waves.

"Did we scare it off?" Shah asked.

"Maybe for now," Raymond said. "That might have been its first experience with bullets. I'm sure now it's just angry."

Shah's face went slack. "Shit."

"Any chance we can go faster?" Raymond shouted at Chaplin.

"I'm giving it all she's got, but as big as that *thing* is, I'm not sure it will matter."

The fanned tail emerged from the water and crashed down in front of the boat's stern, plunging it beneath the water and sending two of the officers into the frothing waves.

"Cage! Sizer!" Shah shouted. "Swim, quick!"

Before anyone could react, the creature's maw rose from the depths and swallowed them whole. It reared back and let out another cry. This time it sounded like the musical cackle of a hyena. The ship came to an uneasy stop and began to lean backwards into the water.

"Fuck," Chaplin said, slamming his hands into the wheel. His skin was waxy, and a sheen of sweat coated his face.

Shah looked to Raymond. "What are we supposed to do? It just swallowed two of my soldiers."

"I saw," Raymond said staring at the gigantic beast outside his window. "What time is it?"

"What does that—"

"Eight-fifty. Evac should arrive in the next five minutes." Greenwood said.

"Can we survive that long?" Peters asked.

"Probably not," Raymond said, "but we have to try."

Shah composed himself, cocked his gun, and said, "Well then, let's make sure this thing has a serious phobia of bullets after this." His hands trembled as he held the weapon. "Greenwood, watch over the Captain."

"Yes, Commander." Greenwood shuffled over and sat down beside Raymond.

"Peters," Shah said.

"Yes?"

"Let's go."

Peters paled, and he crossed himself solemnly as he readied his weapon. He wasn't much older looking than Chaplin. Raymond closed his eyes and offered up as much of a prayer as his disbelief could muster. He opened them and watched the two soldiers go forward.

They exited the cabin, unleashing a spray of bullets in quick controlled bursts. The creature winced and reared back, shrieking and hissing. There was no blood, and no injuries appeared on its scaly skin.

"Aim for its eyes!" Shah shouted.

"It's so high up I can barely see its eyes," Peters shouted back.

"Wait," Shah said, "cover me!" Shah dove to the deck of the boat and crawled to the nearest seat. A long black case was slowly sliding into the water. He snatched it up, popped it open and pulled out the pieces. "One sniper rifle, coming up." The rocking of the boat made the assembly more difficult, but in under a minute he had it assembled.

Shah climbed up on top of the boat's highest point, laid out, and aimed. "Peters, kill your fire."

With the hail of bullets ended, the creature's movements slowed, and it stared down the boat. Raymond thought it looked almost curious.

"Account for the motion, and," Shah whispered, "gotcha." He took a deep breath, held it, and squeezed the trigger. The rifle boomed in his hands. Immediately, the creature shrieked in pain as blood poured from its shredded eye socket. It began thrashing violently, threatening to capsize the boat. A clawed hand rose from the depths and swiped at them, crushing part of the boat in the process. The force knocked Peters over. He cracked his head on the side of the boat, and slid into the water, leaving a bloody trail after him. The creature plunged its head into the water much like an ostrich would the sand.

"Dammit, no!" Shah said, diving into the water after him. "No one else!"

Raymond started, "Shah, he's—"

The commander plunged into the water before Raymond could finish his sentence.

"Do you hear something?" Greenwood said.

"Yeah, I hear that thing throwing a fit," Chaplin said.

"No, listen, behind all that."

Raymond strained to hear. Behind the shrieks and thrashing of whatever it was, he could just make out the pulsing repetition of a helicopter. Shah emerged from the water screaming, cutting his focus.

"Chaplin," Raymond said, "go help him."

The young man ran to the end of the boat and was about to dive in when he saw the purple luminescent glow surrounding the screaming commander. Several spindly legs, different from the giant creature in color and structure, clawed over the man's face.

"Doing something to the water," he gasped out. "Bugs. Acid. Burns. Don't…come…in."

The water reddened around the man as his skin began to bubble and burn, torn away by the chitinous legs that twitched just above the surface of the waves. The commander seized violently, then went still, and sank into the sea while chunks of his   flesh   drifted   on   the   sloshing   waves. Chaplin sank to his knees.

The creature ceased its thrashing, and a harsh rumble echoed from beneath the waves. The sac around its neck began to deflate, and the spines at the end of its frills began to tremble. Without warning, its head snapped to the right, and all the tension in the air around it vanished. The rumble died off, and the sea around the creature grew calm. It let out a slight warble. Raymond followed its gaze and watched a whale pod surface and spray near the horizon. The creature warbled again and dove beneath the surface, sending the ship skidding in the opposite direction and spraying the deck with water. He watched its shadow rush toward the pod and vanish into the distance.

"What just happened?" Greenwood asked.

"I think...it realized it was hungry," Raymond said. He looked to what remained of the stern and saw Chaplin slumped in the rising water. "Go get him, before he throws himself into the waves."

He watched her limp to the young man's side. She put a hand on his shoulder and talked to him for a moment. She helped him to his feet and then returned to the cabin whose floor was now an inch underwater.

The helicopter drew closer; Raymond could hear its propeller over the rush of the sea air and the keening cries of the distant whales. He clenched his eyes shut and committed to memory the face of every lost officer. Shah. Peters. Cage. Sizer. When he finished, and their faces still danced behind his eyelids when he relaxed his focus, he opened his eyes and watched the sea, hoping that the creature wouldn't decide to finish what it had started.

CHAPTER 2

Devonte spun around in his chair and tapped the keyboard at his desk. The computer hummed to life, drenching the dark room in fluctuating shades of red, blue, and green. A single red notification lingered in the bottom right corner of the screen. Devonte opened the message. It was from his forum buddy, D-Base.

Did you hear about the seismic activity near the Mariana Trench,   KK?

Devonte swiveled to face his second screen. He googled "Mariana seismic" and scrolled through the search results. There had been an earthquake of some kind, and an abandoned oil rig sank.

Looks pretty standard to me. Submarine earthquakes are common, he sent back.

He sat back in his chair and drummed his fingers on the desk. D-Base was always online. They'd get back to him soon. Why were they bringing up something so routine? He scrolled through his usual forum, checking for any signs of strange happenings. A man in Hawaii reported seeing massive spikes travelling through foggy waters during a fishing expedition, but further investigation determined that the "spikes" had been rocks connected to a nearby uncharted island. In Japan, a woman claimed to be hunted by several "black, spiky dogs with blue fangs". Her blood had tested positive for LSD, and further investigation was halted.

The chat icon popped up. Devonte clicked it.

That's what I thought at first, but...

But what?

...

It's a challenge. See what you find. Let's correlate! :) Back later.

Just tell me!

D-Base's icon changed to "Away". An emoticon sticking its tongue out replaced the small green "Available" indicator.

"Motherfucker." Devonte rested his head in his hands. D-Base always did this. Whenever they came to a conclusion first it was a game, or a test, to see if Devonte could get there too. He enjoyed the game, just not this early in the morning. "Fine then. I'll do it better."

He pulled up his computer's console and logged into a live satellite feed. NASA's live satellite feed. The backdoor was reaching its expiration date. In a few days the open port would cycle, and he'd have to work his way back in. He wasn't sure if they didn't know, or didn't care about his actions, either one suited him just fine. Each satellite was identified by a lengthy and unique string of numbers. For now, he checked to see which satellite had most recently done a pass over the trench. He pulled up the live feed for the past week. The satellite's connections included a seismometer, an EC meter, and a flow detector. Several other data feeds sent a constant stream of information back to mission control, and to Devonte.

"Time for a good, old-fashioned romp." The program was designed to take in data from a set time period and search for anomalies using his self-made machine learning algorithm. Devonte massaged his temples, looking at the large amounts of data. "It'll need more data."

He expanded the program to pull from the past years-worth of data. It would take much longer, but it would be more accurate.

"And now we wait." He reached for a half-empty water bottle, finished it, and tossed it in the trash can. In a small journal, he made a note to recycle it later. He usually forgot to anyway, but it made him feel better that he was trying.

A few hours passed, and a new notification popped up, an email. He double-clicked it open. There was no subject line, and the email address simply read: user@mailserver.com. Scoffing, he went to delete it, but the message caught his eye.

It read: *I see you're interested in monsters. What if I told you they were real?*

Coincidence? Devonte thought. No. Targeted spam? Probably. He checked his messenger app. D-Base still registered as offline. A prank? No, he and D-Base both agreed monsters were real. Probably some internet troll who'd found some of his posts.

He responded to the message. The word scathing came to mind as he hit send. Basically, it boiled down to a hearty "fuck you, and fuck off".

The reply came almost instantly. *Check for yourself. Your results should be in -Tempest.*

At that exact moment, a second email came through. The notification sound caused him to jump. It was his program. Finished. Devonte glanced back and forth between the two emails. They were received at almost the exact same time. He opened the program response and looked through the data. A single anomaly stood out. A huge one. And from just a few months ago too. Devonte looked at the timestamp and pulled up the correlated images on the data feed and saw...nothing. The surface of the ocean, the thermal images, and the tectonics all looked exactly the same as every other image. That shouldn't be the case. "With that much seismic activity, the ocean should be rife with new activity. Unless ..." He looked at the data again. The image was exactly the same as the image from the previous day. "That's impossible," he mumbled.

Devonte flipped back to the strange email. "Tempest? What does that have to do with—"

A message from D-Base popped onto the screen. *Figure it out yet????*

"Somebody doctored the live feed," Devonte whispered. Another thought came to him. He opened up the messenger app and searched for Tempest. One result. They were online. Devonte cracked his knuckles and sent them a message.

Why would someone change the image feed? And how did you know?

He waited for a minute. No response. He flipped back over to his chat with D-Base. He typed two words. *Of course.*

Tempest's chat popped up. *Should we include your friend?*

The system printed a message. *[User D-Base has been added to the conversation]*

D-Base chatted, *Who's this? A new friend? Did you need help, KK?*

Devonte rolled his eyes. *They messaged me first. About the trench. Thought you were fucking with me.*

When have I ever? ;)

Only all the goddamn time, Devonte thought.

D-Base changed back to the main topic. *Seems like we share an interest though. Can we do the same with information?*

Your friend was on to something, Tempest replied.

Devonte sighed. His stomach growled noisily. *With some help from NASA, I learned that someone changed the image feed of the Mariana Trench on the day with the seismic anomaly.* As he texted, he felt his excitement grow. The chance, even the smallest chance, that the event might be tied to a real-life kaiju quickened his pulse.

D-Base responded, *Really? Suspicious! My information just pointed to the fact that the seismic event that occurred is the greatest in recorded history. It would be an 11.5 on the RS.*

Devonte rolled his eyes. *An 11.5, and no one felt it? Impossible.*

Check your data, picture boy!

Devonte turned back to his program. He scrolled through the information, frowning. He checked the data again. Then a third time.

He scoffed. "Well what do you know."

Not only was the earthquake massive, but the shockwaves dissipated right near the epicenter. "So, no one would have felt it…"

Checks out, he replied. *How does that happen?*

Dunno, D-Base sent back. *Hey Temp, you've been pretty quiet.*

Devonte had almost forgotten about the stranger in their midst. Their icon displayed an ellipsis while they typed.

Turn around…

What? Devonte replied. He swiveled in his chair and looked around his room. No one but him. He looked back at the computer screen. Tempest appeared as offline, but D-Base still showed as green.

Is this joker trying to scare us, D?

KK, there's someone at my door. They're jiggling the knob.

Devonte rolled his eyes. *Really? You're not funny.*

I'm not. I'm scared. I called the police but—

Devonte's gaze locked on that part. He and D-Base got into some sketchy shit. Calling the police would be the ultimate last resort. The message went on.

— they're banging now. Oh god they broke down the door. KK, I'm really scared.

Devonte froze. His eyes shot to the icon next to D-Base's avatar. It went white. Offline. He slammed the power button on his desktop tower and ripped the cord from the outlet as soon as the lights went black. Jumping from his desk, he paced the floor.

"What am I going to do?" he kept repeating as he paced the floor. He eyed the door to his room. And listened. There was no sound except his footsteps. "I have to get out of here."

He grabbed his laptop, a spare he kept hidden in the space between his desk and the wall, and hurriedly shoved it in his backpack. His desk was covered in unopened snack bars that he dropped on top of the laptop.

"What else?" He eyed his wardrobe.

Flinging it open, he dug through his clothes, stuffing some into the bag as he went, until he came to the bottom of the drawer. The gun he got from his father on his last visit, and a hand-sized Buck knife sat against the particle wood. He grabbed the gun and stuffed it into the waistband of his track pants, pulling his shirt down to cover it. The knife he slid into the side pocket of his backpack. A loud knock echoed through his apartment. Devonte froze. *Stay quiet, make them think you already left.*

"This is the FBI, open up." The voice held all of the authority of a federal agent, but the accent sounded fake, like someone trying to do their best interpretation of a cowboy. "Now."

Devonte looked around for anything else he might need, decided "fuck it, I can improvise", and slid open the sliding glass door to his balcony. He surveyed the ground three stories below. The back of his apartment faced a dense wooded area, perfect for his escape. He heard the sound of his door being kicked in, and hopped onto the fire escape, sliding down by holding onto the outside of the ladder. His hands burned as he dropped into the bushes below, crouching amongst the thick green foliage.

From above, he heard someone shout, "He's gone into the woods," in a thick Korean accent.

Two sets of heavy bootsteps clanged on the ladder and thudded to the ground right next to his hiding spot. He cupped his hand over his mouth and held his breath. The two pairs of boots shuffled on the ground nearby before taking off into a run towards the woods. He watched the two men disappear into the trees. When he could no longer see them, he let out a deep breath and relaxed. He lay there for what felt like an hour before disentangling himself from the branches of the shrubbery and set off at a quick pace. As he rounded his building, he saw a black Lexus parked behind his car. With a mischievous grin, he took the knife and slashed three of the four tires.

"Kick down *my* door will you, motherfuckers?" he sneered.

Satisfied with his work, he began his jog to the farthest public cafe within walking distance. He needed to check on D-Base first, then he could try to figure out what was going on, and what it had to do with the doctored photos from the Mariana Trench.

#

It was just before nine, so the cafe was packed. People filled the space in some bastardization of a line, waiting to order lattes and re-heated breakfast sandwiches. Devonte crept in with his hood on and slid into a booth near an outlet. His laptop booted quickly, and he tried to remote connect into his server.

Connection Failed.

"Shit." In his panic to escape he forgot that he unplugged his desktop. He rubbed at the stubble on his face. The hair was coarse and uneven. Even at twenty-one it wasn't growing in like he wanted.

"Dad, tell me you listened to me on this at least," he muttered. In his father's spare room, the one that would have been his if he hadn't moved out, he'd convinced his dad to let him set up a backup server. "You promised not to touch it."

He put in his password. *Connecting...Welcome, Devonte!*

Devonte pumped his fist in a silent cheer, then, noticing the strange looks the other patrons gave him, attempted to make himself less suspicious. He pulled down his hood and adjusted the way he was sitting. The gun pressed uncomfortably into his thigh, so he grabbed at his crotch and shifted it, glancing around, hoping people had resumed ignoring him. For the most part they had, save one older gentleman in the corner who stared intently in Devonte's direction. He did his best to ignore him. *Old people are just like that*, he thought.

On his laptop he pulled up the data and the photos from the morning. "Okay, show me what you got," he said. Most of the time, when a picture is modified, the changes are saved in the new picture. He went and found a tool online that claimed to be able to find that changelog and recreate the original image. The progress bar said it would take at least two hours.

"Public Wi-Fi," he grumbled. At the same time, his stomach growled. He reached into his backpack and pulled out a granola bar, unwrapping and finishing it in three bites. "It's okay, just try and relax."

He logged into the message app that he and D-Base used and saw that his friend still appeared offline. A message popped up on his screen. Tempest.

Where did you go?

Devonte ignored it.

Another message. *Where are you now?*

And another. *Your friend is asking for you.*

Fed up, Devonte responded. *Fuck you, creep. What do you want?*

Just you now.

A chill ran down Devonte's spine. He logged out of the app and closed the software. *It's okay,* he thought, *San Fran is a big city. They won't be able to find you that easily.*

"You're in trouble," a gravelly voice said.

Devonte jumped and reached for the gun in his waistband. The older gentleman slid into the seat across from him.

"You're nervous, and packing," the man said in his smoker's voice.

Sweat beaded on Devonte's brow. He clung tight to the handgun. "I don't know what you're talking about."

The man held up both hands. "I want to get my wallet out." He lowered his voice. "Please don't shoot me."

Devonte nodded.

The man pulled out a badge. A younger version of his face stared out from the picture underneath the words: *Inspector Raymond Dehane.*

"You're police?" Devonte said. "I haven't done anything wrong."

"Yet," Inspector Dehane said.

"The gun is for my protection," Devonte hissed.

"So, you are carrying?"

Fuck, Devonte thought. "My license is in my wallet." He hoped it was still there.

The inspector shrugged. "I feel like there is a bigger issue here, than whether or not you are allowed to carry the gun. Why do you think you need it? Protection from what? Gang violence?"

Devonte frowned. "No, why would it be— oh, you think because I'm black—"

A few heads turned as his volume increased. Devonte scowled and lowered his voice.

The inspector cut him off. "I meant no offense. Please, what is your situation?"

"Why should I trust you?"

Inspector Dehane flipped open his trench-coat, making the inside visible only to Devonte. Inside the coat pocket gleamed a polished silver revolver. "If I thought you were a threat, I could have confronted you in a less polite manner." He gave a tired smile.

Devonte released his grip on the gun with a sigh. "I'll show you," he said, motioning for the man to come around to the same side of the table as him.

He minimized the application running over the photos and re-opened the messaging app. His jaw dropped. All of the messages were gone. His and D-Base's from before today, and the ones that included Tempest. It was like he had never used it.

"What am I looking at here?" the inspector said, leaning into the computer.

"The messages," Devonte whispered, "they're all gone."

"Can you explain without them?"

"Yes, but…"

"What?"

"Now there's no guarantee you'll believe me."

"Let's assume that I will," the inspector said, placing a firm but comforting hand on Devonte's shoulder. "Start from the beginning." He took out a notepad and a red fine point pen and scratched the date at the top of the first blank sheet.

He must have noticed the worried look that crossed Devonte's face, because he said, "Don't worry, my memory just isn't as great as when I was your age. This is just to help me keep the facts straight."

The worry didn't leave Devonte's face.

Inspector Dehane chuckled. "And besides, I'm not a San Francisco detective, I have no jurisdiction here. I'd just like to help, if I can."

Devonte felt a little less tense. "Okay. It started at about 6am this morning." When the inspector's pen stopped moving, he continued with his story. He left out the bits about giant monster theories and hacking into the NASA satellite system. The inspector said he wanted to help, but Devonte thought it unwise to admit to federal crimes and kaiju conspiracies in front of a law enforcement agent.

The Inspector, Raymond, as he asked Devonte to call him, nodded sagely as he finished his story. "That is quite distressing."

Devonte ran his hands through coarse hair. "What am I gonna do?" The words all came out at once.

"We should return to your apartment. Search for clues. And you in particular should stay calm."

"My apartment?" Devonte said, his eyes wide. "Uh, I'm sure there's nothing there worth checking." He wasn't about to just let a random man, of the law or otherwise, into his apartment, even if he claimed to be trying to help.

Raymond raised an eyebrow. "I am not here to bust you for any crimes you may or may not be committing. If your friend was kidnapped, that is a more serious matter in my mind."

Devonte drummed his fingers on the table with one hand and held his head with the other. *Do I have a choice?* He sighed. "Okay. For D-Base."

"Hm. Good, shall we?" He slid his chair away from the table and stood. "Oh, and when we get outside, please hand over your gun."

"What? Why?"

Without turning his head, Raymond glanced at a woman in the corner of the cafe. "Because I believe someone may have called the police. And I've seen the news lately."

Devonte felt his pulse quicken, a fast, but heavy throbbing in his chest. "Yeah, let's get out of here." He packed his bag as fast as he could and scooted his chair back. It scraped noisily against the floor, turning a few heads. The woman Raymond had pointed out narrowed her eyes. Every fiber in Devonte's being wanted to flip her off. He resisted with an equally potent scowl.

The two of them exited, making polite excuses to the people in the line as they pushed through. When they were outside and no longer in view of the glass door, Devonte pulled the gun from his waistband and handed it to Raymond. He muttered something about "terrible gun safety" and slid it into a spare holster at his waist.

"Not a moment too soon," Devonte whispered.

A police cruiser, an old Mustang, whooped and rolled up beside them. The car stopped and they did as well. Two officers, a man and a woman, got out of the car. His badge read "Johnson", and hers, "McGee". Devonte let out an unconscious sigh of relief when he saw that at least one of the officers was black. The man towered over both Devonte and Raymond. The wrinkles around his eyes pinched together as he rubbed at his receding hairline.

"You two come from the cafe back there?" His voice sounded like concrete dragged across hot asphalt. He gave them a tired look that carried all the gravitas of a man who'd been to war.

"They match the description, Lieutenant," McGee said. Her hand went to her hip. To her gun, Devonte thought. He tensed.

"Please don't cause me any problems today," the male cop said. "Just frisk the kid." He turned to Devonte. "You don't mind, do you?"

Devonte knew it would be easier to comply. He tried to lighten the tension in the air with a joke. "Just try not to get too handsy down there." *Are you fucking stupid?*

As soon as the words left his mouth he cringed. McGee scowled at him and took a step forward. Her hand no longer on her gun, Devonte felt himself relax, if only a little bit.

"Now, I believe that is unnecessary," Raymond said, stepping between Devonte and the female officer. His badge was in his hand, on display for them to see. "Interpol. And you're a Chicago detective." It was a statement, not a question. The lieutenant looked Raymond up and down. "We received a call about a suspicious black kid and an older, disheveled looking Caucasian gentleman."

Raymond checked his trench coat and rumpled burgundy suit, then looked back at the officer with a mixture of horror and a deep sense of offense.

"If you don't mind, the caller seemed to be quite afraid of the fact that the young man had a gun. The frisk?" The lieutenant continued, either not noticing or completely ignoring Raymond's reaction.

"Ah," Raymond said, composing himself and refusing to move from in front of Devonte. "A simple mistake." He opened his trench-coat, revealing both his revolver and Devonte's Beretta. "I am the one with the gun...guns."

Lieutenant Johnson gave a heavy sigh. "Sir—"

"If you would like to see my licenses," Raymond continued. "I do believe I happen to have both of them on me."

Devonte shot him a confused glance then quickly fixed his face when he caught the other officer staring him down.

She opened her mouth to say something but was interrupted by a loud musical chime. She frowned and looked at the detective.

Raymond pressed a hand against his jacket pocket. "That...is my work phone. It could be important. Do you mind if I—"

Lieutenant Johnson waved his hand to say, "Go ahead".

Devonte had taken to the staring contest that the female officer initiated. He lost several times as Raymond carried on his conversation.

After the seventh loss, Raymond said, "I'd love to come right in, but I'm currently about to be stopped and frisked, so I'll be in as soon as that is done with."

Lieutenant Johnson scowled, wrinkles etching dark lines across his face.

"You'd like to speak to the officer," Raymond said, ignoring the change in demeanor. "I'll see if he would like to speak to you."

"Give me the damn phone," Johnson said. Devonte half expected him to growl about being too old for this shit. His eyes narrowed as he spoke to whoever was on the other end of the phone. He argued a bit, but the conversation ended with an exceptionally irritated, "Yes, ma'am."

He snapped the phone shut, and tossed it at Raymond, who caught it with a sly look. "So, am I free to go?"

"You are."

Officer McGee stared at her partner in shock. "We can't just—"

Johnson held up a hand. "But the boy is being detained. He was the one who was reported as suspicious, and this is our jurisdiction, not yours."

Devonte felt his heart freeze. He willed himself not to break into a run.

Without missing a beat, Raymond responded, "You can't detain him without detaining me. He is my partner, and is just as needed where I am going as I am." His face turned from sly to defiant, and he crossed his arms across his chest. "Now I've been quite patient with you two, but it's wearing thin now that you're impeding *my* job. You know, international security?" He began tapping his foot.

Lieutenant Johnson glared down at the adamant detective. Devonte thought of the old spaghetti westerns he would watch with his dad as a child. He wondered if either man would actually draw on the other.

The lieutenant grumbled and looked at his watch. "I don't have time for this. I'm supposed to meet the wife for lunch. Let's go, McGee." He turned and headed back to the cruiser.

McGee relaxed. The scowl Devonte swore was permanent melted away. "Sorry for the hassle," she said, and climbed into the passenger side seat.

It was all a tough cop act, Devonte thought. He became painfully aware of the sweat that had soaked through his shirt. They watched the cruiser pull away and turn at the nearest intersection.

"You just lied to the police," Devonte said.

"The police always lie to the police," Raymond said. "At least when we want to actually get something done that is."

"We're not going to my apartment, are we?"

"I'm afraid not," Raymond said. "But where we are going, there will be people who might be able to help us find your friend."

Devonte breathed an internal sigh of relief. "Okay, where are we headed?"

"The Naval Base."

And with that, Devonte wished he could take back that sigh of relief. *Into the lion's den,* he thought. "How are you going to get me in?"

"That we will figure out once we get there," Raymond said. "My car is this way." He twirled his keys around his index finger and continued in the direction they had been walking.

#

The Camaro roared down the road. Raymond was pushing his car at least fifteen miles over the speed limit. Devonte sank into his seat and clung to what he called the "oh shit bar" above the passenger window. He was used to riding in speeding cars, but most of them didn't have quite as much muscle as this one. His dad's Honda could only manage a snail's pace in comparison. When Devonte asked him about it, Raymond responded with a dismissive, "We're in a hurry."

"That reminds me," Raymond said, "should you call...your parents? Girlfriend? Someone? And let them know that you're safe."

"Oh, yeah, I guess I should." He pulled out his phone and scrolled until he found his dad's cell-phone number. The phone rang once. Twice. Three times.

Ay, it's Aaron. Not at the phone right now. Leave a message and I'll hit you back, the voicemail said. Devonte hung up without leaving a message.

"No response," he said.

"Got another number for them?" Raymond asked.

"I do, but..."

"No buts. I don't want to get accused of kidnapping. Call."

"Don't boss me around like a child," Devonte snapped.

Raymond raised his eyebrows but didn't look away from the road.

"Sorry," Devonte said. "I'll call." He took a deep breath. And dialed Alison's number.

The phone rang. Once. Twice. Devonte prayed no one would answer. Before the third ring, a sound on the other side of the phone clicked.

"Devi, is that you?" Alison cooed over the phone.

"Hey Alison. It's me," Devonte said. He switched the phone to his left hand and leaned his head against the car window. "And please don't call me Devi."

"Oh my gosh, Devi, are you okay? Where are you?" He knew her concern was sincere, but the way she spoke made it sound fake. Devonte pictured her painting her nails or checking out her reflection as they talked. His jaw tightened.

"I'm fine. Why wouldn't I be?"

"Well two FBI agents came by the house asking about you, so I figured you got yourself in trouble with all that tracking you do." An exaggerated sigh rasped out of the speaker.

"Hacking," Devonte corrected, then quickly added, "but I only do it on my own virtual— never mind, you said two FBI agents came by?"

Raymond gave him a curious look. He mouthed, "For real?"

"Yeah, a scrawny guy and a guy so fit it made my mouth water. Meow." She giggled.

You're married to my dad, you—

"Alison." Devonte effected his most controlled voice. "What did they look like?"

"Uh, they were definitely Asian. They kept chattering to each other while I was talking to your dad on the phone." He could picture the confused shrug she did as she spoke.

Devonte's mind went into panic mode and he bolted up in his seat. "Are they still there? Where's dad? Is he okay?"

"Whoa, calm down, you're freaking me out. No, they're not here anymore, they stopped by super early and woke me up, and left after I told them where you live."

"You *what*?!"

A startled Raymond swerved into the oncoming traffic lane before correcting himself and giving Devonte a look that mixed frustration and confusion.

"Don't yell at me, you know I'm—"

"Is dad there?" Devonte cut her off. "Put him on the phone."

He could feel her hurt in the silence. "No. He's not here."

"Where is he?"

"Out," she said. "I'm hanging up now. I have a cruise to catch. Buh-bye."

"Alison, no, don't hang—"

His phone beeped to let him know that the call had been disconnected

"Up." He gripped his phone tight enough for his hand to shake.

"Please do not chuck your phone in frustration. It might ricochet of the dashboard and give me a concussion," Raymond said. "Which would probably kill us both, given the circumstances."

Devonte glared at him but stopped when he saw the sympathetic look on the older man's face. He ran a hand through his hair and exhaled a thin stream of air through pursed lips. "She's a bit of a—"

"Bitch?" Raymond offered.

Devonte chuckled. "Ditz is probably more accurate. I think she means well."

"The men that came to your house?"

"She *sent* them to my house. Bought the whole FBI schtick. Probably trying to impress one of them with her immediate and respectful compliance."

"But you said there was a person in your chat room?"

"I had assumed they traced me by IP or something," Devonte said, "but I guess not...they knew enough about me to find my family home."

"Then with your friend they would have had to do the same, right?"

"I was thinking that. It would be helpful information if I knew anything about D-Base other than a username and a general set of interests." Devonte flung his head back against the headrest.

"You've known this person for how long, and you never discussed your personal lives?"

"We...got wrapped up in other things, okay. It just never came up...except, hold on...I think they live in Chicago? Yeah, yeah, cause when Obama was elected president, they were hyped about having a local president."

"Isn't Obama from Hawaii?"

"I tried to explain that, but they insisted that since he currently resided in Chicago it counted."

"Well Chicago is a bit far away for us to do any detecting. Still, the people at the base are sure to have some contacts there, so try not to worry."

"No, no," Devonte said, growing visibly excited. "I know the general area they live! With that I can run over the people who visit the sites I know we both frequented, and back trace their IP address."

"Which would tell you where they live," Raymond said. "Ah, the horrors of modern technology and the youth who understand it."

"You think they'll have decent Wi-Fi at the base?" Devonte asked.

"I believe the question you should be asking is 'Will they let me carry my laptop through the front gate?'" Raymond replied as he turned off onto an exit without slowing down at all. "The answer is probably 'no'."

"But D-Base could be in real trouble!"

"We'll have to see if we can get you access to an internal terminal then."

"There's no way they'd let some random ass dude touch their shit. I mean, come on."

"But they might let the partner of an esteemed Interpol agent 'touch their shit', as you say." Raymond winked, but the cheeky effect was lost since his eyes remained glued to the road.

"You're going to lie...to the American government? For me?"

"No. For your kidnapped friend. Things need to get done."

The adrenaline from the morning must have finally worn off, because Devonte felt the nagging of a question at the back of his mind. "Why are you helping me?"

"I'm a detective. In essence, my job is to help people."

"No, but why are you going this far? I mean, the cafe...the police...now the military! That has to extend beyond the call of duty, right?"

Raymond paused to think a moment, then pulled off to the shoulder of the highway. "Because, I worry I may be at fault for you and your friend's present condition."

INTERLUDE I

The grey-blue ocean lapped around the cruise liner off the coast of Hawaii. Gentle waves lapped at the reflective white paint of the ship's hull as it rested out in the infinite aquatic expanse. Vacationers leapt from the lower deck, splashing noisily as they joined their peers amongst the waves.

"Marleen, come on in!"

The middle-aged woman looked down at the man who'd invited her to come with him. Eric. This was his idea of a date. The ocean. She'd felt a real connection with him over the dating app and when they met for coffee the month before, so she didn't want to spoil the mood by admitting her fear of water. Thalassophobia her therapist called it. She wondered if he thought naming it would help her overcome the fear. In this moment she didn't think it mattered much. Visions of great writhing tentacles dragging her down into the infinite dark filled her head. Her heart raced and she began sweating more than normal, even under the bright noon sun.

"Don't worry," Eric reassured her. "I'll be right here when you hit the water. Just start swimming up as soon as you go under."

But what if I don't, she thought. *What if I hit the water and pass out? What if there's a rock we can't see? What if a wave—*

Her thoughts were cut short by a deep rumbling from beneath the ship. Without warning, the ocean grew violent and the boat teetered from side to side. Marleen fought to keep her balance, gripping to the railing of the ship with knuckles as pale as the white sand beaches they explored that morning.

Another lurch of the boat sent her spilling down into the water. She screamed the entire way. Eric was good to his word. No sooner had she hit the water, his arms were around her and pulling her to the surface. She gasped for breath and opened her eyes, to see Eric's terrified eyes looking over her shoulder.

Marleen heard a sound that made her skin crawl. An animalistic cry akin to a whale, but deeper and angrier, with a hyena's cackle at the end. The air around them trembled with the force of the noise and the waves rose to terrible heights from the force of the sound.

She turned and saw the creature towering over the cruise ship. Part dragon, part turtle, its serpentine neck ending in a reptilian head a good ten meters above their cruise ship.

But that's a fifty-meter ship…

Eric pulled her attention back to him. "Don't look at it. We need to go." The urgency in his eyes reactivated her conscious thought and brought with it the panic. A monster in the water. Her greatest fear, true. She began to flail and hyperventilate, plunging beneath the surface and bobbing back up. Salt-water poured into her mouth and she coughed as it stung her lungs.

"Marleen," Eric said pulling her once more to the surface and holding her up as he treaded water for both of them. "Look at me."

She managed to lock her focus on him, keeping her eyes from darting around in her skull. Fatigue crept over her already.

"There's an island just over there," he said. "We have to get away from the boat." His voice came out in even, calm syllables. If Eric was afraid, he was putting on one hell of a good show for her, she thought.

Just over there was probably a whole football field away. Something about his calm demeanor made her think she could make it. Even as she heard the screams of the people on the ship. Even as she heard the groans and cracks when the creature bit down onto the cruise ship. She began to swim, just behind Eric. There were other people swimming for the island. Marleen could barely see them with all the salt in her eyes, but she could feel them. They all exuded the same panic, a mixture of confusion and pure terror.

She didn't remember making it to the island, but she felt the sand against her skin. Eric pulled her to shore.

"You made it," he said. He smiled, but the smile was worn out and poisoned with sadness.

Everyone else on the island was staring out to sea. She went to follow their gaze, but Eric held her head gently in his hands.

"Don't." He pulled her head to his shoulder and she began to cry. Deep heaving sobs. Her warm tears rolled down Eric's chest as he looked out at what remained of the cruise ship.

He clutched Marleen even tighter. She never did look back, not until the ship completely sank from view and the sun began to start its slow descent. She checked Eric's watch. The whole ordeal had only lasted an hour. To her it had felt like ages.

The creature was gone. It'd fled once it realized the ship wasn't food, but not before taking out its frustration on the imposter. What was once a towering crown of the sea had now sunk slowly into the brine. Smoke plumed up to the sky as fires erupted from the remaining debris. A dark substance spread out from the wreckage. Marleen knew it was oil, but she couldn't help but imagine that something fresh and organic had seeped in with the fuel after the attack. She could make out bodies too. Some of them were swimming towards the small island they now called home. Some just floated and bobbed with the motion of the waves.

CHAPTER 3

The door to the cell slid open, grinding and grating on rusted tracks. Bright light poured into the dark interior of the room. Skylar shielded her eyes as a wiry silhouette stepped into view.

"Are you ready to cooperate with us, Ms. O'Hara?"

"Please, just let me go." Skylar forced her voice to remain calm.

"Now, that is not an answer to the question you were asked." The woman walked into the cell and leaned in close, so her face was only inches away from Skylar's. Her warm breath drifted across Skylar's skin. It smelled like pineapples.

Skylar took a deep breath. "What do you want from me?"

"I told you that online," the woman replied. "A real-life kaiju. Don't you want to study it?"

"I *want* to not be kidnapped." Skylar cursed the edge in her voice and hoped it wouldn't get her in trouble.

The other woman let out a wild, mocking laugh. At the end she covered her mouth and the laugh subsided to a soft chuckle. "You weren't kidnapped."

"You expect me to believe that?"

"What do you believe, then?"

"You broke into my home, threw me in a van, and dragged me here." Skylar's temper flared. "Pretty sure I *know* that's kidnapping."

"Is it kidnapping if it's your government bringing you in for crimes you committed?" the woman whispered. "Say, the FBI?"

"You're not FBI," Skylar protested. "There are rules you have to follow."

The woman flashed a badge. "Agent Jia Ming. FBI. You and your friend were up to some naughty business."

Skylar saw the badge, but she didn't buy it. *My best bet is to play along,* she thought. *Find a chance to...to what? Escape? They found me once before, but if I can work with KK...*

"Where's KK?" she asked. "Let me see him!"

The woman's face soured. It made her look at least ten years older. "Your friend is on the run."

New plan. Bide time. "I see," Skylar said. "So... tell me about this supposed kaiju?"

"Get up." Agent Ming smiled and motioned for the door. "It's right this way."

#

All kinds of people populated the open courtyard as Agent Ming guided Skylar on what felt like a museum tour without the endless stream of facts and commentary. None of them wore suits, appearing more like a crowd of visitors than federal agents. The whole thing made Ming seem out of place.

"This doesn't look like a government facility," Skylar said.

"Look around. Surely you know where we are." Ming waved a hand in the air.

Skylar looked around. A tower pierced into the sky, its white sheen blinding in the open sun. She could smell salt on the air, so she guessed they were on an island. There looked to be the ruins of an older building next to the square grey building ahead of them.

"Alcatraz," she said. "So, these are—"

"Just people. Not federal agents." An enigmatic smile played across Ming's lips. "I told you that you weren't a prisoner."

"Huh. Then where are we headed?"

"We can't conduct our business here in public."

"Don't tell me there's a secret sub-basement to Alcatraz." Skylar's eyes widened despite her reservations.

"There is no secret sub-basement to Alcatraz...but there is a secret passage to a facility that rests inside the island," Ming said.

"Oh my god! That's so cool, I mean a secret underground—"

People turned and stared at her outburst.

Ming cleared her throat. "*Secret* is the keyword."

"Oh right. Sorry."

People resumed their normal sightseeing activities as they entered the retired prison. Rows upon rows of empty cells echoed with the sounds of their footsteps.

"No one's inside. Don't they do tours?"

"We're in between them. Hurry up." The agent quickened her pace and they stopped in front of a cell much larger than all of the others. An oriental rug covered the concrete floor, and several pieces of wooden furniture far too fancy for a prison sat covered in dust inside the cell. Agent Ming produced a different badge from her suit jacket and scanned it against a brick on the wall. There was a beep and a small click. The plexiglass panel sealing the room slid up on hydraulic slides. They entered the cell and closed the panel behind them.

"Okay, so where's the secret door?"

No sooner had she said something, a loud grinding sound rumbled from the back wall of the cell. It began to slide down, slowly revealing a sterile looking hallway illuminated with fluorescent lights. Agent Ming stood holding a nineteen-twenties rotary phone off the hook. When the door opened all the way, she hung it up. Skylar could hear the gears move, preparing to reseal the passageway.

"That's too cool."

"Yes. Now please hurry before anyone comes along."

"Oh yeah." Skylar jogged to the back of the cell and into the sterile portal.

The door rumbled closed behind them and sealed with an echoing thud. An antiseptic smell filled the air, like someone just finished cleaning. It reminded her of a hospital.

Skylar sneezed. Agent Ming walked ahead briskly, disappearing through a door at the end of the hallway. Skylar squeaked and scurried after her, not wanting to be left alone in the empty corridor. She pushed open the heavy iron door and entered a room like something out of her science-fiction novels.

People in lab coats hustled to and fro, while strange devices whizzed and chimed. Some sparked and smoked. The far wall of the room was covered floor to ceiling in monitors displaying what appeared to be various live camera feeds of San Francisco, and other places that Skylar didn't recognize.

In the center of the room, suspended in a vat of fluid, sat a tooth the size of a small person. Blood and tissue floated alongside it as it bobbed in the clear mixture.

"What?" Skylar froze. She shook her head, and rushed to the side of the container, pressing her face against the glass like a child looking through a window at a much-desired toy. "Is this— is it real?"

"Real enough to tear clean through a blue whale." A young man with silver hair and glasses bigger than his head walked up beside her. His golden eyes sparkled as he spoke. "Beautiful, isn't it."

"Doctor Wagner, this is Skylar O'Hara," Ming said.

"*Doctor* Skylar O'Hara," Skylar said extending her hand and shooting the agent a not-so-friendly look.

"Well, doctor," the man laughed, "pleased to meet another person as excited about this discovery as I am. And please, there's no need for formality here, please call me Kurtis."

"Doctor Wagner, until further notice please continue to call me Doctor O'Hara," Skylar said with a smile. "I don't know any of you outside of this supposedly professional environment, so I will do the same."

Kurtis looked taken aback. The childlike wonder of minutes again had dropped completely, and Skylar stared him down with the cold professionalism she so rigorously practiced to survive her male colleagues.

"Well, uh, if you say so," he stuttered, casting a "help me" glance at Agent Ming, who simply shrugged.

"Now then," Skylar said, forcing her tone to be as authoritative as possible. "Tell me about the specimen."

"It's a tooth," Kurtis deadpanned.

Skylar frowned. "Obviously. What have you learned from the tooth? Or the tissue?"

"We don't exactly have those kind of biology experts here at the, uh, FBI." He scratched the back of his head and chuckled nervously. "So, we haven't gotten much beyond that."

Skylar paused. "Which explains why you brought me here." She turned to Ming. "You could have just asked, you know."

"You could have said no." Ming waved a hand dismissively.

"I wouldn't have."

"How could we have known?"

"Well you certainly knew enough about me to know to drag me in," Skylar muttered. "Okay," she said raising her voice back to its normal volume. "I'll need—"

"We set up a station for you just over there," Kurtis said, pointing to a table covered in all kinds of equipment. "You should find everything you could need, but if not let us know. Will you need any assistance?"

Skylar regarded Wagner icily. "No. Thank you."

#

She wasn't sure what to make of the creature. It shared genetic characteristics with reptiles, amphibians, fish, and even sharks, something remarkably impossible. Or at least it would have been, if she wasn't seeing it with her own two eyes. Of one thing she was sure though, the creature's regenerative abilities were astounding. She could see the cells growing and re-growing even as she observed it. It explained the smell: hydrochloric acid. To keep the organic tissue from spreading they were constantly killing it.

"Learned that the hard way," Kurtis said, approaching. Skylar wasn't sure how much time had passed, but she imagined she must have been staring off in thought for a while for him to come and check up on her. He poured a small amount of clear liquid into the petri dish. A sharp burning smell wafted through the air. More acid.

"Huh?" she said, blinking. "Hey!"

He held up a hand. "Your sample is fine, look."

The new cells that had formed during observation dissolved away, but the original tissue remained. As soon as the pungent odor had appeared, it vanished. Skylar mentally marked that down as another oddity.

"When we first got the sample, it had been frozen. Imagine our surprise when, during transport, it began to re-grow. Fast."

"I've never seen anything like this. I mean, starfish, and some lizards, but that takes time; this is insane."

"Is that your best scientific assessment?" he chuckled.

"Is that your best attempt at a joke?" she snapped.

His mouth snapped shut and his shoulders slumped. "You're right, that was in bad taste. I'm sure this is fascinating, and hard to process. Trying to ease the tension, mostly." His mouth twitched like he wanted to smile but was keeping himself from doing so.

"The thing is, the regeneration has no point," she said.

"I would think it's a survival mechanism," he offered.

Skylar squinted at him. "Another joke?"

His mouth opened a minute and he returned her confused look. "Yes? Maybe? Depending on what you say next, I guess."

"That's not how jokes work. But no, what I meant was that the regeneration has no order. Starfish can regrow limbs specifically. Lizards, tails. This is just random tissue growing into more random tissue."

"What does that mean?"

"In theory, as fast as this tissue regrows...this creature is unkillable. Immortal, even." She wasn't sure which of her emotions showed more on her face, fear or excitement, but she could see the terror on the other doctor's face.

"Everything has a weak point though, right?" His eyes were darting around, looking for something.

"Like I said, in theory. What I can say though is that it won't be easy to put it down if we have to. That is what we are researching, right? How to kill the giant monster."

Kurtis gripped the glass acid container so tightly Skylar worried it might shatter and burn off his hand. She reached out and gently took the beaker from his hand, placing it safely in a holder. "Are you okay, Dr. Wagner?"

Her question snapped him out of whatever internal conflict he was having. "Oh. Yeah, right. Do you want to see the creature?" His gold eyes flicked to the door, lingered for a moment, then settled back on her with a pleading look.

"Of course," she said. "I wanted to see if I could determine what type of creature it was first but given these results...I would like to see the owner of the tooth." She gave a small smile. Whatever it was he was worrying about, she had a feeling he would use this opportunity to tell her. At least that's what she hoped.

He gestured for her to follow him to the back of the room. The other people went about their business as they passed. A woman sat behind a computer, her glasses reflecting the green on black image of a terminal. Her eyes flicked up and Skylar made her best attempt at trying to act like she hadn't been staring.

As they reached the back of the room, Skylar realized something she hadn't before. A wall of thick glass separated the monitors from the rest of the lab. A dark-skinned man in a black suit watched them approach from behind blue aviator lenses.

"Jason," Kurtis said. "Gonna show the newbie our beastie."

"You know I have to go in with you." His voice vibrated in Skylar's chest like the bass at a dance concert.

"About that, we were gonna watch the roar, so I understand if you don't want to."

"Shit man, I hate that sound. So loud...and my wife's already getting on at me about fucking up my hearing." He lowered his sunglasses and glanced between the two of them. "Damn, just don't tell Ming, alright? And be quick about it."

"You got it, man." Kurtis held up his fist.

Jason frowned at him, sucked his teeth, and said, "Get your ass in there."

Skylar pushed Kurtis into the room to spare herself any further secondhand embarrassment. The door sealed behind them with an audible hiss.

"Soundproof," Kurtis said, "because some of the videos get a little loud. We can talk in relative privacy here. Just keep looking at the screen. It's interesting enough anyway." He walked over to a panel on the wall, and the lights dimmed. All twenty-five monitors, five by five, changed to the same blank screen. A crystal-clear video appeared; one massive image split across all the screens. Skylar remarked at the video quality.

"I'm sure you know this, but most of us are not here by choice."

"Yeah."

The video showed the ocean, waves cresting and crashing. A shadow appeared beneath the waves, a great black spot that twisted and writhed with the sea. The carcass of a whale breached the surface, staining the water a deep, churning red. Great angry scars wrapped around the blue-grey flesh as the water mixed and frothed with the blood. Birds flocked around, landing on and pecking at what to them appeared as a free meal. She could hear the whale's wounded call, almost drowned out by the celebratory caws of the sea birds.

"Do you know who these people are?" he asked.

"Not the FBI?" she said.

"No. I've tried asking Jason, but he gets pretty tight lipped about it. I do know that the 'agent' is in charge."

"Gathered that. What are we doing here?"

A second, larger shadow appeared beneath the whale. Skylar felt her breath catch in her chest. Three rows of teeth emerged on either side of the whale carcass and snapped together like a bear-trap in slow motion. The razor-sharp teeth tore through the sea mammal's flesh like it was butter, severing it into two parts. Skylar gasped. The head attached to the teeth emerged from the sea and kept rising until it towered outside the frame of the camera. The sea birds screamed and scattered away. Whatever was recording the video adjusted accordingly. Skylar estimated that the creature's neck alone must have been at least sixty meters tall. Taking that, the whole thing must have been at least one hundred meters from head to toe.

"It's terrible isn't it," Kurtis said. "And they want to control it."

"What?" Skylar's head snapped around to look at Kurtis.

"Eyes on the screen." He didn't look at her.

Skylar forced her eyes back to the video screen. "Control it?" She watched as the creature, the Tempest Beast, tore its prey apart. Shark-like teeth carving out chunks of flesh as seagulls dove in and took their chance. The large predator ignored them as they picked off their own bits of the kill.

"These people call themselves Tempest. They believe this creature is a sign of their divine right to rule, as well as their weapon to enforce that rule."

"And they took us…to make us figure it out."

Kurtis nodded and handed her a pair of earplugs. "I suggest you put these in, wouldn't want to damage your hearing."

Skylar complied not a moment too soon. Even with the plugs in she could hear the monster's bellow. She thought at first it might be another whale, but in the middle of the sonorous tone the noise pitched down becoming a harsh basso rumble that vibrated through her teeth and down into her chest. As the bellow ended, the creature let out a cry that reminded Skylar of accidentally scraping a metal fork on a ceramic plate. Only a thousand times worse. She cupped her hands over the top of her already plugged ears until it ended.

The video cut off.

"After that, the battery in the drone died," Kurtis said.

Behind them, the sliding door hissed open, and the clicking sound of heels approached them. "So, what do you think of the creature?" Agent Ming placed herself between them, giving Skylar a questioning look.

"It's," Skylar searched for the best word, "awe-inspiring."

Ming smiled. "Yes. And you get to be one of the first to research it."

Skylar decided to push her luck. "To learn how to kill it?"

Kurtis' eyes widened.

The agent frowned. It wasn't a frown of anger, but one closer to concern. "It would be our preference simply to either capture it or figure out what attracts and repulses it so that we can keep it at bay."

"Really?" Skylar feigned surprise. "I just thought like in the movies, you know, everyone just wants to kill the big scary creature."

"I'm sure our counterparts in the military will be more than likely to take that approach, but we're hoping to accomplish our goal before then. Will you help us?"

Kurtis watched Skylar with interest from behind the agent's back.

"It's been my life's dream to research a real-life kaiju," Skylar said. "What do you think?"

Agent Ming smiled brightly. "Then you have my thanks." She turned on her heel and crossed to the door. "Oh, and Doctor Wagner, try not to distract her too much with your flirtatious advances."

Kurtis' face went bright red. "I, uh, no, sorry, what?!"

"Convincing Jason to let you two have some alone time in the soundproof room," she said with a raised eyebrow.

"Oh...yeah." He rubbed the back of his head and looked away when Skylar caught his eye.

Agent Ming left them there, soaking in the awkward silence.

Kurtis broke the silence. "It's not—"

"We should get to work. Before they suspect us," Skylar said.

"Yeah."

As they exited, Jason gripped Kurtis by the shoulder and half whispered, half hissed, "You owe me."

Kurtis said, "Yeah, you're a good one, man."

#

"Whales?" Kurtis asked. He glanced over Skylar's shoulder at the notes she had taken but must have found her handwriting completely illegible as he squinted in confusion.

"More specifically, whale *noises*," she said, dancing around to the other side of the work bench.

Kurtis spread his arms in a way that said, "Please explain."

"I have never known a predator that won't come where the food calls," Skylar said, frustrated. "Instinct reigns supreme."

"You plan to hijack the whales?"

Skylar blinked. "Physics. Right?"

Kurtis put on a straight face, ignoring the sleight at his profession.

"Okay, imagine this," Skylar said. "You're a giant predator that devours entire whales in a few bites."

"An easy place of mind to put myself," he said dryly.

Skylar continued, undeterred by his sarcasm. "You track your prey by listening for their calls in the depths of the sea, and you use your acute sense of hearing to do so." She paused for a breath. "But what if it's a trick? What if you hear the whale calls but they're fake?"

"How would I know?"

"Exactly!" Skylar tossed her notebook at the other doctor. "You wouldn't know."

"You think we can lure the creature away with fake whale songs?"

"Real whale songs. Fake whales."

Kurtis shrugged. "I can't argue with that logic."

"That's because it's right."

Someone clapped behind her. Skylar wheeled around. Agent Ming clapped again, more enthusiastically this time. Skylar hated the woman's penchant for popping up when she was least expected.

"That is truly brilliant," Agent Ming said.

"Anyone here could have figured it out," Skylar said. She mostly meant it.

"But there's one problem."

"What?"

"That would *attract* the creature, how would we repel it?"

Were you listening to what I said, or weren't you? Skylar thought. "You can use it to the same effect. Just place the whale calls somewhere away from the places you want it to stay away from."

"Ah," Ming said, "and would this work without fail?"

Skylar screwed up her nose. "I don't have much to go off of. A few videos and a giant tooth. I don't even know if *this* is guaranteed to work. We don't know how intelligent the creature is. I'd need more time to—"

Agent Ming interrupted her. "Time is not a luxury we can afford."

"What?" Skylar snapped. "We can't just put something out there that could get people killed. It needs to be fully tested."

The agent fixed her with a cold stare. "People may die, but their sacrifice will not be in vain. Begin a prototype and have it ready for a field test as soon as possible." She turned to Jason. "Make sure they work."

The black man gave a nearly imperceptible nod of confirmation. "They'll work."

"Good." Her smile dripped venom. She turned and gave the same smile to Skylar and Kurtis. The two watched her disappear into another room.

"Does she just sit in that room and come out just to piss me off?" Skylar asked.

Kurtis chuckled. "Be careful, if she hears you say that on camera, she may do it more often."

"Ay, Kurtis, don't make this hard for me, just do whatever thing that crazy bitch wants you to do." He peered over his sunglasses with a look that blended menace and exhaustion.

Kurtis waved Jason down. "Yeah, yeah. We will."

He and Skylar shared a look. "Very slowly," they whispered together.

CHAPTER 4

Devonte stared at the man in the driver's seat, his mouth hanging open, his eyes so wide he thought they might bulge from their sockets and roll to the floor at his feet.

"You're telling me you fought a kaiju?"

Raymond had pulled back onto the road.

"Fought is a strong word. Survived may be a better one."

"And the Yakuza guy?"

"Masahiro Ishii," Raymond said. "Shortly after we finished questioning him, he was found dead in his cell."

"After he spilled what he knew?"

"I have to assume they all know about the creature now, yes."

"Inkanyamba?"

"Say what?"

"We've got to name it," Devonte said. "Figured mythology was as good a place to start."

"Your best friend may be in the hands of the Japanese mafia and that's what you're thinking about?"

"I can't do anything for D-Base until we get where we're going, and I've spent a good eight of my twenty-two years on Earth hoping that kaiju were real, cut me some slack."

Raymond said nothing.

"So…Inkanyamba?"

"Sure," Raymond said as they pulled into the gated Navy compound. "We're here."

The guard scowled at them, one hand resting on his rifle, the other held out expectantly. Raymond handed him his badge.

"I believe I'm expected."

The guard scanned the badge on his terminal in silence. He harrumphed to himself and handed the badge back. "And him?" His eyes shot to Devonte.

"Ah yes, my new partner will need a visitor badge. Where would we go for that?"

"Pull forward until you see the second guard station, then turn left. The building at the end of that road is the visitor center. They'll set you up."

Raymond thanked the guard and pulled forward and turned before the second guard station. The visitor center sat at the end of the road, like the guard said. A squat grey building with as many windows as a prison cell. No sooner had they exited the car they were accosted by a woman in military fatigues.

"Captain Dehane," she called. "Over here!"

Her long blonde hair bobbed atop her head in a tight ponytail as she jogged over. A few loose strands hung down into her face. She looked young, not much older than Devonte, maybe thirty he thought. Ice blue eyes flashed in his direction.

"Who's this?" she asked. It wasn't an entirely hostile question.

"Please, Lieutenant Greenwood, I've said it time and again, Raymond is fine. Devonte, this is Lieutenant Ashleigh Greenwood. Lieutenant, this is—"

"Devonte Rhodes. You were on the boat with Raymond when he saw the kaiju, right?" Devonte said, the words all spilling out at once.

The lieutenant's smile twitched. "You told him about the boat?" she asked.

"Our discovery has affected his life. He deserved to know."

She sighed. "Well, come this way then, Devonte, Captain Dehane."

When she turned her back, Raymond leaned down and whispered to Devonte, "She's not happy with me."

"Are you and her...?"

"No. And you two are horrible at whispering," she snapped.

Raymond cleared his throat as they entered a nearby building, not quite as grey as the visitor center, but just as squat. This one also had no windows.

"The lieutenant was just under the impression that we should keep our encounter a military secret until such time as we knew how to handle it. A sentiment I share."

"Save for a few obvious exceptions," she said.

"Save for one exception in which it might be linked to this young man's missing friend."

"That reminds me," Devonte said, "do you have a computer I can use?"

"Maybe. After you meet the general," Greenwood said.

General MacPherson, a short, stocky woman with obsidian skin, met them at the door to what Devonte assumed was the command room. She saluted them both and made no big fuss about his presence. Instead, after the appropriate introductions, she turned to him and spoke as if he had always been part of her team.

"Are you aware of the situation?"

"Uh, yeah, a sting operation went south, woke up Inkanyamba, and potentially led to my friend being kidnapped. Is that all?"

She shook her head sadly. "There's been another sighting. A cruise ship off the coast of Hawaii completely torn apart. Of the two thousand guests, only around one hundred survived."

Raymond clenched and unclenched his fists. Devonte could hear his knuckles popping with each repetition. He wondered if it would be weird to put a hand on his shoulder, and offer some words of...something, he didn't know what. Lieutenant Greenwood beat him to it.

"It's not your fault," she said, placing a firm hand on the detective's shoulder.

"Were that only the case," Raymond mumbled. He locked eyes with the general. "Tell me we're able to track it now?"

The general locked her jaw and shook her head. "No. It maintains depths beyond the range of our radars and it's too dangerous to send any more subs scouting."

"Any more?" Devonte asked.

"We sent a small nuclear sub, the USS Adeptus, to track the creature. Five minutes after first contact, all communications were lost, and the sub is now considered destroyed."

Devonte's mouth hung open. "You're telling me you sent a nuclear submarine after a giant monster? Have none of you ever *watched* a movie?"

The general's eyes narrowed. "It's standard operating procedure. Do you have a problem with that?" Devonte swallowed hard. "Just seems, uh, you know, like that never goes well...in the movies at least."

"Nor did it here," Raymond intervened. "General, my assistant here has a serious situation that requires the use of a computer, the more powerful the better."

"You can drop the act, Captain Dehane. We both know this young man is not your partner. In fact, I believe we here probably know more about him than you. Should we enlighten ourselves?" No expression crossed the general's face. She held out a hand and a soldier from a nearby desk stood and handed her a manila folder. Devonte's throat tightened.

"Look, uh, ma'am," Devonte choked out.

The general cocked an eyebrow.

Devonte steeled himself and continued. "My friend might be in serious danger. I can help her, but I need your help to do that."

General MacPherson flipped through the folder in silence, as though she didn't hear him. She hummed to herself and after what felt like an impossible length of time she spoke up. "You fancy yourself a giant monster expert?"

"I've been studying them as much as I can. Not many colleges want to take in students majoring in Cryptozoology or the study of fictional megafauna though." He signed air quotes around the word fictional. "But I have published—"

She waved her hand to cut him off. "Can you or can you not help us with our situation?"

He shook his head. "Maybe a little, but I'm basically a glorified fanboy. D-Base can help though. If we can find them. They have their PhD in Zoology and Biology. And I can find them if you just let me use a computer."

The general grunted. "Lieutenant Greenwood, set him up on a workstation."

Greenwood saluted. "Ma'am." She looked at Devonte. "Over here."

Devonte followed her to a computer in the corner. She sat down and logged into the machine then stood and motioned for him to sit. "Try not to do anything illegal," she said as she walked away. There was no humor in her voice.

"I get the feeling you don't like me, Lieutenant," Devonte said. "Did I do something? We've only just met."

She paused, and without turning back to him said, "It has nothing to do with like or dislike. I don't trust you. Captain Dehane feels responsible for your situation. But—"

"You're worried I'll abuse his trust?"

She didn't answer. She walked away.

Devonte sighed, puffing out his cheeks. "Good talk." He turned his attention to the computer screen and cracked his knuckles. "Alright. Don't worry D, I'll find you."

Raymond clapped his hands together once and said in an exhausted voice, "Well, I guess I'm off to Hawaii then."

#

The inspector sighed, stroked through his beard, and stared out the window of the small signal engine plane. Ashleigh crossed and uncrossed her legs in the seat across the aisle, if you could call the narrow separator an aisle. He looked down at the folder in his lap. A woman's face stared back up at him. Marleen Cromwell, a Kung-Fu instructor originally from The Bronx who just so happened to survive the monster's attack on the cruise.

"Why the hell was she on the boat?" Raymond asked.

"What?" Lieutenant Greenwood jumped. A thin sheen of sweat glistened on her forehead.

"Thalassophobia. The lady's terrified of the ocean. It would be like putting an acrophobe on an airplane."

Ashleigh gripped the arm rests of her seat until her hands began to tremble. "Yeah."

Raymond noticed the whitening of her knuckles, the square solidity of her shoulders, and her refusal to even glance out of the window. "Just like an acrophobe...on a plane...why exactly did you decide to come along if you don't like flying?"

"You needed backup."

"For an interview?"

"With all due respect Captain, stop asking me questions before I puke on you."

"Understood." He pulled down the microphone on his headset and radioed the pilot. "Aaron, how much longer until touchdown?"

"About two hours, Captain. Y'all alright back there?"

"Just fine but pour on the speed a bit if you can." He cast a glance at Ashleigh's rigid form. "Sooner we arrive, the better."

"You got it."

Raymond slid the microphone back up and away from his mouth. "Put your seat back, and close your eyes," he said to Ashleigh.

She gave him a confused look.

"Try it. Imagine you're on a float in a pool."

Ashleigh forced out a held breath and put the seat back. She stared at the ceiling for a few minutes, searching for a point to lock onto before closing her eyes. In a matter of minutes, she began to snore softly.

Raymond smiled wistfully as he watched her sleep before going back over the reports of the cruise attack.

#

Raymond and Ashleigh didn't have a chance to catch their breath when they landed in Hawaii. Something was causing a commotion on the beach by the airport. People cluttered the beach, all of them staring towards the shore. As they approached, a group of men were inching away, faces pale and eyes wide.

"What's going on?" Ashleigh said, grabbing the closest man by the arm. "What's down there?"

The man turned slowly, confused and obviously startled at being accosted at such a moment. He shook his head. "I don't know, lady, some kind of...monster."

"It just like...washed up on shore," a second guy added.

The third guy chimed in. "What's real scary though is that it looks like something else killed it. Something bigger, ya know?"

Ashleigh glanced at Raymond and he nodded his head. She let the man go. He and his friends stumbled away from the crowd like drunks at the end of a rave. They disappeared into a nearby bar.

Raymond took out his badge and gun and pressed forward into the thickening mob. "Make way. Police!" The crowd did not disperse, in fact the crowd tightened against their forceful advance.

Ashleigh rolled her eyes, pulled out her gun, and fired three shots into the air. "Everybody, get the hell out of our way!" That did it. People moved aside and stared in a mixture of fear and anger at the two of them.

Raymond caught her eye with a questioning look.

"It worked." She shrugged and strolled towards the beach.

Raymond blinked rapidly and followed after her. The crowd continued to part like the Red Sea. As the shoreline drew closer, the smell of copper and brine mixed with another pungent odor filled the air.

"Calamari?" Ashleigh asked.

"It would appear so."

The crowd parted and revealed the source of the smell. Stretched across the majority of the beach, where the sea touched the sand, sprawled a massive squid-like creature. Ink and blood seeped from ragged claw marks on the mushroom shaped head, staining the sand and water a muddy brown color. Its tentacles bent like elbows at the top and trailed down the beach. Some floated with the ebb and flow of the cresting waves. A single spotlight eye shined pale and glazed in the morning sun.

"That's—"

"Not our creature," Raymond finished.

The local sheriff came over, and Raymond flashed his badge, never taking his eyes off the squid creature.

"Dehane? You're the detective here to see the Cromwell chick, right?"

"Is it dead?" Raymond asked the sheriff.

"Couple of folks say they saw it breathing when it first washed up," he said, scowling at his comment being ignored. "One guy got sucked in, so we had to put up a perimeter." He motioned at the fence around them. Raymond hadn't even noticed it.

"I'm sorry. Sucked in?" Ashleigh asked.

"It's got like...breathing holes on the side, or some shit. Siphons, that's what they're called." The other officer walked up and introduced himself. "Arnett Sanderson. Just a rookie. But I did go to school for marine bio." He extended a hand. "Squids were my thing man, but this is wild."

Raymond shook it, finally refocusing on the people around him. He acknowledged the sheriff for the first time before turning to Arnett. "It's really just a squid?"

"Yeah, shit's just bigger than anything we got on record, and I checked. It's called a Magnapinna. They don't come out to play with the surface much, but also, most of them only get about twenty-six feet long. This sucker's almost three-hundred." He stroked his chin with one hand and cocked his head to the side. "What can kill a three-hundred-foot squid, though?"

"A whale?" the sheriff offered.

"All due respect, Truman, that thing would swallow a whale whole and shit out its skeleton. And no whale I can think of has got claws."

Sheriff Truman shrugged. "Squids weren't that big until today, and I don't think they had bladed tentacles either."

"I mean...you're not wrong." He eyed the lengthy tentacles. The tips flattened into spade-shaped plates made of hardened bone. "It's like some kind of Lovecraftian murder machine."

"Do you have Marleen Cromwell?" Raymond asked, pulling his eyes away from the dead creature.

"She's back at the station, yeah," Sheriff Truman said. "I guess we've left her there for quite a bit."

"We'll fill you in on the way, best we can, then." Raymond turned to walk off. "Your car is this way, right?"

"Station's only about a mile away. We walked."

Raymond let out a groan and massaged his legs, kneading the muscles roughly with his bare knuckles. His back locked up and he collapsed to his knees. Ashleigh rushed to his side and held him steady. Arnett came to his other side and helped her lift him up.

Sheriff Truman rolled his eyes and said, "I guess I'll have someone bring around a patrol car then."

#

In the cramped back of the cop car, Raymond's back felt as though it was on fire. He initially tried to explain the situation but found that each of his words was punctuated by a gasp or otherwise delaying exclamation of pain, so Ashleigh took over.

Sheriff Truman wasn't buying it. "No such things as sea dragons," he kept repeating, shaking his head and frowning.

Arnett took it a bit better. "I mean given what we know about things getting bigger as we go deeper in the ocean, it makes sense."

"No such thing as sea dragons."

"You think that's what attacked the cruise ship?" Arnett continued, rolling his eyes.

"I bet it was the Chinese," Truman interjected.

"Enough with the Chinese!" Arnett said.

"Yes, we think it may have mistaken the boat for a whale, the only thing we've seen it eat," Ashleigh said.

Arnett nodded sagely. "Solid."

"Guess it added squid to its menu," the sheriff mused.

"Unlikely," Arnett said. "The claw marks are deep and meant to kill, but nothing appeared...eaten."

"Did you notice," Raymond gasped for air, "the blood on the tentacles?"

"What?"

"Different. Color. Blue."

"So maybe our big-ass squid tried to eat your—"

"Inkanyamba," Raymond hissed.

Arnett squinted, confused.

"It's what one of ours apparently named it," Ashleigh clarified.

"Zulu storm monster," Arnett said. "I can dig it. Anyway, maybe it tried to eat Inkanyamba and got its shit rocked."

"Or it's all a hoax," Truman said, as if his answer was the most correct.

"By the Chinese," Arnett sighed. "Right?"

"Now you're catching on, kid." The sheriff laughed.

They pulled into the station garage. The aluminum shutter clattered closed as they parked the car. Arnett helped Raymond slide out of the car seat and waved at Ashleigh to go ahead.

"You want me to take you—"

"To the interrogation room." Raymond wrapped an arm around the rookie cop's shoulder and strained unsuccessfully to straighten his back.

"Was gonna say med station, but alright."

"I'm fine."

"The hunch in your back is really selling it."

"Just get me to a chair...please."

It was slow progress just from the car to the garage entrance to the station.

"How are you gonna kill it?" Arnett asked.

"Don't know. Big guns?" Raymond said with a pained laugh.

"Think we'll have to nuke it?" he asked as they walked into the fluorescent lit station.

"God, I hope not."

"God, I hope so," Truman said, coming around with a strap-on heat pack and holding it awkwardly in front of him. "It'll teach whoever did this a lesson they won't soon forget."

Raymond snatched the heat pack and glared at the sheriff. He slid the heat pack under his shirt and fastened it in the front. A few adjustments let the heat radiate up and down his spine. He couldn't help but let out a sigh of relief.

"Yeah, teach the monster a lesson and start World War III," Arnett scoffed.

"We'd win that," Truman chuckled. "We're America."

"Nobody wins that shit, man."

Truman shrugged and shuffled off to his desk. "You can sit in on the interrogation, Sanderson."

"You better save some of that whiskey for me," Arnett shouted after him.

"After all that talk of sea dragons? Maybe I better not." Laughter mixed with phlegmy coughs echoed down the hall.

Arnett shook his head. "That man."

"Seems a bit...stuck in his ways."

"That's one way to put it."

"Oh?"

"He's an asshole, plain and simple, but he means well, and on top of that, he drinks real good." He leaned in conspiratorially. "We put up with him for the whiskey."

Raymond smirked and chuckled. It didn't hurt as much as his last laugh, but he still regretted it immensely. Arnett joined in on the short-lived laugh.

"I hear y'all out there," Truman's voice shouted.

Arnett waved his hand to signal that no, he didn't, and helped Raymond to the interrogation room.

Marleen Cromwell sat across the table from Ashleigh in the small black box of a room. The two women looked up as the men entered. Marleen didn't look like the kind of woman who would be afraid of water. Her thick, well-toned arms rested across breasts that were more muscle than fat. Short, spiky hair stood at odd angles atop a head that slanted into a well chiseled jaw. She clicked her teeth as Raymond entered. He took one of the seats across from her, between Ashleigh and Arnett.

"Name, please," he said.

"You know my name." Marleen's voice was much more feminine than her appearance would have indicated, but with just the right amount of attitude.

Guess when water's not involved this is what she's like, Raymond thought. "That's right Ms. Cromwell, it's just standard procedure, but we can skip it." He opened his folder. "Your boyfriend, Eric Warner, will not be joining us?"

"No. He thinks I shouldn't be here. Says the government will just make us all out as lunatics if it means sweeping this thing under the rug. I think people should know about it though."

"Even if you're made out to be crazy?"

"Am I crazy?"

Raymond didn't know how to respond to that, so he pressed on. "So, you claim to have seen a... dragon?" He didn't want to color her story with his own input, so he feigned ignorance of the situation.

"I didn't see it," she said, shifting in her seat. "Eric did, not that he'll admit it, but I heard it, and I saw what it did to the cruise ship."

"Which is?" Raymond gave a rolling wave that said, "Continue."

"Sunk it, obviously," she said. "With one bite!"

"How do you know it was only one bite, if you couldn't see it?" Ashleigh asked.

"I heard the noise of one impact. A big crunch. The rest was just the boat collapsing on itself."

Arnett jumped in. "Why did it attack the ship?"

"Because it fucking wanted to? I don't know." Marleen gave an exaggerated shrug.

"Can you think of any reason it might have singled out your boat specifically?" Raymond asked.

"Wait," she said, holding up her hands. "Do you guys believe me?"

Raymond and Ashleigh shared a look.

"You could say that we might," Ashleigh said.

"We may have woken up this dragon." Raymond rubbed his temple and scrunched his eyes closed. "More or less."

"So, it's your fault all those people are dead."

Raymond opened his eyes to see her steely gaze piercing into him. She didn't look angry, but the look was harsh and judgmental. He took a deep breath and wrung his hands. "I wouldn't say that."

"I would," Marleen snapped.

"Then you'd be an idiot," Ashleigh bit back.

Marleen narrowed her eyes but didn't respond.

"Should we take a break?" Arnett asked, pushing back from the table awkwardly. "Maybe get some coffee? Whiskey?"

"No, no, it's fine," Raymond said, "she's entitled to feel how she likes. I would appreciate an answer to my last question though. Any reason it might attack your boat?" He steepled his fingers together.

"You mean besides being pissed that you interrupted its beauty sleep?"

Ashleigh tensed, ready to pounce across the table and take the woman with her bare hands, but Raymond waved her down. Marleen tapped the side of her cheek as she thought. A soft hum escaped her lips.

"Were there any whales?" Arnett asked. "We think it eats whales." He looked at Raymond and nodded. "Right?"

Marleen snapped her fingers. "Maybe that's it."

"Enlighten us?" The heat from the pack faded against Raymond's back, and the irritation and pain were beginning to settle in. He needed to lay down.

"About an hour before the attack, the captain had been playing whale sounds to attract a pod he said was nearby." Horror crossed her face. "Oh my god, did it kill the whales?"

"I can't see why it would have attempted to eat your boat had it eaten the pod," Raymond said. "If anything, the pod sensed the creature coming and left the area."

"Smart motherfuckers," Arnett quipped. His laugh was met with silence. "Alright then." He scraped his chair across the floor as he pushed all the way back from the table.

Ashleigh rose in silence and exited the room.

Raymond stood. "Thank you for your time."

"I'm sorry about what I said before," Marleen said. "I just can't stop hearing their screams…"

Raymond gave a solemn smile. "It's quite alright. Trust me, no one blames me more than I do."

Without warning the entire room began to shake. Marleen caught Raymond as he toppled over. Glad he didn't fall, but in agony from the sudden stop, he righted himself against the wall.

Ashleigh bolted back into the room. "Outside, now!"

Raymond ground his teeth and set off at a half-jog, half-limp. Arnett met him in the hallway. "What the hell is this?"

Outside the police station a familiar roar rose above the sounds of panicked people and emergency sirens.

Arnett froze, and stared wide eyed at Raymond. "Is that…?"

"Afraid so."

"Is this the part where we run towards the danger?" he asked.

"Afraid so."

"Fuck." He pulled the keys to a patrol car out of his pocket and jingled them up and down. "Alright, let's go."

CHAPTER 5

The city was burning. Raymond could smell the acrid smoke seeping into the car like aerated poison. He coughed and covered his mouth and nose with his sleeve. Traffic heading towards the city was sparse. So, Raymond noticed, were the sounds of sirens and emergency responders. He hadn't realized how long the drive had taken the first time. His back ached and itched as he fidgeted in the back seat of the car.

"Holy shit," Arnett said, peering past Raymond and out the passenger window. Raymond turned in his seat to look as well. The creature's draconic head could be seen towering above the city skyline, fresh magma still dripping down through the cracks and crags of its skin.

A double row of razor-sharp teeth protruded from its mouth, revealed with each furious roar. Two glowing orange horns crowned its head, the most prominent in a double row of spikes that ran down its neck before shifting form into a plate-armored carapace the color of dried blood. It stood on two thick hindlegs, slightly hunched by the weight of two long arms terminating in three iron black claws each. The creature threw back its head and arms and roared, shattering the windows of several nearby buildings, before lashing out at the air around it.

"That's not our creature," Ashleigh said.

"What?" Arnett asked, turning to look from the monster to Ashleigh.

"She's right." Raymond stared at the creature, as realization dawned on him.

"What the hell does that mean?" Arnett shouted.

"The one we woke up was grey," Ashleigh said. "Like the color of the ocean."

"And bigger," Raymond said. He let the information hang in the air. The weight of understanding threatened to crush them in the silence of the car. "There's two of them."

The creature screamed as if in response to their realization, causing the windows of the car to rattle violently. Arnett swerved to avoid another car speeding down the wrong side of the road. They made a turn and the creature came full into view. It towered at the base of Kilauea, dwarfing the Honolulu skyline with its demoniac form. The torn carcass of the Magnapinna, or what remained of it, had been pulled from the shore, and almost entirely eaten.

"Guess this one was hungry," Arnett said.

He stopped the car and all of them filed out onto the street. Even this far away the creature's presence was overwhelming. A pair of magma-soaked wings draped down its body, like a cape on a king. With a lazy swish of its thorny tail, it toppled a nearby skyscraper. Raymond wondered how many people died as the structure crumbled down onto itself. The thought made him nauseous. Over the roar of the city falling apart, he could just make out the cracks and pops of guns, infantile compared to the creature's power.

Arnett's radio crackled to life. Sheriff Truman's voice came as a staticky shout. "Sanderson, where are you?"

"I'm just outside the city, I— Are you seeing this?"

"Seeing this!" The sound of gunfire punctuated his exclamation. "I'm down here shooting at fucking Satan himself and you're sightseeing?"

"Guess he believes now," Ashleigh said.

"Truman, get out of there," Arnett shouted into the radio.

"We're pulling back now," his voice crackled back. "We got out who we could."

"Tell him he needs to hurry," Raymond said, leaning on the car for support. "Something's happening, and I doubt it's good."

The creature reared back and opened its mouth wider and wider until Raymond was sure he could see it begin to foam at the corners. Its wings spread and expanded, the translucent membranes spreading to show a network of veins. The horns crackled to life before bursting into flames. It beat its wings violently, and as it did, the network of veins began to glow a vibrant red. A hiss like the world's largest gas leak filled the air.

Raymond shivered as the temperature plummeted. Even the guns fell silent as the city froze to see what would happen next.

And then the world cracked in half.

The sound was terrible, like the blast of an atom bomb. Raymond grabbed his ears and felt blood run down the side of his head beneath palms. The air in front of the creature rippled as it whipped its head towards the ground. Trees in the direct path of the shimmering air snapped at their bases and burst into flames, disappearing to ash almost instantly. Buildings nearby that were strong enough to withstand the force reddened and began to melt and sag down to the ground. The rest simply disintegrated on impact. The sky burned an angry red as fire and molten material spread their devastation throughout the city.

A scream crackled through Arnett's radio, but it was short-lived and soon there was no sound but the static. The rookie cop begged the sheriff to respond. He radioed the rest of his squad as well. No one answered. Arnett slumped into a sitting position on the hood of his car. The gunshots had stopped. There were only the deep rumbling noises of the creature, noises that sounded like the laughter of a cruel god.

"How in the ever-loving fuck are we supposed to do *anything* about that?" Arnett shouted, wiping the blood from his ears.

Ashleigh just stood in stunned silence as Raymond said a silent prayer for the dead.

"No, seriously, it just turned the whole fucking city into Michael Bay's version of hell! That thing is a dragon. An honest-to-fucking-god *dragon*!"

"Dragons aren't real," Ashleigh said. Her hands were trembling.

Arnett gestured at the creature mulling about the city. "Then what should I call that thing?"

"Dragons. Aren't. Real."

Raymond interjected, "Aren't they?" He closed his eyes and breathed deep the acrid smoke and the oceanic smell of the nearby shoreline. His jaw hurt, clenched tight to hold back his own feelings.

"Sir?"

"Every story has to start from somewhere, right?" Raymond shrugged. "Why not with this creature, born from fire?" He pointed at the volcano. Half of it looked as though it had burst open from the inside. A steady stream of lava flowed down the slope on a slow path towards the city.

Ashleigh's mouth hung open a little. She frowned and shrugged. "Maybe so."

Raymond put a hand on Arnett's shoulder. The younger man cradled his head in his hands. He looked up with a pained expression.

"We have to get back to San Francisco," Raymond said.

"The airport is going to be impossible," Arnett muttered.

The creature screamed in the distance. The initial hush after the attack subsided and, in its wake, a more unsettling silence cloaked the city. There were no more sirens, no screams, no sounds but the roar of the fires and the earthshaking steps of the creature.

Ashleigh's eyes never left the burning skyline. "Independent airfields? Military?"

The rookie cop returned his head in his hands and stared at the ground. Tears streamed down his face. He didn't answer. "Truman. Shardik. Church."

"Officer," Ashleigh barked, jerking him by the collar. "Pull yourself together." Her voice cracked but it got the desired effect. Arnett jumped and stared into her eyes. "Are there any smaller airfields we can use."

"Oh, um, yeah. Hickam is nearby, it's a military base. Shouldn't you know that?"

"You needed to focus," Ashleigh said, frowning. "Do you want me to drive?"

"No. I'm good." Arnett sighed. "I'm good," he repeated.

Ashleigh nodded sharply and climbed into the passenger side of the car. Raymond eased into the back seat, his pain forgotten amongst the rush of adrenaline, just as the engine roared to life. Six fighter jets screamed overhead as they peeled away from their vantage point. They heard the creature shriek a challenge as the first sidewinder missile roared towards it. Explosions rocked the ground, and Arnett struggled to control the small patrol car. The creature's scream didn't sound like pain. Its fury culminated in the sickening crunch of metal and a quieter explosion. The first plane to be destroyed in the conflict, and, Raymond assumed, not the last. They never heard the others go down, but soon the sounds of conflict died and a roar that oozed with the pride rang out through the air. Raymond turned in his seat to look out the window.

The creature surveyed the molten hole that had been Honolulu. New columns of smoke trailed into the sky. Six of them, from below the horizon. The creature leaned down and scooped up the remains of the squid carcass with its iron black claws. It spread its wings and beat them with a force like a hurricane, spraying magma all around it, before launching into the air and vanishing into the distance.

It's over...for now, Raymond thought.

CHAPTER 6

Devonte pulled up the results of his scan. Four phone numbers matched the criteria. In Chicago. Connected to the chat app at times he and D-base normally talked. And visited similar sites as him. He pulled out his cell phone and dialed each number in order. A Middle Eastern man answered the first number and through a combination of bad connection and a thick accent, Devonte gave up a few minutes into the conversation. The second was an elderly woman who thought he was a telemarketer. He hung up when she began to read him her credit card information. The third phone number reached an automatic response of unavailable connections. Growing frustrated, Devonte dialed the last number.

"Hello?"

Deciding to go with a new approach, Devonte said, "This is Agent Edwards with the FBI—"

General MacPherson shot him a dirty glance. Devonte just shrugged. *If it works...*

He continued. "I'm calling—"

"Is this about my kid again?" A gruff voice cut him off.

"I'm sorry?" Devonte furrowed his brow.

"You lot already called once. I told you, she ain't here."

Devonte composed himself. "Well sir, I'm looking at my records here and I have no information pertaining to…"

"I told your partner, Agent Z, or G, or whatever her name was, the kid is in San Francisco. Left last week. Something about a giant monster fan club, or some shit."

Devonte managed to keep his cool. "Ah, I'm sorry for the inconvenience. Could you please give me your child's phone number?"

The man gave the phone number. "We done?"

"Yes. Thank you for your cooperation."

The call disconnected with three consecutive beeps.

"Asshole," Devonte whispered.

"Finding it hard to make friends while posing as a federal agent?" MacPherson said.

Devonte grimaced. "I got what I needed."

"You found your friend?"

"No." He held up a single finger. "But I am one step closer. D-Base was here in San Fran when they were taken, and I have their phone number."

"You think they have their phone?"

"I think their phone won't be too far away from them." He typed the phone number into the computer, checking for the GPS location.

"Alcatraz?" Devonte scratched his head.

General MacPherson pushed him aside and peered over the monitor. "That's not possible. That's a major tourist hub."

The blinking icon sat squarely in the middle of the ex-prison island.

"That's what the locator says," Devonte said, crossing his arms. "We have to go."

MacPherson wrinkled her nose. "I'm not sure it's such a good idea to go traipsing around such a populated area with a squad of soldiers. Mass panic is never fun."

"And sneaking in after-hours would draw unwanted attention from Tempest," Devonte added. He snapped his fingers. "I'll go."

"Absolutely not."

"D-Base is my friend. I should be the one to get them."

"You're an idiot if you think you could just waltz in there and drag your friend to safety."

"But—"

"Come with me," she interrupted, turning and walking out into the hallway off of the command room. The two of them walked in a frustrated silence, Devonte clenching his jaw. He did his best not to audibly huff and puff.

"Stop acting like a child," MacPherson growled. "It doesn't suit you."

Devonte held his tongue. "Where are we going?"

"The barracks. I know just who to send to rescue your friend."

Devonte raised an eyebrow.

"You'll see."

The barracks smelled like a gym that missed its last two scheduled cleanings. Even MacPherson's nostrils twitched visibly as they entered. The men fell into line, standing at attention. They looked about as Devonte expected. Large, muscle bound men with cropped haircuts and yesterday's five o'clock shadow.

"At ease." MacPherson waved her hand dismissively. "Captain Brannigan, step forward."

Devonte hadn't seen this man at first. He stood out from the rest, not because he appeared bigger or stronger. Wiry was the word that popped to mind when he broke rank. His hair hung sloppily down one side of his head, but the other half remained shaved. Pale green eyes stared out over dark, sleepless bags. Despite his appearance, an ominous presence pulsed off the man in palpable waves.

"What can I do for you, ma'am?" Tired eyes assessed Devonte in the way a hawk might assess a rabbit. Devonte felt a shiver run down his spine.

"A rescue mission," MacPherson said. She showed no signs of acknowledging the man's aura. "Saving a kidnapped person."

"I think I'm more suited to missions where people don't make it out alive." The other soldiers in the barracks chuckled at the dark humor. Devonte found it hard to join them.

"I'm sorry," the general said, "was that not properly phrased as an order? Should I repeat myself?"

Brannigan clicked his teeth and looked away. "No, ma'am."

"That's what I thought." She gestured to Devonte. "This young man will brief you on the situation."

Devonte was left speechless in front of the dead-eyed man. The soldiers in the background snickered. General MacPherson's foot tapped away, awaiting some detailed explanation that Devonte hadn't yet devised.

"Well?" Brannigan's eyes bored into him.

"We have to break into a secret base beneath Alcatraz to save a person who can help us stop a rampaging giant monster." The words tumbled out of his mouth and jumbled their way into the open air. Devonte stood frozen. What he said was true but spewing it out like that made him feel stupid in this room of full-grown adults. It didn't help that Brannigan and the men burst out laughing not moments after he finished his sentence.

The general cleared her throat, and Devonte had never felt more thankful for a person's intervention. "You find your mission humorous, Captain?"

"He's serious?"

"*I* definitely am," she replied.

Brannigan fell back into attention. "Ma'am."

"Gear up, Cade. Take him."

"Ma'am?"

"What?" Devonte recoiled.

"You wanted to go save your friend, right? And you're the one who has the tracking information." She smirked.

"Hell no, a rescue mission is one thing, but I'm definitely not dragging some civilian along." Brannigan's green eyes lit up with fury.

"If you follow orders now," the general said, her voice cool and detached, "I'll ignore the fact that you just defied, and shouted at a superior officer." If looks could kill, the entire room would have dropped dead that instant.

Devonte could see the teeth grinding in Brannigan's jaw as he spoke. "Yes, ma'am." He turned to Devonte. "What's your name, kid?"

"I'm twenty-two, you know?"

"Weird name. Alright, come on, Twenty-two." He saluted the general one more time and pushed past Devonte out into the hallway.

"No, my name is—"

"I can't hear you over the sound of me walking down this hallway," Brannigan shouted back.

Devonte glanced at the general. She shrugged and walked the opposite direction of Brannigan's fading footsteps. "Best catch up. He'll probably try to leave you."

This left him standing awkwardly in the room with the five other soldiers. "Uh, gentlemen." He did his best salute and took off down the hall after Brannigan.

Devonte caught up with him outside of the weapon's locker. The captain had already finished strapping on his Kevlar vest. He looked up at Devonte's approach.

"You know how to use a gun, Twenty-two?"

The new nickname elicited an eyeroll from Devonte. "Dad taught me how to shoot when I was a kid."

"I'll put you in front then," he said, tossing him a gun.

Devonte caught it and eyed the gun. It was the same model his dad had given him; the one Raymond took with him when he left for Hawaii. He stuffed it in his waistband.

"No," Brannigan said firmly. He reached into a locker and pulled out a hip holster. "You wanna end up making the expression 'no balls' a reality?" He held out the holster.

"Oh. Yeah. Thanks," Devonte mumbled. He strapped the holster to his belt and slid the gun into place.

Brannigan muttered something under his breath. It sounded like, "dumbass".

While he waited for the captain to finish his preparations, Devonte transferred the tracking program from his laptop to his phone. He shoved the backpack into one of the empty lockers and sat down on a nearby bench. "How are we going to get there?"

"Quietly."

"Look," Devonte snapped, "I get it, you don't want to work with me. Right now, the feeling's mutual, but can you at least stop being an asshole until we get my friend out safe? Then you can fuck back off to being a badass loner for all I care!"

Brannigan stared at him with no expression, and for a minute Devonte thought he might hit him. Instead the captain grinned wildly. "There are those missing balls."

#

People crowded the docks. Devonte trailed behind Captain Brannigan as they wound a path to a secluded pier on the far end. A small motorboat bobbed up and down on the soft waves as they lapped up against barnacle encrusted wooden pylons.

"Isn't the island going to be crowded?" Devonte asked as he stepped uncertainly into the boat. It rocked as he stepped in, sending ripples through the water and scattering some fish that swam near the surface.

Brannigan grunted as he untethered the vessel. "Probably."

"How are we going to—"

"You ever heard of hiding in plain sight? We're gonna do that. Just act natural." He glanced over at Devonte. "Put your hood up."

The engine roared to life as Brannigan stepped into the boat, and Devonte tumbled unceremoniously into the available seat with the sudden lurching motion. In the distance he could see Alcatraz circled by several ferries, but otherwise alone in the middle of the San Francisco Bay.

Just like the docks, the prison island was jam packed with bodies. Brannigan shouldered his way through the crowd, his leather bomber hiding all trace of the weaponry beneath.

"What does your tracker say?" he asked when they came to a small clearing.

"Says the phone is inside the actual building."

Brannigan nodded and made a b-line for the squat stone structure.

A perky young woman popped in front of him as he approached the door. "Hi there! The next tour isn't scheduled for another ten minutes, if I could have you wait right here until then." She gestured at a sign that read "Line Starts Here" in peeling white paint.

"We're not here for a—"

"Oh, thank you so much," Brannigan said, pouring on all the charm he could muster. "My step-brother here is fascinated by Al Capone, so he's a little impatient." He turned to Devonte and winked. "Waiting for everyone to go in would be the better thing to do, right?"

Devonte narrowed his eyes and said, "Yes, I suppose so."

The time passed quickly and before Devonte knew it, they were ushered into the prison building. Elise, their tour guide rambled cheerily about the history of the prison as they entered the main cell block.

"And now, the moment you've all been waiting for," she gestured at a cell separated from the main hallway not by bars, but by a thick sheet of plexiglass.

"Brannigan," Devonte hissed, yanking on the captain's sleeve, "it says the phone is straight ahead...behind the glass."

CHAPTER 7

It took several hours for the crowds to clear out. The sun had gone down when they heard the tour guides saying their farewells and locking the prison up. When silence covered the establishment, Brannigan insisted they wait just a few minutes more.

"Can we please get out of this closet?" Devonte grumbled.

Brannigan grunted in reply and kicked open the rotting wooden door.

The two crept as quietly as they could back over to Al Capone's cell. A see-through window separated them from the posh holding container. Brannigan looked around, then slammed against the panel as hard as he could. There was a slight groan, followed by a creaking sound, then a pop, but the door didn't budge. Brannigan rubbed his shoulder, and Devonte realized that the pop had come from him.

"Did you just dislocate—"

"No, it does that sometimes." The marine rotated his shoulder eliciting several more of the soft popping sounds. "See?"

Brannigan tried to rattle the cell panel, to the same effect. He sucked his teeth. "Got any ideas?"

"Do they have to involve brute force?" Devonte asked.

Brannigan rolled his eyes at the obvious sarcasm. "It might have worked."

"Every door has to have a knob...somewhere."

Brannigan gave a half-hearted look around. "All plexiglass, no brass handle."

Devonte pulled out his phone. "Not necessarily an actual handle. I just meant a way to open it." He scanned his phone around the perimeter of the glass, lingering over each brick for just a few seconds and muttering to himself. Just when he was considering changing his approach, the phone dinged. "There's something here."

Brannigan peered at the brick in question. "Huh, what do you know? It's a bit of a different color than the rest." He rapped a knuckle against it. "And also, plastic."

It took a little bit of effort, but the Marine was able to wedge his combat knife behind the plastic casing and pop it off the wall. A black ID scanner flashed a light at them like a mechanical red eye, cold and unfeeling. Brannigan positioned his knife to jam it into the device.

"What are you doing?"

"Just gonna short it out so the door will open up," Brannigan said with all the confidence of a man who'd done that very thing a million times.

"Does that work?" Devonte asked. "Ever?"

Brannigan paused for a minute. "Usually we have a guy who breaks into stuff like this, so I don't think I've actually ever tried it."

Devonte pointed at himself. "I'm your guy who breaks into stuff like this. And the answer is no, it won't work. Ever." He looked at his phone. "That'll take too long." He unzipped his backpack and pulled out a screwdriver which he handed to Brannigan. "They do teach you how to use these," he asked, "right?"

"Nope. It's all C4 and rocket launchers, asshole." He snatched the screwdriver. "I'm looking for nails with this, right?" And for the first time, Devonte saw him give a genuine, if not snarky, smile.

Devonte's laptop booted up. He scrolled through several applications. "No. No. No. There you are!" He reached into a side pocket on the backpack and pulled out a long cable.

Brannigan tossed the plastic cover to the scanner. It clattered to the ground beside Devonte.

"Plug this in."

"No 'please'?" Brannigan said.

"Thought you didn't like the idea of working with a civilian," Devonte said as he held the cable out expectantly.

Brannigan barked a laugh. "You're gonna be a pain to keep track of in combat, but you're not useless. I respect that much." He took the cable and tied it into the panel's wiring.

"That may be the nicest thing you'll ever say to me," Devonte mumbled as he double-clicked the device icon that appeared on screen.

"Count on it," Brannigan said.

Devonte found it difficult to crack the code, especially with Brannigan leaning over his shoulder and asking questions. After the fifth or sixth tangent, Devonte stopped and said, "Do you have any experience with computers?"

"Does watching porn count?"

"No."

"Then no."

"Okay, so nothing I say will make sense, and this will go a lot faster if you just let me work."

"Talk about a personality shift," Brannigan said holding up his hands in defense. "Note to self, don't distract the nerd." He flashed a grin. "I prefer putting things together with my hands anyway. Tinkering with actual objects and not just—"

Devonte scowled at him as he continued speaking.

"Okay, shutting up, sir."

Finally, the panel blinked green, and the glass door slid aside so they could enter.

"Nerd: One; Marine: Zero," Devonte said, giving Brannigan a thumbs up.

"Let's not forget who probably would have gotten us kicked out by the tour guides were it not for my quick thinking...*little bro*. I'll be nice and say we're still zero-zero." He laughed and punched him in the shoulder. Devonte refused to let the word "ouch" leave his mouth, so he rubbed the sore spot in silence.

"Now what?" Brannigan said, twirling in a slow circle at the center of the room. "We broke into a prison cell."

"I feel like you're doing this on purpose," Devonte said.

"Doing what?"

"Acting stupid. Are you still testing me?"

"I have no idea what you're talking about," Brannigan said, but his smile most definitely knew what Devonte was talking about. "But I will say, it's strange that most everything in here is covered in dust, except for the phone."

Devonte picked it up off the hook. "Yeah that is—"

He fell silent as a deep rumble filled the room. The stone wall at the back of the cell rose slowly. Bits of dust and chips of stone and paint fell to the floor as it worked its way open.

Brannigan dropped his humor and drew his gun. "Out here was playtime. Now we get serious. Lock, load, and stay behind me."

"And no more playing dumb," Devonte added, drawing his own weapon. He flipped the safety off and aimed at the ground as he and Brannigan made their way into the sterile, fluorescent glow of the underground complex.

A suffocating silence filled the halls, making each echoing step feel like it might alert any and every person in the place. If there were any people. Most of the rooms they checked were empty, completely devoid of anything save the white green light from the overhead bulbs. Brannigan looked almost disappointed.

They turned a corner and heard voices. Brannigan yanked Devonte back around the corner and mimed for him to keep quiet. They peered around the corner.

A door opened and a woman stepped out. Her heels clicked on the ground as she stopped to answer her phone, turning away from them in the process. She answered in Chinese but switched to English shortly after. Her body went rigid.

"Mr. Martin, it's an honor to hear from you," she said. Her voice was a thinly veiled mixture of irritation and fear. "How can I help you?"

They were too far away to make out the voice coming from the other end of the cellphone.

"The scientists are already beginning work on the— when will it be done? Well that's hard to be sure— What? Hawaii? No, we last tracked it in the Sea of Japan."

A tense silence broke the conversation.

"It's gone? Destroyed? No, I can't imagine how much that cost you, sir. Yes, as fast as possible, sir." She paused. "Is there anything—"

The woman looked at her phone. "Bastard," she spat. "And how the hell did the beast get from Japan to Hawaii *that* quickly?" She stomped her foot and cursed, then brushed her long brown hair from her face and strode down the hall away from Devonte and Brannigan's vantage point. They waited for her to turn the corner and followed silently. She opened a door and shouted at someone in the room as the door slid shut behind her.

Brannigan held out an arm to stop Devonte. "You should stay here."

"Excuse me?"

"We don't know who or what is behind that door," Brannigan said, taking off his pack. He pulled out two bricks of C4. "And you've never done a breach. You could kill someone you don't mean to. Like your friend."

Devonte stared warily at the explosive. "But—"

"Nope. No buts. This is where I do my job, and you stay out of the way." He handed Devonte a cylindrical device topped with a small red button. The detonator. "All you have to do is hit the button and watch my back. Can you?"

Devonte wanted to protest, but he knew Brannigan was right. "Try not to die."

"Haven't yet. By that logic, I'm probably invincible," came the marine's terse reply.

Devonte snorted at the supposed logic.

Brannigan crept over to the door and attached the C4, placing both bricks side by side in the center. Devonte watched as he connected the wires that dangled from the detonator to a device on the side of one of the lumps of grey material.

When everything was set up, Brannigan pulled a darkened visor down over his eyes and pulled the scarf he wore around his neck up over his mouth. He completed the outfit with a pair of soundproof earpieces. "When I give the signal, hit the button. Then cover your ears and close your eyes."

Devonte nodded.

Brannigan positioned himself to the side of the door, out of the range of the explosion. He looked at Devonte and gave a questioning thumbs up.

Devonte hit the button, closed his eyes, and covered his ears.

#

Fuck, Brannigan thought, *that was not the signal.*

He recovered from his initial shock and fell into the breach routine. The smoke provided him some cover as he charged the room. To his immediate left, a man in a lab coat pulled out a gun. Cade shot him before he could even aim. Two people ran in front of him and ducked underneath a lab bench. *Not a threat for now.* He saw the woman from before, she looked stunned, but she had a radio in her hands. His shot missed, and he saw her duck for cover, speaking into the radio. *Shit,* he thought. *Backup inbound.*

"If you don't want lead implants," he shouted, "get on your fucking knees."

About half of the room complied. The rest got over the initial shock of the explosion and drew their weapons. *One. Two. Three. Four. Five. Six. And a giant tooth.* Cade counted. He dove behind the nearest lab bench, overturning it and taking shelter next to the first scientist's dead body. Shots rang out inside the room and tiny bits of debris sprayed over him as the bullets pierced holes in his makeshift shelter. The guns died down and he hid in silence, holding his breath.

He heard Devonte's voice from the hall. "Cade. Is it over?"

Dammit, Rhodes!

The woman said something in Chinese, and he heard footsteps head to the door. Then he heard the clicking of her heels. A door opened in the back corner of the room. One he hadn't noticed. It slid closed behind her and vanished seamlessly into the wall.

"Now or never," Cade whispered to himself. He popped over the table and sprayed in a wide arc. A man and a woman went down in a spray of red, but not before one got a shot off. The bullet tore through his arm. It burned at the center of his muscle as warm red blood poured out. Cade clenched his teeth and looked for the last person he'd counted. He found him. The black man was shielded behind one of the scientists.

"Release the hostage," Cade shouted.

"Wait, no!" the scientist said. "Don't shoot." He turned back to the other man. "Jason, please. Put down your gun, you don't have to do this."

Jason's sunglasses made it hard for Cade to read his expression, but he looked conflicted. Which meant Cade wasn't lowering his weapon until he did. He heard movement and glanced to the side. A redheaded woman crawled out from under a lab table. Her frizzy hair bobbed as she shook her head and rubbed her face.

"Is it over?" she said, before freezing at the sight of the standoff in front of her.

"Jason, please." The scientist had his hand on the man's arm. "If you do this, your wife…"

Jason lowered his weapon. "You owe me, again."

"You should consider any debt settled," Cade said. "The man just saved your life."

The sunglasses bored into Cade. "I said he owes me." He tossed his gun to the side.

"It's a running joke we have," the scientist said, "he doesn't mean anything by—"

A gunshot cut the statement short. Cade flinched but didn't feel any pain. His own gun hadn't fired.

"Devonte!" he shouted, sprinting to the hall. No sign of the young man. He backtracked, tracing their steps and found him, covered in blood, slumped next to the corpse of one of the men in lab coats. He was shaking.

Cade knelt down beside him. "Hey."

Devonte's eyes lacked focus.

"Are you alright?" Cade asked.

No response.

Cade put a hand on his shoulder. And for the first time, recognition flashed behind Devonte's unfocused eyes. "He's dead."

"Yes, and you're alive."

"I shot him."

Cade glanced at the body. "Twice it seems. In the chest. It happens."

Devonte swallowed hard. "Is this what you do...every day?"

"No," Cade said. "I aim for the head."

"How can you crack jokes about this?" Tears welled at the corner of Devonte's eyes. They'd regained focus, and something more, recognition.

"Your first time's always rough," Cade sat on the floor next to him. "But think of it this way, did you want to die?"

"No," Devonte's voice croaked.

"Do you think he wanted you to die?"

"Yes."

"Only one of you could have gotten what you wanted then. You did what you had to do to survive." Cade put a firm hand on Devonte's shoulder. He held out his other hand. "Do you want me to take the gun?"

Devonte wiped his eyes. "No, I think I'll keep it. Can I ask you something?"

"Shoot." He saw the look of horror on Devonte's face and winced. "Right. Sorry. Ask away."

"Did you cry the first time?"

Cade chuckled. "No. I did what any self-respecting soldier would do. I climbed so deep in a bottle it almost cost me my life and my career."

"How did you—"

"Get out?"

Devonte's silent curiosity was answer enough.

"I threw myself into the program. Can't drink when you have no free time." He shrugged. "Worked out for me."

Footsteps approached, and Devonte snapped his gun forward, hands still trembling.

"Easy there, Punisher, don't shoot the people we came to rescue." Cade pressed down firm but gentle on the gun in Devonte's hands, pointing it towards the floor.

The redhead, the scientist with grey hair, and the black man in the suit approached.

"No one else wanted to be rescued?" Cade asked.

"Most of them are too afraid to defy Tempest," grey hair said.

"And you?" Cade said to the man in the suit.

"You're alive, which means I failed. They don't like failure." His tone and face remained emotionless. "I'm with y'all now."

"Let me guess," Cade said. "We owe you?"

"No. But if I do die, I'm haunting your asses."

"What about your wife?" Grey Hair asked. "Your daughter?"

Jason stared straight ahead. "I'll make some calls. Got to hope for the best."

The statement hung in the air. No one wanted to say anything.

Devonte spoke up, his voice wavering. "Um, do any of you go by the online name D-Base?"

"Debase?" Grey Hair asked.

"No, D-Base. It stands for Destroyer Base."

The girl with curly red hair raised her hand. "That's me," she said. "But only—"

Her eyes lit up. "KK?" She flung herself forward and wrapped her arms around Devonte, much to his obvious confusion. "Is that really you?" she asked.

"Yep," he croaked. "King of the Kaiju, in the flesh. Good to finally meet you."

She pulled away and extended a hand. "Name's Skylar, and you?"

"Devonte." He fidgeted nervously as she smiled at him with bright green eyes. "You're a girl?"

Cade rolled his eyes. "And your name's Jason, and you are?"

"Kurtis," Grey Hair said.

"Great. Introductions over. Can we get out of here now? Before more people with guns show up."

"Unlikely," Jason said.

The sterile white light turned an angry red, and a siren wailed from speakers hidden somewhere overhead.

"What now?" Devonte asked.

"Protocol dictates that they detonate the base if compromised," Jason said.

"And you didn't say anything about that?" Cade shouted.

"I was supposed to kill you, remember?"

"They're gonna blow up Alcatraz?" Skylar looked more offended than afraid.

Jason nodded. "We should go."

"Can we stop it?" Devonte asked. "I mean this is a historic landmark." His eyes never left Skylar's face.

"Not the mission, kid," Cade said. He hoisted Devonte to his feet. "Let's go."

#

They watched from the boat as the island, prison and all, went up in a cacophonous display of smoke and fire. Devonte felt a pang of guilt. *Did I just cause the destruction of a historic monument?*

He noticed a similar look on Skylar's face, just a hint of discomfort mixed with a lot of sadness. Alcatraz meant nothing to them personally, but to the people of San Francisco, it mattered.

Should I say something?

"It'll never be the same," Skylar said. "Do you think they'll rebuild it?"

"Probably not," Devonte said. "I don't know how you salvage all the history from that."

The stone structure began to crumble into the sea as the island burned and smoke billowed into the sky. Another smaller explosion went off, showering the ocean with bits of debris. Devonte watched as the telephone from Capone's famous cell soared overhead and plunged into the depths of the bay.

"Better report this," Brannigan said. He turned a knob on his radio, and it crackled to life. As soon as it powered up a voice blasted through the speaker.

"Brannigan." General MacPherson's voice cut through the static like an icy knife. "What in *the hell* is going on out there?"

"Uh, what reports are you receiving?" Brannigan said, trying to soothe the general's obvious fury. "Because we extracted the targets."

"Do not beat around the bush with me, Captain. Tell me that Alcatraz prison is *not* currently a smoldering crater."

"Alcatraz prison is currently a *burning* crater," Brannigan said. "That's not better, is it?"

The obvious "no" remained unspoken. "Explain."

"Secret base. Sore losers. Self-destruct sequence. Boom." He tried to sound as disinterested as he could, but Devonte could see how upset he looked.

Silence from the other end of the radio, and then, "Report back. Now."

"En route as we speak. See you soon, General."

An irritated groan crackled from the speaker, and then the radio went dead.

"She's gonna have my ass for that one," Brannigan said, scratching the side of his head. "Fuck."

Devonte turned to Skylar. "What did they have you doing in that lab?"

"The tooth!" she shouted in response.

Kurtis shook his head. "The fire probably burned it away faster than it could regenerate."

"If it's still in there, the coast guard will handle it," Brannigan said.

Skylar nodded solemnly. "We were building a device to attract the creature. They want to control it."

"They?" Brannigan said. "You mentioned something called Tempest earlier, Grey. Care to explain?"

Jason spoke up instead. "Multinational crime syndicate. Believe they are destined to claim the world. Led by seven shadow operatives known as the Hands of Fate. And the fact that I haven't been shot yet means they think I'm dead...for now."

Devonte's eyes went wide.

Brannigan lit a cigarette. "Casual. What do they want with the creature?"

Jason's sunglasses hid his eyes, but Devonte imagined that he had just blinked rapidly in confusion. "Did you miss the 'want to rule the world' part?"

"Nah, just wondering if these guys are as stupid as they sound."

Jason grimaced. "I'm sorry?"

"The megalomaniacs want to use a giant monster as their enforcer?"

"Yes."

"That's like trying to control a hurricane. It's stupid, and one hundred percent going to backfire." Brannigan shrugged as smoke streamed out of his mouth.

"That'll kill you," Skylar said absentmindedly.

"Thank god, can it hurry up?" Brannigan flashed his teeth in a smile.

"Did it work?" Devonte asked. "The device."

Kurtis and Skylar shared a look. "Not exactly…"

Devonte raised an eyebrow.

"We only had one test before you guys burst in," Skylar said.

Brannigan rolled his eyes. "You're welcome."

Skylar narrowed her eyes. "Thank you. But my point is, we had just turned the device on when you blew open the door...and shot it."

Devonte began to panic. "You turned on the device in the middle of the San Francisco Bay?"

"Calm down," Skylar said, holding up a hand. "It wasn't on long enough to have any effect."

Brannigan puffed more smoke into the air. The waves crashed against the side of the boat, and Devonte couldn't help but look out onto the horizon. He expected to see a giant creature rising from the sea, gunning to devastate his home state. Instead he saw the line where the sea touched the sky separated by a thick layer of fog. He sighed heavily. "Okay."

They made landfall without incident. A cadre of Navy officers, including General MacPherson, awaited their arrival. As they made port, multiple vessels departed in the direction of Alcatraz.

"Captain, Mr. Rhodes," she eyed the rest of their group, "the rest of you. Good to see you all made it, despite the...complications." Her eyes flicked to the smoking carcass of what was once the major tourist attraction.

"We didn't know the building was—"

The general cut Devonte off. "What's done is done. We're heading back to base. A more pressing matter has arisen."

CHAPTER 8

Hectic might be the biggest understatement Raymond could use to describe the airfield when they arrived. The creature had taken off into the sky with the remains of its meal, but the military had no intention of letting it get away that easily. Raymond knew that his pleas not to pursue would fall on deaf ears, so he kept his mouth shut as Ashleigh talked with the base commander.

"But sir," she started.

"We have no resources to spare," he said in the way that a parent would speak when ending a conversation with their child.

Another soldier jogged up and whispered in the commander's ear.

"I'll be right there." His glare warned Ashleigh to stay out of trouble, and more importantly, to stay out of his way. "You are dismissed."

"Sir."

"So, when does our flight leave?" Arnett called after the base commander. "Asshole"

Ashleigh stalked over, her fists clenched.

"So, what do we do now?" Arnett asked.

"We *must* get back to San Francisco," Raymond said. The pain in his lower body no longer threatened to leave him in a fit of tears. Still, he leaned on Arnett's shoulder. "To tell them what we know and come up with a plan."

"I *know*." Ashleigh gnawed on the knuckle of her thumb, taking in their surroundings with an analytical eye. Her gaze lingered on a Black Hawk transport. "Fuck it."

The scrambling of the fighters made sneaking around the base an easy task. Eyes were not on them, but on the sky waiting for the creature to return or just trying to get another glimpse. Raymond overheard a soldier lamenting that he missed a photo opportunity.

"Terror and curiosity truly are linked in our minds," Raymond muttered.

"Yeah, see also, stupidity and ignorance of the situation." Arnett readjusted Raymond's weight and practically carried him to the rear of the large aircraft.

Ashleigh signaled for them to wait as she scoped out the inside of the craft. The pilot sat at the console, communication headset on, and did not hear her approach. She took a moment to consider what her next action might lead to. Her chest tightened and her breath came in short gasps. She drew her pistol and pressed it against the back of the pilot's head, tearing the headset off with her free hand.

"Don't move."

The pilot went rigid, but then, to Ashleigh's confusion, he relaxed.

"Lieutenant Greenwood?" he asked.

"Turn around," Ashleigh commanded. "Slowly."

She recognized his face, still young and soft despite his military training. Bright eyes regarded her with nostalgic fondness. Spencer Chaplin stared at her with a grim smile and said, "Guess our past came back to bite us, huh?"

Ashleigh found herself speechless. She wrapped her arms around Spencer. "Thank god I didn't just shoot you."

"That would have sucked," he agreed.

"I need a favor."

"A reward for not killing me?" He laughed.

"Not exactly."

"A flight then," Spencer said pulling away from the embrace. "Commander Lawrence say no?"

"Technically," Arnett said, mounting the ramp with Raymond in tow, "he said you have no resources available. Which would imply a yes, were there resources available. Are they?"

"Good to see you again, Chaplin," Raymond said, settling onto one of the transport's row benches, with his back against the inner hull. "I certainly hope you can help us." He leaned back and closed his eyes, wishing for a soft bed. "If you don't mind, I'm going to close my eyes for a bit. I can't imagine I'll be getting much proper sleep in the days ahead."

Chaplin went to check the craft's log. He flipped through several pages on a clipboard and hummed to himself as he did. The pages rustled as he let them all fall back into place and chucked the clipboard into a nearby bin. "This transport is not scheduled for departure."

"Meaning?" Arnett asked.

"Meaning no one will be paying attention to it," Ashleigh answered. "Will you help us?"

"Of course," Chaplin said, "we're partners."

Ashleigh took the co-pilot seat, felt the rubber against her back, and fastened herself in. "I've never flown before, so just tell me what to do."

"Aren't you afraid of heights?"

She winced. "Very."

Spencer frowned.

"The copter requires two people, right?"

"I don't want to put you in an uncomfortable—"

"Just tell me what to do," she said through gritted teeth. "I'll live."

A moment of awkward silence hung in the air like a lead brick. Ashleigh settled the headset over her ears. Spencer did the same.

"Just watch these indicators," he said, "and let me know if they start flashing red."

"Roger," Ashleigh said, her voice filtering through the headset speakers. "You two settled in back there?"

"I think he's asleep, but yeah, we're good back here," Arnett's voice sounded clear as crystal in her ears. "Just get us off where we need to go."

Spencer started the transport's turbines. Fighter jets roared into the skies around them, leaping from smaller runways and setting off in pursuit of the creature. The large aircraft lurched into the sky before propelling forward and out over the open sea. Ashleigh gripped the arms of her seat and did her best to relax.

A voice came through the headset. "Resurgence, this is Control. You are not authorized for lift-off. Return to base immediately."

Spencer growled with a fake southern drawl. "No can-do Control, I've got a special delivery to make."

"Give me that!" Commander Lawrence's voice blared through the headset. "Listen here, you turn that transport around, or I will have you court martialed, do you hear me?"

Ashleigh mouthed the words, "Are you sure about this?"

Spencer cut the communication channel and shrugged. "Probably a little late for that question. Hold on."

The *Resurgence* rattled and rose unsteadily into the sky. It wobbled and bounced, bobbed and weaved, and Ashleigh swore she would be sick right then and there. But as the ground dropped away beneath them and the transport began to steady, she felt her nerves and stomach reach an uneasy equilibrium.

"Relaxed?" Spencer asked.

"Not the word I'd use, but this is a much steadier flight than the one we took here."

"Single engine?"

"And rickety as all hell," she said. "I was convinced we were going to die."

The two of them laughed awkwardly. Ashleigh shifted in her seat. Her mood darkened.

"You want to ask me, don't you?"

"No."

"Go ahead."

"When we got to Hong Kong you--where did you go? We searched for a week. We thought you killed yourself."

Chaplin winced, and gave a half-hearted smile. He pressed the autopilot button and pushed his seat back from the console. "Look," he said, rolling up his sleeves. Pale jagged scars formed a capital 'T' from his wrist up to the inside of his forearms, one on each arm. "I tried."

Ashleigh gaped.

"I had just watched most of my squad, my friends, get wiped off the face of the Earth by something that shouldn't exist. It was a rough place to be."

"So how did you, I mean—"

"How did I end up here?"

"Yeah."

"Shortly after I did this to myself, as I lay bleeding out in an alley, an old nurse found me. Ji Mochou. I guess she was on her way home from work. She berated me the whole time she patched me up. Stitches, bandages, the works. And then she took me in."

"You lived with her?"

"For about a month. She insisted. Kept saying my head 'wasn't on right'. Guess she thought I needed someone to look after me. I can't say she was wrong."

"Why didn't you come back after?"

"Honestly," Spencer watched the ocean rush by, "I don't know. I took a plane to Hawaii and ended up here. They needed a pilot and I just...settled in. Time got away from me. I'm sorry."

Ashleigh reached across and thumped him on the back. "Don't worry about it. Sounds like you needed the time to yourself. But I am glad to have you back."

"As am I," Raymond said, leaning over the pilot's chair. He cupped Chaplin's shoulder. "Your voices woke me up, so I couldn't help but listen. And I'm sorry that we weren't there in your time of need."

"Thanks. And don't worry about it. I'm alright now," Chaplin said. "But I do have a question."

Raymond raised his eyebrows. "Yes?"

"That's not the same creature, is it?" He glanced between their faces intently.

"No." Raymond's face darkened.

"Did we wake that one up too?"

"I think maybe our creature woke up that one."

Chaplin nodded. "Okay. Do we have a plan?"

"No," Raymond admitted.

Chaplin winced. "Great."

"Try not to worry," Ashleigh said. "We have some people who can hopefully help us."

Chaplin bit his lip. "Hope they're some miracle workers, because if one of those things could level Honolulu with a single breath...two...God, two."

A heavy silence fell over the cockpit.

"We have to stop it." Ashleigh slammed her fist on the arm of the chair. "It's our responsibility."

"That it is," Raymond said. He smiled softly at Ashleigh and placed a hand on her shoulder. "And we will do everything we can."

Ashleigh turned away so Raymond wouldn't see her blush at his touch. "Of course we will. Go rest."

"Yes, I think I will," Raymond said. "Wake me again as we get closer."

"We will," Ashleigh said shortly. She waited until the door closed before she relaxed.

"You still haven't told him?" Chaplin didn't look at her.

Ashleigh stayed silent.

"We don't have to talk about it."

"He has to know, right?" she said after a minute. "He's a detective. If he hasn't brought it up, he knows and obviously wants nothing to do with it."

"I wouldn't say that, necessarily," Chaplin laughed.

"What do you mean?"

"Well you've worked with him in the past, sure, but pretty much every time he's around you, there is at least a slightly more pressing matter going on. Crime lords, giant monsters, you know?" He checked their course on the small navigation screen and adjusted the heading slightly.

Greenwood kneaded her forehead. "I know and that hasn't exactly made it easy to tell him either."

Chaplin rotated his seat and placed his hands on his knees. "Your time will come."

"After we save the world?"

"Or in the post-apocalyptic waste if we fail," he said with a goofy grin.

"Shut up." Ashleigh punched him in the shoulder.

"Hey, don't distract the pilot," he said, flinching away with a laugh.

"Thanks," she said. "Not really the time or place, but I needed that."

Chaplin shrugged. "No worries."

"Wait, what is that?" Ashleigh leaned over the console to look out the window. Chaplin followed her gaze. Something massive, grey, and mottled, carved through the water, slashing its tail back and forth.

"It's so fast," Chaplin said in a hushed tone.

"Does this plane have a weapon?" Ashleigh said, bolting to her feet. "Anything?"

"It has the one rotary cannon, but I don't think—"

Ashleigh was out the door before he could respond. Arnett and Raymond jumped as the cabin door sealed behind her with a thud.

"What's going on?" Arnett asked.

"Contact."

"The creature?" Raymond sat up with some difficulty. "What are you going to do?"

"It's heading the same way as us. I'm gonna stop it." She crossed to the port side of the ship, to a tarp-covered object. Yanking the cover off revealed a mounted rotary cannon. Ashleigh assessed the gun, checking to make sure it could be fired properly. "Bring us around, Chaplin," she said into her headset.

"I'm not sure this is the best idea," he said.

"Bring. Us. Around."

He sighed in her ears as she prepared to open the cabin door. "Strap in, if you aren't," she shouted.

"Is this really the best course of action?" Raymond asked.

Arnett checked his straps once, and then again, before giving a thumbs up. "I mean, really, shouldn't we *not* shoot at the giant monster that isn't attacking us?"

"Yet," Ashleigh said.

Raymond gripped his straps tight and gave a short nod. "I suppose."

The port side door slid open and the wind whipped and roared around their ears as the cabin depressurized. Ashleigh felt her ears fill with pressure and forced herself to yawn to relieve the discomfort. She slid into the gunner seat and checked the gun's range of motion. "All set, Chaplin, show me the ugly bastard."

"Bitch," Arnett said, "most likely, that's the female."

"Still going to shoot it," Ashleigh said.

Something along the lines of "get us all killed" grumbled through the headset, but the transport began to turn in a slow, wide arc. She could see the coast of California on the horizon. Too close to not make a stand.

Inkanyamba came into view. Either it hadn't noticed them yet, or it didn't care. It just kept pressing forward to whatever destination it had in mind. The gun whined as it spun to life. Sweat ran down Ashleigh's neck and sent a cold chill down her spine. Thunder roared and fire rained from the gun barrel to the sea below. The first volley struck the creature's neck, showering the water below in a spray of red. The creature reared its head and screamed at the transport overhead.

"I think it just noticed us," Arnett said. "Hope that's not as bad as it sounds."

"Its eye is back," Ashleigh said.

"Back?" Raymond questioned.

"The one Ira shot out...the right one, it's back!"

"How is that possible?"

"I don't know but it doesn't exactly boost my confidence," she said.

"Keep shooting?" Arnett suggested.

The whine pierced through the air again before being replaced with the repeating thrum of the rotary cannon. This time Inkanyamba was prepared. It plunged beneath the waves, leaving only its shell exposed. So that's where Ashleigh aimed. She tried her best to focus on one spot, hoping to crack the exterior and break to the soft spot beneath. Chunks of the petrified crust blew off of the creature and tumbled into the sea.

A crack appeared in the shell spreading out from a hole the armor piercing rounds had made. The creature's head re-emerged from the sea, the translucent sac around its neck pulsed and its mouth hung open. A choking, clicking sound came from its throat as it tracked the transport across the sky. The air around them began to hum.

"Change our course, now!" Ashleigh shouted through the headset. She slammed the gunner door closed as fast as she could. "Don't follow this path."

"This thing is not made for quick adjustments," Spencer shouted back.

The transport lurched, and even with her harness, Ashleigh was forced to grab onto the cannon's handles to avoid being thrown from the seat. A blinding light flashed for just a moment, followed by a rumble of thunder. Hairs all over her body stood on end, and her limbs began to tingle.

She looked over to see Arnett and Raymond writhing in their seats. *Electrocuting.* Quick as she could, Ashleigh unstrapped herself and stumbled towards where they were sitting. Her rubber-soled boots must have kept her grounded. She looked around for something that would do the same for them. *Parachute? No. Life jacket? No. Think!* Raymond began to foam at the mouth right in front of her. Arnett's eyes rolled back in his head as he continued to shake and thrash about. Ashleigh looked at the floor. *Rubber treads!* She pulled her knife from its thigh holster, making sure none of her skin touched the metal portion. Raymond's straps cut easily. Ashleigh took a deep breath and grabbed him by his clothes.

She'd never been struck by lightning, but she imagined this is what it felt like. Fire coursed through her veins, and every muscle in her body contracted like one massive cramp. If her jaw had been able to unclench, she might have screamed. Instead, she mustered everything she could and yanked Raymond off the bench and onto the rubber floor. The fire subsided, and the cramp relaxed. She checked Raymond's pulse. Soft, but there. He was alive. *Thank god.* She felt like jelly held together by string and glue, but she knew she had to get Arnett too. Her heart pounded in her chest and in her head, everything throbbed like it was about to burst. She clenched her fists and pushed herself up on her hands and knees.

Knife in hand, she cut his straps as well. Hoping for a less painful outcome, she wedged the sole of her boot between

Arnett's back and the wall of the plane, taking care not to touch the metal with anything that wasn't insulated.

"Three, two, one." She put all the weight she could behind her one leg and pushed him forward. The police officer sprawled onto the padded floor.

"Fuck. Tasers," he said between gulping down mouthfuls of air. "Fuck." He collapsed on the floor. "We still alive?"

"I think so," Ashleigh said. "But Raymond...he needs a hospital."

The cockpit door opened, and Chaplin stepped into the cabin. "So, we're crashing," he said in a matter of fact tone.

A soft "fuck" came from the facedown Arnett.

"Can you guide us down somewhere safe?" Ashleigh asked.

Chaplin shook his head. "Whatever that thing did locked the controls."

"Some kind of electrical discharge. Not like the one in Hawaii."

"Fire and Lightning," Chaplin said. "Anyone reconsidering their position on the Bible yet?"

His comment was met with silence

"Not to be that guy, but where are we going to crash land, exactly?" Arnett said, finally sitting up. He rolled Raymond on his side, just in case.

"Can't say," Chaplin said with a resigned sigh, "hopefully nowhere heavily populated. Nothing I can do about it either way. Probably the ocean."

"I did this," Ashleigh murmured. "If I hadn't shot at the creature, tried to be a hero—"

Something hit her in the back and clattered to the ground.

"Handcuffs?" She held them up to Arnett with a questioning look.

"You think you're the bad guy, arrest yourself. Otherwise we don't have time for a pity party. We. Are. Crashing." His frown was stern, but there was no anger in it.

"He's right," Chaplin said, kneeling beside her and offering a hand. She took it and he pulled her to her feet. "We also have another problem."

"Another problem?" Ashleigh cocked her head to the side.

Arnett groaned.

"No parachutes."

"What?"

"I didn't do a flight check before we left. We don't have any parachutes," Chaplin repeated.

"We can't bail out?" Arnett asked.

Chaplin glanced out the window. "Would you want to? With that thing out there?"

"What is the creature doing?" Ashleigh asked. "Never mind, one thing at a time. We're crashing." She pressed her hand against the metal frame of the transport. When she didn't immediately feel electricity rush through her body, she figured it was safe now. The transport must have discharged itself.

"Arnett, make sure he doesn't roll off the rubber," she said, motioning to Raymond. "Chaplin, back to the cockpit, prepare to take control."

"I told you, the controls are dead," he protested.

"I have an idea," she said, leaping back into the gunner seat, and sliding the door open once more. "It might work, or it might just suck a lot."

"Oh god," Chaplin said. "You're not gonna—"

"Copter needs a pilot," she shouted.

Inkanyamba glared up at the plane, the cracked casing of its shell crumbling off in chunks both small and large. This aggravated the creature and it continuously lashed at them and tried to gnaw more of the shell away. With each crunch of fossilized stone, it thrashed about and screamed in rage. It must have been in pain, Ashleigh thought. Good.

Ashleigh pressed the soles of her boots into the floor of the plane. "Alright you slimy bitch, bring on the light show!"

The gun thundered to life again, spraying piping hot bullets onto the creature's scaly skin. For the moment it forgot its shell and returned its attention to the craft. Anger contorted its face. The skin around its upper fangs pulled back and it snarled. A warning, Ashleigh thought, one she chose to ignore. The bullets continued to rain down, punching holes in the creature. Inkanyamba thrashed, not in pain, but in irritation, the way a person may swat at a swarm of gnats.

What if it can't? she thought. *Does it need to recharge? Are we just royally fucked?* Her heart throbbed in her chest, and her breathing became quick and shallow. "Come on!"

Bullets struck shell and scale, head, throat, and eyes, but the creature continued to track them with the same cruel focus. Its tongue lashed about as its wounds disappeared as fast as they appeared. Its eyes narrowed.

"Hit me!" she screamed.

The hum returned, less intense than before, but she still felt it tickling the back of her skull. Ashleigh was quick, not wanting to put her boots through the ringer again, she dove onto the rubber mat with Arnett and Raymond.

The blue light flashed again, dimmer, but still bright enough to white out the world. She clamped her eyes shut when they started to burn. The transport rocked. It creaked and groaned around them sounding like the end of the world. Then it rolled. The few loose pieces of cargo slid across the floor and out the open door. She felt herself begin to slide towards the open portal. Her fear kicked in and her body refused to cooperate any further as it plummeted downward.

"No, no, please!" she shouted. Her eyes darted around for something she could grab onto. Basic motor functions returned, and she began to flail. Fingers brushed metal and rubber, but she couldn't get a grip. She clenched her eyes and waited for the freefall, when she felt a hand close around her wrist. Arnett clung to the straps of the nearest bench with one hand and clung to her with the other.

"I suggest," he said, grunting with the effort, "*not* sliding into the ocean from thirty thousand feet."

Ashleigh began to cry. "Thank you," she kept repeating. Her head was swimming and it was all she could do to keep from shaking. She reached her other hand up and grabbed onto Arnett's arm.

"Heavy," he groaned.

And then Ashleigh heard what she had been hoping for: the engine.

Chaplin crackled over the headset. "Controls...and comms...but barely. Only one of... engines is..."

"Just get us out of here!" she shouted. She knew she didn't need to tell him, but it was the first thing that came to her mind. The transport returned to its proper orientation and she slumped to the floor. Arnett stumbled over and closed the door.

"I'm never flying again," he sighed.

"Can you guide us into the bay?" Ashleigh pressed the mic against her mouth.

Static filled her ears. She repeated what she said. Then again. And again. Still no response.

"Damn it, Chaplin, can you hear me?"

"Yes, I...now please stop ...ting! ...hard to...focus."

Ashleigh breathed a sigh of relief. "Okay. Just give us some impact warning."

"No...just let you figure it...your own."

Ashleigh had to laugh at the frustrated sarcasm. Her body relaxed for the first time since she boarded the transport. Crashing would be easy, she thought, that involves being on the ground and not shooting at a sea dragon.

Raymond groaned and rolled onto his back. He muttered something she couldn't hear. His breathing had grown ragged and it was harder to see the rise and fall of his chest.

"Get ready to hold your breath," she whispered to him. "Don't you die on me."

#

The water battered Ashleigh as she tried to fight her way out of the plane. Raymond was strapped to her back through a series of severed aircraft seatbelts and duct tape from a police utility belt. The crash had plunged them deep into the bay, and in his condition, he wouldn't be able to hold his breath for long. She looked back as she pushed past the onslaught of water and saw Arnett force his way out into the open expanse of green water. Chaplin followed just behind him. The transport continued to sink, as debris and fuel floated into the surrounding water. Ashleigh forced air out of her lungs and pushed down with all her might. The light at the surface barely filtered down this far, but above a strange twilight twinkled as the surface waves distorted the sunbeams and scattered them into the depths. She pushed down again. Her thoughts were fuzzy. Darkness crept in at the edges of her vision. Again. The warmth of the sun was filtering through the water here. Soothing in the cold murk. Her vision started going darker. Her eyes burned. The push was harder this time. And harder still the next. Her body felt limp. Weak. A final push and…

Air. She gulped it down greedily. Behind her she heard Raymond do the same. He coughed and sputtered. His breathing didn't sound good, but he was breathing. She smiled as she continued to take in deep swallows of the salty air.

Arnett broke the surface moments later. "Oh Jesus," he said. "Thank you, Jesus." He splashed at the water. "I never want to do that again."

Chaplin gasped. "Agreed."

Ashleigh scanned their surroundings. She could feel her strength fading fast. Treading water for two people would take its toll quickly. They were near Alcatraz Island. Or at least what remained of it. The smoke billowed off the husk of the island, and where the prison once stood, nothing remained but a few crumbling stone walls. Before she could question the circumstances, a voice called out to her.

"Are you alive?" it asked.

"Yes!" Arnett shouted. "Please tell me that's a boat!"

The coast guard ship slid through fog that emanated from the surface of the water. It shined a light on them.

"How many?" the voice asked again.

"Four," Ashleigh said. "Three swimmers, and one in need of medical attention." She felt the boat bump her and strong arms grabbed her by the soaking fabric of her fatigues. Another pair of arms assisted and hoisted her out of the water. She flopped sideways onto the floor of a small rescue boat.

"How did you know we'd crash in the bay?" she heard Chaplin ask as they pulled him onboard next.

"Didn't," the voice said. "We were heading to the island when your transport hit water. Almost capsized us."

"Sorry about that," Chaplin said.

The man attached to the voice shrugged. "You *didn't* capsize us."

Arnett climbed onto the ship.

"We would've pulled you out," the ship captain said.

"Nah, I was sick of being in the water," he said, resting against the side of the boat. "Can we please just get to solid ground?"

Raymond coughed up water onto the deck. "We have something very important to report," he wheezed.

The men cut him free and turned him on his side so he could expel the rest of the water from his lungs. More of it sprayed out with each cough.

"Don't try and talk," Ashleigh said, alternating between rubbing his back gently and thumping on it to get the water out. "Just take it easy. We'll get where we need to go."

She stood on wobbly legs and saluted the man on the boat. "Lieutenant Ashleigh Greenwood," she introduced herself. "We need to get to Concord Base as soon as possible to report to General Adelaide MacPherson."

"Seaman Greg Porter, ma'am. We'll have you there in no time."

#

True to his word the seaman delivered then to shore and gave them a full escort to the Naval Base. Ashleigh stopped the medic as she carted Raymond past.

"Will he be okay?" she asked.

"Conditions change fast," the nurse said, "we need to get him to the infirmary now."

Ashleigh was about to demand to go with him when she felt a hand squeeze her shoulder.

"I'll go with him, you get where you need to go," Chaplin said.

Ashleigh swallowed hard and gave a curt nod.

"Can I sit down somewhere?" Arnett asked.

"You're with me. Need our eyewitness," Ashleigh said. She turned her back on Raymond's still body and listened as he was wheeled away. When she could no longer hear the sound, she made her way to the command center.

As she opened the door, General MacPherson shouted. She held an empty mug in one hand. "Are we just letting anybody in here now, Greenwood?"

Devonte and two people Ashleigh didn't recognize, a silver haired man and a girl with bright red curls, turned in her direction. Devonte gave her a confused frown. A man in Marine Greens leaned against a wall and chuckled.

"I have a report, and this man is an eyewitness," Ashleigh said, standing at attention.

MacPherson placed the mug on a table and crossed her arms. "At ease. What is it now?"

"There are two creatures." The words hung in the air. She could feel their presence weighing on the mood in the room.

Devonte's eyes widened. The marine cursed silently. If the general scowled any harder, Ashleigh worried she might tear a muscle in her face. Skylar looked absolutely giddy, something that caused both worry and intrigue to play across the grey-haired man's face.

"Do you care to explain that statement, Lieutenant?" General MacPherson's facial muscles pulled against the formation of every word that left her mouth. "We have no reports of a second creature here."

"When we were in Hawaii, there was a disturbance. Captain Dehane, Officer Sanderson, and I went to investigate. The creature was the cause. But it was different from the one six months ago. Smaller, and a different color."

"I can just barely believe in one giant sea dragon, and you expect me to believe that there are two of them stomping around?"

"Is it possible you misremembered the creature?" the grey-haired man asked. "Tempest only has a record of one monster as well."

"I'm sorry, who are you?" Ashleigh asked.

The man straightened himself. "I'm Dr. Kurtis Wagner. A pleasure to meet you."

"Well, Doctor, I know what I saw on both occasions." She didn't try to disguise the edge in her voice. "And the one in Hawaii crawled out of a volcano."

Arnett jumped in. "Not to mention the fact that we engaged in combat with the second creature on the way here."

The entire room seemed to perk up.

"You what?" MacPherson practically hissed the words.

Ashleigh winced. "The creature rose from the sea beneath us, seemingly on the same course we were. Towards the San Francisco Bay. I made the decision to engage in an attempt to deter the creature."

MacPherson tapped her foot. "An interesting decision."

"Ma'am," Devonte said. "General MacPherson?"

"What is it, Rhodes?"

"I pulled up the satellite footage from Hawaii as well as the images of the creature you have on record."

"You didn't have permission to access those images." She pinched the bridge of her nose. "Put them on the big screen."

The differences between the two images were immediately obvious. Horns versus no-horns, no shell versus shell, blood red versus murk grey. Two separate creatures, one engulfed in the flames of a burning city, the other slicing its way through a blue-grey sea.

"I think this proves my point," Ashleigh said, her voice an icy dagger.

MacPherson hurled the empty mug across the room. Her face twitched with rage. "Two," she growled. "We have to deal with two." The loss of composure only lasted a split second, replaced immediately with her normal professional air. "Were you successful in deterring the...original...creature?"

"We crashed, ma'am," Ashleigh replied.

MacPherson stormed across the room. "Do you mean to tell me that one of those things could be here any minute?"

"It's a possibility."

MacPherson held Ashleigh's gaze for the briefest of moments, looked her up and down, and said, "Go get cleaned up." She turned to Arnett. "And do you plan on sticking around? Should I have my men prepare another cot?"

"Honestly," he said, "I need time to get my head around this. I got family in the city. I'm gonna check on them, maybe move 'em somewhere safe before shit hits the fan, but I want to help here. That thing burned my city. I can't let that stand, so I'll be back."

MacPherson looked him up and down. "We'll see, I suppose."

"Yeah, you will," Arnett said. He exited the room and called out to one of the passing soldiers. "My man, give me a lift?"

The soldier looked questioningly at the general, who nodded her approval.

MacPherson watched the man go before crossing the room to pick up the phone. She dialed a number and waited as it rang. The line clicked. "We're on high alert," she said, "send the tank squads to the shoreline near the bay." A pause. "We're going to set up a temporary command center on Angel Island."

She held the phone away from her ear and Ashleigh could hear the voice on the other end of the line shouting. Some politician she guessed. The voice on the other end died down and MacPherson returned the phone to her ear.

"Yes, I know Alcatraz was just destroyed, but we've learned that the creature might enter the bay. That makes the island a strategic location."

Another bout of shouting on the other end indicated that the other person didn't like this answer any more than the initial news.

"What *about* the Golden Gate Bridge?" MacPherson's composure began to slip away again. She gripped the phone so tight her hand shook. "Like I give a fuck about your campaign."

The other end of the line went deadly quiet. Ashleigh couldn't hear what was said.

"Go write a policy banning the monster from the city. Until then I'll be doing what needs to be done to keep us all safe." MacPherson hung up. It rang again almost immediately. She picked it up, said, "We're busy," hung up, and left the phone off the hook.

Ashleigh took her leave of the room before the general could say anything else.

INTERLUDE II

The man sat behind a giant oak desk in front of a picturesque wall of windows looking out over the city of Chicago. He didn't turn to face her when she entered. "What name are you going by now?" he asked.

"Jia Ming."

"Very well, Jia Ming, care to explain to me why our Alcatraz base is no more?" He spun around in his chair and lifted his feet onto the desk. Sunken eyes stared at her from beneath bushy eyebrows. He crossed his hands behind his head, careful not to disturb the perfectly manufactured crop of salt and pepper hair. "I like the new dark hair. It suits you."

"Mr. Martin—"

He held up a hand to cut her off. "Please, call me 'sir'," he said with a smirk.

It took all of her willpower not to ball her hand into a fist and really bring out the grey in his five o'clock shadow by covering his face in bruises.

"Sir," she started again, "the base was compromised. Per protocol, destruction was the correct course of action."

"Please don't reference protocol to me, you know how much I hate it. It gives me indigestion. Protocol is Mr. Nishimura's domain. Business is mine. Do you know how much this affects our business?"

Before she could respond he said, "No, you don't, because you're a glorified grunt."

Ming heard her teeth cracking in her ears. She knew his guards were right outside waiting for any indication of a disturbance. *Could she kill him before they killed her?* she thought. *Probably, yes. Would it be worth it? Certainly.* But she had another task to complete first. So, she smiled. "How have I affected our business?"

She knew exactly what he was going to say. "The tooth. Not only was it our main source of research on the creature, *but,*" he paused dramatically, "it had already been sold to a very high bidder. Someone I now have to placate otherwise." His eyes narrowed. "Money makes the world go around, sweetheart, and you just cost me tons of it."

"I'm sorry." The words tasted bitter in her mouth.

"I don't want sorry. I want recompense. Do you know what that means?" He put his feet down from the desk and hunched over it, fingers spread on the smooth, lacquered wood.

"What do I need to do?" she asked.

Mr. Martin's face split into a predatory smile. "You two, get in here," he shouted.

The door behind her opened and slammed shut. She didn't turn around. The two men trudged past her, a muscle-bound thug of a white man, with a shaved head and a thin, bespectacled man who spoke with a thick Spanish accent.

"You requested our transfer to this location?" he said. Neither he nor his partner turned to acknowledge Jia Ming.

"Senor Hugo Fernandez, Mr. Ivan Cole. Thank you for joining us." He indicated for Jia to step forward. "This is Ms. Jia Ming. Former commander of Storm Base on Alcatraz."

The two men turned to regard her, Fernandez with a restrained respect, and Cole the way one might regard a potential conquest. She knew she'd need to keep an eye on him. For now, she put on a face that meant business. *I will not be intimidated by the likes of scum.* "Gentlemen," she said. "Welcome." To Martin she added, "What are they doing here?"

"They will be accompanying you on your next task."

"They what?" she deadpanned. *Play the part*, she thought, *this doesn't matter.*

Martin steepled his fingers. "Senor Fernandez here is something of a researcher. Certainly more reliable than your plans of kidnapping a biology student. And Mr. Cole is the best there is at what he does, and what he does is kill people. They will assist you in reclaiming the tooth."

"The tooth is gone," Jia Ming said. "Up in flames."

"Wrong. Your ignorance is honestly sad." He drummed his fingers on his desk. "The tooth is *gone*, not destroyed. It's currently in the hands of the American military."

"How do you know?"

"I run the business, and a good businessman keeps track of all his assets at all times."

"There's a mole," she said. *Of course there is. There's always a mole.*

Martin shrugged. "Trade secret." He waved his hand to dismiss them all.

Fernandez bounded up to her like a coked-out puppy. "You've seen the tooth?" he asked, mustache atwitch. "What is it like?"

"It's a huge fucking dinosaur tooth. You know what those look like, right?" she snapped.

He recoiled but said nothing. Cole lumbered towards them with a slow but purposeful stride. "If you intend to be useful, I suggest you up your pace," she spat.

Cole let out a low guttural growl and continued his robotic trudge.

Jia Ming waited until both of them exited before slamming the door and rounding on Martin. "And how do you expect the three of us to infiltrate a fully operational military base?"

Martin sighed. "First, lower your voice. Second, I would never set you up to fail. In order to handle the potential threat of the two creatures the military will be moving to a temporary base on Angel Island, leaving only a skeleton crew to defend the tooth."

"Your asset?"

"My asset." He wiggled his fingers. "Goodbye."

Jia Ming took a deep breath, turned, and left the room.

"You two, come on," she said as she strode past her two new, unwanted partners. "Do you have men?"

"Yes," Cole said. "Many men."

"I tend to prefer to do my work alone," Fernandez said.

"No surprises there," Jia Ming muttered.

"We strike now?" Cole asked.

She ran her hand through her hair. "No, you idiot. It will take time for them to pack up and move out. We'll attack when we attack."

"But," Fernandez started.

"The tooth will still be there. Go prepare. Or more importantly just go somewhere not here."

CHAPTER 9

"I'm not leaving him here." Ashleigh slammed her fist into a desk, snapping Devonte back to the argument that had been going on since the general ordered their move.

"He's a grown ass man who will have a security and medical detail on him until we return." General MacPherson's calm fury made Devonte shiver.

Ashleigh scowled. "I owe him my life!"

"The way I see it, Lieutenant Greenwood, you stole a transport helicopter—"

"On your orders to return."

"All the same, I could have you court martialed. Instead, I'm asking you *politely* to follow a single damn order. Are we clear?"

If looks could kill, Devonte thought. *The general wouldn't stand a chance.*

Skylar tapped his shoulder. He jumped.

"Should we intervene?" she asked.

"Be my guest," Devonte said. "I prefer living."

"True." She paused, biting her lower lip. "I wanted to say thanks for saving me."

"Oh, yeah, it was no big deal. Glad you're safe." He smiled and she smiled back.

MacPherson's voice rose to a forcefully punctuated shout. "If we are going to successfully eliminate the threat, I need everyone involved to cooperate. Shut up and stand down Lieutenant, you have your orders."

Skylar frowned. "Eliminate," she said. "You want to kill them?"

MacPherson stared daggers at her. To Devonte's surprise, Skylar returned them in earnest.

"It is a threat to our country. It must be destroyed."

"It's a brand-new creature!" Skylar said. "As far as we know, it's no more malicious than a shark. We need to learn what it needs so that we can protect us and it!"

"I'm already dealing with one asinine argument. I refuse to cater to this one."

Skylar's face turned as red as her hair. "You what?!"

MacPherson's eyes narrowed. "Are we all on the same page here?"

"No," the other two women shouted back.

Devonte rubbed his temples. *This is getting out of hand.* He clenched his fingers and felt the knuckles pop. "We'll stay," he said.

MacPherson leveled a gaze on him more oppressive than the Eye of Sauron. She said nothing. She didn't have to.

"I mean, it works right? We're not soldiers. Neither is Dr. Wagner. But I also owe Raymond a debt, so I can stay and watch over him. So, Ashleigh can go. Skylar doesn't seem to want to have a part in the death of the creature, so she can stay here and research it. Everyone ends up mostly not hating the outcome." Devonte shrugged. "Maybe?"

He thought he could hear MacPherson's teeth cracking from the tension in her jaw. When she didn't shoot him down, a wave of shock and relief washed over him.

"Fine," she said. "Nothing else on the subject. Greenwood, prepare to move out." MacPherson stormed out of the room.

"Ashleigh. Lieutenant Greenwood," Devonte stuttered, "I know you don't trust me, but—"

"Anything happens to him, it's on you." With that warning, she turned and followed MacPherson out of the room. The door slammed behind her.

"Care to complete the trilogy of being pissed off at me for that suggestion?" Devonte asked Skylar, rubbing his stinging eyes.

"You're not the one trying to kill an innocent creature," she said. "And you're right, I'd want no part of that."

"Not to start another argument, but you do know that the creature sunk a cruise ship and killed over a thousand people, right? And that the other one burned Hawaii?"

"I didn't," she admitted. "But I don't think that makes it evil. We kill so many animals for food and for sport...does that make us evil?"

"Sometimes I wonder," Devonte said. He looked at his phone. Zero missed calls. Zero texts. *A helicopter falls out of the sky and he doesn't even shoot me a message.* He noticed Skylar watching him. "Sorry, I was somewhere else. You're right, the creature probably isn't evil, but it is dangerous."

"It is, which is why I think we should one up Tempest." Kurtis sauntered into the room. "Beat them at their own game."

Skylar looked up. "What do you mean?"

"The device," he said. "We can finish it."

"It got destroyed in the self-destruction," Skylar said. "So did our notes."

Kurtis fumbled with the pocket on his lab coat and pulled out several crumpled sheets of paper.

"The notes!" Skylar clapped her hands together.

"With everyone gone we'll have the peace and quiet to get it done this time!"

"I'm not sure that's a good idea," Devonte said.

Kurtis scowled. "And why not?"

Because fuck you, Devonte thought. He said, "Just seems like asking for trouble to build the thing the bad guys wanted. If they're as omnipresent and powerful as you say, what if it falls into their hands?"

Kurtis clicked his teeth. "What do you think, Dr. O'Hara?"

Flattery? Really? Devonte thought. He looked at Skylar and what he saw made his stomach drop. She was excited.

"If we can get something done before the creature arrives, we can show General MacPherson that we can drive it away and they won't have to kill it!" Her smile lit up her entire face.

"My thoughts exactly," Kurtis said.

"You can help," Skylar said, grabbing one of Devonte's hands in hers. "With a more mechanically minded person we can finish it twice as fast!"

Her eyes bored into him, and he felt his face heat up. "I— I should go check up on Raymond," he said. "You heard what Ashleigh said."

He'd crushed her excitement. It was written all over her face. Her smile dropped and she gave him a flat "ok".

"I can join you guys a little later—"

"Don't worry about it. Him and I did this before, we can do it again." She didn't look at him as she left the room.

"Smooth," Kurtis said as he went to follow her.

"Get fucked," Devonte mumbled. He sat alone, spinning in his computer chair for a little bit. *Maybe she'll decide it's not a good idea after all. Maybe she'll come back.* After an hour he got up and made his way to the infirmary.

Raymond lay on the white cot, breathing softly. Devonte's eyes widened. A mechanical apparatus extended from the base of his spine and wrapped around his waist, extending down his legs. The harness was a complicated mess of straps and thin metal bars. Devonte traced his hand on the frame.

The detective's eyes fluttered open. "I see you've discovered my secret."

Devonte jerked his hand away, embarrassed. "I'm sorry, I didn't mean to—"

"It's fine. There was shame at first, but in the past months I've accepted my new condition. One must always press on."

"What happened?" Devonte tried his best not to stare. He locked eyes with Raymond but found that even more uncomfortable, so he stared over the man's shoulder instead.

"A long fall, and a sudden stop. It shattered...a lot of bones." Raymond struggled to sit up. Devonte helped as best he could.

They sat in silence for a moment.

"What's on your mind?" Raymond asked finally.

"Huh? What makes you think something's bothering me?" Devonte stuttered.

"I didn't ask what's bothering you, but now I know something is. I don't need to be a detective to figure out something is wrong. You wear your emotions like a badge."

"Like at the cafe?"

"Like at the cafe," Raymond affirmed. "Now spill."

Devonte tongued his cheek. "It's Skylar," he said.

"You're crushing on her already?" Raymond grimaced as he chuckled.

"Yes. No! Maybe. Shut up." Devonte ran a hand through his hair. "That's not what's on my mind right now though. It's her and Kurtis. They're trying to build the prototype that Tempest wanted."

"And you're worried they might get their hands on it?"

Devonte nodded.

"Then why aren't you helping them?" Raymond asked.

"Did you miss the part where I don't think it's a good idea?"

"And you told them this?" Raymond said.

"Yes."

"And they decided to do it anyway?"

"Uh-huh."

"So, you can't stop them from doing what they want to do?" Raymond cocked an eyebrow.

"That's why we're having this conversation, yes."

Raymond sighed. He reached out and put a hand on Devonte's shoulder. "Control what you can. Now, go help your friend." He said with a wink.

"I don't—"

"Go."

#

Devonte took a deep breath and opened the door to the lab. Skylar looked up and her face immediately lit up. Kurtis scowled.

"I'm here to help," Devonte said. "You guys need a tech person still, right?"

Kurtis opened his mouth, but Skylar spoke first. "Of course!" She ran over to Devonte. He thought she was going to hug him but instead she punched him in the arm.

"Ouch!"

"That's for making me think you weren't gonna help." Then she hugged him.

Kurtis crossed his arms and pursed his lips.

"So, what is the device supposed to do?"

"We need be able to draw the creature away by calling it with the sounds of its natural prey," Kurtis said. His voice was laced with venom.

"Whales," Devonte said. "Right? But you can't just blast whale sounds over the entire populace."

"Why not?" Kurtis argued.

"Would you want to hear a whale cry at the volume of a jet engine in your city? Not to mention the frequency and the volume would shatter everything glass within a pretty wide radius. That's basic physics, right?"

Kurtis' eyes narrowed. "Of course, but this is just a prototype."

"Well I don't know what you do in physics," Devonte said, looking intently at the tangle of wires and parts beginning to take shape on the workbench, "but when I design a prototype, it needs to function effectively the same as the desired outcome. Otherwise how do you know that it works?" He popped up to check how his comments went over. Kurtis did not look pleased.

"I didn't even think about that," Skylar said. She beamed at Devonte. The smile quickly changed to a frown. "How do we deal with that?"

"Yeah, smart guy," Kurtis said.

"Oh, shut up. Let him think," Skylar snapped.

Devonte couldn't help but smile as he realized what Raymond had been trying to explain to him. "It's actually an easy concept. You can just isolate the portion of the sound that can't be heard by humans, but still draws the creature. There's plenty of software out there that can do it, but to be safe...I can write us one."

#

Devonte watched Skylar wipe her forehead, smearing a streak of grease beneath the tied-up mane of her hair. "I think it's done," she said. "Kurtis?"

The grey-haired man checked over the crumpled notes one last time. "Everything seems to be according to the original prototype specifications." He stuffed them back into his pocket. "All that's left is to see if your friend can solve our volume problem."

"Call me Amazon Prime, because I just delivered," Devonte said, holding up a small thumb drive. "Coded, compiled, and ready for action."

Kurtis reached for the device, but Devonte pulled it away. "Uh-uh, this is Skylar's device, so she gets to plug in the last piece," he said, walking past Kurtis and placing the thumb drive in Skylar's hand.

She beamed up at him. "Let's do this," she said.

At that moment a klaxon sounded, and the base was drenched in a pulsing blue light. Skylar stuffed the thumb drive in her breast pocket before giving a questioning look to the two men.

"The last time I heard a sound like that, something blew up," Devonte said. "I doubt it's ever a good sound."

"What should we do?" Kurtis asked.

"You two stay here," Devonte said. "Keep this thing hidden and safe."

"Where are you going?" Skylar asked.

"I've got to check on Raymond. He just started walking again." Devonte packed up his bag, including the gun Brannigan had left him. When questioned by the general, the captain had said it was lost in the explosion at Alcatraz. "Stay. Here." he whispered.

#

The skeleton crew thumped through the hallways as Devonte made his way to the infirmary. Halfway to his destination, an explosion shook the base; he heard the sounds of gunfire and quickened his pace into a frantic run. In his sprint, he almost crashed right into Raymond, who motioned for him to be quiet and pulled him into a nearby room just as several black clad figures hurried by.

"We're under attack," Devonte said, breathing heavily.

"It seems Tempest did not take kindly to our assault on their base," Raymond confirmed. "Where are the others?"

"In the machine room. I told them to hide."

"And the device?"

Devonte looked down. "It's fully operational once my code is uploaded."

Raymond looked at him expectantly. "I see," he said. "Then let's stop it from being taken. I've already sent word to the general, they will be here as quick as they can. Are you armed?"

Devonte flashed the holster at his belt.

"Good," Raymond said, "I'm afraid we'll need it." He checked outside their room, and seeing nobody, motioned for Devonte to follow.

They stayed close to the walls and ducked down low, moving quickly but quietly. Every time Devonte heard a volley of gunfire, he felt his chest tighten with anxiety. They turned a corner and saw the back of a man in black body armor. Devonte jerked up his gun in response, but Raymond pushed the weapon down. He pulled a knife from a sheath on his boot and crept up behind the man, sliding the blade effortlessly into the exposed space around his neck. The man gurgled, and Raymond twisted the knife, silencing him completely.

Devonte mouthed, "What the fuck?"

"You pick up some things when dealing with the nastier sides of the criminal underworld," Raymond said with a solemn face. "Let's go."

"Not going anywhere," a deep voice said.

Devonte watched as a nearly seven-foot man rounded the corner. His fists alone looked to be about the size of a person's head. He had no weapon on him, but his body armor covered every inch of him. No room to stick a knife.

"You come with me," the man said in his thick Russian accent.

Raymond put himself between Devonte and the man. "And if we refuse?"

"I break you. Then you come with me. In pieces." The man grinned a slow, malicious smile. "Please resist."

Devonte sized up the man, determined there was no chance of beating him, tugged on Raymond's sleeve and said, "Run."

The man was faster than expected. Before they'd even made it a few steps, he was on them. He caught Devonte first, by the back of the collar, and flung him to the floor. The force of the impact forced all the air out his lungs and left his head ringing. Raymond didn't stand a chance as he wheeled around to face his pursuer. To his credit, he put up his fists and prepared to fight anyway.

"Down!"

Instinctively, Raymond hit the floor with a slight exhalation of pain just as the rat-a-tat of the assault rifle sounded off from behind him. The towering man stumbled backwards as the hail of bullets pounded into his body armor.

"Wow, you won't got down easy, huh?" Brannigan emerged from the smoke-filled hallway. "Happy to see me?" He winked at Devonte. "Don't get up, I got this." He tossed his gun to the side. "Now that I've got your attention, bruiser, how about you pick on somebody your own...eh, you know what, fight me you ugly motherfucker."

"What are you doing?" Devonte shouted.

"I'm about to kick his ass while you get away," Brannigan said, dodging a punch that surely would have shattered his skull if it had made contact. "So, get away!" He caught the follow-up punch and used the man's momentum to knock him off his feet. The heavy thud echoed in the corridor. Devonte didn't waste any time; he grabbed Raymond and ran around the fallen man, in the direction of the machine room. He heard the man get up with a bellow of rage as he turned the corner and ducked into the machine room.

CHAPTER 10

Brannigan steadied himself. The other man was certainly faster than he looked. The captain almost regretted throwing away his gun, but the appeal to the other man's bravado had worked all too well. Every punch the man threw was a haymaker, but his training was obvious in the way he moved with each punch. Brannigan wouldn't win this in a fair fight. But he did have an ace in the hole.

"So, what's your name, bruiser?" Parry. Dodge. Counterattack the jaw. Like punching concrete. Uppercut to the solar plexus. Less concrete, more iron. "Please tell me it's Doug or something." He said between each heavy breath.

"You face Ivan Cole, dead man," the man said before landing a solid blow directly in Brannigan's side.

Brannigan felt like one of his kidneys had popped, and he wouldn't have been surprised to learn that it actually had. He staggered back and spat blood on the floor. He grinned at the other man through bloody teeth. "Nice shot," he said. "My turn."

"Take your best," Ivan said, returning Brannigan's grin. He spread his arms wide, taunting and welcoming the next attack.

"I thought you'd never ask."

Brannigan stalked forward, hand clutching his side, until he stood just in front of the man. *Please don't let him change his mind about this.* While he pulled back with one hand, he reached into one of his side pouches with the other. He thrust both of his hands forward, and shouted, "Tag, you're it."

Ivan laughed and kicked him square in the chest, launching him back down the hallway.

Brannigan clamored to his feet and scrambled away from the now approaching man. He put as much distance as he could between them and hid behind a nearby door ripped off its hinges.

"You run, little man?" Ivan said.

"Yeah, but not from you." Brannigan motioned for the man to look down. Hooked onto one of the straps of the man's body armor was Brannigan's ace. One live grenade, pin not included. "On the bright side, at least you're going out with a—"

The sound of the grenade set Brannigan's ears ringing as he was launched backwards by the force of the explosion. He felt the impact of the shrapnel against his makeshift shield that he clung to even as he hit the ground a good fifteen feet from where he'd started. As the dust cleared and Brannigan managed to climb to his feet, he saw the body of the hulking man slumped against the wall at the other side of the hallway; a piece of shrapnel was embedded in his helmet and at least one of his hands was missing. He must have tried to unhook the grenade right before it went off.

"Bang," Brannigan said, and stumbled in the direction he'd seen Devonte and the detective go not too much earlier. He flipped off the man as he went by.

#

"What the hell?" Devonte shouted, looking at the scene playing out before him. Kurtis had one arm wrapped around Skylar's neck, while the other hand pressed a gun to her head.

"Well this is awkward," Kurtis said. "I'd planned to be gone by now." Beside him stood a woman that Devonte didn't recognize, but Raymond obviously did.

"You?" the detective said. "But I watched you die."

The woman sneered. "So, you are the one who killed Bae Ling Zhang." Her face contorted into dark fury. Then she composed herself. "I am Jia Ming. Consider yourself lucky. Today is not your day to die." Her words held a tone that implied she wished it was. She turned to Kurtis. "Where is the tooth?"

"Gone in the explosion," he said, "but I needed you lot to act sooner than if I had just said come get me."

"But Mr. Martin—"

"Mr. Martin believes what he wants, but trust me, this—" he thumped a hand on the prototype device "— and this—" the thumb drive twirled its way between his thin fingers "— are what we really came for."

"What are those?"

"Do we have evac?" Kurtis asked.

"Yes."

"Then allow me to demonstrate." He shoved Skylar over to Devonte, who rushed to catch her before she tumbled to the ground.

"You can't turn that thing on here," Skylar shouted as she righted herself. She started to rush back at him, but the quick response of several guns being leveled on her froze her in place.

"I can, and you made it possible," Kurtis said. "Maybe I am going to fall in love with you after all," he added with a smirk.

Skylar's face reddened in embarrassment. "It's not mutual."

"That'd be a shame." He flicked the switch on the device and plugged the thumb drive into its slot. "Oh well, let's see if our beastie is around."

There was no sound, at least not that Devonte could hear, but the oscilloscope showed the wavelength that was being played, just outside their range of hearing. Devonte quickly realized that while he couldn't hear the sound, he could still feel the vibrations rattling around in his chest cavity. He couldn't help but smirk.

"What's so funny?" Kurtis said.

"You didn't put in the password?"

"The what?"

The device began to spark, and smoke billowed out of it before it caught on fire completely. Kurtis jumped away from the device with a shout. "What did you do?"

"Authorization check. Start the device and it waits for a certain code to be entered, for about fifteen seconds. Sans that it goes straight into a self-destruct sequence, overloading the voltage on all of the internal components."

"You booby trapped our device?" Skylar asked.

"I was going to share the code with you, but then this all happened. Sorry."

"Don't apologize. That's brilliant."

"Oh yeah, of course, you know me," Devonte felt his face grow warm.

Kurtis scowled. "We have the notes. Kill them."

"No," Jia Ming said. "We've been here too long as it is."

"I said kill them," Kurtis barked.

None of the men around him obeyed. They stowed their guns and began to retreat on Jia Ming's orders.

"This is my operation," she said. "We fall back. Now."

Kurtis' hands fell to his side.

"Is this the part where you say we'll rue the day," Skylar taunted.

"I don't need to. You know I'll have my vengeance." Before anyone could react, he aimed his gun and fired. Devonte felt fire tear through his left shoulder. In the next instant he dropped to the ground with a scream. He saw blood draining from the bullet wound near his chest, dripping down to join the initial explosive splatter. He clutched at the ragged hole and slumped down onto his back. His body felt cold. The last thing he heard was a piercing shriek so far away in the distance, followed by the rumble of an unearthly roar. *It worked,* he thought.

#

Devonte fell in and out of consciousness, but even in his dazed state he knew something was wrong. He heard voices and felt like he was gliding through the air. The soft sensation of a medical gurney pressed up against his back. He was being carted around. He opened his eyes, just a sliver, and saw Raymond's face looking straight ahead, dripping with sweat. He looked concerned. Turning his head was so much effort. Skylar was on his right. Above her, he saw the ceiling tear away in a massive chunk, an orange reptilian eye glared in on them. *Am I dreaming?* he thought. *No, the creature,* he remembered. *It's here.* A roar rattled his bones as the glide took a sharp turn to the left. There was another noise. *Fireworks? No. Gunshots.* He remembered more. *I got shot.* He wanted to be sick, but the thought of his stomach sent pain coursing through his body. *Am I going to die?*

"You better not," Brannigan shouted back from his left. "You just finally grew a pair."

Devonte hadn't realized he'd spoken out loud. He tried to give the captain a smile, but the effort sent him spiraling back into the darkness.

#

Incandescent light buzzed above his head as he opened his eyes. The ceiling was pock-marked, chipped, and cracked. It had seen a lot. Devonte tried to sit up, but the pain that shot through his shoulder made him jerk back down onto the cot he was lying on with an agonized groan.

"You shouldn't have done that," Skylar's voice said.

Devonte rolled his head and saw her sitting at the side of his bed. Her eyes were red and swollen. "Don't tell me you were crying over me, D-Base," he said.

"It's my fault you got shot," she said. "I taunted him." Her voice cracked. "I *trusted* him."

Devonte didn't disagree, but said, "Nah, don't worry about it. I had just upstaged his big moment. I was definitely getting shot either way."

Skylar shook her head. "And after you went through all the trouble to rescue me."

Devonte moved his one good arm to put a hand on the top of her head. "Hope this isn't too weird, but, you're my best friend, it's okay," he said. His smile felt stiff, but he hoped it looked as genuine as it was meant to be. "I will admit though," he continued, "getting shot sucks all kinds of ass."

Skylar couldn't help but laugh with tears in her eyes.

"How bad is it?" he asked.

"The field nurse said it looks like just soft tissue damage. You'll need some physical therapy and using it will not be comfortable for…probably a while, but you'll recover fine."

"Damn, and here I was hoping to get myself a robotic arm," he said with a soft chuckle.

Skylar laughed with him, tears running down her cheeks.

"Where are we?" Devonte asked.

"Apparently, there are a lot of secret underground bases in San Francisco," Skylar responded. "This is the second one I've been in and it's only been a week."

"Lucky. This is my first time," Devonte chuckled. "Where is this one located?"

"Beneath Angel Island, I think," she said. "They didn't exactly want to divulge the exact location of the place but given the direction we went from where we were…that's my guess."

"Wait, did they blindfold you?"

She nodded. "You too, even though you were unconscious. Can't be too careful, I guess."

"Huh," Devonte said, "thought that was only in movies."

Outside the door, a voice said, "Sir, you can't go in, he should only have one visitor at a time."

Brannigan's voice barked back, "Yeah, well she's been in there all day, and I want my turn, so move aside." The door swung open and Brannigan strode into the room. "You mean to tell me I go and get my ass kicked by a real-life Batman villain to protect your ass and you still end up getting shot?"

"Sorry?" Devonte said.

"You better be." Brannigan went to punch him in the shoulder but stopped short as if suddenly realizing that punching a man with a gunshot wound might not be for the best. "Right, I'll call it acceptable since you lived." He rubbed the back of his head. "That being said, I come bearing stupid news: the general ordered that you be brought to command as soon as you woke up so," he looked around, "let me go beat some clothes off of somebody."

Devonte looked down, checked under the sheets and realized all he had on were his boxers. "Oh," he said. He quirked an eyebrow at Skylar.

"Don't get your hopes up," she said, "I did not undress you."

The two of them fell into a second shared fit of laughter as Brannigan re-entered with Devonte's jeans and T-shirt with no trace of blood on it.

"What'd I miss?" he asked.

#

Raymond and MacPherson looked up as they entered the room.

Devonte gave a small wave with his good arm. The other rested in a sling. "Not dead yet."

"That's wonderful news," Raymond said, "I'm afraid ours is not."

Devonte looked back and forth between the two adults. "What happened?"

"Alcatraz," MacPherson said through gritted teeth.

"It blew up, yeah, still feel bad about that."

The general shook her head. "Inkanyamba you called it? It's taken up residence on Alcatraz Island."

"What?"

"How much do you remember?" Skylar asked.

Devonte frowned. "Kurtis…he activated the prototype."

"And it worked," Skylar said. "Really well."

"What about the second creature?" Devonte asked.

"I have a name for it now," Skylar said.

MacPherson rolled her eyes. "Do tell."

"Vornax." She paused. "A combination of volcano and Fornax, a Roman god of—"

"Ovens?" Brannigan said.

Skylar blinked in surprise.

"What? I've read books before." He shrugged.

"Yes. Yeah, god of ovens. Look, it sounded cool okay, and I wanted to stick with Devonte's mythological slant."

"No judgment," Brannigan said, "I think it's badass."

"That's all very well and good," MacPherson said, "but we don't *want* this creature to be a badass. We want it dead."

"It's here too?" Devonte asked.

"Not yet," Raymond said.

"Yet?"

"The sound dampeners on the base work exceptionally well," MacPherson said. "Since taking up a position on the island the creature has been…calling out. Loudly."

"How long was I out?"

"Two days, five hours, and thirty-two minutes," Skylar said.

"Wanna throw the seconds in there as well," Brannigan snarked.

Skylar's face turned a deep shade of red.

"Can we see it?" Devonte asked.

The general motioned to one of the other uniformed soldiers who quickly typed something into his computer. An overhead monitor descended from the ceiling and the lights dimmed. An image flickered to life on the screen. Devonte's breath caught in his throat.

The creature perched atop the island was massive. None of the videos or images he'd seen so far had done it justice. Part crocodilian, part turtle, part fantasy leviathan, it was beautiful in the worst sense of the word. It extended its neck and bellowed, a high keening cry that sent shivers down Devonte's spine.

"Is it calling out a challenge?" he asked.

Skylar shook her head. "Tissue samples of the two from their previous attack sites indicate that they are actually from the same species, despite their vast differences. I personally think it's—"

"A mating call," Devonte finished. The air in the room was heavy with the information. "If we assume that they can be classified as reptiles…"

"We're looking at a potential cluster of one hundred eggs," Skylar said, "one hundred new kaiju."

"That is unacceptable," MacPherson growled. "We have to stop this thing."

"At least before it gets fucked," Brannigan chimed in.

The general's jaw tightened in response, and Devonte thought he could see a vein bulge in her forehead. "Yes."

"There's also the problem of Tempest," Skylar said. "It's likely that they will try to capture the creature in this sedentary period."

"Wouldn't that make its boyfriend mad though?" Brannigan asked. "They don't seem to have much interest in him, actually."

"I don't know," Skylar said. "Their plans seem pretty focused on Inkanyamba."

"I think we are all missing the very important question here," Raymond said.

Skylar scowled at the statement.

"How do we kill it?" Devonte said flatly. He searched the room for any inkling of an answer. No one met his gaze.

CHAPTER 11

Kurtis had never seen Randolph Martin as worked up as he was at the present moment. He was actually glad none of the wrath was directed at him, not that it ever could be. Ming, however, was taking quite the reaming. He fiddled with the thumb drive he'd managed to rescue from the prototype before it had burst into flames.

"You cost us our station in San Francisco, an unacceptable number of men including Mr. Cole, who, while alive, is deep in a coma, I'm sure thanks to some failing on your part, culminating with your inability to recover either the tooth or the prototype device." The man's cool condescension had boiled over into an all-consuming rage as he paced furiously behind his desk.

Jia Ming, Kurtis noticed, was trying her damnedest not to respond in kind, but he saw a glint of murder in her eyes.

Mr. Martin's temper cooled as his tirade subsided. "Luckily for you, Mr. Fernandez was able to salvage enough of the junk you brought us to recreate it. A minor success amidst so much failure, but a success nonetheless."

"Orders, sir," Jia Ming deadpanned.

For a minute, Kurtis thought Randolph might actually come from behind his desk and strangle her in a fit of apoplectic violence. He didn't, however, and instead simply said, "Get out of my sight."

The woman flashed an icy look at Kurtis before storming out of the room.

"That went well," Kurtis quipped as the door slammed behind him.

"She needs to learn that failure has consequences," Randolph said, slicking back his frazzled hair.

"I will admit that a good portion of her failure was my fault." Kurtis gave a short apologetic bow.

"Don't act noble," Randolph sneered, "it doesn't suit you."

Kurtis let a smile play at the corner of his mouth. "True."

"I know you didn't come just to offer a fake apology. What do you want?"

"Fake? So suspicious. But yes, there is more." Kurtis paused. "I want the girl."

Randolph quirked an eyebrow. "You want...her?" He pointed at the door Jia Ming had used.

Kurtis shook his head. "The one the military took from us. I want Skylar O'Hara."

"We have the device designs and most of her research notes. What good is she to us now?"

"Not to us," Kurtis said. "*For* me."

A crooked grin cracked across Randolph's face. "You dog."

"No need for praise," Kurtis said, "Just a yes."

"If she is of no further use to us, then you may do with her as you please...not that you needed my permission anyway."

"I prefer not to upset coworkers. It helps keep a more productive work environment." Kurtis turned to leave.

"There is one more thing," Randolph said.

"Yes?" Kurtis looked back at the older man.

"What about the other creature?"

"It's a potential threat to our creature," Kurtis said. "Kill it."

"Of course."

"Anything else?"

"No, sir."

Kurtis nodded silently and exited the posh office, stepping out onto the top floor of The Harrison building. He looked out onto the bay and saw the creature coiled up atop its island perch. The soundproof windows kept its cry from reaching his ears, but he watched as it went through the motion of rearing back its head and stretching open its mouth, razor-sharp teeth glinting in the evening sun. After each attempt it would lower its head to the ground and wait for some reply.

Kurtis pressed a hand to the glass. "Glorious," he said.

#

Kurtis entered the medical room and looked at the comatose form of their best mercenary. He flagged down a nurse. "What's his prognosis?"

"Well," the woman said, "comas are unpredictable, so it's hard to tell. One of our scientists has a theory about using something to stimulate his brain activity, but it's not proven and—"

"Do it," Kurtis said.

The woman looked at him, mouth agape.

"Now," Kurtis said with a smile so fake it hurt his face.

The nurse scurried off, presumably to find the scientist in charge of whatever far-fetched idea she'd been going on about.

"Ivan Cole, if this works, you're going to have a special mission assigned to you. I pray for your sake that you don't fail this one."

The nurse came back with a man in a lab coat stained grey with dust and metal shavings.

"Doctor Felding," the nurse said, "this is the man who asked for you."

"Greetings."

"I hear you have a way to wake him up," Kurtis said.

"Potentially."

Kurtis frowned, waiting for more. "Care to elaborate?"

"I thought you'd never ask!" The man sprang into action, rushing up beside Cole, and placing his fingers on the comatose man's head like some kind of reverse crown. "Nanobots." He waited as if that word explained everything about his plan.

"Full sentences," Kurtis said through gritted teeth.

Dr. Felding sighed. "If we fill his brain full of nanobots that are constantly activating his brain in a fashion similar to the way it used to operate, it is possible to get him up and running again and," he said with a sneaky grin, "we will be able to directly affect his decision-making process via the robots."

Kurtis nodded his head. "And the risks?"

"Plenty." He paused. "We could microwave his brain by accident; the metal particles of the nanobots could be detected by his antibodies which would then begin to destroy his brain; we could overload his sensory experiences, leading to a systematic collapse of his, well, nervous system. I'm sure the nurse here told you—"

"That it's unproven, and now I'm gathering it's dangerous and unethical?" Kurtis said with disinterest.

"Yes."

"Do it anyway."

"I'm sorry?"

"Do it. Make him your first human test subject. If he lives, great. If not, well, he's no less use to us than he currently is."

The doctor didn't seem shocked at the callousness of the statement. "Understood. Nurse, wheel the patient to my laboratory if you please."

The nurse ran a horrified glance back and forth between the two men. "Yes, of course," she said finally.

"Do you mind terribly if I watch?" Kurtis asked.

"Watch? You're going to help me," the doctor said with a manic grin. "This way."

Kurtis followed, silently wishing he'd not started this chain of events, but curious to see where it led.

The laboratory looked like something out of a modern Frankenstein movie, cluttered, grimy, and ionized with the occasional electrical malfunction sparking somewhere overhead. Kurtis pulled on a pair of gloves with a snap.

"Now, coma patients can feel pain, as I'm sure you know," Dr. Felding started.

Kurtis nodded.

"This will be extremely painful. Perhaps the most painful thing a human being could possibly endure."

"Just tell me what I need to do," Kurtis said.

Felding pointed to a screen. "That's his brain scan in real time, whenever this image lights up red, hit the button to your left to flood his body with morphine. Hold it until the orange starts to dissipate."

"How much?"

"Potentially all of it. He's likely to die from overdose, but if we don't manage his pain, he could die from that as well." The doctor shrugged. "I could spend an entire day listing all the ways he could die, honestly."

"Pass. I'll hit the button as needed."

Felding smiled, reached up and pulled a helmet-like apparatus down from just over his head. Tubes, wires, and cables snaked their way up and beyond where Kurtis could see. He fixed the device to Ivan Cole's head and cranked a lever on the side until there was a pneumatic hiss followed by a dull thunk. Ivan's body twitched violently, then settled once more.

"Like an iron maiden for the brain," the doctor mumbled as he spun around and assessed a screen of, presumably, the patient's vitals. "Last chance to back out," he added.

"Do I seem like a person who backs out once a decision is made?"

"Fair enough. Geronimo." He threw a lever and the whole lab rumbled to life. Through the clear tubes affixed to the helmet, Kurtis watched a flood of grey descend into Ivan Cole's motionless skull. The grey material leaked from his nose and tinged the corners of his mouth.

"The morphine!"

Kurtis had been so entranced by the process that he'd neglected to watch the scan. "Shit," he said, slamming the button. The brain scan went from flashing an angry red back to its original blue color. He returned the doctor's irritated stare with an equal measure of defiance. "Continue."

The doctor rolled his eyes before returning his attention to the scans. "It seems like we've introduced enough of the nanodevices to create a large enough synaptic shock to wake him up, theoretically." He glanced over at Kurtis. "I suggest you back away from him. The initial response will almost definitely be violent."

Kurtis wheeled two arm lengths away from the massive slumbering man.

"Synaptic shock, now."

The helmet crackled as if struck by lightning, and Ivan Cole bolted upright with a guttural scream. Every muscle in his body contracted and bulged beneath the surface of his skin as he writhed in agony.

"Ending trial one," Dr. Felding shouted.

The lightning subsided and Ivan collapsed back on the cot.

"Did it work?" Kurtis asked.

"Well his brain activity is certainly maintaining levels that would indicate consciousness." The doctor craned his neck to observe Ivan. "Call his name."

"Ivan Cole," Kurtis said in a raised voice. "Answer me."

The mercenary's eyes flickered open. He didn't speak as he sat up. The doctor came over and removed the helmet carefully. Cole's bald head retained the pinprick pattern from the needles in the headpiece. He rubbed absent-mindedly at the wounds, smearing blood on the top of his head. While doing that he looked down to his left, noticing for the first time that his left hand was missing. A stump wrapped in stained cloth rested in its place.

"Grenade," he said.

"Yes," Kurtis said, "I heard you took a grenade point blank."

"Dead?"

"No, you are alive."

"Not me."

Kurtis looked at the doctor with a cocked eyebrow.

"I believe I was told that the grenade was attached to him directly by one of the people in the military base at the time of the invasion. Perhaps he is asking about that?"

Kurtis thought for a moment before speaking. "No, I'm afraid he is still alive."

The doctor gave him a puzzled look, which Kurtis shot down with a look of his own.

Ivan's face contorted into a grim mask of rage. "Alive?" His one fist clenched tight. "I kill him."

Kurtis smiled to himself. "That's fine big guy, we'll make sure you get the chance. For now, the nice nurse is going to wheel you back to the medical wing and give you a check-up." He motioned for the nurse to take him and go.

When the gurney was out of sight, the doctor turned to him and asked, "How do you know his assailant survived?"

"I don't, but revenge is a great motivator, especially for a thing that seems to only have a one-track mind at the moment."

"I see."

"You disapprove?"

"I simply wonder what the ramifications may be in the future," the doctor said with a shrug. "That's all."

Kurtis shrugged.

#

"We are not launching another attack on them," Jia Ming said. "We lost too many men and walked away with basically nothing the last time."

"Yes, yes, I understand, but this isn't an attack," Kurtis said. "I want to send in *one* operative—"

"To kidnap the girl who watched you shoot her best friend?"

"Well when you put it like that...yes."

"You got us Ivan back, in some fashion, so thanks for that, but as the person presumably still in charge of whatever this clusterfuck mission is supposed to be, I am not wasting that resource on your puppy love."

"Not many people would talk to me that way, you know," Kurtis said coldly.

"If you or any other of the Hands of Fate were going to kill me, you'd have done it by now, but you haven't because despite Martin's shouting and frothing he knows I get results," she spat back.

"Fair play," Kurtis said. "At least until you stop getting results."

"Are we done here?"

"Yes, take Ivan, run your plan, do whatever voodoo you think you can do. We'll talk again after this is all over."

"Hopefully not," Jia Ming said, rising from her seat and exiting the room.

Kurtis steepled his hands in front of his face. "Hopefully not, indeed."

A buzz came through the intercom at his desk. "Mr. Wagner," the voice said.

"Yes, Dr. Felding?"

"It's about our, um, experiment." He sounded nervous.

"Cole?"

"He's gone."

A smile spread across Kurtis' face. "Is that so?"

"I'm so sorry. I tasked the nurse with watching him and—"

"It's fine. How well does the control aspect of your experiment work?"

CHAPTER 12

Brannigan strapped the body armor over his dark grey fatigues. Devonte sat in a folding chair, typing away one handed on his laptop.

"I'm sending the schematics to your GPS unit," he said. "I still don't think this is a good idea."

"Why's that?" Brannigan said. He knew why. This was the fourth time the kid had brought it up…in the last hour.

"Inkanyamba is on that island, and we don't know the full extent of its capabilities. Not only that but—"

"Vornax could show up and we all could die," Brannigan finished the thought. "Kid, we're the Marines. Death is the sugar we sprinkle on our cheerios, okay?"

"Sounds like macho bullshit to me," Devonte grumbled.

"Alright, you want me to level with you?" Brannigan said as he holstered his pistol. "I'm scared shitless. I mean, war is terrible, ghastly business, but there's never been a giant monster involved. Look at me, I'm six feet tall and I have guns that, as far as we know, only piss off that thing out there. I got nothing." He paused. "But I signed up for this shit to do everything in my power to protect people, and if that means walking into the belly of the beast a bit more literally than initially intended, so be it."

Devonte stared at him grimly.

"I'm not gonna lie and say that this'll turn out alright. I definitely might die. All we can do is hope that it's not in vain."

"You can stop now," Devonte said.

Brannigan started to say something else but was interrupted by a knock on the door. "Come on in," he said.

General MacPherson stepped into the room.

"I didn't realize generals knew how to knock," Brannigan said with mock surprise.

The general ignored his jab. "Captain Brannigan, your squad."

Brannigan looked the men up and down. Five soldiers, he noticed, smaller than the standard army size, and much smaller than the thirteen he was used to. They all looked capable enough, but he didn't recognize any of the faces. "Alright gentlemen," he barked, trying to suppress a grin, "let's hear some names and ranks."

"First Lieutenant Hicks," said the first man. He was taller than Brannigan and maybe twice as wide. "And this is my partner, Bowman. Same rank." Bowman, a stout, barrel of a man, grunted in confirmation.

Hicks and Bowman looked promising. They had the experience but none of the arrogance that tended to go along with it. Brannigan nodded in approval. The other three were younger, and obviously less experienced. Brannigan gave the general a curious glance. She gave no physical response.

One of the men stepped forward. "Spencer Chaplin, sir. I was on the boat during the creature's first appearance. It took my friends, and I ran away, but I'm here now and I'm ready for action."

Brannigan smirked. *Make that three promising soldiers,* he thought. "Thank you for your life story, Private, don't disappoint me." He turned to address the remaining soldiers who introduced themselves as Thayer and Collins. "Y'all ready to kick some monster ass?"

The men all saluted in response, and echoed a collective, "Sir."

"The only rank that matters on this mission is mine. I'm in charge. Follow orders, stay alert, and let's get this done."

"Sir," came the collective response again.

Brannigan grinned down at Devonte. "See? We're big, we're bad, and we got this in the bag."

"The schematics are on your device. I've linked your comms and camera to my computer, so I'll be watching and listening," Devonte said with a roll of his eyes. "Try not to die."

CHAPTER 13

The rusted iron door screamed open under the combined force of Brannigan and Bowman's weight. Chaplin fumbled around in the dark beyond the door and found the emergency power switch. He flipped it and nothing happened.

"Typical," Brannigan said. "Torches lit, boys!"

The darkness of the maintenance tunnel shattered apart as six beams of ultrabright light burned into it.

"And this leads all the way under Alcatraz Island?" Chaplin asked.

"Supposedly," Brannigan said. "That's two secret spaces beneath the island in a two-week span."

"This tunnel is actually fairly common knowledge," Hicks said. "What gets me is how there was an entire secret complex down here and no one noticed."

"Easy," Bowman grunted. "They paid off the workers."

"Ah," Hicks said, "that makes sense."

"I'll take point," Brannigan said. "Bowman, you take up the rear. The rest of you stay alert." He stepped into the darkness, flicking his light from left to right, illuminating rusted pipes and long dead spider webs.

The path twisted and wound about, with maintenance doors every hundred feet no matter which direction they turned. Darkness lingered outside the scope of their lights, clawing at the silence broken only by the sound of the soldiers' even paced steps. Brannigan's boot splashed in something wet. He called the squad to a halt.

"There shouldn't be water down here," he said.

"It's under the bay," Thayer replied. "Course it'll be a little wet."

"Have you ever heard of structural integrity?" Brannigan asked.

"He's right," Chaplin said, "if there are any cracks or weaknesses, the whole thing could come down on our heads."

Brannigan angled his light down at the ground. "Good news, and bad news."

"Good news first?" Chaplin said.

"It's not water."

"And the bad news?"

"It looks organic...like mucus."

"Which means?" Shannon asked.

"Which means we ain't down here alone," Bowman growled, sweeping behind them with his light.

Brannigan sniffed at the viscous substance. "Smells acidic." He shined the light on his boots. The mucus had started to eat away at the thick rubber sole. He scraped it off on the floor as best he could. "Don't step in it," he said. "Come on we've only got about a mile to go." As he spoke, a thick glob of the mucus dripped down from the ceiling onto the ground in front of him. "Fuck," he whispered. "Above us."

As he fell silent, he noticed a noise that hadn't been there before, a soft scuttling sound interspersed with whisper-thin squeaks. He slowly raised his light to the ceiling and saw...legs. Hundreds of chitinous legs, writhing and oscillating around mucus-covered, segmented bodies. As the light passed over the shiny black eyes of one of the insectoid creatures, it began to scream.

"What the fuck are those?" Shannon asked.

"Devonte, you seeing this?" Brannigan whispered.

"Unfortunately," came the voice through his headset. "I hate bugs."

"They look like isopods," came Skylar's voice. "Like lice," she finished.

"I've never had lice," Brannigan said, "but aren't they supposed to be smaller?"

"We've captured deep sea isopods as big as a foot."

"How about six?"

"Holy shit," came Devonte's breathy reply.

The first of the creatures dropped to the tunnel floor with a moist thud. Thick, pincer-like mandibles snapped at them with a harsh clicking sound. He could see now that the segmented plates were each covered in a field of wicked spikes. It reared back with a scream, kicking its front-most legs and shivering violently.

Thayer opened fire from Brannigan's right, blasting the creature's head into a thick purple paste. The sound of the shots echoed loudly throughout the maintenance tunnel. "Hold your fire," Brannigan shouted.

It was too late. The whole ceiling came alive with a collective scream, the creatures on the ceiling no longer moved languidly, but clattered to a violent cadence. He heard at least two drop down behind them before Bowman called out to confirm the situation.

"We need to move, now!" Brannigan shouted. "Stay on me." He set off at a sprint, glancing up every so often in the hopes that he'd see an end to the sea of legs and pincers. Behind him, he could hear the ever growing and quickly approaching swarm. "Tell me these things are herbivores."

"Parasitic carnivores," Skylar's voice said. "They *will* eat you."

"Of course they will." He skidded to a stop as the path branched into three separate paths. Confused, he checked his GPS. According to the device there should be a right turn at this junction. Instead the path went left, straight, and back the way they came, but at a left angle. Not right. "Devonte, the hell is up with this?"

"I don't know." His voice sounded panicked. "The schematics were the most recent I could find, from just last year." Brannigan heard loud clicking on a keyboard through his headset. "They should be right, unless…"

"Unless Tempest has been doctoring the schematics for a long time," Brannigan finished.

A human scream from behind interrupted their conversation. Brannigan wheeled around to see Collins, just as a pair of pincers crunched down through his skull. The look of shock and horror never left his face as several of the swarm broke off from their stampede and began to rip and tear at his flesh.

"Open fire," Brannigan called. It was too late to save Collins, but he'd be damned if these bugs got the better of him. The sound in the narrow tunnel was unbearable as the dark lit up in flashes with the rapid-fire volley of the rifles. Bugs showered the walls with their insides as they popped like vile balloons. But they just kept coming.

"We're gonna get overwhelmed if we keep this up," Hicks shouted.

"I know," Brannigan yelled back. "Damn it," he hissed. "Left path."

The soldiers responded and began their escape. Bowman's leg was caught by one of the creatures, dragging him to the ground. Hicks opened fire on the attacking creature, blowing it to bits, but not before several more clamored over the downed man, stripping him of his flesh in seconds.

The swarm carpeted the ceiling and walls behind them, blowing out lights and tearing electrical cables as they stampeded after the fleeing men. Ahead of them was a heavy iron door much like the one they entered through.

"You lot lay down suppressing fire while I get this thing open," Brannigan shouted, shouldering his weapon and immediately setting to grinding the rusted wheel on the door. The echoes of gunfire blended with the high-pitched screams of the creatures as they were blown apart.

"They're getting a bit close for comfort here," Chaplin shouted.

"Keep shooting," Hicks roared in reply.

"Almost got it," Brannigan said as the door swung open on creaking old hinges. "Everyone through, now."

He didn't have to tell them twice. The remaining two soldiers dove through the door, Brannigan was right behind them, dragging the heavy weight with him as he went. The vault-like door sealed shut with an exasperated hiss and a dull clanging thud. Brannigan gulped down air in greedy breaths as he listened to the furious chittering of the creatures on the other side of the door.

"Bugs," Hicks gasped. "I fucking hate bugs."

"Brannigan," Devonte's voice crackled to life through Brannigan's headpiece, "are you okay?"

"Yeah," Brannigan said, "just thoroughly creeped out and…and we're down two men," he added bitterly. "Bowman, and Collins. Fuck." He looked at the three remaining men. Chaplin had been one of the first to encounter the monster they were calling Inkanyamba. He looked exhausted, but mostly unfazed by the loss of their comrades. Hicks looked upset but managed to stay composed. Thayer, on the other hand, was in tears.

"Fuck, man, they came out of nowhere and just fucked our shit," he said. "What the fuck are we supposed to do about that?"

"You haven't even seen the big one up close yet," Chaplin said.

"Oh you think this is funny?" Thayer spat. "Two of our men just died. My friend just died!" He stalked across the room and hoisted Chaplin up by his collar and slammed him into a nearby wall. "And you think that's funny?"

Chaplin met his furious gaze with one of complete detachment. "Of a squad of seven, two of us survived first contact."

"Man, fuck you," Thayer said pulling back for a punch.

Hicks grabbed his wrist and held it just tight enough to hurt. "Enough."

Brannigan watched in silence. Thayer dropped Chaplin and pulled his arm from Hicks' grasp.

"Shit sucks. People are dead. We have a mission," Brannigan said, drawing their attention back to him.

"Yeah, a mission that didn't involve flesh-eating bugs the size of people," Thayer shouted. "And also, your little friend with the schematics isn't doing a very good job either is he? I mean, a left turn being a little early or late is one thing, but not existing at all. The hell kind of intel is that?" He clicked on his comm-link. "Hey computer boy, got any information on those bugs for us? They got acid for blood or something?"

There was silence for a minute, the sound of rustling, and Skylar's voice came over the comms. "At the depths they would have been surviving, near all that volcano material, it is possible they could have acid for blood. Or blood that is so toxic, breathing in the fumes from it could kill you instantly. What is true, however, is that you're panicking and need to shut the fuck up and listen to Captain Brannigan."

"Oh," Thayer said, "oh that's just great, Shirley Temple is sticking up for her boyfriend everyone. Give her a round of applause." He began to slow clap loudly.

On the third clap, Brannigan's fist cracked across his jaw.

"On your feet, Thayer, that's an order!"

"Thought rank didn't matter on this mission," Thayer said, rubbing his jaw.

"It didn't. Now it does. On. Your. Feet." Brannigan extended his hand, but Thayer brushed it aside.

"I'm up," he said. "What next?"

"We press on, of course," Brannigan said dryly. "Devonte, you there?"

"Yeah," came the sullen reply.

"No time for pity-partying, I'll give you shit for it later. Where are we?"

"Hold on, let me check." The sound of keyboard keys clicked loudly through the earpiece. "Your GPS signal is faint because of the dirt and metal and some other interference—"

"Maybe the bioelectrical interference of the insects...or Inkanyamba herself," Skylar chimed in.

"But based on what I've got...you ended up in the right place. I put you right below Alcatraz Island." Another pause. "The schematics I have say there should be an elevator that leads up to the main basement of the prison, but—"

"We'll figure it out from here, kid," Brannigan said. "Thanks. You did good."

Brannigan put his index finger to his lips. "She's right up there, boys. Let's not wake her. God knows she needs her beauty sleep."

All of the color drained from Thayer's face, and he tightened his grip on his assault rifle. "We're beneath it?"

"Yep," Brannigan said. "And the way I see it is, we either go out and face big momma, or we go back and fight our way through those things." He motioned at the door, the creatures still scraping and clicking furiously on the other side. Crossing the room, he flipped a switch and illuminated an industrial elevator so obviously lacking in any form of safety measures, Brannigan wryly thought that its kill count might be higher than his.

"Fuck me," Hicks said.

"Another time, maybe," Brannigan said with a grin. "Shall we?" He made a sweeping gesture towards the rickety elevator.

"Let's not waste any more time," Chaplin said, sliding the dubious safety chain to the side and stepping on to the elevator platform.

Brannigan followed, and Hicks and Thayer pulled up the rear.

#

The first thing Brannigan noticed was the smell, like murky brine left to sit and stew in fetid pools of garbage beneath a brutal sun. Each breath was a fight not to vomit. The second thing was the sheer size of Inkanyamba. From the videos and stories, he knew she was big, but that was an understatement. Her slumbering form towered above them. She was asleep, and each breath set the earth beneath their feet rumbling with tremors. The sharkskin scales that covered her body bristled when she inhaled and relaxed when she exhaled. Her serpentine head tucked itself away, collapsed down for protection. Covering her entire back was a patchwork of fossilized rock, and coral, and sea-life, a jagged shell that cracked and crumbled in chunks.

Brannigan was glad for the encounter with the isopods, because the smell that clung to him and his men matched the smell that clogged the air. She wouldn't catch their scent. Not if they worked fast.

Quiet as they could, they set about planting the explosives, a blend of TNT and PETN, "for a little extra oomph", they'd been told. Brannigan placed the explosives as close to the creature as he dared get, wiring the detonator thread back to the elevator shaft. The others did the same. When all the bombs were placed, they gathered back up at the elevator.

"Alright, boys, let's wrap this up," Brannigan whispered.

"Brannigan," Devonte's voice crackled in his ear.

"We're almost done here, don't worry, kid."

"No, Brannigan, you have incoming!"

At that moment, a shrieking roar louder than any jet engine pierced the silence. Brannigan looked up to the sky and saw the devil himself, Vornax, descending towards Alcatraz Island, cloaked in smoke and fire.

"Everyone down," he shouted, diving behind a pile of rubble that had once been a prison wall.

Chaplin crawled onto the elevator platform and lay as still as he could. Hicks slid into the remains of a cell and ducked as low as he could.

Thayer froze to the spot. He was rooted in place, shaking uncontrollably. Sweat poured down his face.

"Thayer," Brannigan hissed. "Move."

Vornax landed, the smell of sulfur and heat burning away the fetid swamp smell in an instant. It shrieked once more, flexing its wings before folding them flat against its back. Inkanyamba swelled in return, her serpentine neck extending and turning to regard the other creature. Her yawn bellowed like a foghorn as she rose up onto all four feet. The frills along her neck bristled and flared, flexing as she moved. At full height she reigned a good twenty meters above Vornax, looking down at him with reptilian interest.

"Thayer," he hissed again, waving for the man to come towards him.

The soldier slowly turned his head and looked at Brannigan. His eyes were unfocused and darted between the monsters and the captain. Brannigan had seen this look before, and it never meant anything good.

The sounds coming from the creatures now were different, like they were cooing at each other, if a coo could sound as loud as a train whistle. *Mating*, Brannigan thought. He looked past Thayer to where Chaplin still lay belly down on the elevator platform.

The private caught his eye and mouthed, "Plan?"

Brannigan shook his head.

And then Thayer screamed and opened fire. The cooing quickly turned to shrieks of rage and indignation as the two monsters turned to regard what Brannigan thought must look like an ant screaming and spitting at them. Vornax was the first to react, rearing back with an ear-splitting scream before exhaling what could only be described as a pyroclastic cloud at the man. Thayer didn't stand a chance. Brannigan barely had time to affix his gas mask and pray he wouldn't be burnt as well. The heat around him grew nearly unbearable and for a split second he thought that he would meet his end, but then the heat vanished as quickly as it started. With a mighty beat of Vornax's wings, the ash cloud cleared, and from behind his hiding spot, Brannigan could see Thayer, flash-fried like the bodies he'd read about in Pompeii. He looked up, and pulled quickly back into cover. Vornax was now scanning the area, as if expecting another Thayer to appear ready to be ushered into the same fate. Inkanyamba warbled, and Vornax responded, his heavy footsteps lumbering back towards her.

Brannigan took a deep breath and used the opportunity, sprinting from cover and towards the elevator platform. He heard Inkanyamba roar; she'd seen him. He dove on to the elevator platform just as a flash of white light obliterated the wall he'd used for cover. The hairs all over his body stood on end as he slammed the button. The elevator began its slow descent back down the shaft. He watched as Hicks emerged from his hiding cell, sprinting towards them with all his might. It wasn't enough. Inkanyamba's head snapped down like a whip and caught him in her mouth. Hicks screamed a sharp piercing sound before the monster swallowed him whole.

Chaplin gasped.

Inkanyamba turned to regard the descending elevator. Her slitted eyes fixed on the two of them as the platform disappeared from her line of sight. She roared triumphantly, and Vornax joined her with his own hyena cackle.

"Time for a bad idea," Brannigan said, pulling the explosive detonator from his utility belt. "Bye, bitch." The explosion came instantaneously, rocking the platform and snapping the support cables in the process. The last thing Brannigan saw before plunging into the dark of the elevator shaft was Inkanyamba snapping her head around with a roar to see what had happened. He couldn't help but smirk.

"You know," Chaplin shouted, "this is me plummeting to my probable death too many times in such a short period."

"Not gonna die this time either," Brannigan said over the cacophony of explosions and roars from overhead. "Still gonna suck. We got about one hundred and fifty meters of elevator shaft. Pull the cord on your pack and pretend we're base jumping."

Chaplin groaned and pulled the cord. As the parachute opened, Brannigan rushed past before opening his own. The whiplash made him want to puke, and he was sure he heard something in his neck crack. He watched as the elevator platform sped down below them. A few seconds later, he heard it crash into the bottom. A cloud of dust rose up to greet them. Brannigan focused on keeping his parachute away from the sides of the elevator shaft. He had to be precise, or all that jagged metal at the bottom would become an intimate part of his body. Finally, the ground was close enough that he angled his descent and grabbed onto an exposed pipe on the wall, hooking on with a clip attached to his belt. He cut his chute and climbed down the last few feet, dropping down into the room they'd left earlier. Behind him, Chaplin landed with a thud, rattling some rusty metal and eliciting a whining creak from the elevator's remains.

"You good?" Brannigan called over.

"Aside from the tetanus? I'll live," Chaplin replied. "We do have another problem though."

"The bugs."

"How do you propose we get back through that tunnel?"

"On the way in, they didn't grow agitated until Thayer shot at them."

"And we just detonated an unholy amount of nitro over the top of their heads," Chaplin said grimly.

"Bugs either scatter or swarm, right?" Brannigan said, making sure his rifle was fully loaded.

"I suppose that's a fair generalization of their behavior," Chaplin said.

"A few small threats with guns, the swarm, and attack and defend…" He trailed off. "Point is, an earthquake probably set them running."

"One can hope."

"What else are we going to do, wait to see if the island comes crashing down on top of us?" Brannigan made some final adjustments to his gear and jerked a thumb at the door. "Saddle up."

#

The tunnel was quiet save for the rumblings of the creatures overhead. *Death throes,* Brannigan hoped, though something in the pit of his stomach told him it wouldn't be that easy. Beneath his boots the ground squelched, damp from the water now trickling in from above and from the residue left behind by the giant isopods.

"Captain," Chaplin whispered, "look." He pointed at a cluster of large spherical objects lining the sides of the tunnel. "What are they?"

Brannigan leaned in. The spheres were lined, like an armadillo curled into a ball. "These, I think, are our insect friends," he said. He looked down the tunnel, the creatures were curled up and clustered together for as far down that tunnel as he could see. Quietly, he reached out a hand and rapped on the hard shell.

"What are you doing?" Chaplin hissed, bringing his gun to the ready.

"Shush," Brannigan said. "Listen."

The creature, curled tight in its ball, chittered softly, but did not uncurl.

"They're threatened, and this is their defense," Brannigan said. "They won't uncurl until the threat up there has passed."

"Okay, then let's go," Chaplin said.

"We can't let these things live," Brannigan said. "Do we have any explosives left?"

Chaplin rummaged through his pack. "No, but we do have these," he said, holding up five incendiaries. "And one grenade."

"Give them here." Brannigan pressed the firebomb to the side of the creature's shell, wedging it in place. More chittering from inside the shell, but still no activity. "Reach in my pack and give me the bottle."

"Is this vodka?" Chaplin said, doing as he was told.

"It'll work."

"That's not why I was asking."

"Then shut up." Brannigan placed an explosive near the shell of each creature in the largest clusters he could find and poured a trail of vodka between each until all five were placed. On the last one, he looked down and saw a skeleton lying in the dirt, still fresh and red.

"Bowman," Chaplin said. "And over there, Collins."

"Get their tags," Brannigan said. A pang of guilt washed over him as he realized he hadn't been able to get Hicks or Thayer's.

The rumbling overhead was getting quieter. Down the tunnel, Brannigan could hear the isopods beginning to uncurl and skitter to life.

"We need to go, now," he shouted.

The door was only a hundred yards away, and Brannigan had never run so fast in his life. Chaplin pulled up to the door almost immediately after him. They forced it open just as the first scream of the swarm alerted the rest to their presence. Brannigan and Chaplin got as far away from the portal as they could before Brannigan pulled the pin on the grenade and hurled it back into the service tunnel. They bolted through the door and slammed it shut, a spray of rust raining down from the top.

"Three...two...one."

The grenade went off with a muffled boom behind the solid door. Hundreds of screams rose up in agony as the firebombs went off in a series of successive detonations filling the whole tunnel with 4000° flames. Even from behind the door, they could feel the heat. The grenade must have damaged the integrity of the tunnel, since over top of the screams they heard the sound of collapsing concrete and groaning metal. Eventually all they heard was the muted hiss of the phosphorous flames still burning even beneath all the rubble.

Chaplin turned to walk away and Brannigan held up a hand. A bit of the rubble was moving, from beneath dirt and crumbled debris, a lone isopod emerged from the ground to the side of the door, its shell cracked, two of its legs gone entirely, and a purple green fluid leaking from one gaping eye socket. Brannigan lowered his rifle, pulled out his handgun, and put a bullet right in its head.

"Just to be sure," he said, pulling out a flask. He poured alcohol over the creature's dead body, flicked a lighter he produced from another pocket and set the corpse alight. "Eggs or something."

Chaplin shuddered and turned around. "Ah, our ride."

Lieutenant Greenwood emerged from the Humvee, a look of concern and fear blanketing her features.

"And bearing wonderful news, it seems," Brannigan said dryly.

"You completed your mission," Greenwood said, "but...there's been a complication. Come with me."

"Always a fucking complication," Brannigan sighed.

#

The video quality was grainy at best. Brannigan didn't expect much better from a news helicopter. The scene of the explosion was so much more violent from above; two creatures wreathed in an expanding ball of fire, smoke, and debris, shrieking in rage.

"So we got them," he said, a tinge of excitement in his voice.

"Keep watching," Devonte said, leaning in like a man invested in the suspense of a movie.

From the smoke and ash, Vornax was the first to rise, his wings beating away the inky black cloud. He hovered above the island crying down to his mate, and she responded in turn.

"Fuck," Brannigan said, slamming his fist on the wall, "so we accomplished nothing?"

"Keep watching," Devonte said, still refusing to look at the screen.

Inkanyamba rose from the settling cloud of explosive dust, the shell on her back split straight down the middle. She reached around with her neck and took hold of the left chunk, prying it off of her body with obvious discomfort. Vornax dove down and wrenched the second half, tearing it into the air before dropping it into the bay. Inkanyamba shuddered, and something fell from her back, draping the ground around her feet.

"No way," Brannigan said, eyes wide.

The sea creature screamed to the heavens, unfurling a pair of frilled wings that blocked the whole horizon.

"It can fly too?"

"It gets worse," Skylar said. "Look at its back."

Clustered on Inkanyamba's back, in the space between her wings, appeared to be a clutch of eggs, stuck to her skin by a mucus-like substance. Brannigan stopped counting around twenty, but he knew there had to be more.

"She's pregnant," he whispered.

"Technically, she was pregnant," Skylar said. "Now she's raising her young."

"I don't understand."

"From what I can tell, Inkanyamba's species doesn't naturally have a shell. It forms one using materials gathered at the depths of the ocean and seals it with that mucus to protect the clutch of eggs. If she's so willing to part with it now…it must be just about time." Skylar's face was grim. "The eggs will hatch soon."

#

"Behold its beauty," Martin said, gesturing at the on-screen image. "A true storm dragon."

Kurtis nodded. "And a whole ton of babies."

"I want one of those eggs," Martin shouted, practically vibrating with manic energy.

"Not sure you are cut out for the parenting lifestyle," Kurtis muttered.

"But think of it! The Hands of Fate, leaders of an immortal empire enforced by an endless supply of storm dragons. We'd be unstoppable."

"And how do you propose that we remove any one of those eggs from the back of that creature?"

"A discussion for later, for now let's celebrate!"

Kurtis rolled his eyes and raised his glass with as little enthusiasm as possible. "Sure."

"But really, what is our plan for this immortal empire?" Jia Ming said, blowing a stream of smoke from her nose. She put the cigarette out on the arm of the chair.

Martin paused mid-drink and glared at her.

Kurtis knew he couldn't handle another explosive argument but leaving would trigger one as well. "Wait until they hatch," he said.

"What?" Martin said.

"Because transporting a live baby monster would be easier than transporting an egg," Jia Ming said sarcastically.

Kurtis sighed. "I'm no biology expert—"

"And you lost ours," Jia Ming said.

"But…most reptiles that stay alongside their eggs protect them until they hatch, but then…the children are on their own. That's when we can snatch one up."

"Are you going to do that yourself? Because you can count me out. Kill me first."

"No," Martin said, "wait. Kurt, I heard you were fiddling around with that doctor of ours and Ivan Cole. How'd that go?"

"As far as I can tell, it was a success, but—"

"Send him."

"He hasn't been field tested yet."

Martin waved a hand dismissively. "Send him anyway."

Kurtis bit his tongue. He could pull rank on Martin, but the ensuing confrontation would be quite the hassle. *Besides,* he thought, *if this goes bad, the blame's on him. And good riddance.* "Sure," Kurtis said. "I'll go tell him now." He slid his chair back, stood up, and exited the room before anyone could say anything to trap him again.

He made his way down to the hall to the doctor's laboratory where Ivan was being monitored. As soon as he entered the room, Ivan stood from the examination table, pulling IVs and electrodes from his body without batting an eye.

"News?" the Russian giant asked.

"A mission," Kurtis responded. "For you."

A cruel smile curled across his face. "Good."

Doctor Felding bolted from his chair. "Mr. Wagner, as I've already told you—"

Kurtis waved his hand to silence the man. "Not my decision. You want to argue, take it down to Mr. Martin."

The doctor's face paled. "No, that's quite alright, I trust his judgment."

"Makes one of us."

"I'm sorry?"

"Nothing."

"Mission?" Ivan Cole said.

Kurtis sighed. "Report to Mr. Martin's office for your briefing."

Ivan nodded and began a slow march out of the laboratory. When he exited, Kurtis slumped in the nearest chair he could find, with a deeper sigh than before.

"If I may," the doctor started, "what is his mission?"

"Martin wants him to play Pokémon with the monster's babies."

Doctor Felding cocked his head to the side.

"Catch one for research," Kurtis said.

"Ah…" The doctor looked like he was about to say something, but Kurtis cut him off.

"I don't want to talk about it. It's an idiotic idea and we all know it's an idiotic idea. That's that," Kurtis closed his eyes and ran his hands through his hair. "How easy will it be for us to assume control if need be?"

"I managed to fully sync the nanobot frequencies to my control station, so…it should work."

"Good."

#

"What are we going to do about that?" Brannigan asked the silent room. Raymond, Devonte, Skylar, and General MacPherson were lost in their own thoughts. No one offered anything in response. An air of frustration filled the room like a fog.

Devonte said, "If we couldn't take out two, what could we do against hundreds?"

"I don't know," Brannigan said, "but that doesn't mean we give up."

Skylar scratched at the curls atop her head. "Well…let's look at what we know of the creatures."

"They're big and indestructible," Devonte said. "One breathes fiery death, the other somehow generates electrical death. Did I miss anything?"

Skylar punched him in the shoulder. "Not what I meant."

"Well one seems to be attuned more to fire, and the other to water," Raymond offered.

"With electrical properties," Skylar added. "Like a bio-electrical tesla coil."

"The female of the species is larger than the male," MacPherson said.

"She's going to eat him," Devonte said breathlessly.

"What?" Skylar asked, taken aback. Her eyes widened. "She's going to *eat* him!"

"Pardon my what the fuck," Brannigan said, "but what the fuck?"

Devonte gestured to Skylar to let her speak. "The sexual dimorphism."

"Is that some fetish only giant monsters can have?" Brannigan asked.

"No," Skylar said, rolling her eyes, "it's the differences between the two. Remember, they're the same species, but they have a drastically different physiology."

"Oh, yeah, yeah…I follow." Brannigan looked to Devonte for an explanation. The latter just pointed back to Skylar.

"And in almost every species where we see a bigger female in a sexually dimorphic pair," Devonte added, "she eats her mate."

"I thought that was limited to insects," Raymond interjected, "these are…reptiles?"

"That's what we assumed until recently," Skylar said, "but we also have seen this behavior in Anacondas. They release pheromones to attract a mate, do the nasty, and then she eats him."

"Oh my god," Brannigan said, "she literally called him over for dinner."

The general cleared her throat.

"Sorry," Brannigan said, "but this is good for us, right? One less monster to deal with, and I'm sure she'll be in for a nice nap after chowing down on sixty meters of monster man meat, right?"

"The nutrients taken in from eating him may trigger the birth of the offspring," Skylar said.

"Maybe the babies aren't as tough as their mother?" Brannigan offered.

"I suppose it's possible that the scales may not fully harden, but—"

"Then that's a thing we can use, right?" Brannigan interrupted.

"General, there's activity on Alcatraz Island," one of the communication officers shouted.

"On screen," the general said.

INTERLUDE III

Hunger. Gnawing, scraping, clawing. She feels it. Not just hers, but her children's. Throbbing, scared, alive. She needs to feed. Her skin burns from the tiny creatures' fire, but that will fade. The pain always fades. The hunger will not.

Her mate calls out to her. She regards him warily. She called him to her, but…hungry. *Food.* She feels herself begin to salivate. *Hunger.* She lets out a weak cry in response to his. He seems confused. He can't feel the hunger. *Can he?*

She feels the children on her back, so close, so ready to burst into the sunlight and feel the warmth. *And the hunger. Tiny hungers.*

Her mate calls out to her again. Concern? Or a threat? Her children demand protection.

She rises to her full height, looking down on him, his taste teasing her tongue as it flicks the air. Pleasure courses through her. *Food.*

Closer. Her meal slides closer to her, nuzzling against her, smelling so…edible. She can barely resist. Why should she resist?

Eat me, her meal says. Or is that just her desire? *Eat him*, her children say. Or is she just hungry? She leans down, nipping at his wing playfully. *Delicious. More.*

Her meal pulls away, looking up at her. He's confused. The food is confused.

She goes down for another taste, but he moves out of reach, eyeing her suspiciously.

He knows. Her meal is running away with itself. *Rage.* She screams, stretching wings dormant longer than she can remember. *Powerful.* Her meal backs away, trembling, but then steadies, stretching his own wings and roaring with indignation. She lashes out at him, her massive claw tearing through the meat of his shoulder. *Warm. Blood.* Instinctively she springs her neck forward, latching onto the fresh wound. The taste is exhilarating. She hears her meal scream and that only serves to invigorate her more. The pleasure pulls her in until…*Pain.*

Her meal's claws are lodged into the side of her neck. She feels her own blood pouring down her scales. It makes her hungrier. With a flick of her powerful neck, she sends the meal crashing to the other side of the island. She doesn't want a fight, just a meal, but the hunt drives her senses wild. Her children tremble with excitement as well, urging her forward, urging her to feed. She rears back on her hind legs, spreads her wings, and issues her challenge. The noise rumbles in the depths of her core. And she charges.

Her meal is quick, trying his best to take to the sky. She catches him with her forelegs, dragging him back to the ground and holding him there with her weight. She's ready to strike, teeth bared. Her meal opens his mouth too and releases a rush of burning gas directly in her face. It stings her eyes and chokes her lungs. The gas fills her lungs and she stumbles back, hacking and barking. Her meal wastes no time, raking across her face with burning hot claws, tearing her flesh and fanning the flames of her rage. She wheels with the blow, turning slowly, deliberately, until her back is to him and her tail smashes into his side. Bones crunch underneath the force of her blow. She angles her tail down, crushing him into the ground before rounding on him again and driving the claws of her forelegs into the fleshy membranes of both his wings. They tear ragged and bloody as she drags her claws down along their length. Holding him in place, she bites down on a wing, tearing off a chunk and gulping the flesh down greedily. A soft trill escapes her throat. *Pleasure.*

Her meal's body gets hot. Too hot. Burning her. She rears into the sky on heavy wings, hovering above her prey before slamming back down on him. He crunches beneath her, blood gushing from his foaming mouth and open wounds. His body is still hot. She feels the temperature around her rise. *Fire.*

She summons her own power, a stream of electricity courses through her veins. Her muscles spasm before contracting so tight they feel like they're tearing. She tingles from the pit of her stomach to the tips of her wings. Her meal is slow, she hears the clicking that indicates his coming attack. She is not slow. The air crackles around her. She wants this to end. Her jaws sink into the throat of her meal, and she releases her energy. Static fills her head and her teeth buzz with the current. The heat of her meal burns the inside of her mouth. She feels the flesh burning, but she holds on, not letting go. His body convulses beneath her, thrashing and clawing at her. He lets out a violent rattle from his chest, a last, shaky breath. One last weak roar escapes his lips before he falls limp and silent. She's won. Her reward lies beneath her. *Food. Eat.* Her children share her pleasure as she gorges herself on warm flesh, crunching through bones and tearing tendons.

Stop. She pauses. Her children will need food on their own. She looks down at the meal that was her mate, half eaten. They will eat from him as well. Until then, she will sleep. Her children are coming soon. She feels them squirming in their eggs. Soon. She grabs the remains of her prey by the remaining wing and glides into the murky water around her nest searching for a place to submerge completely. The air is drying out her skin and she feels the pain as it begins to crack and bleed. Beneath the surface of the water, her body slows down until no more sensation disturbs her rest. Only darkness and the motion of the currents.

CHAPTER 14

"Holy shit," Devonte said.

"That was…probably the most brutal thing I have ever seen," Brannigan said. "And I have literally been to war."

"Nature is fucking mental," Skylar said.

"All I know," General MacPherson said, "is that we have one less problem to deal with."

"And potentially one-hundred new problems to deal with," Devonte said. "Sorry," he added, seeing the general's scowling face.

"We need a plan," Raymond said.

"Well we've shot it, we've blown it up, and we've shot it some more," Brannigan said, "we've basically exhausted any military-type plans."

"We need—"

"Devonte," Brannigan interrupted with a grin, "if you say science, I swear to god I will call you a nerd for the rest of eternity."

"…science…"

"Nerd."

"He's right, though," Skylar said.

"Like two nerds in a pod," Brannigan said.

"Did anyone else notice the most important thing in the video?" Skylar asked, ignoring him. She looked around the room expectantly.

"Kaiju Smackdown Raw could make a man rich?" Brannigan offered a shrug.

"Brannigan," the general barked, "if you have nothing productive to add, you are dismissed."

"Sorry ma'am, just trying to lighten the mood."

"He's technically not wrong," Skylar said, "but no, Inkanyamba needs to return to the water every so often or her skin starts to dry out and fracture." She rewound the footage and zoomed in on the larger creature and enhanced the image. All along the surface of its scaly skin, angry fissure zigged and zagged, oozing with blood and bodily fluids. "This could be how we get her."

Devonte's phone rang loudly in the small control room. He looked down at the device and grimaced. "Sorry, it's my dad, I have to take this." He wheeled out of the room and into the hallway, before answering. "Hello?"

"D! I finally got access to a phone. Are you okay?" His dad's voice boomed out of the phone speaker. "Alison said you went with the FBI just before...oh my god, you were right...giant monsters...I can't believe it."

That bitch lied to you, Devonte thought. "I can hardly believe it myself. And no, I didn't go with the FBI," he paused, wondering how much was safe to tell, "that was just me messing around. I evacuated with a group closer to my apartment."

"And you didn't try to call? Where are you? Can you get to Carson City? That's where they moved us to."

Nevada, Devonte thought, *good, he's out of state.* "I'm fine dad. I'm...at a military shelter." He tried to shrug his injured shoulder as a test, wincing and gasping slightly at the pain. "I'm safe."

"Where's the shelter?"

On the island across from where the giant monster made its nest. "They told us Carson City was too crowded and so they took us to a place in the Black Rock Desert," he lied.

"Okay. I'll see if I can find a car and I'll come pick you up."

"No!"

His father made a noise of surprise on the other end of the phone.

"I mean, I'm fine here, you should stay and take care of Alison. I'm sure she's freaking out, right?"

"D...Alison didn't make it."

"What?

"There was a cruise ship that left California to go down to Hawaii."

"She was on that ship? The one the sea monster attacked?"

He could hear his dad take a shaky breath. "I tried calling her after I heard the news, to see if she was one of the survivors, but..."

"I'm so sorry dad, I know you...I know she was important to you."

His dad didn't answer.

"Dad?"

"I think that's the nicest thing you've said about her," his dad said with a sad chuckle.

I'm an ass. "Her and I never connected," Devonte said. "Too different, I'm me and she was…"

"Not the brightest, I know. But she was good, D."

"Dad, I'm—"

"It's fine, she never held it against you. Neither did I. But now she's gone and I…I miss her so much."

Devonte didn't know what to say. He never thought he'd be comforting his father on the intricacies of a broken relationship. "You spent the last few years with her. I'm sure that's a normal feeling."

"Yeah." His father paused. "Hey, um, when this is all over, do you think you'd want to move back with me for a while? I know you moved out because of me, but…given everything it would be nice to…you know what, never mind. Stay safe, kiddo."

"Dad, I didn't move out because of you. I just needed—*to get away from Alison*—some time to sort myself out and, you know, pursue my passions."

"So, yes?"

"I don't know about that. I'm used to my independence at this point."

"Oh."

"But I will definitely visit more often and…you're welcome to come over as well. Does that work?"

"Yeah," his dad said, "that works."

Skylar came out of the control room and mouthed, "Everything alright?"

Devonte nodded. "Hey, dad, thank you for calling. It's great to hear your voice, but I've got to go. My phone battery is dying, and I've promised some of the other evacuees here that they can use it to call their loved ones as well."

"You're a good kid, D. I love you."

"Love you too, dad. Stay safe. Bye." He hung up the phone and turned to Skylar. "What do you need?"

"Nothing, just…checking up on my friend," she said with a shy smile. "Making sure the king of the monsters still reigns." She laughed without a hint of awkwardness. Devonte couldn't help but laugh along with her despite the tears rolling down his cheeks.

"I'm here. My dad was just checking up on me. Nothing serious. They moved evacuees to Carson City." He remembered his brief conversation with Skylar's father. "Has your dad...?"

"I doubt he even cares," she said, with a forced smile. "That's...actually why I came out to San Francisco. I ran away."

"You ran away?" Devonte asked. "Do you have family here or—"

"I have a friend here, who I thought might let me stay with them while I try to get my feet up under me." She smiled. "I'm kind of desperate for a change of pace."

"Oh? Where do they live?"

She cocked an eyebrow at him.

"You know, I just thought that maybe I could help you find them after all of this is over." Devonte scratched his head awkwardly. "If you wanted?"

Skylar sighed. "Hey, Devonte, where do you live?"

"My apartment complex is over by North Beach, why?"

"That's where my friend lives."

"Oh, they live near—"

Skylar's frown cut him off.

"Wait, you mean...me?"

"No, I mean the other guy I spend countless hours of my life chatting with online about all the things we have in common." Her smile returned.

"I, uh...yeah, I knew that, I was just messing around," Devonte stuttered. "So you wanted to—"

"You wouldn't mind if I stayed with you for a while after this is all over, right?" she asked. "At least until I can get up on my own two feet. I can help with rent and food and—"

"Of course!" Devonte cursed the eagerness in his voice. He tried to recover what little cool he had. "I mean, yeah, you came all the way out here, I'm not going to turn you away."

Her face brightened. "Really? That's great!" She flung her arms around Devonte's neck. "Thank you."

"Yeah, no problem, but, this kind of hurts."

She jumped back with a gasp. "I'm so sorry."

"It's fine, really, just," he gestured to his present condition, "things are a little rough for me right now. I know it's just a shoulder injury, but everything hurts."

"You're not used to keeping it still for so long."

"I'm pretty sure it's cramping."

Skylar looked concerned. "That's pretty likely. How does the shoulder itself feel otherwise?"

"Like it got shot," he said in a completely deadpan voice before busting out into a fit of laughter. "No, it's…it hurts a lot, but I think the adrenaline from everything else is keeping it under wraps. That and these," he said, rattling a pill bottle. "I'm fine."

"Good."

Devonte cleared his throat. "Well maybe when this is all over, you'd like to–"

"Hey, you two," Brannigan's voice called from the control room, "your evil friend is on video call in here!"

Devonte frowned at Skylar, and she returned his look of confusion.

"Should we go?" Skylar asked.

"Yeah."

#

Kurtis' golden eyes stared disinterestedly out at them from the massive screen.

"You!" Skylar shouted. "How dare you show your face?"

"Skylar—"

"That's Dr. O'Hara to you," she spat.

"Dr. O'Hara, then. Spare us the theatrics, they don't suit you."

"What do you want?" she asked.

"Dr. O'Hara," the general said, "while I appreciate your enthusiasm, Dr. Wagner—"

"Ah, yeah, I'm not actually a doctor. That was a cover," Kurtis said with a laugh.

The general scowled. "Mr. Wagner is here as a representative of The Tempest organization."

"Just Tempest."

"A representative of Tempest. So let's leave the line of questioning to the professionals, as it were."

"Yes, ma'am," Skylar said before flipping Kurtis a distinct finger.

Raymond stepped to the front of the group. "Well, my first question will be the same," he said. "What is it you want from us today?"

"From you? Nothing," Kurtis said. "I came to do something for you."

"Shoot me in my other shoulder?" Devonte said bitterly.

Kurtis smiled. "I do apologize for that. I do abhor violence, you just made me so…angry, and admittedly, a little jealous." He glanced at Skylar. "It won't happen again."

"Mr. Wagner," Raymond said, "your point?"

"Yes, right. My…organization is mounting an endeavor shortly that I think it would be beneficial for both of us, if you were to…intervene."

"What?" Raymond asked.

"A compatriot of mine has decided that trying to steal a newborn from our…Inkanyamba, you called it? That trying to steal a newborn from her is a good idea."

"He wants to take a baby from a kaiju?" Skylar asked. "Is he an idiot?"

"If you ask him, he's a genius. If you ask me…I take your stance."

"And why," Raymond said, jumping back into the conversation, "would you tell us this information?"

"I believe I've made it clear that I do not support this plan."

"So you want it to fail?"

"No, I want it to be thwarted. It makes him look worse."

"And how does this benefit anyone?" Raymond asked.

"Well for you it keeps Tempest from raising a kaiju under their control. For me, it removes an unwanted pest in the hierarchy of an otherwise near-perfect organization." He smiled again, this time flashing his teeth in the process. "Win-win."

"And if we refuse to play along with your stupid games?" Brannigan asked.

"No threats. No ultimatums. Just information," Kurtis said with a shrug. "Do with it as you please. Or don't."

"Why should we trust you again?" Skylar asked.

"Because as always, I'm serving my own self-interest." He looked down at something off-screen. "Not much time left. The man being sent is Ivan Cole." He held up a photo.

"Last I saw him, he took a grenade point blank," Brannigan said, "you sure it's him?"

"Positive. And if you're the one who pushed that grenade on him, I suggest you watch out. He's determined to avenge himself."

Brannigan smirked. "Sounds like a date."

"He'll be using the underground tunnel that leads to the island—"

"We blew that up," Brannigan said, still smirking.

For the first time, Kurtis looked surprised. "Really? So you were the ones who caused the explosion?"

"Guilty as charged."

"I should have known."

"Well then," Kurtis said, "I'm sure he'll try and hijack a boat or something. You have all that military intelligence, figure out how to stop him." The video connection ended.

"Dick," Skylar said, crossing her arms.

"We're not really going to fall for that, are we?" Devonte asked.

The others in the room looked at him somberly.

"We can't risk Tempest getting their hands on even one of Inkanyamba's children," Raymond said, "so we have to fall for it."

"But—"

"Don't worry kid, I took him down once, I'll do it again," Brannigan said.

"He kicked your ass," Devonte shouted, "you won by cheating."

"Then I'll do it again."

"He'll be expecting it this time."

Raymond placed a hand on Devonte's shoulder. "Don't worry, I have a plan."

"What is it?"

"Have I ever told you that I own a boat?" Raymond said with a soft smile.

#

It'd been months since Raymond had set foot on a boat. The *Nakajima II*, a gift from his late wife's brother in Japan, bobbed at the side of the dock. He dragged his hand gently across her rails as he made his way to the helm. Captain Brannigan sat at the stern, prepping his gear before moving down into the cabin in the bottom of the small vessel.

The port had been emptied of all other vessels save this one. If Cole was going to go to the island via the bay, he would have to board here. Raymond fidgeted with his mustache as he surveyed the dock from behind dark sunglasses.

A few hours passed before Raymond noticed a figure approaching the dock. He radioed Brannigan. "I think our guest has arrived."

"Roger," came the captain's voice. He disappeared down the steps into the sleeping quarters of the ship.

In the assault on the base, Raymond hadn't noticed just how tall the man was. He easily towered over Raymond's six-foot person. It was easy to be intimidated, but Raymond stood his ground.

"Not many people want to be on the water, what with them creatures over there," he said, "but then, by the size of you, you might be able to take them yourself." He flashed a winning smile.

"Alcatraz," Ivan said, staring out over the grey waters of the bay. He extended a hand full of crumpled dollars and coins.

Raymond took the money. "So you are here to tussle with the creatures then?"

"Alcatraz. Now." His gaze dropped onto Raymond.

"Strong silent type. I'll get you to the island. Hold tight."

Raymond made his way back to the helm, and radioed Brannigan once more. "Something's off about him. He's only speaking in single word sentences."

"Grenade might have done some brain damage," Brannigan said. "Try not to aggravate him. He might get violent."

"So avoid my usual tactics."

The door to the helm slid open causing Raymond to jump and fumble to hide his radio. "Faster," Ivan said.

"Of course," Raymond said, "just warming up the engines. She's an old girl."

Ivan merely grunted in return, before seating himself on the bench to the back of the helm room. He folded his arms across his chest and stared out towards Alcatraz Island in the distance.

"You know, I heard the creature left the island and sank down beneath the Golden Gate Bridge. Are you sure this is where you want to go?"

"I wait," Ivan replied.

"You think it will come back?"

"Nest."

"Oh," Raymond said, feigning surprise. "Smart man."

"No. Hunter."

Raymond didn't know how to respond to that. "Hunter, right." He needed to make it about halfway to Alcatraz Island for the plan to start. They needed deep water.

#

Brannigan waited down in the captain's quarters, awaiting the signal. He could hear the conversation between Raymond and Ivan Cole through the radio, and the inspector was right, the man sounded different, addled in some way, like he was talking through a fog. They'd been going at a good click for about an hour or so now. Soon it would be time. He checked his GPS. *Correction,* he thought, *now is the time.* He pulled on a pair of rubber gloves and approached the breakers. He flipped the switch Raymond had showed him earlier and heard the engine sputter and die. The boat stopped moving. Through the radio he heard:

"Go." *Ivan.*

"I don't know what's happened. The engine was fine this morning." *Raymond.*

"Go!"

"I can't! The engine is dead, you see?"

Silence.

Did something go wrong? Brannigan thought.

"I check," came Ivan's slow voice through the radio.

"Are you sure? I can call someone to come with another vessel."

"I check."

"I won't stop you then," Raymond said.

Brannigan heard heavy footsteps plodding towards his hiding spot. The door opened and Ivan's boots thumped down the steps. The giant man approached the cabin and examined the panel. Brannigan could see the thick armor covering his entire body. A gun wouldn't work. He picked up a nearby wrench and snuck from his hiding spot, taking great care to be quiet. He raised the wrench above his head and brought it down as hard as he could. A massive hand caught the wrench mid-air.

"Surprise," Ivan said. "You?"

"Hello again. You're not still mad about the whole clipping a grenade to your belt thing, are you?"

"No." A cruel smile spread across Ivan's face. His fist slammed into Brannigan's stomach, winding him. Ivan hoisted him off the ground and tossed him against the stairs leading out of the cabin. Brannigan felt the same ribs from the last fight crack again, and maybe a few others.

"Hey Raymond," he gasped. "We have a problem."

"Big problem," Ivan said, emerging from below deck. "Me."

"Yes, I gathered that," Raymond said, drawing his gun. "Freeze," he shouted.

"No," Ivan said, stalking towards Brannigan as he clamored to his feet.

"That's a first," Raymond said, blinking in surprise. He squeezed off two shots into the man's chest.

Ivan went rigid, before casting a dark glare up the steps. "Armor," he said. "No pain." He continued towards the now standing Brannigan.

"I will put a bullet in your brain," Raymond shouted.

"No," Ivan said again. Still facing Brannigan, he opened up the large jacket he wore.

"Raymond," Brannigan said. "Don't shoot him."

"What?"

"He's got a bomb wired up to his vitals. You kill him, we all go boom."

"Boom," Ivan said, smiling with crooked teeth.

"Damn it," Raymond spat.

"Don't worry," Brannigan said shakily. He emerged onto the deck of the boat. "I got this."

"Not this time," Ivan taunted.

"Three words in a row? Just for me?" Brannigan said in a mocking voice. "I'm touched, really."

Ivan's smile fell. "Die."

"Make me."

Ivan roared, and charged at Brannigan, who just barely got out of the way, tripping the giant in the process. He smashed into the deck with a thud and a grunt. He roared again as he rose to his feet, looking around until his eyes locked onto Brannigan again. He charged again, straight into a right hook from Brannigan. It didn't do much but staggered the man, as though he was surprised at being hit. Pain shot from Brannigan's wrist up into his shoulder.

"He's not fighting," Brannigan said, trying to shake the pain out of his arm, "just charging at me."

#

Kurtis watched the sensory readout for Ivan with interest. "And we've lost complete control?"

"I'm afraid so," Dr. Felding said. "It's like his drive for vengeance is overwriting our control mechanism."

"Shame," Kurtis said. "Shut him down."

The doctor flipped a switch. "Uh…"

"Uh?"

"He should be dead, but…"

"He's not?"

"He's not."

Kurtis sighed. "I guess we just see where this goes then." He stood up. "I need to send word to the rest of the council, informing them of Mr. Martin's failure."

"He hasn't failed yet," Dr. Felding said.

Kurtis flashed a glance at the screen where Captain Brannigan squared off against the reanimated shell of Ivan Cole. "Trust me, he will." He flicked his lab coat out behind him as he exited the room.

#

Can't fight. Can't talk. Can't swim? Brannigan hoped whatever had been done to the mercenary since their last encounter had addled him as much as it seemed. He'd finally started fighting instead of charging, but his moves were sluggish and telegraphed; nothing like before. Brannigan landed a swift kick to the groin that elicited the only real pain response he'd seen from the man since this started. He shoved the man away as hard as he could and sprinted to the side of the ship. He needed the man angry. Angry enough to charge one more time. Brannigan was banking on him being stupid enough not to see what was coming.

"So I blow you up, you live, come all the way back out here to kill me, and you can't even touch me. Tragic." Brannigan spat a glob of blood onto the wooden deck of the boat.

"I touch you," Ivan said.

"Oh? I didn't know we rolled the same way. Sorry though, I prefer my men with a little less space between their ears."

Ivan furrowed his brow in confusion.

"You're an idiot," Brannigan explained.

"No."

"Oh, don't be upset," Brannigan said, dodging a fist the size of his head, "stupid isn't the worst thing you could be. In your case, you're also ugly, so at least you're good at multi-tasking."

Ivan growled a low rumbling sound like a wild animal. A warning the captain chose to ignore. *His emotional reactions are like that of a child,* he thought. *I can literally taunt my way to victory.*

He gave a quick thumbs up to Raymond who still had his gun trained on Ivan in case things went bad enough that sinking the ship would be a preferable outcome.

"Come on, big guy," Brannigan shouted, "let's dance."

Another kick to the groin, followed by an uppercut to the jaw that crunched the bones in Brannigan's knuckles. The strike must have made Ivan bite his tongue because a steady stream of blood now poured from his mouth. The man spat on the deck before throwing a punch that managed to take Brannigan by surprise. It caught him at the temple with enough force to blackout his vision for a few seconds. He collapsed to his knees and vomited.

"What's that...three ribs and my skull you've cracked?" Brannigan shuddered as he tried to rise to his feet. Vertigo almost put him back to his knees, and he choked down a second wave of nausea. *Not good. Concussion, or brain bleed? Both? Can't take another hit. Can't last long either way.* He looked out at the bay to his back. *One last shot at this.*

"Come on, you overgrown fucking oaf! You wanna kill me so bad, stop being a little bitch and do it before I bore myself to death. I'm right fucking here, and I don't have all day." The force of shouting rattled Brannigan's cracked ribs and sent his vision diving down a fuzzy tunnel, but he stood his ground. He got the response he wanted.

Ivan let out a shriek of rage before charging headlong straight at him. Brannigan did the only thing his body would let him do; he collapsed, right as Ivan was upon him. The man tripped over Brannigan's body, sending him careening off the ship and into the water of the bay. Raymond rushed over to Brannigan's side.

"Are you okay?" he asked.

"Depends, is he drowning?" Brannigan choked out.

Raymond looked over the side. "He's flailing. Panicking. Drifting away from the boat with the current."

"How far?"

"Twenty, maybe thirty feet?"

"Shoot him."

"What?"

"Shoot him. In the head. Then get down."

"But the dead man's trigger..."

"Water will stop the shrapnel. Boat can handle the pressure wave. Shoot him, we're not monsters."

Raymond nodded in agreement. He aimed for Ivan's head and squeezed the trigger. The man's flailing stopped, and Raymond dove to the ground. A few seconds passed before the explosion rocked the boat, sending both Brannigan and Raymond tumbling to the other side of the boat. A spray of bay water and blood rained down on them from above.

"Fantastic work, Captain," Raymond said.

"Yeah, not to rush you or anything, but I think I need a hospital." Darkness rushed in from the edges of Brannigan's vision and swallowed him whole. He could no longer feel the deck of the boat, just the weightless sensation of falling into nothingness.

CHAPTER 15

"Lieutenant Greenwood," General MacPherson barked.

"I'm here, ma'am."

"Captain Brannigan has been severely injured in the line of duty. You are hereby appointed to lead any and all task forces in relation to Tempest and the ongoing kaiju threat."

"Ma'am."

"You are dismissed."

Greenwood lingered.

"Lieutenant?"

"Will the captain be alright?"

"His new injuries in conjunction with his previous injuries have put him in a bad way. He's in God's hands now."

Greenwood saluted. "Understood."

"But," the general added, "the man had an annoying habit of not ever staying down. Dismissed, for now."

Greenwood gave a slight grin and stepped into the hallway.

"What'd she say?" Devonte accosted her as soon as the door shut behind her.

"Inspector Dehane called in. Brannigan's been hurt, bad. They had to take him to the nearest hospital instead of bringing him back here."

"Where is he?"

"No," Greenwood's voice hardened. "We need you and your friend here trying to solve our giant reptile problem. Got it?"

"But—"

"No buts. Focus. Brannigan knew what he was getting into. He did his job, now you need to do yours."

Devonte lightly rubbed at his injured shoulder. "And what exactly can I do?"

"What?"

"Brannigan's our best soldier, Skylar's the real kaiju expert, Raymond's the detective, you're an all-round badass, and me...I'm a hacker operating at half speed. You can't beat kaiju with code." He slammed his good fist into the wall. "What the hell is the point of me in all this?"

"Who found your friend?" Greenwood said without missing a beat.

"What?"

"Who found your friend? It's a simple question."

"I-I did?"

"You sure about that? You don't sound sure."

"I found Skylar."

"I thought so," she said. "And who kept Tempest from getting their hands on the monster summoning device?"

"Me."

"Mhmm. Now, who's going to stop whining like a bitch and go make themselves useful?"

Devonte's mouth hung open while Greenwood stared at him. He cleared his throat and said, "I am."

Greenwood cupped her hand to her ear.

"I am," Devonte said louder, glaring up at her. "Thanks, I needed the pep talk."

"I don't know what you're talking about, I just told you the facts. If you were useless, I'd have told you that and sent you on your way."

"Oh."

"The point is, Captain Dehane brought you in because he saw something in you. I'm inclined to trust his judgment. Go prove us right."

"I did have an idea—"

"Don't tell me. Work with Skylar."

"Yes, ma'am."

#

Randolph Martin read the letter with the same visible apoplectic rage with which he did most everything in his life. Kurtis watched his face redden and noticed the veins sticking out in both his neck and his forehead and wondered whether or not the stress would simply kill him where he stood.

"I don't understand," he sputtered.

"I think it's rather plain to see," Kurtis said, "in light of your recent failures, the council has decided that your services are no longer worth the risk and you are hereby stripped of your rank as a member of the Hands of Fate."

"After everything I've done for Tempest? I made us billionaires. I've served on the council for over fifteen years and—"

"Randolph, you know I'm not one for speeches and diatribes."

The man slumped into his chair. "You're here to kill me."

Kurtis raised an eyebrow.

"I'm a liability. I know this organization inside and out. They aren't just going to give me a severance package and let me walk."

"I was told explicitly that I was not allowed to kill you."

"Don't lie to me." Randolph slammed his hands on his desk. "At least show me that respect."

"I'm not lying. I was told that the decision as to your fate would be up to your replacement."

"They've already found a replacement?" Randolph's eyes went wide.

Kurtis nodded his head slowly.

"I'm that easily replaceable?"

Kurtis shrugged. He didn't feel like indulging in the man's pity parade.

"Who is he?"

Kurtis laughed. "Come on in," he shouted. For a moment he wished he had a camera just to capture the look that came upon Randolph's face as his replacement walked in. "Ms. Jia Ming."

"You can't be fucking serious," Randolph shouted, rising to his feet and pointing an accusatory finger. "This bitch is my replacement?"

"This bitch also decides your fate," Jia Ming said coldly. "Play nice."

Randolph looked as though someone had walked across his grave. "Y-you?"

She flashed a saccharine smile. "Not that I haven't already decided."

Kurtis watched the interaction with interest. "Speaking of which, Ms. Ming, you are to carry out your decision immediately, so…if you will."

"Of course," Jia Ming said, her smile turning dark.

Randolph wasted no time. Kurtis wasn't surprised that he tried to run. He was surprised by how far down the hallway Jia Ming let him get before he heard two cracks from her pistol, then a third, for good measure he supposed.

"Drag this filth to the nearest landfill and dispose of it," he heard her say. She re-entered the office, sat in Randolph's chair, and placed her gun on the mahogany desk. "That was cathartic."

"I can only imagine," Kurtis said, dragging his hands down his face. "You realize of course that you now assume his responsibilities in regard to both our financial empire, and—"

"The monster, yes, I know," she said, propping her feet up on the desk. "I'll handle it."

"And as for your personal business?"

"I'll handle that too."

Kurtis rested his chin on his hand and gave her a cold appraisal. "I'm sure you'll do a better job than your predecessor."

Before she could reply, Hugo Fernandez burst into the room. "Mr. Martin, I…" he trailed off "…appear to have missed something."

"A simple organizational change," Kurtis said, "please, treat Ms. Ming as you would have treated Mr. Martin."

"Treat me better," she said with a wry twist of her lips, "or join Mr. Martin in the trash heap."

The man's mousy face twitched, and he wrung his hands nervously. "Of course. I only came in to report that I have successfully recreated the HUD."

"The what?" Jia Ming asked.

"Oh, the device those two kids built. I call it the Harmonic Upscaling Device, or HUD for short."

Jia Ming nodded. "Names aside, it works?"

"I haven't run it yet for…obvious reasons, but all the tests I've run on it indicate that it should work as planned. I do suggest we give the new version a proper test run though."

Jia Ming steepled her fingers and narrowed her eyes at the engineer. "I suggest we test out our creature as well."

Kurtis cocked an eyebrow.

"I'm sorry, what?"

"The Hands," she paused, "*we* Hands of Fate want to control this creature because we feel like it represents our organization's strength, and divine right to rule. I'm suggesting that we should first ensure that," she looked at Kurtis, "what did the others call it?"

"Inkanyamba," he replied.

"We should ensure that Inkanyamba does in fact match our high standards," Jia Ming concluded, leaning back in her chair.

Hugo looked to Kurtis for any indication of the right course of action.

"Don't look at me," Kurtis said. "She's your boss. Think of me as an advisor for this mission."

Hugo snapped his attention back to Jia Ming. "How do you propose we test the monster?"

"We did just see it tear its mate apart with little effort," Kurtis added. "Isn't that enough of a test?"

"It's one thing for a creature to perform well according to its own nature. It's another thing to see it compete against mankind for dominance." She drummed her fingers on the arm of the chair. "So far it's only really been in the water. I want to see how it handles the army. Take it to Las Vegas."

Kurtis' eyebrows shot up.

"We'll test the device's functionality over long distances and also see how our Inkanyamba handles a fully mounted response from this country's defenders."

"And if it fails?" Hugo asked.

"I can punish the creator of the device," Jia Ming said, "and if the creature dies, then it's dead and Tempest will move on."

"You're ruthless," Kurtis said, hiding his displeasure.

"I'm efficient," she retorted. "A word my predecessor most likely couldn't spell."

Kurtis rose to his feet. "I take my leave then. My stomach won't sit right watching all of that unnecessary death."

He heard Ms. Ming scoff and demand that everything be prepped as soon as possible for the "training exercise" as he exited the room. Kurtis scowled as he walked down the hallway. "I wonder how they'll handle this," he said to himself.

#

"The amount of strength required to hold this thing would be—"

"Astronomical," Skylar finished, "yes."

"Do we even have any metals that withstand that force? I mean, we saw her tail lash the other monster across an island," Devonte said.

"If we can use carbon steel bracers to lock Inkanyamba in place, and set up massive heat lamps around her, it should dehydrate her enough to kill her, or at least render her inert…like a frog." She paused. "It seems kind of cruel, doesn't it?"

Devonte nodded solemnly. "If this doesn't work, I have a feeling that our friends in the government will just start dropping nukes on her until she's dead or we all are…or worse."

Skylar looked downcast. She'd seen all the same monster movies as him, and in those, the fallout of the bombs always led to worse. Much worse. "This has to work."

"It's a lot of carbon steel though…"

"Leave that to us," Greenwood said, entering the room. "We can requisition anything you need. I take it you have a plan?"

"We'll need a team of welders," Devonte said.

"Be sure to pay them," Skylar added. "Well."

"Excuse me?" The general frowned.

"People work better when paid, regardless of the circumstances," Skylar said.

"And we'll need their best work," Devonte concluded.

Greenwood rubbed her forehead. "Yes, of course."

At that moment an alarm went off, making Devonte jump and tense every muscle in his body. He winced at the pain that seared through his shoulder. "What the hell is that?"

"That's a bad sound isn't it?" Skylar asked.

But Greenwood was already gone.

"I love her explanations," Devonte said, sprinting after her.

Skylar followed close behind.

The command room was abuzz with flashing lights, rushing people, and a general sense of apocalypse. Skylar had been right; whatever the alarm meant, it wasn't good.

"What is going on, General?" Devonte shouted above the ear-splitting klaxon.

"It's heading inland," MacPherson said, a touch of horror in her voice. "Into the city."

"What?" Skylar said, shoving an intern away from the nearest monitor. "That makes no sense. It should want to stay near the water." She turned to look at Devonte with fear in her eyes. "Unless…"

"The device," Devonte said.

"You destroyed it," the general said.

"Not completely," Devonte said. "The components were all still there, just broken."

"They easily could have reverse engineered it," Skylar said. "Um…search for any ambient infrasound. That will tell us."

The intern from before typed at his monitor under Skylar's intense scrutiny. "There is a repeating pulse of sound at about 10Hz," he said, "it's loud, but out of our hearing range."

"Thank you…?"

"Ensign Matthew Bishop," he said.

"Thank you, Matthew. Now, can you pinpoint the sound's origin?"

"Don't bother," Devonte said, "all that glass and metal is causing reverb in the city. It's practically impossible."

"He's right," Bishop said.

Skylar tapped a foot, obviously irritated. "Well, based off the creature's heading, where do you think it's going?"

The ensign's face went pale. "According to our pathing algorithm, if it doesn't stop or change course, it's going to carve right through Las Vegas."

Devonte looked up from his laptop. "Mine says the same thing."

"How long would it take to evacuate Vegas?" Skylar asked.

The general let out a hoarse, barking laugh. "Evacuate Vegas? You'd have better luck evacuating rats from the New York City subway."

"Well we have to try," Skylar shouted.

"I'll communicate the situation to the nearest base," the general said. "Any chance you two's plan could work in the Nevada desert?"

"Actually," Devonte said, "it would probably work better there than it would here."

Skylar nodded in agreement.

"Then I'll get you those welders too. Lieutenant Greenwood and I will be overseeing the mobilization of our military force to try and head the creature off. I'm leaving you both in charge of your own mission. Think you can handle it?"

Greenwood tapped the general on the shoulder and whispered something in her ear. The general pointed at Devonte. "Before you make your way to the hangar, report to the infirmary. Dr. O'Hara, make your way to the hangar and have the attendants prep the space to your specifications."

Devonte and Skylar shared glances. Devonte gave a short nod and jogged off in the direction of the infirmary. Skylar went in the opposite direction.

#

The hangar was huge, and surprisingly empty. A few helicopters and fighter planes were stored, but nothing like what Skylar had expected. Sparks flew from places where unseen engineers worked diligently on repairs or upgrades. Skylar walked towards one such incendiary shower coming from the side of a fighter jet. The man was at the top of a ladder and was focused on welding a set of panels back to the nose of the craft. Skylar called up to the man. "Do you know who's in charge around here?"

No response. She had to jump back to avoid a spark shower that got dangerously close to catching on her clothes. The glowing embers died silently on the ground.

"Excuse me," she shouted, making her voice as loud as possible.

The man didn't stop welding. He either couldn't hear her or was choosing to ignore her.

Skylar looked around until she found a small hammer. She picked it up and tapped it gently, but forcefully, on the side of the ladder. The man's torch cut off, and he looked down at her over his shoulder, the darkened visor of his helmet scanning her like a cold robotic eye. He clipped his torch and stick welder to a cradle hanging from the nose of the plane and began a careful descent down the ladder until he stood mask to face with Skylar. He held out a gloved hand.

"What?" Skylar said.

He pointed at the hammer then held out his hand once more.

"Oh," Skylar said, placing the tool into the thick leather padded glove.

The man took the hammer and placed it back into his toolbox. He took off one glove, then the next, and finally removed his helmet. A matted pile of black curls came into view, and the man turned around, his icy eyes regarding her with irritation.

"Ain't right to touch a man's tool without his permission," he said with a thick southern accent. "Least of all to start banging up on his shit while he's up doing God's work with ten thousand degrees of heat. Might get a man killed that way."

"Sorry," Skylar started, "I tried calling up to you—"

"Might try waiting next time."

"I don't have time to wait," Skylar said, "I need to know who's in charge here."

"Well now you do," he said with a lopsided smirk.

"You?"

"Me."

Great, Skylar thought. "The general sent me down to—"

"I know," he said, wiping the sweat from his forehead, but smearing grease across it in the process. "General sent down a memo. What's your name, ma'am?"

"Just call me Skylar."

The man took out a folded-up piece of paper from his cargo pant pocket and read over it. "Says here I'm supposed to work with a Doctor O'Hara?"

"Yes, Doctor Skylar O'Hara, me," Skylar said, frustrated.

"Pleased to meet you, Doctor O'Hara. Gunner Kaine, but everyone here just calls me 'Boss'," he said, extending a hand. Skylar shook it, a shiver running down her spine as grease and sweat clung to her hand on contact. She waited for the man to turn away before wiping her hand on her jeans. "What can me and my boys do for you today?"

#

Despite his demeanor, Gunner Kaine was exceptionally intelligent and polite in his own way, Skylar realized. He'd taken her around the hangar and introduced her to the rest of his team, mostly by nicknames. Skid, a thin streak of a man; Bunk, heavier than the rest, but the most well-spoken, Tungsten, who'd lost a finger due to an unfortunate choice of wedding ring, and Jet, who used to be a fighter pilot, but couldn't stand being in the air after witnessing the events of 9/11 from Ground Zero. Gunner swore the nickname was around before the phobia, and Jet confirmed that it was his old air force call sign. He mostly found the irony funny at this point he had told her.

"So wait, you're telling me you need us to make giant...staples?" Skid said, scratching his armpit before wiping his face on the stained wifebeater that clung loosely to his wiry frame.

"To hold that giant monster," Tungsten added. He rubbed at what Skylar thought was 5 o'clock shadow but turned out to be a fine spread of dirt on his face. "In Vegas?"

"Effectively, yes," Skylar said, "we need to pin the creature long enough to fully dehydrate it."

"Goddamn," Jet said. "We're talking at least a hundred metric tons of carbon steel. You'd need a fleet of helicopters to transport these things."

"Is it possible?" Skylar asked. "We have the steel."

"With all due respect, ma'am, we're welders," Gunner said, "we can damn well do anything you need with the right amount of steel."

Someone hemmed at Skylar's back. She turned to see General MacPherson standing in front of a staggeringly diverse group of people.

"Doctor O'Hara," MacPherson said, "the shipments of steel are waiting outside the hangar door." She gestured at the crowd of men and women around her. "And here are all of the welders, blacksmiths, and engineers we could claim from the surrounding facilities."

Skid spat on the floor of the hangar. "Look at all that new blood. Good thing too, I was worried we'd be shorthanded." He grinned his nearly toothless grin. "Welcome to the Mechanic Corps, you lot, hope you like cyborgs 'cause after all this you might well be one."

Skylar turned to Gunner. "Can I leave them in your hands?"

"Don't need no supervision here. This is just a Tuesday for us. You can run along and do whatever you need to do."

Skylar extended a hand. Gunner took it and shook it with a firm grip.

"We're counting on you," she said.

#

As soon as Devonte entered the fluorescent lit infirmary, a moon-faced nurse recognized him and ushered him down a long hallway lined with numbered doors until they came to one marked "54".

"I think he's awake," the nurse said, opening the door for him, "go on in."

Inside, Brannigan sat up on the hospital bed, bandages wrapped around his head, chest and one of his wrists. "Hey, if it isn't my favorite nerd!"

"You know, you should keep the wrappings. Hide that face out of respect for those around you," Devonte said with a laugh.

"Oh, too soon man, too soon," Brannigan said, clutching his ribs with a grimace as he laughed.

"Seriously though, what the fuck happened to you?"

"I made the Russian strongman very angry. Turns out I didn't like him very much when he was angry," Brannigan said. "Lots of broken bones. Maybe a spleen or two."

Devonte rolled his eyes but couldn't suppress a chuckle. "But you won?"

"He's dead. Very dead," Brannigan said. "I made sure this time."

"I'm glad you're okay."

"Hey, me too. How is your shoulder?"

"I've been able to sneak in a little bit of physical therapy here and there to keep it from locking up. I can almost move it without wanting to cry now."

"Progress!"

Devonte flashed a toothy smile. "Yeah."

"So what have I missed?"

"Didn't you hear?" Devonte asked.

Brannigan pointed at the wrap around his head that covered one ear completely and halfway covered another one. "It's a bit hard at the moment."

"The creature is heading to Las Vegas. Tempest recreated our device."

Brannigan started to get out of the bed and get dressed. He fumbled and coughed, clutching at his sides before collapsing back on the cot.

"What are you doing?"

"You lot sound like you need help, so I'm coming back with you."

"No, dude, you're real banged up, you need to rest."

Brannigan didn't stop. Devonte searched the room for the emergency call button. He slammed it, and almost instantly a nurse and two soldiers rushed into the room.

Brannigan narrowed his eyes at Devonte. "Motherfucker."

The three attendants were able to wrestle Brannigan as gently as possible back onto the bed and strap him down. The captain pulled at the straps, eliciting a pained gasp from the captain. Brannigan didn't try again.

"Sorry, but this is for your own good," Devonte said. "You need to take care of yourself and heal up. We'll need you at full swing to take on Tempest for real."

Brannigan clenched his fists. "Just because I know you're right doesn't mean I have to like it."

"You'll be okay," Devonte said, rolling over and gently tapping the man's shoulder. "Marines are tough, right?"

Brannigan barely managed to contain his laughter. "Get going, kid, I'm sure you got shit to do."

Devonte gave the best salute he could. "Sorry it's with the wrong hand, but it's the thought that counts, right?"

"That was entirely unnecessary."

Devonte offered a one-armed shrug as he backed out of the hospital room.

#

Kurtis wondered what kind of person it took to hop on a transport helicopter with a device designed to draw the attention of a hundred-meter monster. He knew for a fact he wasn't that kind of person. Jia Ming also wasn't that kind of person. Yet still, many men and women were perfectly happy to play their role as cannon fodder and bait, either out of loyalty or fear. He didn't care which. He was just glad idiots like them existed.

The outpost was a few miles outside of the city and carved out of the face of a rocky outcrop in the desert. Its observatory could render the city down to the smallest detail, via the use of insect-sized drones that circled the city with omnidirectional cameras, high enough not to be noticed, but low enough not to interfere with air traffic. Kurtis sipped his soda, casting a curious glance at Jia Ming.

"So," he said.

"You're not my type," she responded coldly.

"Excuse me?" Kurtis coughed, choking on the drink in his mouth.

"You've been staring at me since we left San Francisco. I assume you want something from me. I don't pity fuck."

Kurtis blinked. "Odd assumption. Making an ass out of yourself a bit there, but okay. No, I was going to ask if you were sure this was a good idea. And if perhaps you could be dissuaded from something so…over the top."

Jia Ming gave him an icy glare. "I will not change my mind."

"Wasn't asking you to. Just asking if you would. I'm not sure how I feel about wiping out an entire city for a training exercise. Not only does it seem unnecessarily violent, it doesn't exactly scream secrecy."

"The time for secrecy is over. With this on our side, we won't need to rely on the shadows to exist. We will stand above all others with power and pride."

"I see." Kurtis steepled his fingers in front of his scowling face.

"You don't agree with me."

"I'll reserve my judgment for after the demonstration. How much longer until contact?"

Jia Ming looked at her watch. "A few hours."

The 3D render of the city sat below them, like looking down on a model city, perfectly and painstakingly crafted. They could see the army's tanks lined up on the street surrounded by little soldiers, and all manner of other artillery. Fighter jets swarmed the sky, cruising around the hovering forms of at least three attack helicopters. Kurtis could tell this battle would not be in the army's favor.

The hours passed slowly, and in silence. Jia Ming gave no indication of wanting to speak or be spoken to, and that was just as well with Kurtis who grew less comfortable with the events about to unfold as time went on. He was just about to voice his concern a final time when an ear-splitting roar echoed throughout the desert.

"She's here," Jia Ming said. Her blood red lips stretched into a cruel smile. "Let the show begin."

#

Skylar couldn't help but be in awe of the giant metal structures lining the hangar. Only two days had passed, and yet here they all stood, arching over her so high she had to crane her neck.

"Staples," she said. "Giant staples."

The man named Gunner cleared his throat indignantly.

"Not to undermine the accomplishment," she added. "A fantastic accomplishment."

The welder gave a self-assured, half-cocked smile, and clicked his teeth. "You're goddamn right. One hundred meters and god knows how many tons each." He scratched at his beard. "Good luck lifting all that."

Lieutenant Greenwood gestured to a cluster of construction helicopters. "Don't worry. We have that covered," she said. "These will be divided into three groups and given an accompanying military escort to Vegas."

Gunner waved his hand. "I don't need to know your Art of War shit." He lit up his torch. "I got fire, I got steel, and I got the knowhow to make something out of them. That's all I need."

Greenwood flashed a glance at Skylar, who simply shrugged in response.

"Yes, well, thank you for your hard work. Bonus payment will be delivered to the account you provided," Greenwood said. "Dismissed."

The gathered metalworkers trickled out of the hangar one by one until only Gunner and his team remained. Greenwood arched a questioning eyebrow at them.

"We work here," he said. "Most of us didn't sleep to get these done for you."

"Take the rest of the day," she said.

"That's more like it," Gunner said loudly over the cheers of the rest of his team.

Skylar gave them all a quick wink, which Gunner return with a barely perceptible nod. They headed towards the exit past the helicopters.

When all the welders were out of sight, Greenwood turned to Skylar and said, "Are you ready?"

"Ready for what?"

"Lift off. This is your mission plan, you should be in the field to supervise," Greenwood said. She noticed Skylar's look of concern. "Don't worry, our chopper will hang back from the escorts and the construction choppers."

Skylar swallowed hard. "Yeah, I'll go."

INTERLUDE IV

Hot. The heat on Inkanyamba's skin is not unpleasant. Yet. She tracks the silver flying creature. They sound like her prey. *Curious.* She doesn't understand how it can fly. The wind rushes past. Each beat of her wings carries her forward. She roars. The other creature ignores her. She is far from her nest. There is no water, only sand. Light from the sun burns her eyes. Great shining structures stretch up from the sand. Like teeth. The flying prey disappears behind the jagged structures. Inkanyamba follows. The ground shakes as she lands. It burns her feet. *Pain.* She looks around. Mottled green and brown creatures with thin, long necks terminating in a single black eye surround her. Their gaze is fixed on her. Smaller creatures scurry amongst them. She recognizes them. They attacked her nest. *Anger.* She lets out a cautionary warble.

The first noise startles her. She whips her head around. The side of her face burns from the impact. One of the creature's eyes is smoking. More noises, like thunder, sound off around her. *Pain.* Smoking black eyes stare at her. They move forward, threatening her. *Fight.*

Inkanyamba lowers her neck to the height of the creatures and screams. The force of her lungs knocks over the smallest creatures and pushes the larger ones back a great distance. A high-pitched sound draws her attention back to the sky. Flying creatures drop things on her from above. *Pain.* She digs her feet into the ground to keep from stumbling backwards. *Fight.*

She swipes out with a clawed foreleg. One of the long-necked creatures crumples under the impact. Smoke and sparks pour out from within. She launches it into a crowd of the small, scurrying creatures. Their tiny sounds are cut off when it crushes them. She knocks the crumpled creatures into another of its kind. It also bursts into flames. The smaller creatures are afraid. She can smell it.

Hundreds of little pops fill the air. They bring a series of itches that bounce off of her scales one by one. She slams her tail down on the offending creatures. The pops fall silent.

Pain. Dry skin tears at the base of her tail. *Water.* She scans her surroundings and sees no water. She beats her wings. The creatures at her feet are blown away as she rises. In the distance she sees water. A small lake lit up in several strange colors. Geysers erupt in a rhythmic pattern across its surface. She glides towards it and lands. *Water.* It only covers her feet. *Rage.* She stomps at the geysers. The stone lake crumbles under her feet. She lashes out with her tail. It crashes through a structure almost as tall as her. Debris tumbles down from it as it collapses. She thrashes her wings, kicking up water and dust and raining it down all around her. She screams. Thunderous sounds snap her from her tantrum. The creatures from before have caught up to her. She hisses a warning. It goes unheeded, and they attack. She rears back to strike. Slamming her forelegs back down, she charges forward. Her head swings back and forth, knocking the creatures out of her way. Many more are crushed under her feet. She slides to a stop and whirls to face the remaining enemies. She bares her teeth.

Pain. It crackles like electricity across her skin. Her scales tear free from her drying skin. The frills on her neck rattle. *Anger.* A low, repetitive pulse tickles her sense. She glares up at the sky. More flying creatures. These are larger, and their wings spin above their heads. Large arches hang beneath them. They move until they come to a hover above her.

The creatures drop their loads. Three heavy forces slam into her back. A sound. She doesn't recognize it. Three heavy weights slam down on her. *Stuck.* She thrashes. She can't break free. She cranes her neck. Three shining rings hold her in place. She screams, snapping and biting at them. Her teeth scrape against the cold material. *Pain.*

Her skin hurts. It tears, red lines cracking all over her body. She's slow. The dryness sucks her strength. *Fear.* Skin rubs off as she shifts inside her bonds. The sun beats down, hot and unending until…*Cool.*

The shade covers her before she can see the cloud. It's in the distance now, but it's there. A massive, puffy cloud. The kind that brings rain. *Water.* Inkanyamba relaxes her muscles. The pain in her skin diminishes at the thought of a refreshing downpour. She waits.

CHAPTER 16

"We got her!" Skylar cheered. She turned to Greenwood for a high-five, but the older woman just nodded at her with a stoic look in her eye.

"Now we wait?" Greenwood asked.

Skylar tapped her cheek thoughtfully. "Actually," she said, "do you think we could set down near the creature?"

"Why the hell would we do that?" Greenwood asked with a frown.

"General MacPherson asked me to gather some samples so I could further research the creature past its…expiration date," Skylar said, doing her best to look serious. "I'd only need a few minutes, and all of my equipment is on one of those construction copters. We just need to radio them down so I can grab it."

Greenwood kneaded her forehead. "Wish people would communicate these things to me," she said. "Just make it quick." She walked up to the pilot. "Put us down close but not too close, and radio the construction copters to bring down the doc's equipment."

The pilot gave a sharp thumbs up, and the copter began to set down towards the midpoint of the creature's body, out of reach of its head and tail. Skylar hopped out and gave the pilot a thumbs up. The military copter lurched back up into the sky.

"You have one hour," Greenwood called down from the chopper.

The construction copter set down next to them. Five men in helmets hopped out of the transport and waited for the equipment to be lowered to the ground.

"Gunner, is that you?" Skylar said.

The first man nodded and said in a slow drawl, "That's right; what do you need from us, ma'am?"

She pointed up towards the creature's back. "I need an egg from up on the creature's back. I know it's dangerous, but…"

"That explains the strange request for ladder rungs on the structures," Skid said from underneath his helmet. "Well Jet's probably the best climber of the lot of us," he added.

Jet looked the makeshift ladder up and down. "Ten minutes up, time to remove the egg, ten minutes down. Got something to put it in?"

"The trunk with the black locks," Skylar said. "You'll probably have to lower the egg with the helicopter's cables."

Jet nodded. "That'll take three of us. Bunk to pilot, Skid to operate the wench, and me to get the egg."

Gunner glanced at Tungsten. "What are you gonna need us to do?"

"You're going to help me down here. I need skin and blood samples."

The two men shared a confused glance.

"I'll get the blood, you lot scrape off some of the scales and put them in one container, and then cut out some of the flesh underneath the scales to put in another container...if you can."

"What if she don't like that very much?" Gunner asked.

"We're small enough that she shouldn't feel it. Think about how you just barely notice an ant crawling over your foot."

Tungsten nodded. "Where are the scalpels?"

"Use the hunting knife over there," Skylar said. "I doubt a scalpel will do anything."

Skylar looked at the assortment of needles packed in with her equipment and sighed. *Neither, for that matter, will any of these.* She sifted through the equipment until she came upon a drill one of the mechanics had brought. She picked it up along with a second hunting knife, a length of tube and a set of stopped vials. Her steps towards the creature wobbled as her knees refused to cooperate with her brain. The sickening smell of spoiled fish, blood, and sea salt made her gag violently. Nothing she'd ever worked with had smelled this bad. Finally she made it to the creature's side. She placed her equipment on the ground before casting a cautious glance up to where the creature's head lay flat on the ground, eyes closed, like it was sleeping. A sense of unease ran through Skylar's body. She looked up and saw that Jet had made it to the top and was working on extricating an egg from the bulbous sac on the creature's back.

Why isn't she reacting? Her children are being threatened.

She pushed the thought from her mind and set about her task. She pried off a patch of scales with the blade of the knife. Then, taking the drill, she pressed it into the exposed flesh, turning her head to avoid the spray of blood. Quick as she could, she inserted the tube into the makeshift hole, taped around it, and placed the first vial at the other end. Her gloved hands pressed into the area around the wound, sending a fresh stream of blood pumping into the vial. She repeated this process six times before removing the tube and tape. Her first instinct was to gauze and tape the wound, as she would with any other animal, but almost as soon as the tube was out, the wound had healed, and fresh scales were already growing into place. She placed a gloved hand on the creature's side.

"I'm sorry it had to be like this," she whispered.

Jet's shout pulled her out of her quiet moment. "Item secured. Descending."

"Good." She handed her vials to Gunner and Tungsten. "Take these and the egg back to my lab on the base. Have Devonte watch over them." She handed Gunner a check worth ten-thousand dollars, something from her secondary savings account.

He smiled and thanked her.

"What are you going to use it for?" she asked before she could catch herself.

Gunner's face turned serious. "My wife and I want kids, you know? But, well, there's a complication." His face reddened. "I can't do it."

"You don't want kids?" Skylar asked.

"I can't have them," he said in a hushed tone. "I'm—"

"Oh," Skylar said. "I see."

"This money won't cover the adoption fee, but it will really help us." He looked around. "And I'll make sure the boys get a good split as well," he added with a wink.

Skylar smiled as the man hopped into the helicopter. Her hair and coat blew around her as the craft lifted into the air and headed off towards San Francisco. As it was taking off, the military craft with Lieutenant Greenwood began its descent towards her.

"Get everything you need?" Greenwood asked.

Skylar smiled, "Just about."

"You sent the copter back with your gatherings? Good idea."

"Yeah," Skylar said, her face falling, "something seems off here and I wanted to make sure it was safe."

"Off how?"

"Let's get up in the air first." She watched the creature with growing concern as the helicopter lurched up into the sky.

"So what's up?"

"Tigers pace back and forth when you put them in a cage. Have you ever tried to pin down a predator? Capture it and hold it in place?"

"Not animals, no."

Skylar's eyes widened.

Greenwood shrugged. "Interpol."

Skylar nodded. "My point is…why isn't she resisting?"

Greenwood frowned.

Inkanyamba lay pressed to the ground, unmoving. Her head was angled up at the sky, mouth slightly agape.

"She looks relaxed," Skylar said. She tracked the direction Inkanyamba was looking and saw, almost on top of them, a dark cumulonimbus cloud lingering in the sky. Its shadow stretched across the ground, darkening it and dropping the temperature at least six degrees. There was no rain, no wind, it wasn't a storm. The hair on Skylar's arms began to stand on end. "We need to go," she said. "Probably best if it's now."

"We were ordered to ensure Inkanyamba's defeat."

"She isn't going to lose."

"What are you talking about? She's pinned and drying out as we speak."

"No, no, no, she's *waiting*!" The electricity in the air began to tingle and hum. An itch began to spread from the back of Skylar's skull until her head felt like it was full of bees.

Inkanyamba let out a soft warble, her body alight with electric currents. Her eyes locked onto the clouds overhead. She lowered her head, then whipped it up, straining her whole body against her oversized restraints before screaming out as white lightning erupted from her whole body. The lightning spread throughout the cloud like misfiring synapses. A bolt struck the top rotor on the helicopter and shorted out the engine. The pilot seized in their seat, smoke pouring out of the console. Skylar choked as the smell of burning flesh filled her nostrils. The helicopter stalled in the air for the smallest fraction of a second before beginning its drop to the ground below. She grabbed onto the side of the craft as it spiraled downward at a dizzying speed. She could barely make out Greenwood's voice over the rush of wind. Most of the words were lost, but she heard "I got you" and "jump". She felt something wrench her grip off the makeshift handhold. And then she saw nothing but the open sky, grey and foreboding, with the first drizzles of rain.

Rain, Skylar thought. She felt the final tug, the opening of a parachute, pulling her up into the sky before settling her into a slow downward drift. She watched the helicopter slam into a nearby building, carving through glass and steel, leaving a jagged lopsided smile in the side of the skyscraper. It crashed, erupting into a massive fireball several yards away from where it had started in the sky. *Rain. She's rehydrating herself. She made it rain.*

The ground was approaching, fast, but not dangerously fast. All of the adrenaline from the crash coursed through Skylar's veins, numbing her to panic and sensation. She didn't even realize when they touched the ground until Greenwood unclipped her from the parachute and she toppled unceremoniously to the ground. She bounced up almost immediately.

"She's going to get out," Skylar shouted. "We can't be here!"

"But she's bolted in place."

"Those restraints relied on her being weakened by the heat and dryness in the air. The rain will revitalize her, and I doubt she'll be happy."

"Fuck," Greenwood said. "I'll call one of the other choppers to come get us."

"I don't think you will," a familiar voice said over the roar of the rain. Skylar turned to see Kurtis, accompanied by four men in full SWAT armor, guns trained on the two of them. "Good to see you again, Dr. O'Hara." He paused. "You look beautiful as always."

"We'll see how beautiful I look covered in your blood, asshole."

"Red does seem to be your color." He smiled. "If you don't mind, accompany me to safety?"

"I'd rather take my chances with the monster. I'm sure it at least has feelings."

At that moment, Inkanyamba let out a terrible roar. Her muscles flexed and she strained against her restraints, warping them and filling the air with the sound of buckling metal.

"Are you sure about that?" Kurtis asked. "At least you know how I feel about you."

Skylar ground her teeth, looking back and forth between Inkanyamba and Kurtis. Before she could respond, Greenwood put her hands above her head and said, "We'll come with you. It's not safe out here."

Skylar's jaw dropped, she wanted to scream, but instead, she grumbled her agreement as well. "Gonna put us in handcuffs now?"

"Only if you ask for it," he said, smirking.

Skylar's face went hot in the ice-cold downpour. The four men walked her and Greenwood to a nearby Humvee, black with an electric blue hurricane decal on the hood. They slid into the backseat while Kurtis and his men climbed up front. The engine roared to life, but the noise was cut off by an even louder roar, the sound a building makes as it crashes to the ground. Skylar turned around just in time to see Inkanyamba break free from her restraints, lightning flashing around her as thunder pealed with a sound like the end of the world.

"And the seven thunders uttered," Kurtis said grimly. He turned in his seat to face them. "I'm honestly sorry about this, but security is always a concern in my line of work." He held up a small aerosol can and, before Skylar could react, sprayed both her and Greenwood directly in the face. Immediately her world went fuzzy and she felt as though her mind were being sucked down a drain, whirling slowly into the blank emptiness of unconsciousness.

"You won't be harmed," Kurtis said, his voice a million miles away.

"Can't...say the same...for you," Skylar said before succumbing to the effects of the spray.

#

The cell, which Skylar only called a cell because that's what it felt like, was grander than any apartment or hotel room she'd ever stayed in. Lush wool carpet, so thick her feet sunk into it, covered the floor. All of the furnishings were handcrafted from real wood and appeared to be quite old. A desk in the corner was completely fitted with all the necessities for writing, including a laptop, albeit, one not connected to the internet. Greenwood wasn't here with her. They'd been separated. Which made her nervous. What made her more nervous was the canopied four poster bed that sat on the far wall of the room. The implications made her shudder.

There was a knock at the door to the room.

"Leave me alone," she called.

"It's me," Kurtis' voice said in reply.

"Oh, well, in that case, go to hell," she shouted, slamming her fist against the door.

Silence from the other side of the door, and then, "I have the key, and I'm coming in. Back away from the door. There are two men out here who will shoot you if you disobey."

Skylar huffed, and backed away, crossing her arms across her chest.

The lock clicked and Kurtis stepped into the room, closing the door behind him and locking it again. "Comfortable?"

"Where are your bodyguards?" she snapped.

"I lied. It's just me. I was worried you'd do something rash."

Skylar's jaw tightened and she nodded her head. "Right, rash. Like kidnapping and roofying me?"

"I couldn't let you know the way to this place."

"Got to keep your little Tempest hideouts secret, right?"

"This is actually my house," he said, rubbing his head with embarrassment. "My room, even."

Skylar's face and temper flared. "You kidnap me, drug me, and lock me up in your room? What the fuck kind of creep are you?"

"I understand your displeasure at the circumstances…"

"Displeasure," she screamed. "If you so much as look at me wrong, I will break as many of your bones as I can before your men kill me."

"They are only under orders to subdue you," he said.

"Then I guess you'll have a lot of broken bones," she spat.

"Perhaps," he said flatly. "There is a reason I brought you here, and it is not what you may be thinking."

"Where is here?"

"I drugged you so you wouldn't know, and you think I'll just tell you?"

"Worth a shot."

"I brought you here because—"

"Hush," Skylar cut him off and listened intently to the silence. "I can't hear Inkanyamba. If we were still in or near Las Vegas we'd hear her rampage."

"You are correct." Kurtis blinked slowly. "May I finish?"

"If you must."

"I can no longer in good conscience support the actions of Tempest," he said. His eyes locked on to her intensely, waiting for a response.

Skylar sat down on a satin upholstered stool with a scowl. "I don't believe you."

"One of our newest leaders has veered the organization in a direction that I believe is counter to our overall goals.

Surprisingly, the others support her. I am the only dissenting opinion."

"What do you want me to say?"

"I need your help."

"No."

"Please."

"Fuck you."

"Dammit Skylar, I'm serious, I can't do this anymore." The faintest hint of tears glistened at the corners of his eyes. "We were supposed to capture the creature and use it as a threat to allow us to operate as we wanted without any threat from the world governments. A safeguard against things like Interpol interference. But Jia Ming wants to burn the world and let Tempest rule what remains in the ashes. I have no stomach for murder, especially not on this scale."

"So your gang gets too violent and now you want to tuck and run. You're a coward, Kurtis." She stood and shouted at him. "You shot my best friend. How many people did your raid on the base kill? Or the people in Vegas who couldn't get out?"

"These weren't my plans," he shouted back.

"But you did nothing to stop them, did you?"

"They would have killed me."

"Well then they'd have done something right for a change."

Kurtis' face went pale. He sat in a chair on the opposite side of the room. "You're right. I'm a coward. My whole purpose in this organization is...was...to keep us from the limelight, and minimize the ripples of our actions, so this...this is egregious to me." He gave her a pained look. "I don't expect you to trust me, not right now, maybe not ever. But I'm not lying to you and I want to stop this." He rose, brushed off his slacks, and gave her a solemn smile. "Someone will be by with dinner shortly."

Skylar failed to resist the urge to cross the room and slug him right in his pouting face.

He toppled to the ground and rubbed his jaw. "What the fuck?"

"We're nowhere near even," she said.

"You could've taken my head off," he said. "I have a bo—"

He cut himself off. "Ow," he finished.

Skylar scowled and waited until he left the room. When the lock clicked, and she no longer heard his footstep in the hall outside the door she began her search of the room, looking for anything that could aid in her escape. Nothing. Everything heavy was bolted to the floor, and the room had been stripped of anything conducive to freedom.

"Skylar," a voice said, barely audible and muffled sounding.

She searched around for the source of the voice until she came to a small vent down by the side of the bed.

"Skylar," the voice said again. "It's Ashleigh."

"Ashleigh, oh my god, you're okay?"

"Yeah," she said.

Skylar slumped to the floor down by the vent. "Did Kurtis come see you?"

"No, but I heard you talking to him."

"He said he wants to help us."

"Do you buy it?"

"No," she spat, then softened. "I don't know."

"Can you keep him engaged? Maybe get us out of here?"

"I can't stand him!"

"He likes you though. We can use that."

Skylar put her head in her hands. "Do I have to?"

"Of course not, but I'm not sure how we get out of here without you playing along," Greenwood said. "And, if he does actually mean what he's saying…"

"We need all the help we can get against Inkanyamba," Skylar said with a sigh.

The silence from the other end of the vent was all the answer she needed. She ran her hands through her hair, stood up, and began pacing back and forth in the room. There was a knock at the door. Skylar straightened out her shirt, and said in a flat voice, "Come in."

The door opened and Kurtis entered with a burger on a large purple plate. Skylar almost laughed when she saw that there was a knife and fork alongside the meal.

"I thought you said someone else would be by with dinner," she said.

"I said someone would be by," he said, "I'm someone."

"You are indeed." She looked at the burger. "I don't eat meat."

"You told me back in the lab. It's a veggie burger. Vegan cheese?" He put the plate on the desk and turned to leave the room.

"Kurtis," she called before he left.

He turned and raised an eyebrow at her.

"Let's say I believe you…you'll have to give me more to go on than your word."

"Like what?" He closed the door again, and leaned up against it, with his hands buried deep in his pockets.

"Tell me who's in charge of Tempest."

"You know I can't do that."

"You're planning on betraying them anyway," Skylar said. "The only way we can really stop them is if we know who they are."

Kurtis took a deep breath and stepped away from the door, walking across the room until he stood directly in front of her. "You're right."

Skylar's heart skipped a beat.

"I'll tell you about the one we need to stop first. Is that okay?"

"For now."

Kurtis rubbed his face. "There are seven of us, The Hands of Fate. Each hand has something in its grip, a function that only it handles. You know me. I'm the Hand of Shadows."

"You keep the secrets," she said.

"Until now," he said with a grim look.

"And who is the new hand that made you have a change of heart?"

"The Hand of Gold."

"Money?"

"Business and logistics, more accurately," Kurtis corrected.

"And why does the business lady have control of the kaiju plan?"

"If we collapse to world governments and take charge, we control the economy. Not only that, but rulers can demand tribute from their people. We'd have all the money, and no one could stop us."

"Megalomania," Skylar mumbled. "Plain and simple."

"Exactly." Kurtis brushed his hair out of his face. "Ever since her sister died, she's been ruthless. Cruel and demanding, with no room for dissention. She lured your creature—"

"Inkanyamba."

"—to Las Vegas as a test to see how easily it could destroy the armed forces here."

Skylar felt a spike of anger in her chest. "That bitch."

"Do you see why I need your help?"

"Let us go."

"I'm sorry?"

"Me and Lieutenant Greenwood. Let us go back to San Francisco and talk to the people there, so we can bring her down…together," she added begrudgingly.

"I can't do that. You won't keep your word."

"Kurtis. If you want me to trust you, you have to trust me."

He thought for a minute. She saw the logic running behind his eyes as he stared at the opposite wall. "Okay," he said, "on one condition."

"What condition?"

"You're getting sprayed again."

"No. Absolutely not."

"On the chance that you decide to betray me, I need to know that my home is safe and secure out of your people's reach," he said. "You get the spray, or you have to stay."

Skylar sucked her teeth. "Fine."

"I promise it's completely harmless," he said with a reassuring smile. "And you'll be back in no time."

"When I wake up, you're getting decked."

He shrugged. "I probably deserve it."

"Fuck you," she said.

#

For the second time in too short of a span for her comfort, Skylar had woken up from a drug induced sleep. This time, however, she was pleased to find that she had not woken up in a strange man's bedroom. She chuckled at the fact that a sterile medical room brought her more comfort than plush carpets and fancy furnishings. She turned her head to see Devonte sitting in a chair beside the cot.

"How the tables have turned," she said, realizing how dry her throat was in the process. She swallowed hard to try and get some moisture.

"We've got to stop meeting like this."

The two shared a laugh before settling into an overwhelming silence.

"What happened?" Devonte asked. "We all saw Inkanyamba break loose on TV, and I thought—"

"How did I get here?" Skylar asked.

"Some guys in SWAT gear said they found you passed out near the wreck of your helicopter. They brought you here on Lieutenant Greenwood's orders they said, but she was also unconscious when you arrived. It doesn't add up." He looked at her expectantly.

Skylar took a deep breath. She knew this wouldn't go over well, but she wasn't about to lie to her best friend. "It was Kurtis," she said. "He…rescued us."

Her friend stared at her in disbelief. "He what?"

"Our helicopter went down when Inkanyamba summoned the storm. We crashed and he was there."

"And you went with him?" Devonte grew agitated, his grip tightening on the arms of his chair.

Skylar felt her own temper flare. "It's not like we had a choice, he had guns and we were disoriented. He took us to a safe house or something. Devonte…he said he wants to help us."

"Help us? Is that what he was doing when he shot me?" Devonte shouted.

"No, but I think things have gone too far even for him."

"Oh that's great, so now that he's not happy with the plan he decides to switch sides?" he seethed, not looking her in the eye. "And you believe him?"

"Yes. No. I don't know." She averted her eyes as well. "I don't *trust* him. But what if he really does want to help? We could use his resources."

"And what if he decides to betray us *again*, and this time he kills me, or…what if he does something to hurt you?"

Again, for the second time in far too soon, Skylar felt her face flush with embarrassed warmth. She looked away from Devonte. "We'll just have to keep an eye on him."

"An eye, or a gun," Devonte muttered.

"If we can convince everyone else, it will probably be both," Skylar said.

"Good," Devonte said.

"You didn't see how upset he was about everything, D. I don't think we'll have to worry too much about him."

"Then I'll leave that to you," he said in response, "I intend to worry about him, and fuck him up if he steps out of line."

"Yeah, you and your last remaining arm."

"Hey," he said, "I tried to talk the doctor into hooking me up like Raymond. Apparently, it 'wouldn't work for soft tissue damage and would also be irresponsible for her to use bleeding edge technology on a civvy'," he said, doing his best impression of what Skylar could only assume was the doctor.

"Like Raymond?" Skylar asked.

"Yeah, I wanted her to turn me into a hard-boiled detective with a real soft spot. I even promised to narrate my thought process out loud all the time if she did."

"Raymond doesn't seem like noir kind of detective," she said, "now stop being an ass and tell me what happened!"

"Science happened." Devonte kicked his feet up onto the desk. "Do you know what happened to Raymond's back?"

"I heard that he broke it," she said thoughtfully, "but I noticed he gets around pretty well. Always wondered how."

"Cybernetics. Think of it like a highly advanced shock absorber." He tapped a few keys on his computer and pulled up the schematics for something that looked like a cross between a claw and a metal ribcage. "Just a heads up, but you didn't see these details," he said with a wink. "Basically it supports his spine while also negating almost all of the potentially harmful vibrations that travel throughout the body whenever he moves."

"Fantastic!" Skylar said leaning in. Devonte felt his face begin to warm as she drew closer to him. Her arm brushed against him as she took control of the computer mouse. She hummed intently as she read. "This would still mean that continued exertion would eventually cause discomfort and potential exacerbation of the injury."

"Uh…yeah," Devonte said, closing the schematics. "It looks like it's actually the foundational research for something else, but whatever it is, it's locked behind so much security even I'm struggling to access it."

Skylar's eyes widened. "That's exciting!"

"That's what I thought as well," he said, his face reflecting her enthusiasm.

They shared their theories on what the full research might be for a few minutes, with the ideas growing wilder and more insane. When Devonte suggested that it might be geared towards realistic sex robots for soldiers on deployment, the two of them agreed that *obviously* that was the only possible answer.

Devonte was the one to change the subject "By the way, Gunner left a trunk for you in the lab."

Skylar nodded. "Did anyone see it besides you?"

"No. Why?"

She leaned in and whispered what she did.

"You what?"

"Hush!" she said, covering his mouth with her hands.

"Did you tell Greenwood?"

"Of course not. She'd lose her shit."

He nodded. "True."

Skylar swung her legs off the side of the bed and sat up. "I want to get started with it now," she said. "You can join me if you like."

"You probably need to go talk to Raymond and the general, first," Devonte said. "I'll head over to the hangar and get everything prepped."

Skylar smiled with a nod and a bob of her crimson curls. "Okay."

#

"Absolutely not."

Skylar stood stock still next to Lieutenant Greenwood as the general shot down their request. Raymond looked over the conversation with great interest. Skylar noticed that his face didn't show as much adversity to her suggestion as the general's did.

"He says he wants to help us," Skylar continued. "We could use his resources."

"Forty-seven."

"I'm sorry?"

"Forty-seven of my men. My soldiers. My *family*. That's how many his raid on our base killed. And you think I would ever let him in here in anything short of a body bag…"

"An eye for an eye leaves the whole world blind," Skylar quoted.

"Don't you quote that shit at me," the general snapped. "My people are dead, and if I have my way, he will be too."

"Captain Dehane. Raymond. You see what I'm saying, right?" Skylar said. "Detectives have informants. You work with bad guys to take down bigger bad guys all the time, right?"

Raymond rubbed his stubble, which now threatened to be almost a full beard. He said, "All the time is certainly an overstatement propagated by movies, but we do on occasion use resources outside our purview."

"And would you ever pass up a resource this valuable?"

Raymond cast a cautious glance at the general. "I would not. However, this is not an Interpol led mission anymore." He raised an eyebrow. "Is it, General MacPherson?"

The general sighed and rolled her eyes. "No. It isn't."

"Then I suppose we will have to pick apart Tempest from the outside, without the potential help of Mr. Wagner."

"But—"

Raymond cut her off. "We'll work hard, and though we may accomplish nothing without inside knowledge, we can say we did our best." He ended with a smirk and a sage head nod.

"I know exactly what you're doing," the general said.

"Yes, but you also know that what I just said is true. We won't find them without help."

Lieutenant Greenwood stepped in. "Ma'am, if I may. Skylar is suggesting that we use his help and resources. She is in no way implying that we trust him or give him free reign. We bring him in as a prisoner, he gives us intel, and then…"

"He goes away with the rest of them," Raymond concluded. He scanned Skylar's face for a reaction, but she gave none. "That is what happens to informants. They are still criminals, after all."

"That's fair," Skylar said, and she meant it.

General MacPherson mulled it over. She huffed. "He is on full lockdown from the moment he sets foot on this campus until someone comes along to throw him into the deepest pit the American government can dig."

"Thank you."

"Don't. We'll lock him up, but he's your problem while he's here. We're not wasting a single resource on him."

"Yes, ma'am."

"Is there anything else we should know?" Raymond asked.

"Actually yes, the chick who's doing all this…she seems to be out for revenge, for the death of her sister. Do you know anything about that?"

"I knew she looked familiar," Raymond said. "I thought I was seeing a ghost back then."

"The woman on the oil rig," Greenwood said.

"The one I failed to save."

"She attacked you. It was her own fault that she fell."

"Her twin doesn't seem to see it that way."

"And as we just learned," Greenwood said, "she's crazy."

"She has a point," Skylar confirmed.

"Yes, I know," Raymond said, "I just can't help feeling like I failed in my duties…to serve *and* protect. With her, the monster, and all."

"You're doing fine," the general said. "Even better once we catch these people and stop that monster."

Raymond inhaled sharply. "Right." He ran a hand through his hair. "Sorry."

Greenwood put a reassuring hand on his shoulder, which he clasped in his own. "Things are rough right now," she said softly. "Sometimes the world feels like it's burning down around us, monsters on the streets, evil, cruelty, and god knows what else." She paused, and their eyes locked. "But we've got to keep our heads up. The second we lose hope and give up, everything will spiral straight to hell."

"You're always there for me, Ashleigh," Raymond said. "I mean, Lieutenant Greenwood."

"Ashleigh is fine. And I'll always be there for you…Raymond." She leaned in and kissed him, and he kissed her back.

Skylar couldn't help but smile. Even the general didn't interrupt with a bitter or condescending remark. She looked at Skylar and mouthed, "It's about time," with a roll of her eyes.

Awareness of where they were flooded back into the two new lovebirds, and Greenwood practically leapt to put a respectable distance between herself and the detective. "I'm sorry, that was inappropriate," she sputtered.

"Forgiven," the general said.

"I'm sure there are plenty of rooms in this base for you two to find," Skylar quipped.

Raymond's face was completely placid, but Greenwood turned a brilliant shade of red.

"Anyway," Raymond said, "we should figure out how to contact our informant."

Skylar pulled out her phone. "I have a feeling…" she thumbed through her contacts and saw one she didn't recognize labelled "KW". "I think I have his number." She looked at the people in the room. "So should I call him?"

CHAPTER 17

Devonte ran his hand down the slime coated surface of the kaiju egg. As moist as it felt, his hand came away dry, but tingly, as though electricity was dancing across the skin of his palm. He replaced his hand and held it there. Inside the leathery shell he could feel the movement of the unborn creature, slithering in some viscous fluid.

He'd set up all of the necessary machinery for their research with the help of Gunner and his men, and now he just had to wait for Skylar. A chittering cry from inside the egg drew his focus. The egg distended in a shape that vaguely resembled a clawed hand. Once. Then again. The cry grew louder.

"Oh no," Devonte said. "You're way too early." He looked around the makeshift lab in the hangar. The cage he'd commissioned was still incomplete. Gunner estimated a few hours, and that was just thirty minutes ago. Sweat accumulated on Devonte's brow and around the nape of his neck.

An iron black talon tore through the leathery egg sac, spilling blood and amniotic fluid onto the floor at its base. Devonte stepped back to avoid getting any on his shoes. The creature's serpent-like head, no bigger than a football, snaked its way out of the shell. Gooey clumps of afterbirth plopped to the floor as it shook itself free. It was everything Devonte could do not to vomit when bits of it splattered over his body and face.

The first thing Devonte noticed was the creature's color, red, like Vornax. It heaved more of its body out and into the open air, hissing and screaming. The creature favored its father in color. Long fore limbs clicked along the ground as it sniffed the air walking on four powerful legs like a wolf. It had its mother's head, but a shorter neck, complete with vestigial gills, and neck frills that flared with each sucking breath.

No wings, Devonte realized.

The creature pawed at the ground and let out a dark, guttural sound.

Devonte let a small noise escape his throat.

The creature's head swiveled around in his direction, and that's when he realized that an opaque film still covered its eyes. It warbled as it stepped towards him again.

Devonte wanted to run. He wanted to call for help. His body was frozen to the spot, rigid with fear and awe. The creature leaned towards him and sniffed. Another soft warble, and then it licked him, wriggling its tongue around his face, slurping up the egg fluid and soaking him in briny saliva. When he opened his eyes again, the creature had sunk into a stretched position, with both fore and hind legs tucked up beneath its body. It cocked its head to the side, its eyes still covered.

Oh, this is going to be stupid, Devonte thought as he reached out his hand. He touched the side of the creature's head and received a gentle hiss in response. His hand stopped, but he didn't jerk it back. The creature chirped at him, which he took as permission to continue. He stroked his way up the side of its head until he got to the clump of tissue over its eye. Gingerly, he ran a finger over it. The sound of his heartbeat was louder than anything else in the room. He took ahold of the film and pulled, revealing a yellow eye with a red, slit-like iris. It stared at him for a second, taking him in, before angling its head to the other side. Devonte pulled the other film away as well, leaving him eye-to-eye with the young creature.

"Hello," he said.

The creature flicked its long tail, wrapping it around itself.

"I know you can't understand me," Devonte continued, reaching out slowly, "but my name is Devonte." He placed a hand on the cold, scaly neck of the newborn. Its eyes flickered over him, watching and wondering.

The fact that he hadn't lost his hand, or his life, filled Devonte with a greater sense of bravery. He began circling the creature, taking in all the similarities and difference between it and its parents. Whereas Inkanyamba looked like an eel crossed with a turtle and a dragon, and Vornax favored a fictionalized demon, the offspring favored a drake, a strange hybridization of the two.

Devonte circled back around to the front of the creature and took several steps back, taking in the sight. The creature rose with a noise, and for the first time Devonte noticed its size. At its shoulders, it stood around two meters. Raised up, its head stood another half meter. As it moved, cat-like, towards Devonte, it looked down at him the entire time. It made the distance between them the same as before, before settling down and watching him once more.

Devonte backed away. It followed. They did this dance around the inside of the room for a few minutes, before Devonte sat down to think.

"Holy fuck," Skylar said from behind him.

The creature let out a furious screech and rose on its haunches, hissing and spitting, frills all a tingle. Devonte leapt to his feet and held his arms out between Skylar and the creature. "Easy, easy," he said. "Skylar, back up. Slowly."

Skylar did as he said, and Devonte turned to face the creature.

"Hey, boy...girl? Hey...you." He reached out a calming hand. "It's okay. She's a friend." The creature's eyes narrowed suspiciously but he was able to place a hand on the side of its neck and gently stroke, careful not to slice his hands open on the razor-sharp scales. "Approach slowly," he said to Skylar without turning around.

The girl's breath hitched in her chest behind him.

"So far it hasn't bit me," he said in a comforting voice.

"I'm pretty sure it was just about to tear my face off."

"You scared...him?" Devonte cast a glance down at the creature's nether regions but saw nothing to confirm or deny his assessment.

"He scared me!"

"*Everyone* is scared," Devonte said. "Come pet the damn monster."

Tentatively, Skylar approached the creature. It watched her lazily, its eyes barely tracking to follow her. As she got closer, it shook out its frills and turned to look her head on. Devonte's hand never left its neck. Skylar reached out a slow, trembling hand and placed it on the creature's snout. It gurgled in response.

"Now that it's not trying to kill me..."

"It's kind of adorable right?" Devonte said with a laugh.

"Yeah."

"I thought of a name for it."

"Do tell."

"Akuma."

Skylar made her best "not bad" face, and said, "I can get behind that." She looked up to the creature. "What do you think, Akuma?"

The creature, now informally dubbed Akuma, cocked its head to the side.

"I think he likes it."

"There is one pressing matter," Skylar said. "How are we going to get it into the cage now?"

"Maybe we could lure it with fish?" Devonte shrugged.

"And after that we can go study radioactive earthworms?" Skylar said, sarcasm dripping from her voice.

"I mean, if the big ones eat whales, I just figured the little ones—"

"Also probably eat whales…caught by their parent," Skylar finished with a know-it-all smirk.

"Fish worked for Matthew Broderick," Devonte grumbled.

"Did they really though?" Skylar's pocket buzzed. She pulled out her phone and grimaced when she saw the message displayed across the top banner. "He's here," she said. "Kurtis." She looked up to see Devonte's scowl. "I take it you don't want to come."

"Can I hit him?"

"Probably not."

"Have fun, then." Devonte turned back to the creature, pretending to give it an extremely detailed investigation. "Now," he said, "are you a boy or a girl?"

"Right," Skylar said with a sigh, "do me a favor though. Get a blood sample. I want to check out this thing's DNA because," she looked it up and down, "I have a feeling there is something weird going on in there."

"Sure thing," he said with a wave.

#

Kurtis was locked down like Hannibal Lector or the Joker. Skylar almost couldn't help but feel a little bad for him. She was sure this wasn't what he had expected when they'd agreed to work with him. He gave her an inscrutable look as they led him down the hallway to his "consulting office" as the general called it. A prison cell is what it was.

"Is all of this really necessary?" she asked.

The guards escorting him said nothing in reply.

She followed them on the long trudge down the winding corridors until they came to the cell. Kurtis was wheeled into the room, his restraints were undone by one guard while the other kept his gun trained on him. He was shoved to the wall opposite the door, and the two guards backed out of the room before locking it and tucking the two keys away, in each of their pockets.

"He's all yours," one guard said in a gruff voice before sauntering off. The other guard posted himself by the door to the cell.

Skylar looked through the reinforced glass window into the cell. "Can he hear me?" she asked.

"Yes, he can," Kurtis said, before the guard could answer. "I will admit, this is not what I had in mind."

"They don't trust you. You can't blame them."

"And you?"

Skylar stared at the ground. "Try not to betray us again," she said, fists clenched. "The mission leaders will be by soon enough to begin planning our actions." She turned, excited to get back to Devonte and Akuma.

"Where will you be?"

Skylar froze.

"Skylar?"

"Busy." She exited the holding area.

#

Kurtis took a deep breath and sat cross-legged in the middle of the cell with his eyes closed. "So," he said, "are you going to kill me now or...?"

"Shut up," the guard said, "General's orders are to keep you alive."

"And Tempest's orders?"

He heard the guard shuffle uncomfortably outside his cell. "You live."

"She's going to use me to get information on their plans to counter her plans." Kurtis frowned. "Through you?"

"I was hand chosen for this mission."

"Just you?"

Silence.

"I'll take that as a yes," Kurtis said. "Are you the one who took my watch, by the way?"

The guard grunted in the affirmative.

"Do you think I could have that back? I'd like to know how much time I end up wasting here."

"Can't. You aren't allowed any technology."

"My watch is analog, look at it!"

He heard the guard's sharp sigh, and the sound of rustling. "Brown leather band?"

"That's the one."

"It's got a lot of buttons for an analog watch."

"It's a very expensive watch. Maybe a bit above your paygrade. You're welcome to mess with all the buttons to ensure there is nothing high-tech about any of them." *Please be as stupid as I assume you are.*

An irritated grunt was all the response he got, so now he just had to wait. Soon enough, a soft beeping rang out through the holding area.

"What is that noise?" the guard barked.

"It's just the alarm." Kurtis smirked to himself. "It'll go off soon enough."

There was a loud buzzing sound, and the smell of ozone filled the air. The guard let out a choked gurgle. Kurtis heard him collapse to the ground. The scent of burning flesh wafted over the top of the ionized air. Kurtis let out the breath he'd been holding. *This won't curry me any favors with the people here*, he thought. "Hey! If anyone can hear me, I think this guard just died!"

The general, whom he'd met once, rounded the corner in conversation with an older man, Raymond, Kurtis remembered, and the female soldier he'd taken in with Skylar, whose name he couldn't place. The general froze when she saw the dead guard and Kurtis in the cell looking completely placid. Her face immediately contorted into rage.

"Wait, wait, wait," Kurtis said, holding up his hands and instinctively backing away from the glass screen. "He was with Tempest."

"Why the hell should I believe you?" General MacPherson slammed her hand on the window. "That's another one of my people you've killed."

"Actually…"

"Don't you dare get smart with me."

"Yes…ma'am." Kurtis swallowed hard. The general had not been this frightening the first time he met her. "You want proof? Okay. By the looks of him, he's just a peon. All of them have the Japanese character for 'substitute' on their backs. Check him."

The general's suspicious glance switched back and forth between Kurtis and the dead guard. She made no move to check him.

"I'll check," Raymond said, walking over to the body.

"What if it's a trap?" the female soldier said.

"I'm sure it's not, Ashleigh," Raymond said, eyeing Kurtis for any indication to the contrary. He leaned over the body and rolled the man over, stripping off his body armor, and lifting his shirt. There, in sweeping calligraphic strokes were the two kanji that Raymond assumed must mean "substitute". "He has the mark," Raymond said.

The general's face twitched with rage. "Lieutenant Greenwood. Organize a check for everyone in the base. Anyone with that tattoo or anyone who refuses to be checked, throw them in a cell."

"General?"

"Did I stutter, Lieutenant?"

"No," Greenwood said, "I'll get right on it."

"Inspector Dehane," General MacPherson said, backing away from the cell window. Her face tightened in an obvious attempt to control her fury. "I leave the interrogation to you."

"I thought I was working with you guys on this," Kurtis said.

The general gave a humorless smile. "That would be in your best interest. If you'll excuse me, I have an operation to run."

"That just leaves me and you," Raymond said. He searched the area for a chair and found one behind a nearby desk. He dragged it over to the cell window and sat down, stretching his back in the process.

"Did you actually kill her sister?" Kurtis asked.

"I'm supposed to be asking *you* questions," Raymond pulled out a pack of caffeine gum and put a piece in his mouth. "I haven't slept properly in a while," he said. "But no, I did not kill Ms. Zhang. In fact, I tried to save her life." He closed his eyes for a minute. "Death before dishonor she told me as she fell into the churning sea below."

"You didn't strike me as a killer."

"I'd rather not be, if I can afford it." Raymond said. "But that's not why we're here. Please, if you will, Ms. Ming's plans?"

INTERLUDE V

Darkness. Movement. Birth. Inkanyamba knows it's happening. Here. Now. In the dark, saline sea. She had brought the storm and saved their lives, and now it was their time. The ocean streams around her, bristling with life, but barbed with death. Sharks rush past, pursuing the multitudes of fish she feels, pulsing in the water with each twitching forward push. Her back burns. The eggs stuck there are tearing off, floating into the water. She hears every heartbeat of her myriad children kickstart, pulsing in a chorus of percussion. The first one tears its way out and swims back down to join her, landing on her back and sinking its claws into her flesh to hold on. Then the next. And the next until finally all her children are present. Inkanyamba roars, a scream of exuberance that churns the water and frightens away all manner of sea life. Her children follow suit, sucking in that first breath of sea water and crying out alongside their mother. She appraises them. They look nothing like her, but they are hers. She can smell it on them. Her own scent, and that of their father.

The children bite into her back, tearing little bits of flesh, and pawing at the wounds. They are hungry, she knows. Her nest, where lay the corpse of their father, their first meal, is not far from here. She snaps at them, and they stop their biting. A shark, drawn by the scent of blood approaches, and is easily devoured by a pack of her children. The rest pine for the scraps. She calls to them and they return to her. Her powerful tail moves like the waves and propels her forward, her wings gliding through the water as easily as through air. They cling to her, but several drift off, snatched up by the water's unrelenting force. She doesn't go back for them.

Inkanyamba rises from the water and climbs her way up the slope of the island to the ruins that make her nest. Vornax's remains lay amidst a patch of dried blood and discarded remains.

She slumps and allows her children to disembark. They leap, howling and screaming, descending like a swarm over the decaying carcass, ripping, tearing, and gorging themselves on the flesh. Inkanyamba watches, surveying the nest and her spawn. A sound overhead calls her attention. One of the flying creatures from before hovers above, its spinning wings beating the air with a pulsing thrum. It isn't making the whale noises, but she doesn't trust it. She knows what happened the last time this creature was involved, and here it is now, near her newborns. She won't have it. *Protect. Kill.*

She stretches out her long neck, feels the thrum of her electric heart pulse through her body, and opens her mouth. Concentrated electricity arcs from her mouth, a blue so pale it might as well be white. Her vision goes for a split second. She hears the explosion before she sees it, the creature plummeting to the ground and erupting in a ball of smoke and flames, still crackling with her electricity.

She sees more approaching, coming from the metal forest. These new creatures attack. They rain fire down on her and her children. The attacks do not hurt her, but her children scream in pain as several of them are blown to pieces by the assault.

Rage. It boils up inside of her. She lets it out in a scream that shakes the foundations of her island nest. Her mighty wings shudder with the force of their own strength as she lifts herself into the air.

Two faster creatures, silver winged streaks, roar towards her, unleashing more fire towards her nest. She catches the rain of fire with her own body, shrugging off the pain. One of the creatures clips her wing. It hurts her, but the creature careens to the ground and explodes on impact. The second one she burns from the sky with an arc of lightning, she whips it across the sky, dragging it into a nearby spinning sky creature. Its wings seize, locking in place, and it begins to dive towards the ocean below.

She scans the sky, swinging her head back and forth. Six spinning creatures, and four more silver screamers. Inkanyamba won't let them touch any of her children. The clouds above spark with her electric current. She feels a fresh rain begin. The first peal of thunder echoes above. She cries out over top of it, challenging her attackers. They accept.

Lightning arcs from her wings, turning the sky a blinding white. With a gust like a hurricane, she takes off towards them. The force of her flight sucks two spinning creatures into her wake, crashing them into each other in a shower of debris and fire. The screaming creatures rush her, spraying her body with burning pellets. She feels it, like tiny pin pricks on her skin. They pass her. She looks over her shoulder to see them bank and come around for another pass. She waits until they are right up on her and then…a thrash of her tail crushes through one. Her wings flare, stalling her in the air. She feels the second one collide with her adamantine scales. She drops back down to the ground below, devastating the metal forest around her. Giant structures crumble and crash to the ground, sending plumes of dust into the air. She lashes her tail around, completing the devastation and clearing a space for combat.

She whips around to face the remaining attackers. Two remaining silver wings and four spinners. She bares her teeth, feeling them slide out of her gums and lock into place. *Fight. Win. Kill.*

The silver wings roar away into the distance. She tracks them, ensuring they stay away from her nest. They do, and so she lets them live. The spinning creatures stay, they whir to life and the burning pellets resume for a moment. Then come the fireballs. Neither hurt her. The creatures stop their attack. They turn towards her nest.

Fear. Her shriek shatters all the remaining glass in the area, as she launches herself back to the sky. She rears her head to the sky and lightning courses from her throat up into the storm clouds. It courses through the sky, arcing and jumping before descending in four separate lightning bolts, each striking one of the helicopters to devastating effect. Four sparking fireballs plummet to the ground. Inkanyamba roars in triumph. She knows that she has won. Her children are safe.

Or are they?

She hears another noise. A high pitch whistling that grows louder each second. She sniffs the air. Her head swings from side to side. Scanning. Searching. She notices a black speck on the horizon. As the sound grows, so does the speck. She doesn't know what it is, but she senses the danger immediately.

Her jaw unhinges, and her frills stand on edge. Lightning strikes her body and courses along her spines, sparking across her scales. Her whole body is wreathed in lightning, and crackles with power.

The speck is near now. She can hear its roar, the sound of it rushing through the wind.

Danger.

A crack of thunder sounds as lightning arcs out from her mouth, dancing along the air and impacting the object directly on its nose. The noise is deafening, a sound like she has never heard before. Light, brighter and hotter than the sun, blinds her. She cannot see, she cannot hear, the air around her burns. The force of the explosion staggers her. The crumbled remains of buildings turn to dust in an instant. She feels scales ripped from skin. The pain is beyond anything she's ever felt. Her scream is drowned out by the roar of the flames.

CHAPTER 18

"What the hell was that?" General MacPherson shouted.

"That was a MOAB," a soldier shouted in response.

"Who authorized that?"

"The strike came from Warren Airforce Base in Colorado," said another soldier.

"Who's in charge there?"

"General Corden."

Dammit. "Get him on video call, now."

The screen flickered to life. General Corden's weathered face came into view, all hard angles and aged discipline. "Diane," he said.

"Marcelle. Care to tell me why you just dropped a MOAB on my city?"

"It should be obvious. Your people failed to take down the creature. We took matters into our own hands."

"You have no right to decide that!"

"Actually, I do."

"On whose authority?"

"The president's."

"You can't be serious. There's no way the president would authorize that kind of strike on American soil."

General Corden turned off screen. "Captain Sanders, send General MacPherson the document, please."

A message blinked onto the screen in the bottom right corner. It expanded to reveal a document stamped with the Presidential Seal. General MacPherson's eyes darted over the words with disbelief. It was all there.

"I presume that will be enough to confirm my statements."

General MacPherson clenched her jaw so tight she worried her molars would crack. "It does." She turned to her men. "Get me a status report on the creature, now."

"The smoke and debris are making it near impossible to get a read."

"Did I ask for excuses?"

"One of our drones is getting video and sound, but just barely. Putting it on screen."

To say the image quality was fuzzy would be an understatement. With all the dust swirling around from the explosion, hardly anything could be seen. The air in the room hung heavy, everyone waiting to see the outcome of the strike. A keening roar belted and blended with the sound of the static feedback.

"Is that…" General MacPherson clenched her fists.

On screen, General Corden's stony façade crumbled, and his eyes widened in shock as another roar, clearer this time, resounded through the video feed. As the dust cleared, the shape of Inkanyamba could be easily seen. And she was moving. The shadow was sluggish but still moving.

"It's still alive," General Corden said in a hushed tone.

General MacPherson's face went to stone. "And if it's still alive, soon enough it'll be fully healed."

"What?"

"Did you even research the creature?"

General Corden's face failed to hide his shock and offense taken. "I was ordered to launch a nuclear strike on a threat *by the president*."

"The creature known as Inkanyamba has the ability to regenerate any and all damage at an alarming pace so long as its body remains hydrated. Successive nuclear strikes *may* have been effective were the creature not right next to the goddamn water." Her calm disposition melted into shouting at the end. "Only a fool would strike without knowing their enemy."

It was General Corden's turn to grit his teeth.

General MacPherson suppressed the urge to smirk. *Now is the time for more important things than petty satisfaction.*

"Then we'll fire again," Corden said, "harder. We'll nuke the creature until it can't drag its charred, irradiated husk anywhere near the water."

"And what of the civilians?"

"San Francisco has long since been evacuated, correct?"

"What about the people in Las Vegas, and other neighboring states? The fallout would cause irreparable harm to hundreds of thousands of our own people." Her fingernails dug into the flesh of her hands, and she felt the first trickles of blood pool in her palms.

"The needs of the many outweigh the needs of the few. There are three-hundred million people in this country. If a few hundred thousand have to suffer for the good of the rest, so be it. This creature poses a threat to all American lives. I will act to preserve our nation."

Ice cold calm washed over General MacPherson. She folded her arms across her chest. "Prepare all anti-ballistic missile defense systems. From this moment forward, anything that enters our airspace without my authorization gets blown out of the sky. Do you understand?"

A resounding "Yes ma'am" echoed around the control room.

"What did you just say?" Corden's face went ashen with fury. "Interfering with acts of national security is treason. This order comes from the President of the United States."

"False."

"What?"

"The document you showed me has you authorized for a single strike *with a Massive Ordinance Air Blast*. Paragraph two, line four. Not two strikes, and not a nuke." General MacPherson allowed herself to smirk this time. "Unauthorized launch of nuclear weapons, especially on American soil...what do you think that will get you?"

Corden let out a sound halfway between choking and growling. The video feed cut out. General MacPherson relaxed and allowed her shoulders to slump.

"He seems nice." Lieutenant Greenwood stepped into place beside the general. "Aren't you worried he'll fire anyway, or just go and get an amendment from the president?"

"He won't risk his own neck by firing without authorization. And the president...well, there is a reason it took him this long to take any real action thus far."

"Congress?"

"Incompetence," MacPherson deadpanned.

Greenwood blinked away her surprise.

"This is no time for politics," MacPherson continued, "the president will undoubtedly authorize Corden's plan eventually. We have to take Inkanyamba down before then."

"How long?"

"A month would be generous." MacPherson' face turned grim. "Do you think your original plan could work with the right circumstances?"

"I would have to brainstorm again with Dr. O'Hara, but we have a more pressing matter I believe."

"More pressing than San Francisco becoming a nuclear wasteland?"

"Our drones scanning Inkanyamba's island nest have confirmed that she has given birth," Greenwood said plainly. "So, yes. If those things get loose…"

"How many?"

"At least a hundred."

MacPherson willed her jaw not to drop at the number. "One hundred Inkanyambas storming around the world?"

"Not quite. The offspring favor neither parent. They appear more like…reptilian hyenas. At their present size they stand about twice the size of a man."

The general rubbed her face. "Can *they* be killed easily?"

"I ordered a test strike. We learned two things. First, is that the creature has a great maternal instinct. Second, at present, the creature's scales have not hardened as to be invulnerable, nor do they seem capable of regeneration. Yet."

"Small victories."

"That being said, the wrath of the mother is something to behold."

"Yes, we all saw that."

Greenwood shuffled her feet. "If we want to take out the children it will have to be done covertly, and while the mother is expressly occupied. Or dead."

"You're suggesting—"

"Attack the nest, yes." Greenwood stood rigid and without looking at the general. "We need to send in a strike force."

"And simultaneously attack Inkanyamba?"

"We have to kill Inkanyamba, or she'll destroy everything in her rage."

General MacPherson scratched at the tight curls atop her head. "Well—"

A solider with a torn uniform and a haggard appearance skidded into the room. "General, ma'am, we, uh, have a situation in the hangar." He caught his breath for a moment. "You'll probably want to come see this."

#

"Please tell me that I am not seeing what I am seeing," the general said as she watched Devonte, Skylar, and four other men wrestling against cords holding the two-meter tall reptilian in place. Devonte's one-armed contribution was doing little to help the overall containment of the creature, but despite the pain contorting his face, he was doing his best to help.

"We gotta bolt these wires in place," Gunner shouted over the top of the creature's rebellious shriek. Just as they managed to get one bolt in place, the creature's thrashing ripped another out of the ground. By now, a circle of armed men had gathered around the ruckus, guns primed and ready to fire.

"I'm afraid I'm seeing exactly what you are, ma'am," Greenwood said with a sigh. "Goddamn it, Skylar."

The general turned a suspicious eye on her. "You know something about this?"

"Don't shoot him," Devonte shouted. "He's just scared."

Greenwood steeled herself. "Dr. O'Hara claimed to have permission to gather tissue and blood samples from Inkanyamba during our initial stratagem. Apparently, she brought back a little more than discussed."

"I see," the general said, stepping forward. "Would anyone care to explain to me what exactly is going on here?" Her words hung like icicles on her tongue.

The group had succeeded in pinning the snarling creature down. It let out a disgruntled grumble before settling down.

"We were trying to take some blood and tissue samples, and Akuma here," Skylar turned around, "Oh…"

MacPherson gave a frigid smile. "Oh indeed."

Skylar looked to Devonte for help. The young man half shrugged. She rolled her eyes and let out an exasperated sigh. "Such help. Wow." Skylar turned back to the general. "I'm not going to apologize for acting for the advancement of science," she said. "I will apologize for letting science rampage inside the hangar."

MacPherson scanned the large open space. "What's the damage?"

"None," Gunner said. "We were able to mostly pin him as soon as we realized he was fixin' to throw a fit." He paused. "Slippery bastard just managed to give us a bit of a fight."

The general nodded. "Are you aware that there are almost a hundred of these things crawling over the island formerly known as Alcatraz?"

"They all hatched?" Devonte asked. "I suppose that makes sense…eggs are laid and hatch in clutches." His eyes widened. "Did you say one hundred?"

"I did. And are you aware that the mother of these bastards seems to have one nasty protective streak in her?"

"No?"

"No." The general folded her arms behind her back. "Keep it secure."

Devonte and Skylar both blinked in bewilderment.

MacPherson took a brief moment to relish in their uncertainty. "As Dr. O'Hara stated, this is for the advancement of science. Not everyone in the military wants to shoot first and ask questions never."

"But with Inkanyamba…"

"Inkanyamba is a skyscraper-sized creature that has been actively threatening our nation. She needs to be destroyed." Her eyes flickered over to the pinned creature. "For now, this one can be wrestled into submission by two young adults and a cluster of welders. Low threat." Her face darkened. "But understand this: once it becomes a threat, it will be terminated without hesitation."

"About that," Devonte said, "Akuma here is…surprisingly docile. Almost like a cat. Like I said earlier, he only lashed out because we hurt him."

"What are you suggesting?"

"It's only my theory. I'll need to work with Skylar to truly determine the possibility, but given the fact that the creature seems to have imprinted on me when it hatched, and its general relaxed disposition, we may be able to…train him?"

"You want to make *that* your pet?" MacPherson resisted the urge to pull at her hair.

"We were actually thinking more like as a defensive measure," Skylar added.

"It's highly unlikely," Devonte continued, "that Inkanyamba will be the last kaiju threat we see. As unlikely it is that she was the first."

"Don't tell me that," the general said. "Please don't tell me that."

"Sorry," Devonte said, "but it's true. In fact, whatever caused Inkanyamba to wake up might lead to more awakenings."

"Or aliens," Skid interjected.

"Excuse me?" the general said, spinning on her heel. She fixed a look halfway between confusion and frustration.

Skid sputtered. "You know. If the aliens have been watching us all along, and they see that we can barely handle an overgrown moray, they might come on down with their probes and plans for world domination!"

The general was glad to see that even Devonte and Skylar were as taken aback as she was by the idea of an alien invasion. "All that aside," she said, "do you really think that we'll see more Inkanyambas?"

"More kaiju? Yes. More like Inkanyamba? Probably not, but maybe." Devonte punctuated his response with an exaggerated half shrug.

It was Greenwood's turn to ask a question. "But Inkanyamba woke up because we dropped an oil rig on her. We don't make a habit of that."

"That's most likely not what woke her up," Skylar said. "It was just the proverbial straw that broke the camel's back."

"Then what did wake her up?"

"My honest opinion?" Skylar asked. "Global warming."

"Or pollution," Devonte said.

"Or irradiation from nuclear waste."

"Or—"

"Okay," Greenwood said, "next time, just say you don't know."

The general clapped her hands together. "We don't have time for idle chatter and speculation. There. Is. A. Mission." She pointed at Devonte. "Can you train it?"

"Uh, yes?" Devonte said.

"Do it. O'Hara, help him."

"Yes, ma'am."

"Greenwood, is Brannigan able?" the general barked.

"If you ask him, yes."

"Get him to the briefing room. He and Raymond are going to lead the assault on the nest."

"You'll lead a task force in an improved version of the Las Vegas plan." The general smirked at Skylar. "I think I have an idea to failproof your plan, Doctor."

"Ma'am!" Greenwood snapped to attention and gave a full salute. "What about the prisoner?"

"Captain Dehane should be finishing up his interrogation as we speak. I'll have him meet us in the command center."

#

"They plan on capturing and enslaving several of Inkanyamba's children to create a monster army," Raymond said, "on top of their original plan to control Inkanyamba. Kurtis seems to think they will make an attempt during our next attack on the mother."

"Well then," General MacPherson said with a smirk, "for once we are ahead of the enemy. On two fronts, even."

Raymond quirked an eyebrow, glancing between the general and Greenwood.

"Devonte and Skylar have an infant creature in containment in the hangar," Greenwood said. She kneaded her forehead with her fist. "They're trying to train it like a pet."

Raymond couldn't help but let out a deep belly laugh. "That's…that's magnificent!" He wiped the corners of his eyes. "So that's one, what's the other?"

"A two-pronged attack," the general said tersely. "On Inkanyamba and the nest on Alcatraz Island."

Raymond nodded. "They'll never see us coming on the island. Kurtis claims to be their strategic mastermind. Without him, he seems confident Tempest's actions will suffer in quality." He paused. "I'd like to request being part of the Alcatraz Island assault force," he said.

"Already planned that way." She eyed him suspiciously. "Why?"

"On the off chance that Ms. Jia Ming is present I would like an attempt to explain the situation behind her sister's demise."

Greenwood gave him an incredulous look. "Are you insane? She wants your head on a pike."

The general held up a hand to quiet Greenwood. "And if she isn't inclined to listen?"

"I will do what I need to do to defend myself."

"Captain Dehane," General MacPherson narrowed her eyes and dropped her voice to a whisper, "if she is unwilling to cooperate, my men would shoot her dead. I expect the same from you."

A thin, somber smile crept across Raymond's face. "I'm afraid you have no jurisdiction over me or my actions. With all due respect of course." He watched the general's right eye twitch slightly before she turned to address the other soldiers in the room.

Greenwood pulled him aside and hissed, "What are you doing?"

"My duty is, and has always been, to serve and protect. I took this job *knowing* my life is on the line. But to resort to violence is always foolish, and wasteful." The sad smile reappeared on his face. "I won't shoot, ideally, ever. But if need be, I'll never shoot first."

"If you don't shoot first, these people will kill you."

"And that assumption has led to how many wars?"

Greenwood clenched her jaw. "Just come back to me, okay?" She wrapped her arms around his neck and pulled him in close. He could smell the vanilla shampoo in her hair. It brought a real smile to his face.

The door slid open behind them, and Brannigan sauntered in. "Oops. Sorry to interrupt…whatever's happening here," he said. "General, you called for me?"

"Captain. How are you feeling?"

"A couple of things click a bit louder than I'd like, but the world ain't spinning and breathing doesn't make me want to hurl quite as much. You got a mission for me?"

"I do."

"If it involves fist-fighting giants, I'm going to have to hard pass, ma'am."

"How about kaiju hunting?"

Brannigan glanced up at the screen, on which Inkanyamba had nestled down in a city-sized crater where a large portion of San Francisco had once been. "Found her."

"I don't appreciate a smart-ass, Captain."

"Yeah, you do, else I wouldn't still be here."

The general seethed silently. "You and a team will be going back to Alcatraz Island to exterminate Inkanyamba's newly hatched young. Spencer Chaplin will join you again, and this time you will be accompanied by Captain Dehane."

"And me," Arnett dropped his bag on the floor as he walked into the control room.

"You came back," the general said.

"I said I would."

"And I thought you wouldn't."

"I had to drive," he said. "After what happened in Vegas, the army guys weren't so keen on giving me a ride."

"Well that's practically a dream team right there," Brannigan said. "Who else?"

"No one else."

"Excuse me?"

"All remaining hands will be needed on deck to handle the assault on Inkanyamba, the incumbent threat of a secondary nuclear strike—"

"We were nuked? How did I not feel that?"

"Small bomb, and we're underground, and people will also be needed to guard the base, just in case. We've lost a lot of men, soldier."

"Four people against…a fuckton of baby's first kaiju? That's impossible."

The general held his gaze silently. "Jet, the welder has military experience. We can probably spare him."

"Ah. Five. Perfect." Brannigan grimaced.

"We make do with what we have, Captain. I have faith in you. Prep your team." She glanced at the video screen which indicated an incoming transmission. "I have to take a call."

Brannigan glanced at Raymond with a lazy smirk. "Ready to die, old-timer?"

"Always."

"So Zen," Brannigan scoffed. "Come on, Siddhartha, let's go find the others."

Raymond gave Greenwood one last look of longing and a wave before turning and exiting the command room. He'd barely made it a few steps down the hallway before Greenwood called out and jogged up to him. Before he could speak, she had him, her lips pressed against his, hands running through his hair. He returned her passion just as fervently. When they finally broke apart, all he could manage was, "Well then."

"Consider that a see you later," she said before jogging off to prepare for her portion of the mission.

"Goodbye," he whispered when she was no longer within earshot.

#

Don't think about him. Don't think about him. Don't think about him. Greenwood trudged her way back to the hangar. *He'll be fine.* She cleared her throat and focused on the general's newest addition to the dehydration plan. Industrial-sized heating coils used in the removal of moisture from grains. The copper coils would be set around the arches that pinned Inkanyamba and heated to the point that even rain would evaporate before touching her skin. It would also theoretically speed up the dehydration process.

"One kaiju raisin, coming up," she mumbled to herself, "I hope."

She watched as Gunner, Skid, Tungsten, and Bunk set about reforming the arches from their first attempt. When they finished, they'd wrap each structure in as much inch-thick copper tubing as possible.

"You're gonna have a problem with this though, lady," Gunner said as he scaled down from atop the structure. "Too hot."

"Too hot?"

"Steel won't be as strong. The bitch might just tear her way right through it."

Greenwood ran a hand through her hair. "Solutions?"

It was Bunk who spoke up. "Personally, I think we should make use of her weakened state to penetrate her limbs and pin her to the ground. Tungsten rods would probably work." He scratched his head thoughtfully. "It's brittle but she won't be able to move enough to break it."

"I got your Tungsten rod right here," Tungsten chuckled. "And it's damn good at penetrating."

His joke received an uproar of laughter from the other men. Greenwood pursed her lips.

"While the joke is funny," she said, "it's not really the time. Bunk, can you make those spikes happen?"

"It will definitely take more time, given the size, any order will have to be custom made."

"You have two days."

"I hope that's enough," he said.

"It better be."

He shrugged. "It's out of my control."

Greenwood opened her mouth to respond but realized that the man was taking everything she said literally. "Thank you," she said. "Your input may have saved this mission."

Gunner put a hand on his hip. "He just said it first," he griped. Then he grinned and said, "But he's right. That's our college grad for you, showing off that big brain." The group of men fell into another fit of laughter, Bunk included. Greenwood felt a smile creep at the corner of her lips.

"I'll leave you to your work," she said.

#

Kurtis had paced the length of his cell at least a hundred times and walked the perimeter just as many. Twenty steps across, eighty in total to complete the square. He was beginning to wonder if turning himself in had been a bad idea. Expecting them to trust him completely was out of the question, but he'd expected a little quid pro quo. Even if he did still plan to betray them. The fluorescent lights were threatening to give him a migraine. He shielded his eyes. The door to the holding area slammed shut, pulling him from his reverie.

"Finally," Kurtis fumed, "somebody!"

Skylar scowled. "Shut up. You don't get to be impatient."

"Oh, it's you." Kurtis visibly brightened at her presence and flashed her a winning smile. Skylar fidgeted uncomfortably at the gesture.

"They aren't going to let you out," she said.

His face dropped in mock disappointment. "What?"

"The general said that once this is done, you'll be handed over to be tried for crimes against humanity." Skylar stared at the floor. "That's me paraphrasing by the way. Her list went on for a long time."

"They're going to put me up for the death penalty." Kurtis' face went pale enough to match his hair. He ran his hand through the ashen strands with a nervous laugh. "You know, I never once considered I might get caught." His eyes drifted to meet Skylar's. "You have to help me."

Skylar took a startled step back. "Excuse me?"

"Skylar, they are going to kill me."

"You'll get a trial, and whatever they decide on to be your punishment...well that's that," she said, crossing her arms. "Justice."

"I don't deserve to die. Do *you* think I deserve to die for what I've done?"

"Kurtis, I don't *know* what you've done," she shouted. "You ran a fucking crime syndicate."

Kurtis' face steeled. "No."

"No?"

All of the panic had melted away from his face. The calm and in-control persona had returned. "Sorry. I've never experienced the fear of death before. It threw me off my game there for a second, but no, I'm not going to die. I'm going to escape." He stuck his fingers in his mouth, reaching as far back as he could.

"What the fuck are you doing?" Skylar panicked. "Someone," she shouted, "the prisoner is trying to escape."

Kurtis flashed her a furious glance as he ripped out a tooth from the back of his mouth. He twirled the loose molar between his fingers. "Do you happen to know what is behind this cell wall?" he asked, spitting blood to the floor.

Skylar didn't stop shouting for help. She fumbled for her phone, but realized she had no one's number who could come help. Her arms dropped to her sides.

"No? Pity," he said. "I would plug my ears if I were you." He pressed his back against the bulletproof glass panel, looking over his shoulder to be sure that Skylar had heeded his advice and chucked the molar at the cell's back wall. There was barely enough time for him to cover his own ears, and even through his fingers the deafening sound threatened to blow out his eardrums. He coughed through the debris and brushed the fragmented rubble from his clothing.

"Skylar," he said, turning back to face her. Where he'd had the panel to keep him upright, Skylar had tumbled onto the floor, and was staring up at him from the ground. "I do love it when you look up at me like that," he said with a smirk. He blew her a kiss. "Afraid I have to go now. We'll see each other again."

By now, soldiers flooded into the holding area. Greenwood stormed in behind them.

"Get that cell open," she ordered. It was too late however, Kurtis had vanished into the walls of the compound. The soldiers filed in after him. "Don't worry," Greenwood said, "they'll find him."

"No," Skylar said, "they won't."

Greenwood gave her a curious look. "They'll sweep the entire compound, and if they can't bring him back alive…"

"I don't want to hear it," Skylar said. "This man ran an organization that nobody knew about until a few months ago. He'll be long gone."

"You shouldn't fall for a man like him," Greenwood said, putting a hand on Skylar's shoulder. "He's just another criminal."

Skylar brushed her hand off. "I'm not falling for him, damn it, I just…he's clever and smart. Smarter than us. I respect that." She clenched her fists. "And I hate it. And I hate him."

One of the guards came back. "Ma'am, there's no sign of him in the walls and we've received no visual confirmation from the rest of the compound." His frustration ran through the creases in his face. "He's gone."

Greenwood glanced at Skylar who shrugged in response. "If what he said about wanting to see me again is true, we'll have another opportunity to catch him."

"The general will be furious," Greenwood said.

"Isn't she always?"

"You know what?" Greenwood jammed a finger into Skylar's chest. "You're talking about respecting that con man, but you know who you should respect? General Diane *fucking* MacPherson. She's kept a level head during an unprecedented catastrophe, managed to evacuate the city of San Francisco in nearly a moment's notice, and has gone along with you and your friends' plans despite everything about you two screaming that she shouldn't."

Skylar pursed her lips, then exhaled. She counted to ten. "You're right," she said finally. "I'm sorry."

Greenwood relaxed as well. "It's fine, just think before you criticize the person with the world on their shoulders."

"Thank you for your support," General MacPherson said, stepping into the room with her hands folded behind her back. She glanced at Skylar. "Both of you. I teared up." Her eyes slowly made their way back to the now empty cell. "Our prisoner?"

"Gone," Greenwood said.

"He had a bomb in his teeth," Skylar said. "Who does that?"

"Spies, terrorists, mafia," MacPherson said. "I ordered the guard who brought him here to check, but it turned out he was Tempest." She sighed and the relaxation of her face betrayed the sleepless nights and stress that had been eating away at her. "Guess he never got rechecked."

"I think he's going to keep his word," Skylar said. "He said he doesn't want to die. Tempest would kill him if he went back."

The general regarded her with narrow eyes. "An organization can be predicted, and given the right circumstances and talent, controlled. A rogue element on the other hand is *always* a fucking problem."

"Right," Skylar said.

"Ma'am, she had nothing to do with his escape," Ashleigh said.

"Why were you in here, Dr. O'Hara?" MacPherson asked.

Skylar straightened. "I came to tell him your decision on his fate—"

"My *confidential* decision, the knowledge of which, I assume, prompted his escape?"

"Yes."

The general nodded. "Please return to the hangar with Devonte and continue your work on pacifying the creature. And Dr. O'Hara...if you jeopardize my mission or the safety of this nation again, I will have you tried right alongside that white-haired son of a bitch." She didn't look at Skylar when she spoke, but her seriousness dripped from every word. "Lieutenant, I believe you also have business to attend."

The two women made their excuses and apologies and exited. In the hallway, Greenwood stopped Skylar.

"I'm going to nip this right now," she said.

"What?" Skylar didn't look her in the eye.

"This whole thing. His escape. It's not your fault."

"You heard the general—"

"Yes, I did, I also know where she's coming from. But listen to me, he came into custody with a bomb in his teeth. He planned to escape from the start. We weren't giving him what he wanted. He'd have figured it out eventually and then no one would have been there to bring help."

"You would have heard the explosion."

"Yes, but you called for us before the bomb went off."

"And it didn't help at all."

Greenwood sighed. "But it could have been the difference between him escaping and him being caught. Not your fault he's as slippery as he is slimy."

Skylar chuckled at that. "He's a fucking sleaze."

"That he is," Greenwood said, "and you're better off without him. Now go to the guy who really cares about you and help him feed his overgrown cat."

"Devonte? No, he doesn't think of me that way…he thought I was a guy for seven years apparently!"

Greenwood shrugged. "Call it a hunch."

"You're in a much better mood now that you and Raymond are official, you know?"

"Don't you start," Greenwood said, her icy demeanor returning before cracking again into a laugh. "Get back to the hangar before you actually make me like you." She gave Skylar an affectionate shove.

"Isn't that where you're headed too?"

Greenwood paused for a moment. "Oh, yeah."

"Give me a five-minute head start so we don't have to walk awkwardly down the hall together?" Skylar asked.

"That sounds good, now go."

CHAPTER 19

The creature was smarter than Devonte had expected, the past two days had proven that time and again. With positive reinforcement in the form of steak or tuna, Akuma was motivated to learn simple commands.

"Stay," he said, holding up the piece of raw meat in a gloved hand.

Akuma, who had been approaching what he thought was his next meal, paused and perched himself back on his haunches, head cocked to the side. A low rumble, purring Devonte called it despite Skylar's constant reminder that reptilians lack the necessary organs to actually purr, came from his chest. Devonte assumed it conveyed happiness, since there had yet to be a negative response associated with the noise.

"Good boy," Devonte said before tossing the meat at the large drake.

Akuma caught it midway and gulped it down without chewing. He let out a satisfied sound, a cross between a bark and a honk.

Skylar pushed her chair back from the makeshift computer desk they'd set up and said, "I have cool news. Can't say it's good, but it's cool."

"Hit me."

She walked over and slugged him affectionately in the arm. "Akuma's regenerative factor is slowly starting to kick in," she said. "It's nowhere near the level of his mother's yet, but I imagine soon enough he'll be just as hard to kill."

"But we're not going to have to kill him, right?"

"The training seems to be going well, so here's hoping," she said.

Devonte picked up the small sidearm he kept at his workstation. "There's also this," he said, firing at the creature's side. Akuma recoiled at the noise, but the bullet fell harmlessly to the ground at his feet. "Sorry, buddy." He shrugged at Skylar. "Bulletproof. His scales hardened."

"Drawing blood just got five times harder."

"Ah," Devonte said, waving his hand dramatically, "I considered the possibility and installed a port beneath his scales before they hardened. Did it while you were out—" he floundered and almost said, "with Kurtis". Instead he finished with "and about".

"And you say you're only good with computers," Skylar chided, not noticing his hesitation.

"A good programmer plans for weird edge cases."

"Do you apply computer logic to everything?"

"It's served me well so far."

"Even with the ladies?" She gave him a wry smile.

Devonte was glad that his face's complexion wouldn't give away his embarrassment. "Not so much."

"Seems like faulty logic then," she said, striding over and giving him a smug look.

"Well, I mean, I—"

His sentence was cut short by Akuma letting out a dry choking sound. The two of them wheeled to see the creature writhing and scratching at his throat. A strange whimper filled the makeshift research station.

"Is he choking?" Skylar asked.

"He always gulps down his meals and he's never choked before." Devonte rushed to grab his chair and propped it up in front of Akuma. "Open up," he said, reaching for the creature's mouth. Akuma snapped at him, narrowly missing Devonte's arm. "That's new."

"Maybe you should get down from there," Skylar said.

"I'm not going to let him choke," Devonte shouted. He held up his hands and tried to pacify Akuma in the way he always did. "Let me help," he said, his voice calm and even. "Open your mouth." He opened his own mouth wide to demonstrate what he wanted.

Skylar stood on the side and watched the events unfolding when something caught her eye. Akuma's tail was sparking with blue lightning as it thrashed about. Fissures between the scales emitted a light that grew in intensity from a muted blue to almost white in color. As she watched, she felt the temperature in the room rise. She turned to Devonte, mouth hanging open as she realized what was happening, but the words wouldn't come out.

Akuma made another choking sound.

"What's wrong?" Devonte asked the creature.

The next few seconds were a blur. She bolted at Devonte, knocking him from the chair and audibly knocking the wind out of him. The words "what the fu—" were drowned out by a sound like thunder. A beam of energy so hot she thought the skin would melt from her bones erupted from Akuma's mouth, vaporizing the space where Devonte's face had been just a few seconds prior. Akuma reacted just as surprised as they had, panicking and jerking its head upward. The energy that had melted a hole in the ground a few yards away now burned through the tent canopy and the ceiling of the hangar. Akuma held this position for what felt like hours before the light around its tail faded, and the beam grew weaker and dimmer until all that remained was a sound like a gas leak that trickled off into silence.

A wreath of electricity coiled around Akuma's head, which he shook away in irritation. He blinked, that thin reptilian film glazing his eyes momentarily, and turned to look at her and Devonte toppled and tangled together in a mixture of horror and confusion. He scratched at his throat again, grumbled and settled himself on the ground. Almost immediately his breathing slowed, and he was fast asleep.

"That's very new," Devonte broke the silence, repeating his earlier sentiment. He looked down at Skylar who lay pressed against him, head turned to stare at the creature. She smelled like cherry and disinfectant. He pushed the thought from his mind. *Not the time,* he thought, then, with a hint of sadness, *not a chance.* He cleared his throat, drawing her attention back to him. "Guess we're even on the whole saving each other thing, huh?"

"Yeah, I guess so," Skylar said. It took a second, but she also realized that her body was practically draped across his. She leapt up, face a red beacon of embarrassment.

There was an awkward pause, which Skylar eventually broke by saying, "I suppose we shouldn't be too shocked that Akuma is capable of discharging some kind of energy since both of his parents did it." She extended a hand to Devonte.

"I'm not shocked by that," Devonte said, gripping her arm and pulling himself up. He made no comment about the fact that he landed on his injured shoulder, or that the pain had turned his vision blurry. "I'm shocked that I almost lost my head to said discharge."

"You're welcome," Skylar said, then gasped. "You're bleeding."

Devonte glanced down at his shoulder. "Yeah, it does that when things get too rowdy. I'll clean it up after we make sure Akuma's alright."

Gunner and Skids burst into the research tent. "What in the goddamn hell..." they said, practically in unison.

"...is going on?" Gunner finished as he noticed the molten hole in the concrete hangar floor and the still burning roof of the tent. He craned his neck and saw the hole in the ceiling that practically dripped down to the floor below. His eyes scanned down the tent landing on Devonte, his shoulder now slick with fresh blood, and the deer in headlights look that he and Skylar both shared.

"Well fuck me sideways," Skids said, letting out a low whistle. He looked at Akuma. "That thing do all this?"

"Yeah," Devonte said, struggling to his feet. Skylar lent him a helping hand. "Puberty is hard."

"All kinds of discharge," Skylar said.

The two of them couldn't contain their laughter and broke down into fits of it, clutching their sides and doubling over.

"I almost died," Devonte said, still cackling. "And you're making jokes."

Skylar put a hand on his good shoulder for stability. "I'm sorry," she said, "the setup was too perfect."

The two men stared at the cackling researchers with a mixture of fear, concern, and a side of confusion. They gave each other a look.

"I think they've lost it," Skids said. "The stress was too much."

"It's the shock," Gunner said. "Nerves."

"We're fine," Devonte said in between deep heaving breaths. "Just..."

"Just give us a second," Skylar finished.

"Okay, okay," Devonte said finally catching his breath. "I'm good. I'm good." He turned to Skylar. "You good?"

She coughed, sputtered, and then steadied herself. "Yeah." Another deep breath. "Yeah, I'm good."

They turned and regarded Akuma, who slept soundly.

"First time is always exhausting," Devonte said, threatening to send Skylar into another laughing fit. She controlled herself enough to prevent a full-fledged breakdown.

"You gonna muzzle that thing?" Skids asked, interrupting the laughter.

"No," Devonte said, offended. He regained a more serious composure.

"We're trying to keep him as placid as possible," Skylar said, "any restraints beyond the few he seems comfortable with at the moment may trigger a negative response."

"Like firing a death ray all throughout our hangar?" Gunner asked.

"From what I can tell that was more of an overproduction. Like how baby rattlesnakes can't control how much venom they inject," Devonte said.

"That's actually a myth," Skylar corrected, "but given Akuma's alarm it does seem like it wasn't intentional. I don't think *he knew* he could do it."

"Is the rattlesnake thing really a myth?" Devonte asked.

"Yeah. Babies have less venom," Skylar said. "Basically, now that he knows about it, he should be able to regulate it." She noticed the skeptical look on the two men's faces. "Biologist," she said, gesturing at herself. "Welders," she said, gesturing at them. "Trust me."

"I guess baby skunks don't spray, right," Skids said. He shrugged.

"Let's get back to work," Gunner said, taking in the devastation one last time. "The lieutenant's already on our ass. Wants to mobilize within the hour." He gave Skylar and Devonte a once over. "Try not to bring the house down on us."

Devonte scratched his head with a laugh. "We'll do our best."

#

Brannigan cursed as he descended into the sewer system for the second time in the past few months. The stink of rot and excrement hadn't left his nostrils from the last time. He barely reacted while the detective and younger soldier coughed and choked on the sickening fumes.

"Come on kid, we basically just got back from here," Brannigan shouted to the soldier climbing down just below him.

"Still smells like shit," Chaplin replied, "and some other less pleasant things."

Raymond pulled the collar of his trench coat over his mouth and nose. "Like an open grave."

"Lot of experience with that, copper?" Brannigan looked up at the man above him.

"More than I'd care to remember," came the reply.

Brannigan realized he didn't have a response to that answer. "Cool," he said. "Or…not cool." The rifle hung heavy around his shoulders. His feet touched down on the slick tunnel walkway. "So I've got bad news," he said.

"You mean aside from the mission we're walking into," Arnett said, his voice carrying down from the top of the scaling rope.

"*Wading* is probably the more accurate term for what we will be doing. The path here doesn't lead to Alcatraz, but," he shined his light on the sluggish brown river that oozed its way past them, "that does."

"Fuck," Chaplin said.

"I hate everything about that," Arnett agreed.

"You're the one who told the general you wanted to help in any way you could," Brannigan said, grunting with the exertion of climbing down into the murky pit. "What about you, Jet? Anything witty to say?"

"We're in deep shit," came the welder's reply.

Raymond cast a disgusted look at the liquid, though he hesitated to call it that. "Glad I wore layers."

"Hope you bastards are up-to-date on your vaccines." Brannigan cranked the bolt on his rifle and flicked the safety off. "Now get in the water."

The sensation of jumping down into the sludge was worse than anything Brannigan could have imagined. They didn't splash, they glopped into the mixture. It was his turn to retch. *This is going to be a long walk*, he thought.

The sewage path was much less of a straight shot to the island than the service tunnel. He pulled out his map and looked at the winding path they had to take. Flood deposits, drainage pits, and much more meant circumnavigating essentially the entire bay before looping back and emerging from the maintenance room in the remains of the prison. *All while hunting down baby dragons.* He glanced over his shoulder at his four compatriots.

"Fuck me," he hissed. His flashlight beam illuminated the dark tunnel. *Not to mention Tempest possibly lurking around every shit-soaked corner.* He noticed that Jet held his finger on the trigger of his rifle. "Trigger safety," he called over, "and keep the gun down."

Jet apologized, lowering the weapon. "Coast guard," he said, "never actually used one of these."

Brannigan gave him a quick tutorial, cursing in his head the entire time. When he finished, he said, "Got it? That's about as simple as I can make it."

"Well enough to point and shoot," Jet said.

"Which way do we go first?" Chaplin said, sweeping the dank sewer intersection with his flashlight.

Brannigan checked the GPS device on his wrist. "East, for a while."

Chaplin aimed his beam down the right path. "Well, it looks no worse than any of the rest."

"I'll take point," Brannigan said, "Jet, up with me, don't need you shooting us in the back. Chaplin and Sanderson take rear. Detective, you're in the middle." He looked down at the revolver primed in Raymond's right hand. Brannigan had insisted he take an assault weapon, but he'd refused vehemently. He had no training with the weapon and no desire to learn. The revolver had served him well thus far, he said, and he wouldn't replace it for anything.

"Well then, let's get started," Raymond said, rubbing his back.

They walked in silence, stopping every now and then to listen for the sounds of any lurking threats. There never was anything, but the nature of their mission had them on edge. They'd been walking for nearly an hour when the first thing went awry. Brannigan rounded a corner and spotted one of the newborn creatures only a few yards away. It looked up when it heard him gasp, a noise he cursed himself for making. The creature immediately bristled, its scales raising and sticking out like spiked mail.

"I don't see any others," Chaplin said. "Looks like it's alone."

"Take it down," Brannigan roared as the creature charged them. Even with suppressers on their rifles, the sound was unbearable in such tight quarters. The muzzle fire lit up the dark space as bullets pounded into the rigid scales armoring the creature's body and clinked to the ground.

Jet sprayed a volley of bullets that decorated the wall behind the creature, missing its body entirely. Chaplin moved up alongside him getting direct hits along the creature's side.

"It's like shooting a tank," Chaplin said pushing Jet aside, leaving him just enough time to roll out of the creature's razor-sharp reach.

"Tanks don't have teeth," Brannigan said, unloading another burst of gunfire on the creature from behind. It whirled to face him with a snarl.

"My gun isn't doing shit," Arnett said. He ducked to avoid the sweep of the creature's tail. "Watch out, Cade."

"Care to join in, old timer?" Brannigan felt the wind leave his lungs as the tip of the creature's tail caught him in the ribs, flinging him against the wall. He slid down into the grey water, soaking halfway up his chest.

Raymond stood away from the action, his revolver aimed carefully at the creature. "Face it this way and then hold still."

Arnett opened fire on the creature as it stalked towards Brannigan. It turned to face him, teeth bared malevolently. "Well, it's facing you now," he said. "And I'm definitely sitting still for a bit."

The burst of noise from the revolver echoed throughout the sewer like thunder. An inhuman shriek of pain followed. The creature reared back on its hind legs, scratching at its face before toppling over backwards and slamming into the ground. It twitched a few more times before finally falling still. Brannigan saw the gaping wound where its left eye had once been, now pouring purple blood to the already slick surface below. He looked at Raymond who had lowered the gun and was now staring at the dead creature.

"The eye was the first time we hurt the mother. I assume her size and complete healing ability is why it didn't make contact with the brain and kill her. Apparently, it works on these." He stepped around the body and offered a hand to Brannigan, helping him up.

"Could've used that information a little sooner," the captain said, rubbing his side. "But I'm not bitter, that's one demon down."

"Demon?" Raymond asked.

"The kid named the one back at base Akuma. It's Japanese for demon. So I call these little bastards demons."

"I suppose that make sense," Raymond said.

"What, everyone else gets to name a monster, but the minute I do, I get shit for it?"

Chaplin chimed in. "I think no one would have expected you to care what we called these things. You know, more of a 'doesn't matter what we call them 'cause they're going to be real dead real soon' kind of guy," he said, slipping into an impression of Brannigan in the process.

Raymond nodded, doing his best to stifle a smirk. "I do like the sentiment though. These are lesser demons compared to our Akuma. You put a lot of thought into that?"

"Alright, fuck you guys," Brannigan said, "let's just try and wrap up this mission without me putting bullets through your eyes."

"I think we should discuss something important," Chaplin said, changing the subject. "There are a hundred of these things crawling around here. His revolver has six—"

"Five," Raymond corrected.

"Five shots left." He let the statement stand as its own question.

"We're going to do a whole lot of suffocation," Brannigan said setting his pack down on the ground. He pulled out several explosives and set them on the ground next to several unmarked containers.

"Drown them? But they can survive underwater."

"Nope," Brannigan said. "The dy-nerd-mic duo said that the gills on the side of their head only kind of work. They're more like dolphins. Limited underwater breathing with a need to resurface for air. The little demons take after their father it seems. He didn't like the water much either."

"So we're gonna blow the retaining wall and all possible escape routes with bombs to fill the nest with water," Arnett said. "So what's in those containers?"

"I'm glad you asked," Brannigan said, tossing one at the other man. "Glue bombs!"

Arnett fumbled with and dropped the container into the murk. "What the hell, man? What if it went off on me?"

"It's more likely to go off from hitting the ground," Brannigan said.

Arnett stepped warily away from the container which rested on a thick film on the surface of the sludge. "So, glue bombs."

"Effectively, they're grenades that, instead of shrapnel, coat the surrounding area in a quick drying cement," Brannigan explained. "Dries almost instantly."

"I didn't think we had anything like that," Chaplin said. "You raid someone's secret stash?"

"I made them," Brannigan said. He walked over to where Arnett dropped the adhesive bomb and knelt down to pick it up and put it in his pack.

"You made them?"

"Well not the cement solution, I outsourced for that but the combining that with the exploding stuff, yeah, that was me." He realized that the other three men had gone completely silent and looked up to see them all staring at him. "What? I like tinkering."

"That's brilliant, man," Arnett said, clapping him on the shoulder in excitement.

"Thanks. I can't wait to test them."

Arnett's face dropped. "What?"

"No test like a field test," Brannigan said, strapping the pack on his back and setting off in the direction they needed to go. "Keep up."

Arnett looked at the other two men. "Is he always like this?"

Jet shrugged and jogged after Brannigan.

"While I don't generally approve of recklessness," Raymond said, "his often seems to pay off."

"There's a reason he's one of the top soldiers," Chaplin said. "And to think, he was supposed to be here on vacation, and he hasn't complained about it once."

"Vacation?" Arnett asked.

"Supposedly he just got back from a tour in the Middle East. California was his rest spot before the next one."

Raymond made sure to keep a measured distance, so Brannigan couldn't hear their conversation. "He never said so much as a word about it."

"Not his style, I guess." Chaplin shrugged. "He makes his jokes, but he takes his job seriously."

"Respect," Arnett said.

"You four better not be hanging back in hopes that I get attacked first," Brannigan called back.

"We're right on your ass," Arnett said. "Don't worry."

"I could only hope," came Brannigan's reply.

They walked in a loose formation, checking corners and darkened tunnels for any signs of life. Eventually they began to hear the roar of rushing water and came upon a massive drain. A wireframe bridge stretched across the gap, leading out from the sludge channel from which they emerged. All around, mud-colored water poured from openings, and rushed down into the darkness below.

"So I just looked down," Arnett said, "and I really wish I hadn't."

Brannigan scoffed. "If you can't see the bottom, at least you can be sure you'll die on impact."

"Is that supposed to make me feel better?"

"The alternative is hitting the bottom, breaking everything, and literally wallowing in pain and shit for God knows how long." He took a cautionary step onto the rusted bridge. It creaked under his weight, but he didn't plummet into the darkness.

Arnett swallowed hard. "Fair."

"One at a time, just to be sure," Brannigan said. The bridge creaked with each of his heavy footsteps. It felt like forever but eventually he made it across. "Next," he called across. "Arnett."

"If I die—"

"You can haunt me so long as you pay rent," Brannigan said.

The police officer frowned in confusion and disbelief, shook his head silently while muttering under his breath, and took his first step onto the bridge. "Oh, I hate everything about this." Halfway across, the bridge made an angry groaning noise as it settled into place. "Please God, don't let me die soaked in shit and other people's garbage," he said.

"Hurry up," Brannigan said.

"Will you hush," Arnett said, taking three steps in a hurry, and then sprinting the rest of the length of the bridge. He pressed his palms into his knees, then flashed a quick thumbs up. "Made it."

Raymond went next, followed by Jet. Chaplin went last. His first step made the whole structure shudder. Brannigan watched the man suck in a deep breath. Chaplin took another hesitant step, to the continued protest of the bridge. The two locked eyes, and then the bridge dropped. It swung free from its back hinges, sending Chaplin sliding down to its bottom.

Brannigan rushed to the edge of the pit and looked down. "Chaplin!"

Chaplin hung from the bottom, white knuckling on the rusted metal brackets. A jagged piece embedded itself through the palm of his hand. "Definitely going to need a tetanus booster after this," he said with a nervous chuckle. "Damn, that stings."

"Can you climb up?"

"I was lucky to grab hold like this. My hands are fucked."

The bridge creaked against its last two support brackets.

"I don't think this is going to hold on much longer." There was no panic in his voice. He spoke like he was talking about the weather or the daily news.

Shit. Brannigan began to unspool the rappelling rope they used to enter the sewer.

"Brannigan!" Chaplin shouted.

"What?"

"Stop."

Brannigan froze. "What did you say?"

"It's not worth it."

"My squad is worth it," Brannigan replied, "every time." He handed one end of the rope to Arnett. "Tie this to something stable."

Arnett found a thick lead pipe and looped the cord around it, tying it in the tightest knot he knew. He posted up next to the pipe and gripped the rope tightly for extra support. Raymond took hold of the rope halfway between the pipe and the ledge.

"Brannigan, you still there?" Chaplin's voice just barely sounded over the rushing water.

"Shut up, I'm trying to rescue you."

"If you come down here and the bridge goes, you're going to drop with me."

"Cable's tied to a pipe on the wall. I'll be fine."

"We both know that a sewage pipe can't hold two grown men."

"God damn it, Chaplin, I'm—"

"Here I'll make it easy for you," Chaplin said. The bridge clanged against the brick walls of the drainage pit and shuddered one last time. Brannigan's blood ran cold. He felt his heart pounding away behind his eardrums. The rappelling cable spilled from his hands and into the slime infested water. He took one nervous step towards the ledge, then another, hoping that what he knew had happened hadn't actually happened. His legs carried him to the ledge, but he couldn't bring himself to look down. He felt a hand on his shoulder.

"He's gone," Raymond said, "you don't have to look."

But Brannigan knew he had to, or he'd never forgive himself. He peered over the ledge into the abyss below and saw…nothing. No Chaplin, just the rushing waterfalls of sewage and darkness. "That's four," he said. "Four too many."

Arnett stepped forward. "If you need a minute—"

"We have a mission," Brannigan said, turning away from the pit. "One we have to complete. Leave the cable, we won't need it." He pretended not to notice the other men's looks of concern as he walked into the tunnels. *Mission now, mourn later.*

Within an hour, they began to hear animalistic sounds echoing throughout the tunnels. Brannigan motioned for them to stay low and stay quiet. He crept forward, sticking to the shadows as much as possible.

The tunnel opened into a wide chamber with a high ceiling. Demons crawled over every open surface in the chamber. They padded across the slick stone floor, several clung to the ceiling, digging their talons into the brick surface.

Brannigan scanned the area from his hidden location. "I count five exits."

"And I count hundreds of demons," Arnett said.

"We knew that before we came."

"It's just a lot to take in in-person."

Brannigan nodded. "Yeah."

"How have they not smelled us?" Jet asked.

"Smell your sleeve," Brannigan said, and smirked to himself as he heard the other man quietly retch at the scent coming off his own clothes. "We smell like shit. Just stay quiet and stay hidden."

"What is the next step?" Raymond asked.

"We observe, and we wait for your girlfriend to tell us their mother won't smash us to pieces so we can start our attack," Brannigan said.

#

This was too many times in too many days that Greenwood had found herself in the air. On the plus side, her crash landing had stripped away the bigger portion of her panic. Surviving had made her brave. On the other hand, the portion that remained was a deep-seated dread. Her mind reeled about everything that could go wrong, and the consequences if it did. The thoughts competed in intensity only with the steady pulse of the helicopter blades overhead.

"We have full visual," the pilot said, "the creature appears to be recovering."

The rain had stopped, but water had gathered in the puddle after the explosion. Inkanyamba lay partially submerged in the brown liquid, taking deep, heaving breaths. Greenwood couldn't hold her gasp as she took in the sight.

The damage from the bomb was stark against her murky scales. Angry red radiation burns pulsed and oozed across her entire body as whatever strange science brought her into existence continued to knit her back together. Her face was hardly recognizable, stripped of flesh almost down to the bone. Greenwood watched with morbid fascination as flesh and scales began to reform across the wound.

"Amazing," the pilot said.

"It really is," Greenwood said. She changed communication channels. "Gunner, are your choppers ready?" She looked out the flanking windows and saw three squads of four helicopters each, carrying the massive steel brackets. There was enough space between each set of helicopters that Inkanyamba would at least have to sweep with her head to take them all out in one blast.

"You goddamn bet they are," came the distinct drawl. "Time for horseshoes round two."

"Tungsten, how's the ground looking?"

"A steady roll. We have visual on the crater now. Looks like mama's stirring," he said.

Greenwood peered out at the crater and saw Inkanyamba's head rise, glaring at their approach like a rattlesnake on the defensive. Greenwood swallowed hard. *A single lightning blast would wipe me out right here and now.* Her heart dropped as Inkanyamba's jaw stretched wide, her chipped and jagged teeth sparking with electricity. Even in the cockpit she could feel the static gathering in the air…

Inkanyamba choked and screamed out in agony. Lightning wreathed its way around her body, and she seized before slumping back down into the water. Her breathing came in hard, fast gulps and foam gathered at the corners of her mouth.

"The hell was that?" Gunner's voice crackled through the radio.

"I have no clue," Ashleigh admitted, "maybe the bomb did some internal damage that hasn't been repaired yet."

"Well color us lucky bastards today," he said. "Ain't gonna look a gift eel in the mouth."

"Right," she said. Watching the creature writhe in pain, Greenwood felt a pang of guilt. Inkanyamba didn't ask to be this way. She knew they had to kill her, but in that brief moment, it didn't seem fair. Raymond's comments on violence rang in her head. "Damn it." Greenwood steeled herself. *This is the only way.*

"Bunk," she said, switching channels one more time. "How's our *piece de resistance*?"

Silence.

"Bunk?" she asked again.

"Sorry, Lieutenant," Bunk said in his unfailingly even tone. "The sailors on this ship are not so easy to work with despite all that hangs in the balance." Someone chattered in the background, but Greenwood couldn't make out what was said. "Yes, you have to fire them all at once," Bunk said to the unknown voice, irritation just barely evident in his own voice. "Just one leaves a window for escape." A pause. "Do you *want* the monster to escape? No? I didn't think so." More muffled conversation. "Lieutenant, are you still there?"

"I'm here."

"The ship's railguns are primed and ready to fire. *All* of them. Six tungsten piledrivers at your service," he said, then after a short pause added, "but they won't let me push the firing button."

"It's protocol. Don't let it get to you."

"I understand, I'm just disappointed."

Greenwood opened all channels. "All aspects of Operation Red Sun are in play, prepare to strike."

Inkanyamba hadn't stirred since her failed electrical strike, but she watched them with reptilian eyes that calculated their every move. Just as Greenwood was about to give the order to begin, a panic of chatter came through the radio headset. It was Tungsten.

"We're under attack down here," he shouted. "Unmarked soldiers in all black. Face masks with red goggles." The explosive sound of gunfire roared over the headset. "At least thirty of them. They're aiming at the dehydrators. We outnumber them, but the ambush…"

Tempest. Greenwood clenched her teeth. The ground force had sixty fully trained soldiers on guard. "Continue your advance," she ordered, "take out or repel the enemy. This mission cannot fail."

But if they knew of the plan, and attacked the ground force…

The roar of a jet fighter made Greenwood snap her head up. The sleek black craft roared out in front of her helicopter and began to turn to face them.

Shit. All of their fighters and gunships had been destroyed in the skirmishes with Inkanyamba. There was no one up here to defend them. With the steel brackets suspended between four helicopters there was no way to take evasive action. They were all sitting ducks.

A high-pitched whistling noise caught Greenwood's attention. She barely saw the rocket blur past before the fighter jet erupted into a ball of flames. The wreckage spiraled downward, slamming into the devastated remains of a skyscraper, bringing the whole building down on top of it.

"Lieutenant, didn't I impress upon all of you the importance of stopping Tempest?" The voice that came through her headset was modulated to sound deep and robotic.

"Who the hell?"

"The men who are still loyal to me are on the ground as we speak. They will stay on as supplemental escorts."

"Kurtis?"

The robotic voice sighed. Something clicked and Kurtis' regular voice said, "Did you consider that maybe I did the voice thing for a reason?"

"You stuck around?" Greenwood asked, ignoring his irritation.

"Sadly, no. Some people wanted me dead, and that doesn't fit in with my schedule at the moment."

The source of the missile from earlier made itself visible. Six fighter jets, two for each of the three squads of helicopters, descended from the cloud coverage above and rushed past, circling back around to fall into sequence alongside them. Each jet bore the symbol of a black hand with a blue, open eye in the palm. The pilots wore all black, and made no motion to acknowledge her, keeping their eyes dead ahead.

"This doesn't change what you did," Greenwood whispered into the headset.

"Did I ask for redemption?" came the cold reply. There was a loud click, and static buzzed through the headset. Greenwood switched channels to hear Tungsten panicking on the other end.

"I'm here, Tungsten."

"Those soldiers I told you about, well—"

"More soldiers appeared and eliminated them?"

"Yes, and now they've encircled us but haven't fired. We were waiting to hear from you and—wait how did you know?"

"Those men are—*Are what, Greenwood? Not a threat? On our side? Neither of those are true*—going to escort you to the action zone," she said. "Do not engage them."

"Understood. ETA five minutes. Holding position until everything else is in place."

"We'll be set up before you know it." She peered out towards the crater and switched channels. "I see helicopter squad one in place. Others confirm."

Gunner's voice said, "Squad two right where we need to be."

"Yeah, we're here," came Skids' reply.

Inkanyamba lowered her head, submerging her neck in the water. A sound like an earthquake rumbled from her chest. They maintained a position out of reach of her head, just in case.

"Deploy brackets," Greenwood ordered.

The sound of several braided steel cables being severed filled the air. She heard the rush of wind followed by the thunderous boom as the copper wrapped arches impacted the ground. Each one had a pair of seismic drills attached to the bottom. As soon as they made contact with the ground, the drills activated and embedded the arches as deep in the ground as they could before splitting apart into heavy-duty anchors. The three brackets locked Inkanyamba in place. The creature struggled against the braces, and while the structures screamed and groaned, they held fast.

"Raise altitude," Greenwood said. "Bunk, it's your turn."

Inaudible chatter, followed by, "I'm told all the guns are firing…now." Six thunderous roars from the distance were all the confirmation Greenwood needed. A whistling sound grew louder as the projectiles approached. The impact would be devastating. She waited for them to drop. Six blurs of black passed in front of the helicopter's window. The sounds of their impact were drowned out by Inkanyamba's shriek of rage and agony. She thrashed around, causing fresh streams of blood to pour from the wounds where the tungsten rods tore clean through her body, further pinning her to the ground. Despite her previous failed discharge, the creature began to charge up again. Greenwood watched the sparks course through the copper coils, grounding Inkanyamba and beginning the heating process of the coils.

"No matter how much electricity you muster, it won't matter," Greenwood said. Then, as another pang of guilt stabbed behind her chest, she added, "sorry." Her radio crackled static. "Tungsten. Move in."

"You got it."

A few minutes passed before Greenwood could see the dehydrators, giant microwave generators on fifty-foot poles, rolling across the craggy remains of the San Francisco streets. She knew the ex-Tempest soldiers were present but seeing their black body armor, like something out of a far-flung dystopia, interspersed amongst the fatigues of her brothers-in-arms was still jarring. *They're helping us*, she reminded herself. *For now.*

She watched the difficulty in setting up the dehydrators, keeping them out of Inkanyamba's range and staying away entirely from her thrashing tail. Seeing the small lake of water, she was glad that General MacPherson had insisted on her taking two drainage trucks that began the process of pumping the water out of the crater. The microwaves kicked on, their red-orange light bathing Inkanyamba in a way that made her wounds look all the more gruesome. Her thrashing grew more sluggish almost immediately. Greenwood wasn't sure if it was the blood loss or the suddenly intense heat, or a combination of everything the creature had been through up until now that was taking its toll, but she was thankful that this was proving to be a fairly easy endeavor.

"Radio to Captain Brannigan. Tell him he is good to engage his targets," she said to the pilot.

#

Brannigan had been hoping for no more issues during the mission when the call from Lieutenant Greenwood gave him the all-clear. He knew that it was a stupid hope, as stupid as hoping that the silver-haired bastard had lied to them about Tempest's plan to capture and use Inkanyamba's children to their own ends. The sudden appearance of soldiers dressed like the nightmare version of Wolfenstein solidified his newfound belief that hoping for good in the midst of bad just made things worse.

The idiots had come in quietly enough, but upon seeing the creatures, they began playing the whale noises Tempest had used to manipulate Inkanyamba. All of the demons perked up at the sound.

"Are they stupid?" Brannigan hissed through clenched teeth.

"What's wrong?" Arnett asked.

Raymond answered in a hushed tone, "The whale noise worked on Inkanyamba because she remembered that whales had been her prey at one point. Her children have no such understanding. To them it's just an intruder, and—"

"They'll attack," Brannigan finished. "Stay low."

The screams and gunfire started at the same time, right when the first Tempest soldier lost his head down the throat of one of the demons. His body was swatted aside and sank into the sludge.

Several bullets pinged off the walls near where Brannigan crouched in cover with his squad. "Don't move."

A lone soldier, deserting the rest of his men, sprinted towards their tunnel. Brannigan's face darkened. As the fleeing soldier planted his foot just to his right, he shot out and grabbed the man by the head, ripping his mask off and plunging him face first into the sewage. The man struggled, his writhing and thrashing drowned out by the gunfight going on in the main chamber. His body twitched a few more times before succumbing to stillness. Brannigan met the horrified looks of his squad. "An enemy behind you is always a threat," he said.

"But that was…" Arnett started.

"Quiet?" Brannigan said. "Yes. And also brutal, I know. But personally," he hissed, "I'd rather not have a bunch of those things swarming me right now." His eyes scanned the assembled faces. "That's what I thought."

The gunfire had already died down, with the demons having made short work of the unsuspecting soldiers. Now, Brannigan noticed, all the creatures were on alert, scales and spines bristling as they scoured the chamber, sniffing and searching. They'd be caught if they didn't act soon, but they'd most definitely be caught if they acted now.

He pointed at the tunnel across the chamber. "The retaining wall is down that one. All our detonators are long range frequencies, and that one will have to be detonated last. I have enough glue bombs to incapacitate most of these fuckers, but I don't know for how long. Each of us will have to take one tunnel, and we'll save this one for last. All you have to do is blow the tunnel entrance. Easy."

"I vote *not* taking the one on the other side of the pit of dragons," Arnett said.

"No, I'll take that one," Brannigan said. "Jet take the left, Arnett the right."

"And me?" Raymond asked. "The remaining one?"

"No, you stay here," Brannigan said. "With your back you shouldn't even be on this mission let alone trying to outrun monsters. I'll take two tunnels."

Raymond began to protest, but Brannigan cut him off.

"I don't want to hear it. You've been clutching at your back almost the entire time we've been down here. Stay here. Keep watch. Radio if things go to shit."

Arnett put a gentle hand on Raymond's shoulder. "He's got a point, man. If your back goes out on you with one of those things on your tail…"

"I would most certainly end up dead." Raymond frowned. "Yes, I get it." He pulled back the hammer on his revolver. "I'll watch your backs."

Brannigan nodded. "I'm going to try and get as many of those things clustered in the center of the room as possible before lobbing my glue bombs and hoping they do their job right."

"How are you gonna do that?"

Brannigan pulled something off the body armor of the drowned man. He held up the speaker for all of them to see. "Whale call," he said. "Now, everyone go in my pack and get your bombs."

When the three others had explosives in hand, Brannigan set his own two explosives to the side and pulled out his homemade glue bombs.

"Here goes," he said. He pressed the button on the speaker and hurled it into the center of the chamber. Within seconds, the sonorous cry of the blue whale filled the room. The demons perked up once more and stampeded to the center of the room, thrashing and gnashing at the sound whose source they could not find. Brannigan primed his first glue bomb, depressing a button and pulling a pin. He chucked the grey metal container into the tangle of reptilian bodies. As soon as the first was out of his hand he repeated with the second, and then the third one, aiming them so that they landed in the center and near the edges of the crowd. The sound was less of an explosion, and more like the sound of a boulder being dropped into a lake. It happened three times in quick succession. The creatures howled in confused panic as the sticky grey matter coated their skin and dried almost instantly. A few near the edge had avoided the majority of the blast and wheeled around to charge Brannigan. From his crouched position, he fired two bursts in quick succession, piercing straight through the eye of one creature. Raymond stabilized his revolver on his opposite arm and fired twice. The first took down a second creature, but the second shot glanced off the horned skull of another.

"Got any more grenades?" Arnett asked.

"Should be at least one," Brannigan shouted, opening fire again. The bullets caught the creature in the mouth mid-shriek. Its jaws snapped shut, and it skidded to a stop.

Arnett rummaged around and pulled the last grenade from Brannigan's pouch. He waited for one of the creatures to let out its blood-curdling screech before lobbing the grenade into its mouth. The creature swallowed in surprise, and then exploded, showering scaled chunks of flesh all over the chamber.

The last creature leapt towards them, landing on Jet and toppling him to the ground. The sound of his ribs cracking echoed in the tunnel. His scream came out as a rasp, the damaged bone having punctured his lung. He willed his arms up and jammed the barrel of his rifle into the creature's mouth and unloaded his entire clip. The creature wheezed out a weak roar before slumping down on top of the man, dead. It took the combined efforts of Brannigan, Arnett, and a now strained Raymond to force the carcass off of Jet, who climbed gingerly to his feet. He attempted to take a deep breath but gasped in pain before breaking down into a coughing fit that spewed blood into the sludge water below. Brannigan sat him up against the tunnel wall.

"You rest here, soldier," he said. "Take short, shallow breaths, and try not to move too much." He turned to Raymond and handed him Jet's explosive. "You get your wish. Take Jet's tunnel."

"How long until those bastards are free?" Arnett asked.

"No clue; better hurry," Brannigan said, scooping up his two explosives and bolting towards his first tunnel. As he passed the cluster of concreted creatures, he could already hear the sounds of their violent struggle beginning to weaken the concrete. As he entered the tunnel to the retaining wall, he heard the first of the detonations from his compatriots followed by what sounded like a cave in, signaling that one of the exit tunnels had been sealed.

The retaining wall stood a whole two heads above him in height and was made entirely of concrete. A few meters past that was a forged steel grate that let water in and kept things out. *Or in,* he thought.

The wall had just been resealed to repair damage done by erosion from the ocean tides. He almost felt bad undoing all the construction team's hard work. The feeling didn't last long as he stuck the explosive to the wall. "Just making more jobs," he mumbled to himself. "On to the next one." His return sprint was punctuated by the second detonation. *Good,* he thought, *now get back to cover you two.*

He emerged from the tunnel to see the creatures cracking the concrete. They weren't free yet, but they'd be out soon, and they would not be happy. His next tunnel was close. He slid to a stop at the entryway, placed the explosive about halfway up the curve of the arch, and bolted back to the tunnel they'd entered through just as the first creature broke free. His thumb slammed down on the detonator for the tunnel and the explosion caused just enough of a diversion for him to dive into the sludge and shadows of safety.

Raymond had already set up the last explosive on the arch of their own tunnel and now sat slumped against the wall next to Jet. "I thought it might be helpful if that was already done when you got back," he said.

"Good on you, Inspector. Can you walk?"

Raymond rose to his feet. "Enough. Jet, however—"

"Arnett and I will carry him. We need to get away from here before the demons notice us." He hoisted the injured man to his feet and beckoned Arnett over to help him.

As if on cue, the sounds of crumbling concrete and furious reptilian shrieks filled the air.

"Move," Brannigan said.

The creatures were still disoriented and hadn't located them yet, but Brannigan knew that once they realized all other paths were gone, they would flood down this one like a tide of teeth and claws. They needed to put distance between them and the entrance so they could blow it before that happened. He heard at least one creature shuffling around at the entrance to the tunnel.

Damn. It's too soon. He gritted his teeth. "Heads up, I'm blowing the tunnel now." He passed Jet off entirely to Arnett who almost dropped the man. He fumbled around in his pouch and pulled out the detonator. His thumb jammed the button. The explosion knocked them all off their feet. He heard the structure crumble, and the one creature's shriek was cut short underneath the cave in.

Brannigan spat out a mouth of sewer sludge and vomited into the waste. He heard the others doing the same. *One last thing*, he thought. His pouch had slid into the water. It was empty now, save for the last detonator. He reached in and pulled it out, flicking open the button cover in the process.

"So long, you poor little bastards," he said, pressing the button and waiting for the explosion. The sound was drowned out by the immediate sound of rushing water. Brannigan grinned at the success of his plan. He heard the confused cries of the demons cut short by the merciless flood of sea water.

"We did it," Arnett said.

Brannigan nodded. "I sent the signal to our ships to monitor the gate past the retaining wall. Anything that tries to get out will get blown straight to hell."

The sound of multiple footsteps splashing through the water and coming towards them made them all tense. Four figures emerged from the darkness of the tunnel.

"You," Raymond said, whipping his revolver up in front of him.

Jia Ming, her hair now a bright red, flanked by three armored soldiers stood in their path, blocking the way back to their exit. "Hello, murderer," she said. "Thank you for packaging my creatures so nicely."

"Drop your weapons." The soldiers all had their weapons primed and aimed at them. Brannigan cursed letting his guard down, even for a second. He slowly lowered Jet to the ground before standing back up with his hands raised above his head. Arnett followed suit.

"I tried to tell you before," Raymond said, "your sister chose her own death. I tried to save her."

The woman's look of contempt darkened into a black fury. "She died on your watch. That puts you at fault all the same, old man." She raised her pistol and aimed it at his chest. "My soldiers asked you to drop your weapon."

"They won't kill me," he said. "That wouldn't get you your revenge." He smiled. "Vendettas are rather predictable I'm afraid."

Jia Ming let out a hearty laugh. She squeezed the trigger, blowing a hole right through Raymond's lower abdomen. His mouth gaped in surprise and then contorted in agony. He dropped down to one knee and spat blood into the water.

Jia Ming loomed over him, her gun pointed at the top of his head. "Do you feel that? That pain is nothing like what I experienced when I lost my sister, my *twin*," she said. "I can't give you that, but I will make you suffer."

"Too close," Raymond muttered.

"What was that?"

"I said, 'you're too close'," Raymond said. He reached up to grab her gun and jerked it to the side just as she pulled the trigger. Using her surprise to his advantage, he spun her around in front of him and torqued her wrist, making her drop the pistol. Her soldiers all redirected their guns at him.

"You would shoot her?" he asked them.

That was all the opening Brannigan needed. He scooped up his rifle and opened fire at what appeared to be the weakest part of the soldier's gear, the legs. The three men went down with cries of pain, dropping their weapons in the process. Brannigan rushed past Raymond and finished off each of the soldiers one at a time. He turned to Raymond, whose blood was spilling in a heavy flow down his stomach onto Jia Ming and into the sewer water at his feet. It was taking everything in his power to hold the woman in place, his revolver pressed against her head.

"Finish her off, and let's get you to a hospital," Brannigan said.

"No," Raymond grunted, "she comes with us. She gets," he took a labored breath, "a trial."

"Damn it, man," Brannigan said, "we can't carry you, Jet, and her."

"I've got her," Raymond said, his grip loosening.

Brannigan saw it happening but couldn't react fast enough. Raymond's grip slipped just long enough for Jia Ming to break free. She dove for her pistol, rolled onto her back and fired four times directly into Raymond's chest. Brannigan squeezed the trigger of his rifle and a burst of gunfire sprayed Jia Ming, her body rattling with the impact.

Raymond fell face-first into the sludge: dead.

"We'll see you in hell," Jia Ming said, her crimson blood gurgling at the back of her throat. She coughed, spraying her face red, before going limp. Her head lolled to the side.

"Idiot," Brannigan roared. He kicked at the nearest dead soldier and shouted at Raymond again. "You *fucking* idiot!" He stormed over to the man's body and fell to his knees. "You could have just pulled the trigger and you'd still be alive." No tears ran down his face as he hung his head by the side of the dead man.

Arnett made sure that Jet was situated, then walked over to Brannigan and knelt down beside him. "It wasn't who he was," Arnett said. "I mean, I hadn't known the guy for that long but, as far as cops go, he really took the justice thing seriously, and that is rare these days."

"And it got him killed."

"He knew that his life was on the line the moment he took the badge. And I think he would have rather died than take an innocent life, regardless of the circumstances." Arnett rolled the inspector over and wiped the sewage from his face. "He would have rather died than dishonor the oath he swore to uphold. He was a good man."

"He certainly was." Brannigan took a deep breath. "Can you help Jet? I'll carry his body."

The journey back was slow and silent, the two men struggling with the added weight of their incapacitated allies.

Brannigan used the GPS to find them a path that circumvented the bridgeless drainage pit. After what felt like hours, they made it out of the sewer via a path that didn't require any climbing.

Brannigan pressed the button on his earpiece. "General MacPherson, can you get a fix on my location and send a rescue squad? We have one dead, and one in need of medical attention. And we lost Chaplin in one of the drains…if we can spare a search team…" He didn't even listen for a reply, instead he lay Raymond's body out on the ground and lay out on his back, exhausted. "It'll probably take a good thirty minutes for them to get here," he said to Arnett. "Keep watch, I need to rest."

Arnett settled Jet against a nearby wall, checked that his rifle was still functioning, and perched himself on a nearby guard wall. "I got you."

Brannigan gave a lazy mock salute before crossing his arms over his chest and closing his eyes.

#

This was taking longer than Greenwood had thought it would. An hour had passed, and while Inkanyamba's thrashing had deteriorated into low moans and sporadic twitching, she was still very much alive. The creature had tried a few more times to generate a storm with her electrical abilities only to be thwarted by a combination of her own injuries and the grounding effect of the copper wiring.

Greenwood tried not to let her mind wander to Raymond and his mission. She'd given them the go ahead and hadn't heard any reports since. Radio silence was necessary for their safety down in that serpent's lair, so she couldn't check in with them. She forced the worry from her mind. *He's fine*, she thought.

"Lieutenant," the pilot said, "we just got pinged by the general."

"Patch her through."

The general's voice burst through the headset. Her tone was crisp and urgent. "Lieutenant Greenwood, evacuate the area around Inkanyamba immediately."

"General? What's the situation?"

"Corden got his go ahead from the president. Another nuclear warhead is inbound as we speak. A larger payload launched from Colorado. I repeat, evacuate the area immediately."

"Shit." Greenwood slammed her hand on the helicopter console and received a nasty look from the pilot. "Take us out of here. Gunner, Skids, we've gotta pull out."

"What about Tungsten and the ground crew?" Skids' voice was an earnest panic.

"Fuck."

"General MacPherson, how much time do we have?"

"Minutes, at best."

Greenwood hurled the headset to the floor of the helicopter and barked at the pilot. "How many people can this thing hold?"

"Thirty, safely," he said.

Greenwood did the math in her head. Fifty soldiers. Thirty-five engineers. She paused. *What about the Tempest soldiers? How many of them are there?*

"Am I taking us down, Lieutenant?"

"We're not leaving them behind," she said, stabilizing herself as the helicopter began its descent. "Gunner, Skids, get your squads out of here. Mine's going down for a rescue."

"You sure about that?" Gunner asked. "Might need more people storage."

"I'm not risking civvies. Get out of here."

The helicopter bounced violently as it set down on the cracked pavement in the midst of the cities crumbling remains. Greenwood leapt out before the craft fully settled on the ground.

"Everyone, leave everything where it is and get on board one of these helicopters." The roar of the propellers drowned out her voice. The pilot called out to her through the headset. She turned just as he tossed her a megaphone. Greenwood repeated her statement and added, "There is a W-80 nuclear warhead due to strike any minute now. *Move your asses!*"

Tungsten climbed into the helicopter followed by a team of engineers and several soldiers. Spaces were filling up quickly.

She turned to the pilot. "Anything on the radar?" she asked.

"Nothing yet."

Greenwood sighed with relief. If they detected the ICBM on the radar and weren't already out of the blast radius, their quick and fiery deaths would be unavoidable. She gazed out over the swarm of people clamoring to get aboard one of the four helicopters and noticed that Kurtis' soldiers maintained posted positions by the equipment detaining Inkanyamba. She raised the megaphone back to her mouth.

"Soldiers formally associated with Tempest," she said, "in a gesture of good faith you are welcome aboard our helicopters. Regardless of your actions, you do not deserve a nuclear death."

A few of the soldiers turned their glowing red goggles towards her, before immediately returning their attention to whatever task occupied their attention. A lone soldier waded his way through the crowd to approach her.

"I am Caine," he said, his voice digitally altered by the mask, crackled like a cross between the Terminator and Robocop. "I speak for these men, on behalf of our Hand."

"Caine, tell your men to please board the helicopters in a quick and orderly fashion. There is enough room."

"Grant us immunity."

"I'm sorry?"

"Give your word as a soldier of this nation that we will both board and disembark your crafts as free men."

Greenwood frowned. *Is now really the time for this?* "I can't promise that."

"That is unacceptable," Caine said in his same robotic tone.

"I mean to say that I can't make that call. It would be up to General MacPherson."

"Communicate our wish to her."

Greenwood wanted to scream. A nuclear bomb would be turning this place to ash within the next ten minutes, and this man wanted to bargain with her. *I could leave you. I could leave all of you, and I wouldn't lose an ounce of sleep over it.* She knew that was a lie. She'd never forgive herself. "Is the general still on that line?" she asked the pilot.

"Yes ma'am."

Greenwood clicked over. "General, there's a minor…snag," she said.

"That bomb will hit in ten minutes," she snapped, "this better be important."

"There are soldiers here that follow the escaped prisoner, Kurtis. They assisted our mission and—"

"Get them onboard and out of harm's way."

"That's the snag. They won't board without guaranteed immunity." Greenwood listened to the static that filled the silence on the other end of the communication line.

"Grant it." MacPherson's voice was pure ice. Greenwood couldn't help but shiver at the sound of it. "And get out of there."

"Ma'am."

Caine stared at her expectantly, his red lenses never wavering in their focus on her face. "The conclusion?"

"Granted. Now move your asses," Greenwood said.

Caine nodded. He pressed a button on the side of his helmet. "Phantasms. Abandon your posts and board the helicopters. Our duty here is done." Immediately, and at once, all of the black clad soldiers ceased their actions and set a quick pace towards the four choppers. Two minutes later and everyone had boarded. Seconds ago, the missile had entered radar range. Time was running short.

"Get us out of here, now," Greenwood barked into the comm channel.

The helicopter lurched upward. Rising slowly while also beginning to cruise in the forward direction. Within seconds they were above the tops of the toppled buildings and zooming through the air. Greenwood fidgeted in her seat.

#

Even facing the other way, the flash of light from the bomb was nearly blinding. Every sound was muted at first, rising from a low rumble to a thunderous crack, like a mountain splitting in half. The force of the explosion itself started as light turbulence before turning into a powerful concussive force, knocking the helicopter off its axis. Greenwood felt her stomach drop to the floor, her fear of heights returning in spectacular fashion. The only thing that kept her from screaming was the rush of pressure forcing all of the air out of her lungs. She saw the other helicopters from her squad, who left several minutes before hers, in the distance. They made it out of the bomb's range in time.

The helicopter spiraled out of control while the pilot wrestled with the controls. "I'm not going to be able to stabilize," he said. "We're going down."

"Can you still get us out of the blast radius?"

"I have *no* control. The radiation blew most of the controls."

"What's our distance?"

"We should be out of the severe damage zone, given our initial speed."

"Then put us down as gently as you can."

The pilot raised an eyebrow behind his aviator sunglasses. "I'll do what I can."

Greenwood clamored her way into her seat and strapped in. Tight. She used the helicopter's PA system. "We are crashing. On impact, we need to make double time to the nearest structurally sound building. If there's a basement, get there as fast as you can, otherwise gather as close to the center as possible."

"About that building," the pilot said, "brace for impact."

Greenwood looked up just in time to see the bank fill the front windshield of the helicopter. She bent her head forward and ground her heels into the floor until the bottom of her feet hurt. The impact slammed her back in her seat. The screech of metal cut through the air as the propellers caught in the concrete supports of the building and wrenched themselves off the top of the helicopter, tearing the top of the craft off with the sudden stop. G-force caught Greenwood off guard, slamming her back into the seat and holding her there until she felt like her lungs would pop. The pressure released and she gasped for breath as the helicopter skidded to a stop in the center of the building. Greenwood unfastened her seatbelt and turned to the pilot, only to see that a chunk of the rotary blade had lodged itself through the front of his head and out the back of the seat's headrest. Blood painted the wall behind him a red splatter. She pulled his dog tags from his neck and shoved them in her pocket.

The headset didn't work, but she heard the sounds of movement from the passenger section of the helicopter. She opened the door and saw that the soldiers, hers and the ex-Tempest soldiers, were already going through the process of assessing the dead, while assisting the living or injured. She counted seven bodies slumped in their seats, unmoving.

"Everyone out," she shouted, "head to the vaults." She knew they had maybe two minutes before the rest of the nuclear bomb effects caught up with them. "Go. Go!"

They hadn't made it even halfway when the true force of the explosion hit the building, knocking them all to the floor. It felt like the worst earthquake she'd ever experienced. The noise burned its way down to her ear drums. The building screamed, that was the only way to describe it. The building screamed as it was battered and burned by the tiny sun that just exploded near the horizon, and Greenwood wondered if she was screaming too.

CHAPTER 20

"The EMP effect has cut communications, General Macpherson. Three helicopters are confirmed to have returned. Lieutenant Greenwood was not onboard any of them. We have nothing on her status."

The general's face contorted into a mask of rage, one which she directed at the man on screen. "Well Marcelle," she said, her tone even but full of venom, "that's at least thirty American soldiers that *you* just dropped an atom bomb on."

"A small price to pay for the safety of *all* of our people." Corden's voice lacked any hint of remorse.

"That's *if* it worked," MacPherson spat back.

"Diane—"

"That's General MacPherson to you," she said icily.

Corden's face darkened. "General MacPherson," he growled, "the American military is the most powerful force in the world, answerable only to God himself. The bomb will work."

"And my soldiers?"

"A sacrifice well within the acceptable bounds in regard to destroying that creature."

"And the now displaced citizens of San Francisco?" MacPherson asked, searching for any hint of concern in the man's wizened face.

"That is not *my* concern."

No, MacPherson thought, *of course it isn't.* "Get this son of a bitch off of my video screen," she ordered. The screen froze on Corden's offended face then blinked black. "Can any of our drones get live feed out of the city?"

"None. Anything we send in immediately succumbs to the radiation," the comms officer said. "It'll probably be a day or more before the effect clears up."

"God damn it!" she roared. "We don't know the status of our squadron, we don't know the status of the enemy. Is there anything we do know?" She scanned the assembled soldiers with a furious eye. As her gaze ran across each of them in turn, they averted their gaze. A silent, and unanimous, "No".

She kneaded her forehead. "Fuck this," she muttered, "come get me when we have any new intel. I'm going to go check on those two headaches and their monster."

The two headaches were all aflutter when she entered. She pretended not to notice the sudden drop in energy as she entered the makeshift research station. She also pretended not to notice the heat-fused hole in the floor and the gaping hole in the hangar ceiling. General MacPherson was here for any form of good news, and neither of those things leaned in that direction.

"So," she said, spreading her arms, "what have you learned?"

Skylar cleared her throat. "Well given the resilience of the hybrid's DNA and cellular makeup—"

MacPherson held up a hand. "English, please."

"When Akuma grows up, he'll be more powerful than both of his parents," Devonte said. "He's already capable of discharging plasma in the form of a directed energy beam. It's...actually relatively weak right now despite how it may seem." He gestured awkwardly at the damage the general was trying so hard to ignore.

Akuma had watched her as she entered. He gave no indication of threatening behavior. But he watched her. An idea sparked in the general's mind on this observation. She stormed over to Devonte, grabbed him by the collar of his shirt and slammed him against the nearest workstation.

"You mean to tell me," she shouted, "that you've been raising this thing, knowing damn well that it is an even greater threat than the thing out there that we've yet to succeed in killing?" *Guns didn't hurt it,* she thought. She caught sight of a syringe on the desk. *Right.* Still holding Devonte in place with one arm, she snatched up the syringe with her other and jabbed it toward his neck, stopping just before contact. The boy let out a panicked shout, and then she heard it. She spun around, syringe still at Devonte's neck, and faced Akuma.

"General, what the hell..." Devonte started.

"Shut up," she hissed in his ear.

Skylar spoke in a pacifying voice, "General we were going to report back, and..."

"Hush and look," she said.

Akuma had risen from his lounging position and now stood at full alert. His reptilian hackles were fully raised, and his frill was extended to full, crackling with electricity. A menacing hiss seeped out of his throat, and his eyes were narrow slits. He was primed to attack, and his eyes were fixed on the general.

"The damn thing didn't just not eat you," the general said, "it thinks you're its family." She slowly released Devonte from her grasp and backed away from him. Akuma hissed and tracked her every move. MacPherson placed the syringe back on the desk and held up her hands in a placating manner. "It's okay," she said. "I'm sorry I threatened him." She moved to the other side of the room, opposite Devonte. Akuma stared her down for a long while, but eventually relaxed.

"So wait," Devonte said, glancing back and forth between Akuma and the general, "that was all a test?"

"An experiment, yes." MacPherson crossed her arms. "I suppose I owe you an apology as well."

"That's...brilliant," Skylar said, her eyes lighting up with excitement. "He's like a guard dog."

"So that means he's not a threat, right?" Devonte asked.

"No," MacPherson said, "he is quite distinctly a threat to anyone who would threaten you." She eyed the creature warily. "But he didn't immediately attack me, which shows quite a level of self-control."

"Akuma is exceptionally smart. He is able to respond to simple commands like a dog, but he also shows a reasonable level of problem-solving ability." Devonte swelled with pride, like a parent boasting about their child.

He's attached, MacPherson thought with a heavy sigh. "You realize that once the government at large gets wind of...Akuma...we won't be able to keep him here. He'll likely be given to a professional team of researchers..." she trailed off as she watched both Skylar and Devonte visibly deflate. "It's not a pet you know," she continued, "but as of recent, I've seen the...competence of our government in a stark new light, so all I will say is this: if no one finds out, no one finds out. Take that as you will."

"General," Devonte asked, "what do you think we should do?"

"I believe the most effective safety precaution for any weapon is for it to be in the hands of a reliable and trustworthy person who knows what they are doing," she said. "Learn as much as you can about this creature, and make sure that yours are the right hands."

"I will," Devonte said. "How are the missions going?"

"Nothing to report," the general said tersely. "I'll update you when we know anything." She watched their faces for any sign of suspicion and then said, "I should report back to command." As she turned to go, she paused and without facing them said, "Good work, you two," and left.

#

The roar had finally ended, and Greenwood no longer heard screaming. She pushed herself up onto her elbows and looked around the hallway in which she lay. Portions of the ceiling had collapsed. She recognized Tungsten, most of his body buried beneath a pile of rubble, his glassy eyes staring out at nothing. A pang of guilt and sorrow stabbed through her heart. She climbed to her feet and surveyed her surroundings. Several soldiers were also coming to, helping each other up and assessing the situation.

"American soldiers, sound off," she said.

Eleven voices confirmed their presence. She had counted fifteen when they boarded.

"Civvies?" she called.

Four. There had been six.

"Lieutenant Greenwood," Caine's electronic voice crackled through the settling dust. She noticed that his black uniform was dark and drenched on the left side. He was bleeding. "There were nine of us aboard the craft." He paused and made a noise that sounded mournful. "Only two remain."

"You're hurt," Greenwood said.

"It is fine. Only the flesh is damaged."

"Lift up your vest and let me check it out," she said.

The man hesitated, an electronic buzz coming from his mask speaker. "Okay," he said.

A bright red gash arced along the man's umber skin, carving its way from the middle of his abs down around to his lower hip. He was wrong; the cut was deep and angry enough to be an immediate concern, but the amount of blood pouring from the wound was even more concerning to her.

"Wait here," Greenwood said. She retraced her path to try and find the remains of the helicopter. It was where they had left it, perched on the ledge, halfway in the building, halfway out. She climbed into the passenger seat, holding her breath to not gag on the smell of the fried flesh of the pilot. The first aid kit lay cracked open on the cockpit floor. Greenwood grabbed the gauze, medical tape, and rubbing alcohol. She leapt down from the cockpit and heard a crack as the portion of the building supporting the helicopter broke away and plummeted down to the street below. The floor beneath her feet cracked and splintered; she dived away from the ledge just in time to avoid dropping to the ground below as well.

"That was way too close for comfort," she said.

When she got back to Caine, he had sat down against a nearby wall and taken his mask off as well as his upper body armor. He was younger than she thought, closer to Devonte's age than her own. His face was drenched in sweat and he looked up at her with sunken eyes. "It hurts a bit more than I expected."

"The adrenaline's worn off," she said. "Stay still, this will hurt more." She poured the alcohol along the gash. Caine's muscles seized and he hissed in pain as the liquid seeped into the bloody wound. Greenwood pressed the gauze onto the wound and stuck it down with the medical tape. "No painkillers in the helicopter, sorry. But on the bright side, you won't bleed to death."

"Thank you," he said, then, "Do you think it's dead?"

"Inkanyamba?"

Caine nodded.

"I don't know," she said, "but I'm sure we'll find out soon enough. For now, we need to focus on getting out of the city. You can practically smell the radiation in the air and I'm already feeling nauseous. On your feet, soldier."

"Give me a minute," he said, replacing his mask. "I need to give you something." He limped off and disappeared around a corner.

While Caine was gone, Greenwood went around checking on the survivors and organizing them into a group that was ready to travel. They would have to walk out of the city at least as far as it took to get their communication capabilities back. It was a few more minutes before Caine returned. He held seven masks by the straps and carried a sack on his back.

He handed her a mask, set the pack on the ground and pulled out one of the Tempest soldiers' uniforms. Greenwood had a distinct image of seven naked soldiers lying dead somewhere in the building. She shook the thought from her mind.

"Put it on," he said, "it's lined with lead. It will keep the radiation out. There aren't enough for everybody though."

"I don't—"

"Don't argue. I will give the civilians four and," his red lenses gleamed at her, "there are no more after that."

Greenwood found herself shocked by the ruthless efficiency of the soldier. Of course they both knew there were two left over, but they also both knew that giving two safety suits to eleven scared and injured soldiers would only lead to trouble. She took the suit and mask from him, stripped out of her military fatigues, and slid into the oversized black regalia. It was heavier than it looked, but still surprisingly mobile. The mask covered her face, and she couldn't see anything.

"Wait," Caine said. She felt his hand by her throat and tensed. He pressed a button and the lenses flickered to light and she could see clearer than she could with her naked eye. A minimal heads-up display indicated her heart rate, the current radiation level, and her current heading.

When she spoke, her voice sounded in that same metallic monotone as Caine's. "It's hot in here."

"You won't get used to it," Caine said. "But it will keep you safe."

#

The city was devastated. It was already a wreck after Inkanyamba's attack and the first nuclear strike, but now, Greenwood could count the buildings still standing on her fingers. And they were barely managing. Almost everything was reduced to rubble, and the ground beneath her feet was craggy and uneven. It blistered in some places and dropped into wide sinkholes in others. She looked back to where Inkanyamba had been and saw only a lingering cloud of ash and dust, a thick rust-colored haze swimming around it. *Is it still alive?*

"Alright," she said, still wincing every time she heard the harsh mechanical bark of her new mask. "We're at the southern end of Soma now. That means we have about a three-mile walk to Fisherman's Wharf, through a nuclear fallout zone." She paused, taking in the terrified faces of her soldiers, their guns trembling in their hands. "We made it out of range of the worst effects, but that does not mean we should linger any longer than we have to."

Caine approached her. "News," he said.

"Don't wait for an invitation," she said, "tell me."

He showed her the readout on a Geiger counter.

"Yeah, I'd imagine the air would be radioactive after a nuke went off."

"Five minutes ago, the number was double what it is now," he said. "The radiation is disappearing far quicker than it should be."

Greenwood looked at the swirling cloud at the epicenter of the bomb drop. "She's alive."

"I know." Caine followed her gaze. "We should go."

"Alright everybody, let's move out," Greenwood called.

The trek was straightforward, and uneventful, but Greenwood couldn't shake the feeling that she kept seeing glimpses of motion out of the corners of her eyes. Shadows that skittered away as soon as she tried to focus on them.

"You see them too," Caine said.

"What are they?"

"Formicaleon," he said. "Giant bugs that feed off of the great dragon. The Hand of Legends called them that."

Greenwood considered which to address first, the giant insects stalking them or the potential new intel she could glean from Caine. Her military instincts took over. "That's three of these Hands I've heard of now," she said casually. "The Hand of Gold who you believe is a traitor. Your boss, the Hand of Shadows, and now a Hand of Legends, who I'm assuming is…like the pope?"

"That would be an accurate comparison. He preaches and indoctrinates. Much like any government, control is Tempest's highest goal." He stopped mid step, before returning to his original pace. "You're trying to get information out of me."

"Yes."

"You'll get no more."

"I don't understand," Greenwood said. "You and your boss both want to end Tempest now, right? So why not work with us to do that?"

"He does not."

"What?"

"The Hand of Shadows does not wish to *end* Tempest. He wishes for Tempest to return to what he considers the true path. This required us to work with you to that end."

Greenwood bit her tongue. She'd suspected that Kurtis didn't really intend to end Tempest, but hearing it said so plainly made her blood boil. He was a con man through and through.

"I, however," Caine said, "believe Tempest should end." Even through the mechanical distortion, she could hear the young man's anger.

"Oh?" Greenwood said.

"He would have left us to die in that explosion had your general not extended amnesty," he said. "Seven of us did die in that explosion. I thought he was different than the rest, but we are as expendable to him as we would be to her. We are drones expected to serve our purpose and die."

Greenwood let out a sad sigh. "Sometimes," she said, "I feel the same way. The general is great, but the higher ups…can I trust you?" she asked.

"That is not for me to decide," he said. "But know that I stand with you now because of your kindness, not because of my orders."

"And your friend? The one who survived?"

Caine's tone darkened. "He did not survive.

"But you said—"

"His loyalty to Tempest was unwavering. He still intended to betray you."

"You were going to betray us?"

"Just you. He views you as a threat."

"Figures," Greenwood said, "I'll try not to hold it against you."

"I appreciate—Get down!" Caine tackled Greenwood to the ground. She gasped as the air left her lungs. A chittering, clicking mass screamed over their prone forms and skidded to a stop on the other side of what remained of the road. Slimy mandibles snapped and gnashed at the air. The insect only had a moment of menace before eleven assault rifles opened fire, ripping it to shreds and splattering the concrete a sticky green.

Caine rose to his feet and offered a hand to Greenwood. "There will be more," he said. "Formicaleon travel in swarms."

"We'll have to hurry then," Greenwood said, "and thanks, I owe you one."

"No," Caine said, "now we are even."

"Keep a lookout soldiers, there's more of those hostiles where that came from," Greenwood shouted. "We've only got about a mile left to go."

A chorus of chitinous cries rose up around them, a frenzy of discordant harmonics. The Formicaleon poured out of the twisted metal husks of buildings and rushed towards them, hundreds of them.

"We won't outrun them," Caine said.

"New plan, stand and fight," Greenwood said, "they go down easy enough." She raised her rifle and clicked off the safety, ready to fight. As the creatures approached, they split and swarmed around the small group of survivors, ignoring them completely. She watched as the swarm headed for the harbor and disappeared into the crashing waves. "What the hell?"

"I've seen this before in rats," one of the engineers said. "They're running from something."

"Oh fuck," Greenwood said. "Run for the docks, now."

No sooner had she finished, Inkanyamba's ear-splitting cry cut through the air, rattling what remained of the city with the force of her lungs. She emerged from the rust-colored fog, blowing it aside with a single beat of her shredded wings. Heat and radiation had burned her skin an onyx black and fused her scales into one solid armored carapace. Her frills had burned off and her eyes turned a bloodshot red. The arches still clung to her back like a metal exoskeleton. Lightning sparked in the air around her, coursing through the wiring and crackling with each step she took. Greenwood had been afraid the first time she'd encountered Inkanyamba, but the feeling that ran through her veins as Inkanyamba stood before them now froze her to the core. She couldn't move, she couldn't breathe, all she could do was watch as the titanic form loomed over them like a god incarnate. The creature didn't even notice them as it raged in the city center, crushing everything that stood in its way.

"Something's wrong," she said. Inkanyamba had been a devastating force, but her actions had always been instinctual, like an animal. This was violence for the sake of violence. "The radiation must have affected her mind."

"That makes her all the more dangerous," Caine said. "Come on."

"Wait," Greenwood said, "look, there."

In the center of Inkanyamba's chest was a gaping hole that pulsed red with every beat of her massive heart. It glowed like a fire in the center of her onyx form.

"That's where one of our rods went through her. It cracked open and didn't heal properly," Greenwood said. "Which means—"

"She can be killed," Caine finished.

Greenwood's comm-link came to life, "…Greenwood…status…repeat…report…"

"Come in," Greenwood said, "I'm here. Can you repeat the message?"

"Lieutenant," the general's voice crackled through the static. "Are you okay?"

Caine motioned to her that they needed to move. Greenwood nodded, and the group broke into a run towards the Fisherman's Wharf.

"We're here," Greenwood said as she ran. "We lost thirteen and Inkanyamba is still alive. The mission was a failure. We are retreating to Fisherman's Wharf. We'll evac as soon as possible. But there's something more important."

"Then report it, Lieutenant. We haven't got all day."

"Inkanyamba is weakened. There's a wound leading to her heart that hasn't healed. I think striking there will take her down."

Greenwood could hear the general's smirk as she spoke. "I'll send a gunship your way. We *will* bring this monster down. Double time, soldier."

Inkanyamba wasn't chasing them, she hadn't once looked down at them, but her rampage through the city carried her in the same direction as them, and with each of her heavy footfalls, she drew closer to their small group. The harbor was in view now, as was the battleship waiting for them in its waters. Greenwood recognized it immediately. The general had sent the largest ship in their personal armada, the *USS Winguard*. It floated alongside the *USS Velocity*, the railgun-fitted ship that Bunk had launched the tungsten spikes from. As they approached the dock, several sailors shouted out for them from a smaller transport vessel. They piled on board, with Greenwood going last, after ensuring that no one had been left behind. The boat cast off for the main ship, just as Inkanyamba broke through the last few buildings between her and the dock. As they approached the boat, the guns began to swivel to aim at Inkanyamba.

A smile spread across Greenwood's face. *This is it*, she thought.

INTERLUDE VII

Fear. It runs through her like an electric surge. She screams. Her bellow shakes her surroundings. Chunks of rock and debris crumble all around her. *Fear.* Her skin burns and the smell of flesh and fire set her heart racing. She cranes her neck to the sky to check for another fire-bringer. Her skin cracks and tears. Warm blood leaks from the wounds, steaming from the heat radiating off of her. *Pain.* It hurts. The dryness covers her entire body. Each motion opens new wounds. *Rage.* She swings her head at the remains of the nearest standing structure. Skin scrapes off her neck as it crashes through it, hoping the abrasion might bring relief. The pain only grows. Her scream sounds like the cry of a weaker creature. Of prey.

She raises her head, stone and dust raining down to the ground below. Her eyes dart around, but she sees only ruin.

She cries out for her children.

Nothing.

The wind stings against her heart. Its beating draws her attention. She sees the exposed red of her most vital organ. The wound is there, red, and angry, not gone like usual.

She doesn't understand.

Blood. The scent is in the air. Her scent. *Fear.* Her wings twitch. *Pain.* She reels. A gargled roar escapes her dry throat. *Dry. Pain.* The thought comes unbidden. *Water.* She rights herself. Her head rises. Blood and flesh drip to the ground. *Hurt.* The sky is clear. No clouds. Just blue.

She turns. Through the dust and ruins lies the sea. It's gold in the sunlight.

The sound of the waves draws her. *Calm.* Her pulse slows. The fear abates. *Water.* She lumbers forward, letting out an excited shriek. The sky fire has not taken the water. *Home. Safe.* Each step tears at her. Her skin steams as blood runs down feverish skin. Nothing stands in her way. Her bulk crashes through the ruined place. The stone towers scream and fall as she rams through them in a headlong charge towards the water. Her eyes burn. Dust and debris sting in the creases and crevices around her eyes. She does not flinch or waver. She emerges on the shore. The water laps at the ground. Beckoning. Tiny figures look up at her from the shore, and in the distance, three grey creatures with tall necks drift lazily on the surface of the water.

Water. Safe. She trills. The salty spray of sea water soothes the burning sensation crawling across her skin. Her trill turns to a triumphant roar as she moves towards the sea.

Danger. Something strikes her on the left. *Fire. Pain.* She stumbles back. Broken stone crumbles beneath her as she falls. The next attack misses. *Fight.* She looks towards the sea. The grey creatures.

Fear. Rage. The two emotions swirl together inside Inkanyamba and she shrieks at the feeling, righting herself quickly despite the pain. Her head swivels in time to take a blow to the side of her head that blinds her with light and heat. The skin on her face burns. She claws at it, tearing flesh. She remembers the grey sea creatures. When she woke up there had been one. A small one. It had attacked her too. These were bigger. Full grown. They *hurt* her.

She dodges the next attack. *Rage.* Energy courses through her body. It sparks through the cracks in her skin. *Pain.* Her mouth opens, her jaw unhinging at the bottom. She raises ravaged wings in a show of intimidation before letting loose a stream of crackling electricity towards the closest grey creature. The sparking stream engulfs the creature. It shudders and groans before bursting in a brilliant display of fire and smoke. Inkanyamba waits for the rest to retreat in the face of her superiority. Still they linger. A confused warble bubbles from her throat. *Rage. Fear. Flee.* The attack has drained her. She roars again but the sound breaks in the air, falling to the ground, flat and empty. The smell of salt and brine calls to her. It isn't far now. *Safe.*

The next impact strikes closer to her heart. She reels from the deep pain that blossoms in her chest. *Run.* She takes a single, staggering step towards the sea. *Fear. Tired. Weak.*

The grey creatures don't stop. Impact after impact burst against her weakening body. *Pain. Pain. Pain.* She screams. The ocean is there. *Water. Safe.* It's so close. She rears back to dive in when a new pain blossoms in her chest. Every muscle in her body seizes. *Cold.* Blood pours from her body, warm against her cooling skin. Her heart is silent. She can't feel it. *Gone.* She twitches. Her skin no longer burns. Her head drifts in the direction of the other creature. It stares at her with cold black eyes still smoking from the attack that Inkanyamba knew had killed her.

She doesn't understand.

Her mouth opens and closes. The ground trembles with her phlegmy grumble. Numbness sets in. She looks down at the sea. *Home...Safe...*

So close.

Too far.

It rises to greet her as she falls. It beckons still but stays cruelly out of reach as her head slams into the hard, cracked ground. She tries to pull herself to the water, but her limbs won't move. *Tired.* A weak warble breaks from her throat. The sea blurs out of focus. Her vision darkens. The numbness grows. *Tired.* She takes a shuddering breath in; wet and ragged. She exhales one last time and sinks down into the cold, murky darkness. *...Scared...*

CHAPTER 21

The *Velocity* had sunk beneath the waves. Bunk and a full crew of sailors dragged down to the depths. But at that cost, Inkanyamba was dead. As the boat gained distance from the harbor, Greenwood did the only thing she could think to do for all of the fallen. She stood at attention and gave a full salute. *Even to you, Inkanyamba.*

No words of her own seemed appropriate, so she tried to think of what Raymond would say. After a moment of silence, she said, "To a war well fought, and to an enemy worthy of respect." Greenwood wasn't sure how much she meant what she said, but it sounded right. She turned away from the steaming corpse of the fallen creature just as they reached the *Winguard*. Any second she expected to hear Inkanyamba's distinct roar, a final declaration that the battle was not over and never would be, but the sound never came. Not when they boarded the ship, not as they sailed to the base, and not as they disembarked to head in for their debriefing. Inkanyamba was dead, and though they had won, Greenwood could pull no joy from the victory.

CHAPTER 22

A black cloud of mourning hung heavy over the entire naval base. Devonte sat beside Greenwood on a bench in the hallway. Soldiers filed past, preparing for the massive funerary ceremony in two days' time.

"He's really gone," Devonte said, breaking the silence that had hung over them for the past hour. "Just like that."

"That's how it always is," Greenwood said. Her voice faltered halfway through the sentence. "Here, and then gone. Just like that."

"I'm so—"

"It's not fair," Greenwood snapped. "Five years," she said. "Five years I pined away after him and then I finally got him. We finally had each other. And now…" she trailed off. "Now I've got jack shit but a broken heart." She looked down at the list of people killed in action and read the names aloud. "Captain Raymond Dehane. Private First-Class Spencer Chaplin. Timothy "Tungsten" Todd. Gordon "Bunk" Banks."

She kept reading, there were many names, but no more that Devonte recognized. Finally she stopped, and the silence returned like a wall between them.

"I can't stand this silence," she said. "Say something. Anything."

"Did you know he had a sister?" Devonte asked.

"No. He didn't talk much about his personal life."

"She was killed during a drug deal gone wrong. Guy didn't like her price, decided he was just going to take it. She was eighteen."

"Why are you telling me this?"

"I was looking to see if he had any next of kin. But there's nobody still alive."

"New subject."

Skylar approached them. "Skids is leaving," she said. "Did you guys want to come see him off?"

Devonte cast a concerned glance at Greenwood. "I—"

"Go," she said, "You're terrible at comforting people anyway."

"I'm sorry," Devonte said.

"So am I," she said.

Devonte walked alongside Skylar in silence until they were out of earshot of the lieutenant.

"Is she okay?" Skylar asked.

"Would you be?" Devonte replied.

"No." She stopped him by stepping in front of him and putting a hand on his chest. "Are *you* okay?"

"To be honest," he said, "I don't know. I only knew him for a few months, and he was basically a stranger. But…"

"But you're sad."

"Very." Devonte had never been one to shy away from shedding tears. He'd held it together for Greenwood but now they came out in full force. His eyes stung as he spoke. "He didn't have to go out of his way for me, but he did."

He didn't resist as Skylar pulled him into a hug. She squeezed him tight, and he squeezed her back, and for a minute the pain felt a little less. Eventually he did pull away and forced a small smile. It almost felt genuine.

"Come on," he said, wiping his eyes, "we don't want to miss Skids."

Everyone else was already in the hangar when they arrived. Devonte found Brannigan, Gunner, Jet and General MacPherson near the front of the assembled crowd of welders and soldiers.

"It's too late, you missed him," Brannigan said as they approached. "Go back to whatever you were doing."

"Fuck you," Devonte said before giving Brannigan a quick fist bump. "Where is he?"

"Packing up his Jeep. He'll be back shortly."

"He's back now," Skids said, dusting off his hands and shoving them deep in the pockets of his overalls. "Gonna be gone soon though."

"Gonna miss you, brother," Gunner said. The two men clasped hands and pulled each other into a tight embrace.

General MacPherson stepped forward and extended her hand.

"What? No hug?" Skids said with a lopsided grin.

"Anything I can do to convince you to stay?" the general asked as she shook the man's hand.

His smile faltered. "No," he said. "With Tungsten and Bunk gone I just…I can't be around here anymore. Too many good memories turned painful." He scanned the crowd. "Jet?"

The other man stood with his arms folded across his chest. When he heard his name, he looked away.

"Right," Skids said. "I'll miss you, man."

"Not enough to not run away," Jet said.

"Hey," Gunner said, "cut that shit out."

"Nah," Skids said, "he's right, I'm running away. But it's what I gotta do for me. If you ever forgive me—"

"Oh shut up," Jet said, "I don't hate you. Just take care of your damn self."

Skids gave another lopsided grin. "Knew you'd come around." He waved over at Devonte and Skylar. "Y'all keep that wolf-dragon bastard thing from wreaking havoc, you hear?"

"Akuma?" Devonte said. "He wouldn't hurt a fly."

Skids let out a single, loud "ha" as he climbed into his Jeep. "I'll remember that one," he said. He grew solemn. "It was truly an honor to work with all of you. Take care." The Jeep's engine roared to life, and the tires squealed as he floored the gas pedal and roared out of the open hangar.

"All them engine theatrics," Gunner said," just to load the damn thing onto a boat."

The comment received the first genuine bit of laughter Devonte had heard since Inkanyamba's defeat, and all the losses that came with it were reported.

#

"By the way," Skylar said as the two of them sat side by side and leaned against the desk, watching Akuma sleep. "Where are you going to go now that all of this is over?"

"That's right," Devonte said, "my apartment probably blew up, didn't it?"

Skylar nodded.

"I have no clue," he said. "And shit, I promised you could stay with me, didn't I?"

"Don't worry about that," she said. "I can go back to Chicago."

"With your dad?"

"It'll be like I never left," she said, staring at the ground. "He probably didn't even notice I was gone."

"Knock knock," Brannigan said, tossing aside the flap of the research tent and striding in.

"Most people wait for a 'come in' after knocking," Devonte said dryly.

"Why? Are you two getting inappropriate in here? And in front of the baby," he said, dramatically pointing at Akuma, who snorted at the sudden loud noises interrupting his sleep.

"How are you as cheery and cheeky as always?" Skylar asked.

"Kid, I learned a long time ago that there's no sense in dwelling on death," Brannigan said, sliding down the wall and sitting next to Devonte. "And besides, most people need a good laugh when times are hard."

"I do appreciate it," Devonte said. "I think if you had broken down, that would have been the end of it for me."

"Yeah," Brannigan said shortly. "I couldn't help but overhear that you both are having a 'my home has been destroyed in a fire' crisis."

"No," Skylar said, "I—"

"I heard that too. That's not a home, so you're in the same boat as him," Brannigan said. "Anyway, I can't say anything yet because it's a secret, but don't worry about all that yet, just stick around a bit."

"What's that mean?"

"You might have a place to stay after all," he said, rising to his feet. "Talk to the general."

#

"Let it be known, Mr. President, that when General Corden informed me of his plan to launch a nuke on American soil, I protested," General MacPherson said.

"Mr. President, it was on your orders that I launched that nuclear bomb. It was a necessary action to ensure—"

"Marcelle, I'm going to cut you off right there," the president said. "I did not *tell* you to launch that missile. I simply authorized that a nuclear bomb *could* be launched. The way I see it, you made the choice."

"That's preposterous," General Corden shouted.

"Preposterous," the president said, "is the belief that it would ever be acceptable to endanger our great nation by unleashing a weapon of that power on our own city. People had homes in that city."

"Sir, I—"

"As restitution for the good people of the city of San Francisco, and the American people at large, you are hereby stripped of your rank as general and furthermore, dishonorably discharged from the Armed Forces." The president stamped a seal on a paper on his desk and held it up to the camera, so it was on full display on his screen. "Your replacement should be on his way to relieve you."

"Mr. President, I—"

"Goodbye. This is a conversation between high-ranking officials. You are not privy to this information." The president fiddled with the laptop on his desk and Corden's image blinked away. "Now, Diane, can I call you Diane?"

"With all due respect, sir, I prefer to be addressed by my rank," General MacPherson replied.

"That's great, Diane, I think the voters will love me as the president who removed a corrupt and warmongering general from our military's ranks."

MacPherson neglected to remind the president that he had appointed Marcelle Corden in the first place. She was sure he knew. "Mr. President, there is a serious matter I would like to discuss with you."

"Serious? We won! We should be celebrating. I could throw you a parade; would you like a parade?"

"No sir." MacPherson took a deep breath to calm herself. "It's about the kaiju."

"The what now?"

"The—the giant monster, sir."

"Oh, why didn't you just say that?" The president spent a few seconds fixing his hair in the camera. "What about it?"

"We were woefully unprepared for its arrival."

"But we came out on top. Like we always do."

"Sir, we just barely survived out here. We need to be prepared for—"

"For what? Next time? There won't be a next time."

"We can't be sure of that." She slammed her fist on the console, an action she immediately regretted. "Apologies, sir."

"No, no, you might be right. I can spin this. America is afraid, I can give them confidence." He flashed a grin at her. "What do you need?"

"I want to put together a taskforce dedicated to the research and, if need be, extermination of threats like this."

"Yes, good, I like it. I can get some people—"

"Sir?"

"Yes?"

"I already have a list of people, and one more thing…"

"What?"

"This team needs to be outside the hierarchy of the armed forces. It needs to be able to make its own decisions and act unilaterally without being bogged down in bureaucracy." She clenched her jaw and waited for the disapproval.

The president narrowed his eyes and scrutinized her, eyes darting around her face, looking for something. "Let me get this straight. You want to put together a team *you* created to fight monsters, that also comes with built in plausible deniability for me?"

"I suppose that is one way of putting it, sir."

"You would no longer be a general in the United States Navy."

"I know, sir."

The man leaned back and kicked his feet up on the large wooden desk. He folded his hands across his lap. "Sure. I'll sign something today. You will be your own little monster island out there. Put together your team."

"Thank you, sir."

The video screen went dark and General MacPherson let out a heavy sigh. "Fuck that man."

"That looked stressful as hell," Devonte said. The general jumped at the sudden vocalization. "Sorry, didn't mean to startle you."

"How long have you been standing there?"

"Um, *we've* been here since 'plausible deniability'," Devonte said, sharing an awkward look with Skylar. "We weren't eavesdropping, we were just…"

"Eavesdropping," the general said.

"What was that about?" Skylar asked.

"Brannigan sent you, didn't he?"

"Will he get in trouble if we say yes?" Devonte asked.

The general sighed and walked over to a nearby computer chair, slowly easing herself into the leather seat. She rolled her neck, letting each vertebrae crack and relieve the tension in her shoulders. After this, she planned to sleep for a week. "You need a place to stay, right? Both of you?"

The two nodded.

"And I'm assuming most places won't accept a three-meter tall dragon as a pet."

"How'd you guess?" Devonte said with an awkward chuckle.

"That conversation was about putting together a team to do what we did here over the past few months. A kind of response team," she said. "Would you be interested?"

"You're offering us a job?" Devonte asked.

"A job doing what we've been passionately doing for the past few years of our lives," Skylar clarified.

"Don't take this lightly," the general said, her tone hardening. "You've seen firsthand what the risks are. This will not be a game. It will presumably be life or death in any situation we go up against."

"I'm in," Devonte said. "Akuma may not cooperate without me, and risky or not, this is what I've always wanted to do."

"I'm with him," Skylar said. "He wouldn't survive without me."

The general let a small smile play across her face. "Well then, welcome aboard."

"Thank you, General," Devonte said.

"You won't be calling me that for much longer," she said. "It will certainly take some getting used to on my end."

"I'm sure you'll get used to it, Diane," Devonte said with a grin.

MacPherson shot him the nastiest look she could muster and watched him wither under her stare. "You won't be calling me that, either," she said.

"Right." Devonte stared at the floor. "Oh, am I allowed to talk about this with, say, family?"

"No specifics, but yes."

"Then I need to make a phone call," Devonte said.

EPILOGUE

"So, this is what you've decided?" Kurtis' face was cloaked in shadows as he peered down at Caine through the video screen. "I wondered what happened to you."

"It is," Caine said down on one knee in the darkened room. He looked up at the screen. "I... wish to step out of the shadows."

"And why tell me this? I could have you killed in the next ten minutes and call it tying up loose ends." Kurtis steepled his fingers in front of his face. "Traitor."

"If that is what you wish."

"You didn't answer my question."

Caine hesitated. "It was...the honorable thing to do."

"A Phantasm with honor? Novel." Kurtis let out a long sigh and flicked on the lamp that sat on his desk, illuminating his face. "What have you told them?"

"Nothing, I—"

"*What* have you told them?"

"They know about the Hand of Legends."

"Burke? That pompous zealot?" He leered down at Caine. "That's all?"

"It came up in regard to Formicaleon. That's all, I swear."

"Ah, yes, the lice." Kurtis rubbed at the newly developed stubble on his chin. "What happened to them?"

"They fled into the bay, and presumably returned to the depths."

"Good. Too many legs on those things." He cocked his head and gazed upward in thought. "Okay Caine, here's what is going to happen."

Caine stiffened.

"You get to live. Surprise," Kurtis continued, "but on one condition."

"What condition?"

"I want to control Tempest, as you know, to make it what it should have always been. The other Hands, however, are not known to listen to any reason but their own. Logically, this means they have to go."

"You want them dead."

"It doesn't matter to me. You can throw them into the Siberian wilderness for all I care. I just want them gone, somehow, someway."

"And you plan to do this?"

"No," Kurtis said, a cold smile stretching across his face. "I want *you* to do it. You and your new team."

"But I can't tell them about this. They'd never trust me."

"Oh, don't worry, you won't have to. You see, if I know Tempest, and I *do* know Tempest, they won't take so kindly to the death of two of their Hands...three if you count Randall. Yes, by the way, they think I'm dead. Let's keep it that way."

Caine nodded his agreement. "Understood."

"Tempest will want to take their pound of flesh in return." Kurtis closed his eyes and took a deep breath. "You all have a target on your back now, which gives you justification and a necessity." He spread his hands. "Works out pretty well for all of us, don't you think?"

"Is there anything else?" Caine said, keeping his tone as even as possible.

"Ah, yes. How is Skylar?"

"I'm sorry?"

"The redhead," Kurtis said, growing visibly impatient.

"I've only recently been introduced and," he noticed Kurtis' growing irritation, "she seems well. Her and the other young man seem close. That is all I can gather from my observations."

"Close with Devonte?" Kurtis said, his jaw set tight. "Pathetic."

"I suppose," Caine said flatly.

"Try not to agree with me too enthusiastically."

"Never."

Kurtis slumped back in his chair. "Well, she'll come around," he said. "One way or another."

Caine said nothing.

"That's all," Kurtis said. The screen went blank.

"So those are his true colors?" MacPherson said, emerging from the shadows to the right of the screen. "Traditional megalomania, narcissism, and a hyper-fixation on our biologist. Lovely."

Caine didn't know whether to address the woman by her former title or her new one, so he spoke around having to use either. "You now know what I told the Lieutenant," Caine said, "right from his very mouth."

"Yes," MacPherson said, "you've earned, not my trust, it's still too early for that, but you've earned my acknowledgment."

"What are we going to do?"

"Exactly what he asked you to," MacPherson said. "You'll check in with him regularly with my supervision and try to glean as much information from him as you can. When we have enough, we'll drag him down into the pit with the rest of his organization."

"So I am still stuck in a world of shadows and lies," Caine said, his voice a despairing whisper.

"War is a game of shadows, Caine," MacPherson said. "But what you're doing now, is dragging it kicking and screaming into the light. And when it's done, you'll be there too."

Caine looked up, the first hints of tears burning at the corners of his eyes. "Thank you," he said.

"Don't mention it." MacPherson paused for a moment as if working through a difficult problem. At last she said, "And let's keep this operation between us for now. Too many voices, and secrets start spilling."

"I understand."

"Good," she said, "now get going, the government liaison should be here any minute for the inauguration ceremony, and you still have to change into your new, official uniform."

"The masks?"

"Not for these. Our tactical gear for combat situations utilized the tech and a version of the design from your masks. The technology inside was a step ahead of our own. I guess that's what happens when you kidnap or blackmail so many of the world's greatest minds."

"People will work very hard to ensure their safety and the safety of their family," Caine said.

"Yes, I suppose they would." MacPherson moved to the door. "Go change, be back here in no more than ten minutes."

"Yes..." Caine paused, stuck again on the rank and title.

"Commander," MacPherson said.

"Yes, Commander."

"And Caine?"

"Yes, Commander?"

"Welcome to the team."

As Caine walked down the hall to his quarters, he realized that, for the first time in a long time he was smiling. He had new purpose. *And perhaps*, he thought, *I have found people who value me for more than just my usefulness.*

#

Devonte pulled at the tight uniform. "Are jeans and a t-shirt really not an acceptable uniform?"

"You know, when I invited you to be my roommate in this place, I didn't expect you to complain so damn much," Brannigan said. "Buck up, this is mostly a formality. Unless we've got something important going on, I doubt anyone will care what you wear."

Devonte fiddled with the pin, sticking himself as he tried to put it on. The blue lightning bolt slicing through the black circle glistened on his uniform. MacPherson had told him it was a tribute to Inkanyamba, the first kaiju they ever defeated. Brannigan had then made a joke about the team name, which had earned him an ice-cold glare.

"Six months, huh," Brannigan said. "Feels like forever ago."

"No," Devonte said. "I think it's all happened so fast...like everything with Inkanyamba was just yesterday."

Brannigan opened the room door. "You gonna stare at yourself in the mirror all day, or are we going to get this over with?"

"I definitely can't just stay here?"

"Do you want to get booted before we even get officially started?"

Devonte grumbled, adjusted his collar one more time and followed Brannigan into the hall. "Is the president going to be there?"

"No, heard he's on vacation. Suppose it will be the veep doing the honors."

"Small blessings," Devonte said.

"I hear you."

They entered the room to find everyone else already gathered. Several familiar faces turned to greet them. Devonte scanned each one of them. Skylar, MacPherson, Greenwood, Gunner, Arnett, and a dark-skinned man Devonte didn't recognize. The man seemed to notice Devonte's lack of recognition and strode over to him, hand extended.

"Caine," he said.

"Devonte."

"It is a pleasure to meet you."

"Yeah," Devonte said, "how do you fit in to all of this?"

"I betrayed Tempest to join you."

"I see."

"Rhodes," the commander called, "you're already late, care to not hold us up any further?" She gestured for him to join the group.

The commander had been talking to a man in a perfectly fitted tan-suit. The Vice President of the United States. His weathered complexion was complemented by a short crop of salt and pepper hair. He gave a genuine smile as Devonte approached and the whole team gathered around him.

"Well look at this," he said. "What a fine group of people here today."

"They've proven their mettle," the commander said, "and they have my trust."

"Then they have mine," the vice president said. "Well, shall we get this thing along?" He looked down at the document in his hand. "Huh, so that's the name he decided on?"

The commander forced a smile. "The acronym fits, at least."

"I suppose it does."

"You wouldn't be able to change—"

"I'm afraid not."

"Of course."

The vice president cleared his throat. "It is my great honor to appoint on this day, by the power invested in me by the people and government of the United States of America, the official creation of the Strategic Taskforce Against Titanic Intrusive Creatures. STATIC." He folded up the document and gave them all a warm smile. "And that's it. You guys are official. I have faith you'll do great work here."

The vice president practically jumped out of his suit as a loud siren blared throughout the room. "What on earth?"

"Sorry, sorry," Devonte said, "that's my early warning system." He regarded all of the confused faces staring at him. "It's something I programmed and installed with Brannigan's help."

"Did you feel that, Devonte? That bump was you running me over with the bus you just threw me under," Brannigan said, rolling his eyes.

"It scrapes the web looking for...weirdness that could be related to kaiju. The alarm lets us know there is something we should check out..."

"Well?" Commander MacPherson asked.

"What?"

"Go check it out!"

"Oh, right," Devonte jogged over to the computer terminal and pulled up the alert on the big screen situated at the center of the room. "Seems like there have been a lot of bodies turning up in the Everglades with all of the fluid drained from their bodies." He clicked another link. "Oh, there's a video." He hit play.

On the screen, a man appeared to be spearfishing in the shallower waters of the swamp. He stabbed down into the water and a warbling shriek crackled through the speakers in the room.

"What the fuck was that?" the cameraman asked.

"Probably just some bird or somethi—wait, something just touched my leg."

"Man, don't mess with me like that," the cameraman said.

"I'm not, something definitely just slithered past my leg."

"It's a snake, man."

"No, it's way to bi—"

The man stumbled backwards and fell into the marsh water.

"Jason," the cameraman shouted.

Jason's body came back into view as something like a long rope lashed up out of the water. The black tendril had latched itself onto Jason's face. His muffled screams were clearly audible on the video.

"Oh my god. Oh fuck. Oh…oh god," the cameraman kept repeating. "What do I…what is that?"

Jason kicked and struggled against the tendril latched onto his face, but it didn't last. There was a sound like water being flushed down a drain, and Jason's body began to shrivel until only a mummified corpse remained. The tendril whipped Jason's body around, finally releasing it and flinging it away into the distance with a splash.

The cameraman had started backing away slowly, and the footage became shakier, his hands obviously trembling in fear. There was another warbling shriek and several of the tendrils rose from the swamp like periscopes on a submarine.

"Please god, no," the cameraman said as the tendrils swiveled in his direction. Each one had a mouth on the end. These mouths all screamed in unison and slithered their way towards the cameraman.

One of the tendrils lashed out ahead of the others and suctioned itself to the camera lens. Several rows of needle-thin teeth were visible for a few seconds before the cameraman jerked the camera free of the tendril mouth. At this point the cameraman lost the rest of his bravery. The rest of the video consisted of footage of the man's furious sprint back to the airboat he and his friend used to get about, his panicked efforts to climb into said airboat, and the escape from the marsh. All the while, in the background the shrieks of whatever caught his friend rang out like a banshee shrieking, chasing him through the swamp.

"Supposedly," Devonte said scrolling through a new article, "the cameraman is being held in prison in Sunset, Florida on suspicion of killing his friend and fabricating the video as a cover-up. I don't know about you guys, but face-hugging tentacles seem up our alley, right?" He looked up at his teammates.

"Well," the vice president said, "I think I should let you all get to work. I'll see myself out."

"Thank you for coming, sir," Commander MacPherson said, then flipping her switch from polite to commanding, she barked, "Alright STATIC, this is our first real mission. Load up the mobile base, prep the jet, and let's do our damn jobs."

"What's the plan, Commander?" Brannigan asked

"Well for starters, it looks like we're going to Florida."

END

ACKNOWLEDGMENTS

Monsters often are sympathetic creatures at heart. Sure they ravage, devastate, and destroy. But oftentimes they don't mean it, they simply can't help it. When I started writing, I started down one path, but at the end of the day, I simply couldn't help but write this kind of story. Giant monsters are in my blood, in my soul. I love them. This story owes itself to that love, but to many of the people in my life as well.

Thank you of course to my parents, without whom there's no guarantee I'd know what a kaiju is. From one film to a lifelong obsession with giant monsters is not necessarily an expected step, but hopefully one that you appreciate and are proud of!

A thank you to Luke and Lauren, who read every draft of every wild-brained idea I wake up with. Almost 100K words later, I'm sure they didn't completely expect the depth to which my brain plumbs. I appreciate your willingness to read the roughest of drafts and offer kind and useful critiques.

A huge thanks to everyone who has contributed to the Kaiju genre in all of its mediums, paving the way and generating the interest that makes books like these possible.

To everyone at Severed Press whose hands touched this book on its way to production, thank you. Without you, this wouldn't be a real thing. Your efforts are greatly appreciated.

And finally, Stephanie, who read this book knowing what it was and knowing that she wasn't a fan of the genre, and came out loving it. You encouraged me, and offered sound advice on how to make a better monster story by making a better story. You're the best.

About the Author

Vaughn A. Jackson is a writer of speculative fiction, and author of both *Up from the Deep* and the upcoming novel *Touched by Shadows*. He is also a member of the Horror Writers Association.

Vaughn lives near Baltimore with his girlfriend and two grumpy gremlins who disguise themselves as the cutest kittens in the world. He is still waiting on an alien of pure light to give him a transformation device that allows him to fight giant monsters. It's bound to happen soon, right…?

Find Vaughn on Twitter via @blaximillion or at www.thevaughnthewordslinger.weebly.com

Check out other great

Sea Monster Novels!

Michael Cole

SCAR

Scar is a killing machine. Born from DNA spliced between the extinct Megalodon and modern day Great White, he has a viciousness that transcends time. His evil is reflected in his eyes, his savagery in his two-inch serrated teeth, his ruthlessness in his trail of death. After escaping captivity, the killer shark travels to the island community Cross Point, where prey is in abundance. With an insatiable appetite, heightened senses, and skin impervious to bullets, Scar kills everything that crosses his path. His reign of terror puts him at war with the island sheriff, Nick Piatt. With the body count rising, Nick vows to protect his island community from the vicious threat. With the aid of a marine biologist, a rookie deputy, and a bad-tempered fisherman, Nick leads a crusade against Scar, as well as the ruthless scientist who created him.

Rick Chesler

HOTEL MEGALODON

An underwater luxury hotel on a gorgeous tropical island is set for an extravagant opening weekend with the world watching. The only thing standing in the way of a first-rate experience for the jet-setting VIPs is an unscrupulous businessman and sixty feet of prehistoric shark. As the underwater complex is besieged by a marauding behemoth, newly minted marine biologist Coco Keahi must face off against the ancient predator as it rises from the deep with a vengeance. Meanwhile, a human monster has decided he would be better off if Coco were one of the creature's victims.

Check out other great

Sea Monster Novels!

Matt James
SUB-ZERO

The only thing colder than the Antarctic air is the icy chill of death... Off the coast of McMurdo Station, in the frigid waters of the Southern Ocean, a new species of Antarctic octopus is unintentionally discovered. Specialists aboard a state-of-the-art DARPA research vessel aim to apply the animal's "sub-zero venom" to one of their projects: An experimental painkiller designed for soldiers on the front lines. All is going according to plan until the ship is caught in an intense storm. The retrofitted tanker is rocked, and the onboard laboratory is destroyed. Amid the chaos, the lead scientist is infected by a strange virus while conducting the specimen's dissection. The scientist didn't die in the accident. He changed.

Alister Hodge
THE CAVERN

When a sink hole opens up near the Australian outback town of Pintalba, it uncovers a pristine cave system. Sam joins an expedition to explore the subterranean passages as paramedic support, hoping to remain unneeded at base camp. But, when one of the cavers is injured, he must overcome paralysing claustrophobia to dive pitch-black waters and squeeze through the bowels of the earth. Soon he will find there are fates worse than being buried alive, for in the abandoned mines and caves beneath Pintalba, there are ravenous teeth in the dark. As a savage predator targets the group with hideous ferocity, Sam and his friends must fight for their lives if they are ever to see the sun again.

Check out other great

Sea Monster Novels!

Michael Cole

CREATURE OF LAKE SHADOW

It was supposed to be a simple bank robbery. Quick. Clean. Efficient. It was none of those. With police searching for them across the state, a band of criminals hide out in a desolate cabin on the frozen shore of Lake Shadow. Isolated, shrouded in thick forest, and haunted by a mysterious history, they thought it was the perfect place to hide. Tensions mount as they hear strange noises outside. Slain animals are found in the snow. Before long, they realize something is watching them. Something hungry, violent, and not of this world. In their attempt to escape, they found the Creature of Lake Shadow.

C.J. Waller

PREDATOR X

When deep level oil fracking uncovers a vast subterranean sea, a crack team of cavers and scientists are sent down to investigate. Upon their arrival, they disappear without a trace. A second team, including sedimentologist Dr Megan Stoker, are ordered to seek out Alpha Team and report back their findings. But Alpha team are nowhere to be found – instead, they are faced with something unexpected in the depths. Something ancient. Something huge. Something dangerous. Predator X